Crater's Edge

Lucy Andrews

First published 2017 by Solstice Publishing

Published 2019 by Treeberry Press

Copyright © Lucy Andrews 2017

Publisher's Note:

This is a work of fiction. All names, characters, places, and events are the work of the author's imagination.

Any resemblance to real persons, places, or events is coincidental.

ISBN 9781916297012

Crater's Edge

A science fiction novel by

Lucy Andrews

Chapter One

Kalen Trinneer arrived at his supervisor's office in the domed city of Central and paused before the closed door. To one side, a green light on the panel indicated that she was expecting him. The well-lit corridor was empty but he could hear voices and footsteps nearby, audible over the constant hum of the air supply units.

"You're never alone in the settlements," he muttered ruefully.

He hesitated before pressing the entry plate and considered what he would say. He had avoided calling her for two weeks and now she would want to know why. As a senior engineer in the Ea-Zone Colonisation Division, he had continued to submit his official reports. Now his divisional manager had personally summoned him to Central, so it must be important. Was he prepared to tell her the truth or let things ride for the moment? He felt a creeping apprehension as he punched the entry mechanism with the heel of his hand and the door slid open with a gentle sigh.

Halle Rison was seated before a computer screen and looked up as he walked in. Was it his imagination, or was she looking older than her early thirties now? She was dressed in standard issue tight blue jacket and trousers, which she had brightened up with a pewter belt to show off her tiny waist. The top of her jacket was undone just enough for Kalen to glimpse the promise of her ample cleavage. Her blue eyes matched her outfit and her blonde hair had been cut into a neat bob that glistened in the artificial lighting. Kalen could see that her pants were stretched so tightly across her bottom that the material clung to her thighs. He reflected that only Halle could wear a uniform that way. When she saw him, a fleeting expression of concern washed over her delicate features before she constructed a careful smile.

"Morning, Halle. You look well."

"I've missed you. Where have you been?" she asked, as she got up and came towards him, her eyes searching his.

Before he could reply, she wrapped her arms around his neck and reached up to kiss him.

"I hope you haven't forgotten me," she whispered. Her breath was hot and moist on his neck. She pressed herself against him, and he found himself bending his head to respond.

He inhaled her perfume. It triggered a long-buried memory of roses that he had only ever smelled as a small child. He realised that she must have bought the scent on the black market, as it was almost impossible to get in the colony. Kalen slipped his arm around her waist and pressed his hand into the small of her back. Her body felt soft and warm. Almost pliable, he thought, as he used his other hand to pull her hips into his. He gently returned her kiss and she took a step forwards so that one of her slim legs was squeezed between his own. She wiggled slightly and rubbed herself against him. For a few moments, he was aware of nothing but his growing desire for her.

Halle pulled back suddenly. "We shouldn't be doing this here. If you'd called me, we could have spent some time alone."

She's teasing me, reminding me of what I'm missing when I'm not with her, Kalen thought. That was typical of Halle. She played games, but he had to admit, she still had her attractions. Although the initial excitement had worn off, he still enjoyed the physical side of their relationship. A year ago, it hadn't mattered to him that he reported to her. He had only seen her light side and had had no scruples about starting an affair with her. He had needed her then. She had filled a vacancy, a deep void, with her humour, playfulness, and an erotic quality quite unlike anything that he had experienced in his previous relationships.

"You know I've been busy, Halle."

"So busy, you couldn't make time to call me? I kept thinking you'd call, and when you didn't, I wondered if you were seeing someone else."

"There isn't anyone else. We've been through this before. How could I meet someone else at a works site? You have all the records. You know who I work with." Kalen tried to keep the exasperation out of his voice.

"You do still love me, don't you?" Halle tipped her head slightly to one side and looked at him quizzically.

"Of course I do," Kalen replied, pulling her to him. He folded her in his arms, her head resting against his chest so that she couldn't see the lie in his face. "Now, why did you ask me to come in?"

Halle stepped back and assumed a serious expression. Taking a seat by her console, she motioned him to sit opposite her. He noticed that her taut trousers crinkled into little creases at the tops of her legs when she sat down. A curious idea crept into his mind. I wonder if her Duplicate is anything like her? But that was ridiculous. The Duplicate that shared her job in the alternate time zone could be any age or sex.

"I need to talk to you about your next posting. You're being re-assigned, effective immediately, to sort out problems at Area Twenty. Work has virtually stopped there. Over the last few weeks, they've had a series of power failures and several rock-falls. Nearly all of their systems below the thirtieth level have been affected. The upper levels are largely okay so it's still being treated as a mining problem at the moment."

Kalen recalled what he knew about Area Twenty. "That's the site with the three large craters?"

"That's right. It's situated in a remote part of Taidor. The Division considered it ideal for development because of the craters. It's known unofficially simply as Three-Craters."

"Why the sudden urgency? I heard that the power supply there had been playing up for quite a while."

Halle frowned. "They can't find the cause of the power failures. Problems have escalated since work started on the new level. They're down to the forty-sixth. It's deeper than we've ever gone before."

"That's not unusual. As we dig deeper, the more challenging it gets."

"There's more to it than that. The drills and ancillary machinery keep breaking down for no apparent reason. The malfunctions are causing interruptions to the air supply as well as contamination. Heating and lighting have been affected." Halle paused.

"Go on," Kalen said.

"The situation is now critical. There are serious safety issues. Miners have got trapped several times and there could be trouble with them."

"Why do you think there could be trouble? I've never known miners to get worked up about dangerous conditions. They're used to it."

"Morale is low on site. The miners have been asking for transfers or refusing to work in some areas which they claim are jinxed."

"Come on, Halle. I've heard rumours that the place is cursed, but surely it can't be as bad as that?"

"It is. Even the security personnel and staff at the base have started to become unsettled." She looked away, and then back to his face. Her eyes seemed to have turned a darker blue but he couldn't quite read the expression in them.

"What about the other zone?"

"The feeling is pervading the U-Zone as well, so far as we know, but to date, investigations have turned up nothing to explain what's happening. You need to find out what's going on, and get things running again as quickly as possible."

"Don't worry, Halle. I'll get to the bottom of it."

"Our site commander has even suggested sabotage, but so far we've found nothing to support this. Now the miners also think they're under suspicion so the atmosphere is very tense. You'll need to tread carefully."

"What about sabotage? Is that possible?" Things must have got pretty bad for the site commander to suggest it.

"There's no evidence of it. It seems unlikely given that the incidents are occurring in both zones. Someone would have to be working with a counterpart in the other time system, and what would the motive be?"

"You never know. I'll keep an open mind."

"When you get there, you'll need to speak to our mining captain, Jorge Narve, who'll fill you in on all the details. There's also a good geologist on site, Sera Ethern, who you'll want to talk to, although she's got a reputation for being difficult."

Kalen raised an eyebrow. "What does that mean?"

"She questions orders and goes her own way. You may find it hard to get her cooperation. She had to be transferred from her last posting after some trouble with the miners. The reports were vague."

"I'll bear that in mind when I meet her." He pictured an aggressive independent woman, the sort who usually worked at the sites.

"This may be your toughest assignment since the accident."

A dark memory hit him unexpectedly. No, no—not again! For an instant, he was back in the mining works at Area Nine after the rock-fall, amongst the swirling acrid dust and screaming that didn't stop. Eighteen months and he could still smell the fear and the panic of the miners—still feel the cloying dust strangling his lungs, the blackness squeezing him, invading his mouth and throat until he couldn't breathe. Without thinking, he placed his hand in his pocket and curled his fingers around the small packet of Narquum he carried there. A gnawing in his gut told him that he would need another pill soon. He blinked his eyes to bring Halle into focus and pushed the hellish images out of his mind. She was looking at him curiously.

"Are you all right? You looked a bit distant for a moment."

"Yes, I'm fine," he lied.

"You're still blaming yourself for Area Nine, aren't you?" she asked intuitively.

"I still don't know how it happened. The section that collapsed had already been strengthened. I should have suspended construction until I was sure it was safe."

"You must put that behind you. It's just one of Taidor's sites that went bad. It's over. Finished," Halle snapped. "Pull this one off and you'll be in line for promotion."

"Promotion?"

"Yes, promotion!" Halle leaned forward, fixing him with her blue eyes. "You've got the opportunity now to prove yourself. There are only a handful of engineers with your qualifications and expertise. The Division thinks you're the best man to send to Three-Craters. If you can resolve the problems there, promotion will be on the cards."

Halle's eyes sparkled with excitement and he caught her mood. He felt a stirring of ambition, a feeling that had evaded him for months, tempered only by the realisation that she saw her future with him. He would deal with that when he had to.

He smiled. "That would be wonderful, Halle. Let me see what's going on at Three-Craters. It's about time we were called in."

"Your Duplicate, Luther Stonway, is already en-route. I've sent you all of the information and details of the travel arrangements and…" Halle hesitated.

"What is it, Halle? Is there something else?"

"I've heard something, unofficially. I can't talk about it here. You must speak to Jorge Narve when you get there." Halle shifted slightly in her seat. "It's important that it doesn't get out."

"Okay, Halle. I understand." He wondered what Jorge would tell him.

"Good, the transport leaves tonight at twenty hundred hours."

Chapter Two

Kalen passed several people in the corridor after he left Halle's office. Service personnel in uniform mingled with brightly dressed civilians visiting the Division's headquarters, colourful against the pale apple green of the walls. The women chatted as they passed him, occasionally throwing a glance his way. He was wearing his formal uniform and he gave them a quick smile as he went by. Carrying his hat in his hand, he swung it rhythmically as he strolled.

Halle had extracted a promise from him as he left, that he would call her regularly. He groaned inwardly to himself. She constantly tried to control him. But perhaps she was right. If he could sort out the problems at Three-Craters, he might be able to put the accident behind him. Promotion! Could that really be a possibility? But he still had unanswered questions about Area Nine and the guilt weighed heavily on him like an open wound, preventing closure. Suddenly his vision blurred and he began to shake.

"That Narquuum!" he gasped under his breath.

There was a bathroom ahead and he ducked into it. Gripping the lip of the nearest washbasin with both hands, he took a deep breath. Cold sweat had sprung out under his collar, soaking the back of his shirt. He could feel his heart racing, his heartbeat pounding. It pulsed through him, getting louder and louder, until it throbbed in his eardrums.

***

His drumming heartbeat merged into the harsh hammering of the drills at Area Nine. It pounded mercilessly in his ears as he listened to the mining captain. They were at the work face discussing new plans that had been drawn up to avoid weak areas, after several minor rock-falls.

"If we change the design, this is going to put us behind schedule," the mining captain yelled over the din, as a truck carrying equipment rattled past. "It could cost us two or three weeks."

"The Division won't like that. Can't you make up the time?"

A miner riding a mobile drill swung around them, resuming his original path once he was clear.

"Not with these designs. The whole section will need restructuring."

The man's obstinacy irritated Kalen. It was always like this. The miners objected to the extra work, forcing him to go through a process of reasoning, persuasion, and then outright bribery until eventually, a compromise was struck. The timescale was nowhere near two or three weeks and somehow, he had to find the balance. Usually bonus incentives greatly reduced delay.

"So give me your best estimate, with all shifts working extra time."

"We'd have to put…"

A thunderous groaning sound cut off the man's words and his mouth moved mutely as Kalen stared at him in momentary incomprehension. Then the ground shuddered and a deafening roar blasted Kalen's ears. The captain stopped talking and glanced upwards towards the noise, his expression contorting into fear and disbelief. He turned to run, but before he could move, the roof caved in above him. A rain of slashing shards and huge boulders hurtled downwards, smashing the captain until he was obliterated. There was only black rubble smoking with dust where the man had been standing.

The ground shook beneath Kalen's boots. Everywhere he looked, dark rocks rained down, the black storm felling machinery and people around him. The hovering rubble trucks jerked and pivoted as they were struck, and the mobile drills threw their riders as they spun and danced under the heavy downfall. The cavern shuddered as massive rocks crashed downward destroying everything in their path, trapping men under stone and machinery. Huge boulders and rubble crushed equipment and people indiscriminately, hurling up clouds of choking dust that stung and blinded his eyes.

Thick dust swirled around Kalen, blanketing his vision. When he tried to call out, he swallowed it. He could hear screaming nearby, someone desperate for help, and he tried to move toward them, but the dust shrouded everything. Then something struck the back of his head with such force that the blow threw him forward sprawling onto the hard ground. Searing pain swept across his skull and shoulders as a dark avalanche engulfed him, and everything went black.

Grimy dust clogged his mouth and nostrils, suffocating him, and a terrible weight pinned him to the ground, squeezing his lungs so that they were paralysed. Excruciating pain accompanied his struggles to inhale, each breath bringing further agony to his crushed torso. In his mind's eye, he saw a large black crow. It sat on his back, gripping him with sharp talons, its dark wings outstretched to cover his shoulders like an evil cloak. Every time he tried to take a breath, the crow's talons impaled him more fiercely and its wings tightened their hold on him. The bird began to bore into the nape of his neck with its beak and wave upon wave of unbearable pain swept through him until the darkness fell.

***

"Hey, are you sick?"

A man dressed in the overalls of a cleaner was peering into his face. The crow had gone and he was at the washbasin, his shirt sodden with sweat. The accident wouldn't let him go, but he still had a feeling that his memory was incomplete. Something about it continued to elude him.

"I'll be okay, thanks. I just got a little dizzy there for a moment," he replied, straightening up.

"Are you sure? You don't look well."

"I'll be fine, really." He wished the man would go away.

"I can get a medic if you want," the man persisted.

"I don't need a medic; it's just something I've eaten. I'm feeling a lot better now." It wouldn't take a medic long to work out that he was an addict.

"If you say so."

The man turned and left, the door sliding closed behind him. Kalen fumbled in his pocket for his packet of Narquum and shook the contents into his hand. He stared at the two small green pills in his palm and shook the packet again, but it was empty.

"No!" he gasped. Three-Craters was still in construction, nothing more than a building site. He would never get a supply there.

He swallowed one of the pills and shoved the other back into the packet. The Narquum chafed his dry throat as it went down, but within seconds the warm relief coursed through his body and his mind cleared.

***

Kalen checked the contents of his bag and then glanced around his room. It occurred to him that his permanent accommodation here at Central wasn't much larger than the rooms he usually occupied on the construction sites. Looking around the small living area, he reflected that he would need a family to qualify for a larger unit, but he couldn't see that happening for some time. A large screen on one wall simulated a picture window and filled the apartment with light. It showed images of Taidor's capital city below, fed to it by cameras mounted high on the terraces around the east side of the crater. Kalen studied the throngs of people choking the main streets and wondered how long it would take him to get to the transport terminal.

He caught sight of himself in the mirror. He was still dressed formally from his meeting with Halle in a dark burgundy jacket, tailored over neat trousers and fastened at the front with invisible magnetic clips. His senior rank of chief engineer was denoted by silver vertical stripes on the front of his jacket, placed just below the shoulders. He quickly changed into a casual shirt and pants and bundled his uniform into the bag. Looking at his watch, he saw that it was nearly eighteen hundred hours. He hurriedly switched off the lights and set the door to lock as he left.

Kalen walked briskly along the empty corridors, his footsteps muffled by the spotless chrome floors, but his right leg ached. *Another reminder of the accident,* he thought bitterly. Turning into another corridor, he saw his elderly neighbour, Travis Reinhard, hobbling towards him. Travis was stooped with a shock of grey hair, a large nose, and rheumy eyes. He wore slippers and baggy trousers.

Kalen broke his stride. "Good evening, how are you?"

"As well as can be expected—it gets lonely here, but my daughter and the children should be back soon." Travis's forehead creased into deep furrows over his silver eyebrows as he peered up at Kalen.

"I think most people are in town at this time," Kalen replied politely.

Travis eyed Kalen's bag curiously. "You're off again?"

"Yes, I've been reassigned."

"You're never here very much. Will you be away for long?"

"I don't know. It all depends on the job, but I expect it will be a few weeks at least. I'm on my way to catch the transport now." Kalen hoisted his bag over his shoulder.

"Goodbye then," Travis said dolefully.

Kalen nodded his head and carried on walking, immediately immersed in his own thoughts. Where was he going to get more Narquum? His usual dealer wouldn't be around until late that evening, so he would have to use someone else. He was taking a risk. For an instant, he imagined getting caught, the shame of incarceration and dismissal from the Division. Even Halle wouldn't be able to save him. His career would be over, but only Narquum stood between him and the bottomless black pit that perpetually tried to suck him in. He hated himself for his addiction, but he didn't want to fall into the void just yet.

***

Kalen exited the building at an upper level onto a high terrace, one of several that ran along the front of the Ea-Zone accommodation complex overlooking the central hub of the city. Sunlight filtered through the dome high above the vast expanse of buildings, shops, and moving walkways that teemed with people, some eight kilometres across. He could hear the babble of voices and sounds of movement that were always a constant in the city, and despite the integral air supply units, he could still smell cooking from the restaurants. He peered out at the opposite wall of the crater, imagining the U-Zone apartments located there on the west side that were too far away for him to see.

Using the stairways between the terraces, Kalen dropped down until he could go no further, and re-entered the building. After a short walk along another corridor, he boarded an internal elevator to descend through the last few floors to ground level. After leaving the elevator, he made his way through more passageways until he came to an exit into the city.

A young female security guard stood at the checkpoint in front of a large metal framed gateway. She had bright purple hair piled high on her head, fastened by a gold band, and had drawn circles of gold and purple around her eyes to enhance them. It gave her a sort of owlish look, Kalen decided. She smiled as Kalen approached and he tried to recall her name.

"You're looking very nice today, Ije," Kalen said, returning her smile.

She giggled and blushed, and then recovered her composure. "Thank you. Are you leaving, sir?"

"Yes, work, I'm afraid. I won't be back for a few weeks."

"That's too bad, just a moment, sir." She turned and pressed buttons on a control panel on the wall, continuing to flush under his gaze.

"You'll need a pass out. Otherwise you'll be registered as missing when the Gate closes tonight."

"I wouldn't want that to happen," he said, with mock seriousness.

"Personally, I can't think of anything worse," Ije continued cheerfully. "I mean, imagine finding yourself locked out of the Ea-Zone in a city full of strangers."

"I thought Security searched before the U-Zone came in and brought any stragglers back at day end?"

"They do, and if they find someone deliberately out of time, there are penalties. But sometimes, something happens; illness and so forth, and people actually do go missing, or at least for a while." She frowned, looking thoughtful. The light on the control panel glowed orange and she stepped back from it. "There, it's set now. You can go through."

"I'll be back soon." Kalen winked at her and she giggled again.

He held up his identity card to the scanner and after a moment, the light changed to green. He gave Ije a wide grin and stepped into the imposing portal. The Gate subjected him to a full body scan but he felt nothing as he walked through it. An unbidden thought niggled at him. What would life be like without the Gate? What would it be like to be free to come and go all the time instead of being trapped in the accommodation blocks every night?

Kalen stepped out of the other side of the Gate and emerged into the bright light of the dome. He paused to enjoy a brief moment of solitude, turning to look behind him. Above the Gate, a large sign proclaimed the legend 'Early Colonial Time System' in bright red lettering. The dark aperture of the gateway looked like a black scar in the sheer wall of the crater. It soared up to the first of the many terraces that extended up the crater's sides for hundreds of metres until they reached the gentle curve of the transparent roof of the dome, far above. Kalen stared up into the dizzying heights, admiring the construction for a moment longer. He turned and walked into the first square where he quickly found himself swallowed up in the crowds.

Chapter Three

Throngs of people filled the main street and Kalen was jostled as he made his way through. He tried to ignore the noise and the smell of sweat but the heat from the press of bodies made him uncomfortable. Taking a side turning that he recognised, he found himself in the middle of a huddle of people pushing and shoving to board an escalator to the level above. When he got to the top, he stepped onto a moving walkway that crawled towards a parade of shops at the far end of the mall. A teenage boy barged past him, catching him a glancing blow.

"Watch it!" he exclaimed, but the boy was long gone. He decided to get off and walk.

The pharmacy was where he remembered it, in a discreet location on a corner at the end of a row of shops, with an entrance in a small side alley. As he approached it, his hands went clammy and the strap of his bag began slithering about in his palm. Tightening his hold on the bag, he continued walking towards the shop. Stopping at the entrance, he glanced over his shoulder before going in, but only met the blank stare of strangers.

The shop was empty except for a young man with short mouse-brown hair and a smooth round face, who stood behind the counter. He looked up expectantly as Kalen came in and assumed an attentive expression. Kalen didn't remember him.

"I'm looking for Ron? Is he in?"

The assistant narrowed his eyes a fraction and twisted the corners of his mouth into a faint smile. "The pharmacist…"

A voice suddenly boomed from an open door behind him, "I'll be out in a minute."

"I'll wait." Kalen put his bag on the floor with relief and hoped that the man wouldn't be long.

The assistant looked disappointed. He turned his back on Kalen and busied himself tidying the shelves. Kalen waited silently and within a few minutes, a balding middle-aged man emerged from the back room.

"That will be all, Mark. I can take it from here," the man said, and his assistant scuttled into the back room. He looked astutely at Kalen, as if assessing him. "I'm Ron. You asked for me?"

"Yes, I bought some medication from you a few months ago."

The pharmacist made no reply and waited for Kalen to go on.

Would Ron sell to him? He had to take the risk. "You were very helpful. I needed some painkillers but had lost my script."

"What type?" Ron eyed Kalen speculatively.

"Narquum."

"I remember you now. How much do you need?"

Thank the Planets! Ron remembered him. "Three packs will do it. Are they the same price?"

"There's a small increase, but it's been a while, hasn't it? Anything else you need?"

"No, that's all."

Ron disappeared into the back room and then reappeared with three small packets that he put on the counter in front of Kalen. At that moment, Kalen heard the hiss of the shop door open behind him and saw fear in Ron's eyes. Ron pushed the packets towards him and then with a fluid movement held up his calculator so that Kalen could see the price on the display.

"Here are your purchases," Ron said meaningfully.

Kalen heard footsteps beside him and glanced around. A large man in a security guard's uniform stood at his elbow, watching him. Kalen nodded to him. *I must act naturally, as if it's a normal transaction*, he thought. *Do nothing suspicious, otherwise I'm finished*. He picked up the Narquum and put it in his pocket. He could feel sweat prickling his forehead. Fishing out his card to pay, he hoped that the guard hadn't noticed his trembling hands. Then the guard was gone; he had wandered away to look at something else in the shop.

Ron took payment, all the time keeping his eye on the guard.

"Thank you." Kalen put his card away and prepared to leave.

Ron gave him a hard look, as if memorising his face. "I'm always here if you need me."

***

A big board hanging over the escalator flashed the time. Nineteen hundred hours. He barely had time to reach the terminal, he thought desperately. Trust Halle to book him on the last transport out that evening. If he missed it, he would have to provide an explanation. That was unthinkable. The Division might discover that he had bought Narquum.

He set off northwards, keeping to the upper levels that were quieter than the streets below, breaking into a jog where he could. Overhead, a small transport glided smoothly along a monorail that wound through the buildings, in the direction of the terminal. He wished he could bluff his way onto it but its use was restricted. He had nearly two kilometres to cover and his right leg threw out stabs of pain when he ran.

The roar of a ship's engines echoed high above him and he looked up. An interplanetary ship was leaving the city. It had ascended on its docking platform towards the roof of the dome, through a complicated system of air locks, and stood waiting to leave. As he watched, part of the transparent dome began to slide open, glinting in the sunshine. Kalen kept going. He turned a corner and saw the terminal for the underground transports ahead of him.

At the terminal, hundreds of people milled around the central concourse in a noisy confusing mass, forcing Kalen to check his pace. Lines had formed in front of the ticket offices that ringed the concourse and at the departure gates, while other people moved about haphazardly between them. People shouted directions to each other and small groups waited in corners. Kalen scanned the concourse until he spotted a large board displaying that evening's departures. He studied the listings and joined a line moving slowly forward towards a ticket inspector at the barriers.

Behind the barriers, Kalen saw people boarding his transport, but he was still some way from the gate. He counted ten people in front of him. *I'm going to run out of time*, he thought. Each minute he waited seemed excruciatingly long. He shuffled with impatience. Surely they wouldn't let the transport go with people still waiting? Two people went through and then another two. He tried to quell his anxiety as the minutes crawled by.

Now there were only four passengers between him and the gate. Another two went through and finally only a middle-aged woman stood between him and the inspector. At the platform, he could see guards closing the doors of the waiting transport. It was due to leave within minutes. *Please, please move, lady*, he silently prayed.

Suddenly an ear-splitting wail screamed over the terminal, cutting through Kalen like a physical force. Everyone around him seemed to freeze. The ticket inspector paused with a pass in one hand, his voice cut off mid-sentence. The guards on the platform stopped moving about and stood still, throwing glances towards one of the boards that displayed the time.

After a minute, the noise ended abruptly and the inspector shouted, "First siren of day end."

The inspector resumed checking the woman's pass.

"Wrong date!" He waved her away.

"What do you mean, wrong date?"

"Your ticket is for tomorrow, not today."

"But I have to go today!" She looked distraught.

"I've told you, you're not scheduled on this departure," the inspector barked. "Now stand aside."

Kalen cursed silently to himself and willed her to move.

The woman stood her ground. "Isn't there anything you can do?"

"You can't travel tonight. Now leave and let these other people through!"

The woman turned around and brushed past Kalen, her face a mask of annoyance. Kalen stepped forward, quickly breathing a sigh of relief. He said nothing while the inspector checked his travel pass against the list.

The inspector looked up. "You should arrive at Morten just after eight hundred hours tomorrow. Change there for Cherer. Once you're in Cherer you'll need to get an air shuttle out to Area Twenty. It's a long trip. I reckon it will take you nearly twenty-four hours."

"Thank you," Kalen said, as the inspector returned his pass and motioned him through the barrier.

Kalen hurried across the platform and boarded the transport. On-board, he searched for his compartment, squeezing by other passengers in the corridor. When he found it, he slung his bag on the floor and settled on the narrow bunk. Reaching into his bag, he took out his assignment briefing. He could hear people scurrying in the passageways outside and the clatter of luggage being stored.

"Doors closing in two minutes," the public-address system droned.

Kalen got comfortable and looked out of the small window. Only a handful of people were still on the platform, hastily trying to board the transport.

"Doors closing in one minute."

The doors hissed closed and everything went quiet. Moments later the harsh wail of the siren suddenly erupted again, penetrating Kalen's thoughts. Twenty hundred hours and day end. In the tiny compartment, the noise bounced off the walls. Outside, the terminal had emptied apart from a small number of transport officials. Several minutes passed, and then the machine rose and moved forward. Kalen braced himself against the gentle tug of the vehicle's acceleration before it settled into almost imperceptible motion as it picked up speed.

He glanced out of the window and gasped in surprise. The transport was passing the outskirts of the city, but the streets were empty. The restaurants and shops were closed. Where had the people gone? Then he saw security guards in smart grey uniforms and peaked hats moving along the streets. He caught a glimpse of one of the open Gates. A clutch of guards stood by it, underneath large red lettering that proclaimed 'United Colonies Time System.' The U-Zone population hadn't come into the city yet. Then his view blinked out as the transport entered a tunnel.

***

The briefing notes that Halle had supplied were comprehensive. Kalen read them with enthusiasm, absorbing every word, memorising every fact. The development of Area Twenty had started the year before in 2234 and at first, the construction work had proceeded normally. Later, at the lower levels, power failures and rock-falls began to occur. In itself that wasn't unusual, but something about this posting disturbed him. The words on the pages jumped out at him: 'there is now a deep sense of suspicion amongst the miners;' 'this could be a flashpoint;' 'possible mutiny;' 'many believe the site to be cursed.'

The miners now demanded that work be suspended until safety could be assured. Hostility from miners often occurred in these situations, Kalen thought. Problems at the work face had usually crushed morale by the time he was called in, and it would be imperative that he persuade the miners that he was on their side. He would liaise mainly with Jorge Narve, who was waiting for him to arrive. An experienced miner who had worked for the Colonisation Division for twenty years, Jorge could be relied upon to give an objective appraisal of the situation. Kalen would ask him about the other problem that Halle had referred to.

He would also have to talk to the geologist, Sera Ethern. Would she cause him problems? The file told him that she was twenty-eight years old and unmarried with no known attachments. She was probably ugly. The construction sites attracted plain women. They were greatly outnumbered by men at the sites and it gave them better odds of finding a partner. But he would still need her co-operation, ugly or not.

A sense of anticipation gnawed at his innards. He had a challenge ahead. Somewhere, his Duplicate in the U-Zone, Luther Stonway, was also reading his briefing notes and travelling to Three-Craters. They would work together, but he had never met Luther and probably never would. The system prohibited it.

A flash of light from the window caught his eye and he looked out. The transport was passing the perimeter of another city, still lit up by Taidor's eighteen hours of natural daylight. For a moment, he caught a glimpse into the U-Zone and it was morning there. Crowds of people moved along the streets. Kalen got the impression they were all walking in the same direction. Before he could get a good look, the transport entered another tunnel and it went black again outside. He pulled down the window blind and prepared to go to bed. With no intermediate stops before the transport arrived at Morten, he had time to sleep.

Chapter Four

Sera Ethern stretched out to her full length in the hole. The beam from her torch broke up the suffocating blackness, jumping about haphazardly as she moved, illuminating rough surfaces and deep creases in the granite around her. Trying to get purchase with her toes, she used her elbows to drag herself deeper into the fissure. The oxygen supply was thin here and she sucked greedily on the breathing tube at the corner of her mouth.

"Ouch!" Something sharp jabbed her stomach and she wriggled to find a more comfortable position.

Holding her torch in her right hand, Sera extended her arm along the crevice. Ahead, the beam from her torch picked out the glitter of tiny blue crystals in the rock face, each no larger than a centimetre in diameter. In some places, they were concentrated in twinkling clouds, but in others, they were sparsely distributed. Looking closer, she saw that the blue stones had perfect symmetry and were shaped like little pyramids, their colours varying from light blue to deep indigo.

Sera tried to estimate how many of them there were, thousands perhaps. How beautiful! And strange—shapes that she hadn't seen before occurring naturally. Discoveries like this made it all worthwhile. This was the reason she had become a geologist, to discover the unknown. She remembered her mother's reaction to her decision. It was still fresh in her mind.

"Science is a rejection of God!" her mother had screamed, and no amount of pleading would make her see otherwise. But with Father dead, there had been no reason for her to remain in the tiny colony on Borle, so she had left to pursue her dream.

Tingling with excitement, she shone her torch in an arc across the wall of the cavity in front of her. As she swept the beam across the rock, the small crystals shimmered in a glittering colourful array. The stones sparkled in the torchlight and for a moment she forgot the continual sound of the drills that reached her, even here. Inching nearer, she took out her cutting tools and sliced away several for analysis.

"Hey! What's this?" she muttered. The rock around the crystals was serrated, and little grooves ran between the tiny blue stones, connecting them.

In the distance, the mining machinery continued to throb, sending tremors through the rock, vibrating the cold surface she lay on. Shifting her weight, she twisted awkwardly onto her back. Her shoulder brushed a rough edge and she heard a tear as the material of her top snagged on it.

"What now?" she murmured, still engrossed in the jutting, star-like pinpricks that stretched across the granite face.

Inches above her, the jagged roof of the tunnel pressed down, leaving little room to manoeuvre. When she turned her head to one side, she caught her breathing tube against the rock. It popped out of her mouth and dangled against her chest. She tried to grab the tube with her right hand but there was a low protrusion in the way and she knocked her torch hard against it. The torch flew out of her hand and rolled away in the darkness.

"Oh no!" She let out an involuntary squeal that sounded loud in the enclosed space.

She couldn't get hold of the breathing tube with either of her hands. The ceiling plunged downwards above her chest leaving no room for her to slide her right hand across, and her other arm had become wedged between the wall and her body. The oxygen in the air was too thin for her to breathe properly and every intake she took left an unsatisfying ache. Using her heels, she wriggled back towards a wider part of the tunnel and turned over onto her stomach, but when she squirmed around, her breathing tube got tangled. She heard the sound of snapping rubber.

The ache in her chest was getting worse each time she inhaled. She remembered how she had crawled into the crevice from the rough-hewn passageway and squeezed along it as far as she could go. She had to get out quickly. No one knew she was there. How far had she crawled? Surely it couldn't have been far?

Using her arms, she shuffled backwards on her stomach, scraping her elbows. She ignored the cuts and concentrated on pushing herself over the abrasive surface. It was farther than she thought. The tightness in her chest made it difficult for her to breathe. Her head spun and she started to gasp for breath. A faint glimmer of light glowed behind her but it was too far away. She wasn't going to make it.

Suddenly, strong hands clasped her ankles and she felt herself being dragged out.

"Don't worry, Sera! I'll get you out of there in a moment," a man's voice boomed behind her.

The man gave a firm tug and she slithered free into the corridor. Catching her about the waist, the man stood her on her feet, and turned her around to face him. He was a big man with a broad chest who exuded an innate brute strength. He looked amused. Sera recognised him immediately. Lars Mason.

"Are you all right? I heard a noise and came to investigate. Stuck in a hole, were you?" Lars laughed, and peered into her face, still holding her.

"Thank you," she gasped between breaths. She was shaking and her lungs were burning. The air in the passageway was breathable, but dusty and thin. She reached for her breathing tube but it was ripped and unusable. Tears welled in her eyes and she fought them back.

"You don't need that," Lars said genially. "There's enough air in here for both of us." He pressed his huge bulk up close to her. He was a lot taller than she was and his stocky build dwarfed her.

"I'll be all right if I can get back to the main corridor." She tried to move away, but his hands still held her.

"Steady there. You need to rest for a few minutes, and give yourself time to recover." He moved his hands to her shoulders.

She coughed and looked up at him. He stood smiling in front of her. *He's enjoying the whole thing*, she thought. That was just like him. He always seemed to be gloating about something. He was one of those macho types who thought the job was too tough for a woman. He'd been waiting to see if she would slip up in some way and now she had. She coughed again and put her hand up to her mouth. It was bleeding and so was her knee, but the terrible ache in her chest was easing.

"It isn't every day I get to pull a pretty girl out of a hole," he joked.

"How did you know I was here?" They were some distance away from the main site. The crevice was too far away for anyone to hear her. He must have followed her along the corridor or come looking for her. There was no other reason for him to be down here.

"I was just passing. You sounded like you were in a bit of a bind, all that scuffling and coughing."

"I need to get back now."

"There's no hurry. Why don't we spend a little time together?"

He suddenly lowered his face towards hers as if he was going to kiss her. She squirmed away from him, but he had hold of her shoulders in a vicelike grip and his mouth connected with her cheek.

"Come on, you like me really, don't you? One little kiss won't hurt, will it?" One of his hands moved across her chest and squeezed her breast.

"Stop it!" she shouted, trying to wriggle free.

"Oh, come on! I thought you would be grateful."

He laughed as she tried to disengage herself and then he lunged at her again.

She hated men. They were all the same. Angrily, she kicked his shin hard with the steel-tipped toe of her boot. Surprised, he grunted in pain and lessened his grip on her. Seizing her advantage, she gave him a sharp shove and wrenched herself free.

"Damn woman!"

Spinning around, she ran down the passageway towards the main site, but he made no attempt to follow her.

"You can't get away from me that easily," he shouted after her.

***

The small shuttle reduced height as it came in to land at Three-Craters. The ride had become bumpy and the craft shook violently as it fought its way through one of the dust storms that were prevalent on the planet's surface. Kalen peered out of the viewing hatch near his seat. Earlier, he'd seen the shadows of the craters, but now he could see nothing except swirling dust. The shuttle suddenly jerked and pitched forward and the passenger in front of him let out a startled yell, but then the pilot regained control and pulled it back. The dust seemed to thicken as they dropped altitude.

Sitting back in his seat, Kalen checked that his seat belt was fastened tightly for the landing. It was going to be rough. The shuttle was full and held a dozen passengers plus a crew of two. His fellow passengers were all Division personnel, returning to relieve the crews at the works. The craft pitched wildly for several minutes and then steadied itself for its final run into the landing site. Another jolt hit the craft as the pilot switched to automatic, and the ground sensors took hold to pull it in on a straight trajectory.

The craft shook and shuddered; then there was a bump as it came to rest on the docking base and the engines fell silent. There was an air of anticipation amongst the passengers as the docking mechanism secured the vessel and the platform was slowly lowered downwards into the bay. The passengers watched from the viewing hatches as the shuttle descended until it was fully underground and the roof closed over the craft to seal the aperture against the alien atmosphere. Kalen could see the maintenance crews standing at the perimeter of the docking bay with fuelling and loading apparatus.

He waited for the instruction to disembark and then made his way out of the craft along with the other passengers. After security checks, he was directed to an office at one side of the docking bay where a middle-aged man with a chiselled face and short sandy hair was waiting. Although he wore the basic miners' kit of light coloured jacket and pants, the insignia across his chest marked him out as a mining captain. He had a confident bearing and when he saw Kalen, he extended his hand in welcome, appraising him levelly with hard eyes.

"You must be Chief Trinneer. Welcome to Area Twenty. I'm Jorge Narve."

Kalen shook hands. "Good to meet you, Jorge. I'm looking forward to working with you."

"I'll show you to your quarters. I think you'll find everything you need," Jorge said, leading Kalen away from the docking area.

Kalen kept pace with him. "There are a lot of things I want to discuss. I'll also need a full tour of the site."

"We'll do that tomorrow. In the meantime, we can talk en route."

Kalen remembered what he had read about the layout of Three-Craters. The living quarters were located in the upper levels away from the main works, on the other side of the docking bays. Eventually, when construction was complete, these quarters would be used as offices and accommodation for the port staff. Until each section of the development was finished, the living accommodation would be kept separate, so it would be unaffected if there were an accident. This was normal practice, and in a lot of respects, Three-Craters was similar to sites he had already worked in.

Jorge was about the same height and build as him, but his face had the deep lines that came from years of working at the rock face in inhospitable environments. His sandy hair had a few grey streaks, but there was toughness about him, and he moved with the energy of a man in his twenties. Kalen recalled from his briefing notes that Jorge had a family, but Three-Craters was a single posting. He had accepted the assignment to Three-Craters at its inception, some eleven months before, despite it leaving him little opportunity to see his wife and children.

Jorge led Kalen along a brightly lit corridor. The floors and high ceilings were constructed out of a brushed alloy that had been burnished to make it smooth underfoot. The walls were painted peach, but Kalen knew that steel girders ran underneath the pleasing décor. Structural integrity was important and the materials that were used could withstand a severe earthquake. Although the levels were numbered prominently, he saw that each level was painted a different colour.

At the end of the corridor, Jorge led Kalen down an escalator to a lower level where the walls were painted a pleasant yellow. The sound of their footsteps was muted and Kalen recalled that the new building incorporated features to reduce the noise of interior living. They emerged into another brightly lit passageway and then took an elevator down several floors. When the doors opened, Kalen heard the more familiar sounds of the station. The air supply units were noisier than before, as if labouring under strain, and he could hear the relentless distant drumming of the drills. The air had also become cooler.

"The temperature fluctuates," Jorge explained. "It will be some time before the system is properly balanced because the areas to heat are changing on a daily basis as we mine."

"I've read the reports. It seems that temperature fluctuations are the least of the problems here. My primary concern is the power failures."

"The energy demands change daily as the site expands. Sometimes we lose heat and air accidentally and it takes us time to find the leak. That can strain our energy resources, and the system automatically shuts down non-essential functions to conserve life support in the main sections. Of course, once the development has been completed, each zone will have its own power supply to feed its accommodation blocks, and there will be a separate supply for the city itself."

"I read that some of the machines are being run off portable generators but they are still shutting down?"

Jorge nodded. "That's true, but the portable generators aren't always reliable."

"What about the accidents with the machinery?"

"It's likely that the power outages and surges are messing up their programming."

"From what I've read that wouldn't explain everything."

"The rest could be coincidence. Statistically, there are always a number of accidents that occur anyway."

"Are the miners still working?"

"They've been given assurances and they're working at the moment. There's been pressure to call you in, but I'm still not convinced that the power failures aren't simply caused by variations in demand. I tend to think that the most obvious answer is usually the correct one, but of course, it's your call. You'll get a better idea once you've been around the site."

Kalen found his quarters to be sparsely furnished, but there was a desk and computer screen in the corner of the room. No luxury, but he didn't need more, he thought. He looked the room over and sat down at the desk, to place a call to Halle. Her face appeared on the screen and her dainty features lit up when she saw him.

"How was the journey?" She tilted her head to one side flirtatiously.

"The journey was fine, Halle."

"When did you arrive?"

"I got in just a few minutes ago." *As if you didn't know already*, Kalen thought. She knew exactly when he had arrived through her sources; she monitored all of his movements. He tried to shrug off his increasing resentment at her control.

"Have you met any of the miners yet?"

"I've met Jorge Narve, but that's all. I'll be meeting his team tomorrow and taking a tour of the site. It's nearly day end so I can't do much tonight."

"I've been told that Luther Stonway is already on site. He should inspect the works tonight and report to my Duplicate by tomorrow morning."

"I'll send you my report after I've been around the site tomorrow."

"Be careful, Kalen." A flicker of anxiety crossed her face and then she resumed her normal confident expression. "There seems to be a lot of interest in this case."

Kalen looked at Halle sharply. Anyone else would have thought it was a casual remark, but he knew her intimately. Something was wrong. Beneath her flirtatious exterior, she was a ruthless and supremely competent woman who didn't get ruffled easily. It was unlike her to show any anxiety about an assignment. She usually dealt with problems pragmatically and he had never seen her worried before.

She held a powerful position within the Division, and had risen through the ranks with a swiftness that hinted at the keen intelligence she masked by the feminine façade. She had a charisma that most men found irresistible and no doubt, she had used it to get to the top. No, Halle was not someone who worried without good reason. He had to find out what else was going on here.

"Can you give me any more information about the situation?" Kalen asked.

"I've been told nothing further. The priority is to get construction under way again, as quickly as possible. The worst outcome would be any further delays."

"Okay, I'm on it."

Halle lowered her voice seductively. "You know I'm always thinking about you."

"I think about you too," he said gently.

"We can do something special when you get back," she whispered.

"I'll look forward to it."

She tried to hold his gaze, her large blue eyes guileless, her face framed by a halo of golden hair. She reminded him of a little girl begging for sweets. A buzzer sounded behind her, and she jolted upright.

"I forgot I had another appointment. I have to go."

"Bye, Halle."

The screen went blank and he sighed with relief. She tried to dominate everything he did. He couldn't do anything without her knowing about it, well most things, he corrected himself. She didn't know about the Narquum yet, but that was only a matter of time. When she found out, would she shield him? He doubted it. Even Halle would baulk at putting her career on the line for him. No, they would be finished. She would have no option but to report him and his career would be finished too.

Chapter Five

Kalen got up early the next morning, looked at the site plan briefly, and left his quarters. His footsteps crunched softly on the spotless floor, barely audible over the heartbeat thud of the drills pounding far below him. He found the regular beat reassuring; work was continuing normally. It was the silences that were dangerous. That's when you knew something was wrong.

Now how to find the Ea-block canteen? The walls were all dark blue on this level and he had reached the end of the corridor. He had expected the canteen to be here, but there was only a junction with another corridor running at right angles to the one he was on. A few metres away, a security guard stood in front of the doors to an elevator.

The guard stared at Kalen's uniform as he approached. "Morning, sir."

"Morning. Is it usually this quiet? I'm looking for the canteen."

"Most of the men eat in the main mess hall after day change." The guard nodded towards the end of the corridor. "The canteen's down there if you want it."

"Thank you," Kalen said, and continued walking.

After a breakfast of porridge and biscuits, Kalen returned to his room and studied the site plan again. He had already memorised it, but now he pored over the plan to decide which areas it would be crucial for him to see. If he let Jorge suggest the route, he would see which sections Jorge thought were important to the investigation. It would be interesting to note whether Jorge's view accorded with his own. He would also need to speak to the geologist, Sera Ethern, about the strata of the lower levels and inspect the malfunctioning machinery. He imagined a tall, big boned, heavy woman and smiled to himself. Halle really had no need to worry about him straying. There was little chance of it in a place like this.

The first siren of day start sounded, the harsh noise invading his tiny quarters. He heard miners leaving their rooms, the patter of soft footsteps soon multiplying into the drumming of a heavy storm. He carried on studying the site plan for a few more minutes and then checked that he had everything he needed for the day. When the sound of footsteps became a trickle, he left the room and took the nearest elevator to the upper levels, where he joined the last of the miners walking towards one of the Gates. The blast of sirens suddenly echoed around him again. It must be eight hundred hours, he thought. The Gate would be open by the time he got there.

***

The mess hall in the central hub was already half full when Kalen arrived. A number of miners sat at tables eating while others moved about collecting food from the dispensers. He spotted Jorge on the far side at a table, talking to a small wiry man with dark wavy hair. They appeared to be in rapt conversation. As Kalen watched, a young woman of average height moved gracefully between the tables and joined them. Her shoulder length, dark brown hair was tied back with a band and she looked slim beneath her work clothes. A big man, a miner, brushed past Kalen and made his way across the room. The man stopped briefly beside Jorge's table, nodded to Jorge and the others, and settled at a table nearby.

Kalen walked over to the group, ignoring the suspicious stares of several miners whose eyes passed over the insignia on his jacket. He was nearly at the table when Jorge saw him. He immediately broke off his conversation and stood up.

"Good morning. Let me introduce you," Jorge said, turning towards his companions. "This is Chief Engineer Kalen Trinneer. And this is Sera Ethern, our geologist, and

First Engineer Daniel Beidenbeck who heads up our engineering team."

The woman had brown eyes rimmed with thick black lashes and a pale flawless complexion. A deep vertical frown line creased her forehead between her eyes. It was the only thing that marred her beauty and gave her a serious studious look. She sat with stiff shoulders, clasping her hands tightly together in her lap. *So this is the troublesome geologist*, Kalen thought. He sensed the interest of the large miner who sat at the next table and had a gut feeling that the man was listening to them. Perhaps Sera's discomfort had something to do with him.

"I'm pleased to meet you," Sera murmured, twisting her mouth into a half smile. A strand of hair had escaped from the band and flopped over her forehead. She nervously brushed it away with her hand and gazed up at him with a hostile glint in her eye.

Not very friendly, Kalen thought. *She looks like a cold fish.* He gave her his most winning smile and then focused his attention on the engineer. Dan Beidenbeck was a small man, but despite his lack of stature, he had a muscular build and alert expression. Kalen judged him to be about forty, but he suspected that he could still hold his own in a fight against men twice his weight. He gave Kalen a cheerful grin as he rose from his seat and extended his hand in welcome.

"Good to meet you, Chief," Dan said brightly, shaking his hand enthusiastically. "I hope you can get to the root of our problems here. My team have been driven half-crazy by the systems failures."

"It's a nice change to be welcome. Usually the engineering teams don't want me interfering," Kalen replied, laughing.

Dan smiled broadly. "The more eyes on the job, the better, I say. We can really do with the help."

"I thought it would be a good idea if Dan and Sera came around the site with us," Jorge said, glancing towards Sera, who still sat. "They can tell you about their work better than I can, and be on hand to answer questions. Is that okay with you?"

"That's fine," Kalen agreed.

"Have you had breakfast? Do you want to get anything before we go?" Jorge motioned towards the food dispensers.

Kalen shook his head. "I've already had breakfast, thanks. I'd like to get started as soon as you're ready."

"Then let's start with an inspection of the equipment that's been affected, and the places where there have been incidents. You should already have full details, but you can see it for yourself and Dan can answer any questions. Sera can clarify the geology of the different sections as we go along. Or would you prefer to start somewhere else?"

"No, that's okay. I'll let you lead the way. If there's anything else I want to see, I'll let you know."

"In that case, we'll start at the thirty-ninth level." Jorge prepared to leave. "But first I need to update you in my office. Dan and Sera will meet us at the elevator in twenty minutes."

***

Jorge closed the door to his office behind them and leaned back against his desk, resting both palms on the edge and flexed his fingers.

"Have a seat." He gestured towards a chair on the other side of the room. "There's something else you need to know. It isn't common knowledge yet and officially the problem doesn't exist, but the miners have been getting sick."

Kalen remained standing. "What does that have to do with me? I'm an engineer. Illness is outside my brief."

"It could be linked to faulty machinery possibly giving off toxic fumes." Jorge leaned forward slightly. "The symptoms are consistent with poisoning. The men suddenly become weak and feverish. That can last from a few hours to three or four days and then they recover. The site doctor can't find the cause."

"How many cases?"

"At first, we had one isolated case and then there were three the following week. After that, the numbers keep growing."

"Have they all been working in the same area?"

"No, it's site wide. But no one got sick until we broke through to thirty-nine. That was about five weeks ago. Other than that we can't find a link."

"So how many cases altogether?"

Jorge dropped his voice. "As of today, over forty." He grimaced and continued, "Yesterday another man reported to sick bay with the same symptoms."

"That's a hell of a lot!" Kalen snapped. "I thought that anything over twenty cases was classed as an epidemic and quarantine was imposed?"

Jorge gripped the edge of his desk. "You're right. So far it's been covered up by both zones to avoid closing the site."

"What if it's infectious? It could get out into the general population." Kalen could feel his anger rising.

"The doctor doesn't think so. If he did, I wouldn't let the men work," Jorge replied, folding his arms across his chest. "The doctor thinks that it might be chemical poisoning. If the ventilation system is faulty, something could be getting into the air supply. It could cause a reaction and then dissipate quickly from the body, so that by the time he examines a patient, there's no trace of it."

"That's possible; toxins can get into the supply." Kalen's annoyance subsided a little.

"So far, the cases have been treated purely as a routine site matter, logged as unconnected and played down. In reality, the symptoms are strange. The men completely lose it; they can't recognise their surroundings and start hallucinating."

"When they recover, are they fit to return to work?"

"Yes, they seem to get back to normal and there have been no relapses so far. None of them have any idea how they got sick."

"What about the U-Zone? How many are getting sick there?" Kalen asked.

"From what I've heard, they've had about the same number of cases as us."

"The site commanders are responsible for overall safety. What's the official line?"

"Our site commander is stalling for time. If it's chemical exposure, he's hoping the source can be traced before he's forced to declare the site under quarantine. You know what that would mean: all work would stop."

"The air supply could be contaminated," Kalen agreed.

"It seems likely. Even if you can't trace the source of contamination, if you can find anything to support that theory, the commander can use it to keep the site open." Jorge gave Kalen a sharp look. "It's important that we're not shut down."

Kalen thought quickly. No one wanted the site shut down unnecessarily but they risked an epidemic if disease spread. As mining captain, Jorge would usually look out for the welfare of his men first, but here Jorge was taking the company line. At this stage, he didn't have enough information to form a reasoned view, and anyway, he needed Jorge's cooperation to find out what was going on.

He looked Jorge straight in the eye. "No, we don't want the site shut down. I'll see what I can find."

***

Sera waited at the elevators with Dan, until Jorge and the chief engineer arrived. The lifts were large enough to hold thirty men at a time, but most of the miners had already gone below and they boarded an empty car. She studied the new engineer as the car dropped towards the booming sounds of the drills and digging machinery that echoed up through the lift shaft. In the canteen, he had given her a wide smile, exposing a row of perfect white teeth and appraised her with bright eyes that seemed to see right into her. His even features and strong jaw were complemented by dark brows and short black hair that gleamed in the lights of the elevator car. He reminded her of another man that she'd once known. A good-looking man who knew it, she decided. The type she disliked intensely.

He stood on the other side of Jorge from her, lightly resting one hand on the handrail, self-assured, frowning from time to time as he leant forward to hear what Jorge was saying. The drills and lift mechanism muffled their conversation and Sera moved nearer to Jorge so that she could hear them. She wished that she could have avoided this tour. The blue crystals were waiting in her laboratory for analysis and she was impatient to get back to them. She listened as Jorge described the site to Chief Engineer Trinneer.

"The port and shuttle-docks are located to the north-east of the main crater. It's the largest of the three and known as Crater One. We're going south to the area that runs adjacent to the main crater's edge."

The lift slowed to a crawl and began to judder. Sera tightened her grip on the handrail while she followed the conversation.

"The roof of the main crater has been completed but the interior is still largely undeveloped, although the city streets have been mapped out," Jorge continued.

"I've read the reports so I have an idea of the layout," Chief Trinneer replied.

"The terraces on the east side of the main crater haven't been finished yet either. The other two craters lie to the north. A roof has been installed over Crater Two but there was a fatal accident at Crater Three and the roof is only halfway finished."

"Was that where one of the workers fell from the rigging?"

Sera recalled hearing that a roofer had fallen hundreds of metres to his death. It had been the talk of the mess hall.

"That's right."

"He didn't have a safety harness on when he fell, but everyone said that he'd been wearing it at the start of his shift," Dan added. "The harness was never found."

"He must have taken his harness off. Those guys like to take risks," Jorge said, shrugging. "Anyway, first we're going to level thirty-nine where the mining is finished and the construction of the internal accommodation is under way. That will give you some idea of the dimensions of the levels, pre-completion."

"I read that a miner was nearly crushed on the thirty-ninth?" Chief Trinneer asked.

The new engineer is well informed, Sera thought. *He must have been given a full briefing about the site before he got here. I wonder what he's been told about me?*

"Yes, he was riding one of the mobile drills," Jorge replied. "It got rammed from behind by another drill that was running on automatic without a rider. He hit the rock face and injured his shoulder."

"We inspected both machines. Someone must have turned the second drill on remotely, but we couldn't find anyone who had access to the remote," Dan explained.

"I thought all the drills ran on different frequencies to avoid setting them off by accident? Can't the operator be traced through its programming?"

"That's the funny thing," Dan said. "According to its programme, no one switched it on. It hadn't logged the episode at all. Its record showed that it was stationary when the accident happened."

"That's impossible! What about its sensors? It should have stopped automatically before it hit the other drill."

"We checked all that. The machine was in perfect working order."

"There must be a rational explanation for it," Jorge interrupted. "We just haven't found it yet."

The lift slowed to a stop and Jorge opened the doors, letting in a rush of cold air. Sera shivered; she could never get used to the temperature changes between levels. She followed the others out of the car into the building site. The accommodation had been hollowed out, but the complex was still a steel skeleton. Numerous workers milled over a vast area between girders and machinery, and the roof of the cavern was many metres above. Most of the heavy building was being undertaken by machines operated by men riding the apparatus, with others directing them. The sound of machinery and cacophony of human voices made it difficult for her to hear what Jorge was saying.

"Welcome to the thirty-ninth. This level is about halfway to completion. My mining teams are working on the lower levels now. The men you see here are the construction crews. I think they have the softer jobs!" Jorge yelled, leading the way through a mass of steel structures and moving machinery towards the far end of the cavern.

Some of the workers glanced at their party, but most ignored them.

"This is where the rogue drill smashed into the other one." Jorge paused and looked about them. "There isn't anything to see now."

"Is there anything out of the ordinary about this spot?" Chief Trinneer asked.

"Nothing that we know of, it's relatively near the crater's edge but that's all."

Chief Trinneer turned to her. "What about the mineral composition here?"

Sera had barely heard his question above the noise. Now his eyes were fixed on her and the other two had turned towards her as well.

"It's the same as the rest of this area. At this level it's mostly solid granite," she replied.

"What about the floors immediately above and below?"

"The same, nothing unusual, but I've just found an unusual mineral formation on the forty-seventh. A strange type of crystal I don't recognise but I haven't had a chance to analyse it yet."

"We'll take a look at it when we go down there," Jorge said, setting off again.

The ground underfoot was uneven and her hard-soled boots crunched over rubble. She walked beside the chief engineer, her head reaching his shoulder. When Jorge quickened his pace, she lengthened her stride, but the toe of her boot hit a rock and she stumbled. At that moment, a firm hand on her upper arm pulled her back up.

"Are you okay?" Chief Trinneer asked, removing his hand as she steadied herself.

Turning her head to acknowledge his help, she met the chief engineer's eyes. Knowing eyes, she thought. She could still feel the place where his fingers had gripped her, his touch somehow intrusive despite her thick jacket.

"Thank you," she said curtly, and looked away.

In front of them, Jorge had stopped at the entrance of a wide tunnel.

"Let me show you the main crater now," Jorge addressed Kalen. "I think you'll find this interesting."

Chapter Six

Kalen followed Jorge into the dimly lit tunnel, towards a blaze of light shining a hundred metres or so ahead of them. As they walked towards the light, it became blinding and Kalen found himself forced to look away. They were approaching the exit from the tunnel and the light was coming from beyond it. He thought it was too bright for daylight but before he had time to think about this further, he found himself stepping out of its mouth onto a wide terrace overlooking the crater.

Intense light hit his eyes sharply and they smarted. He used his hand to shield his eyes from the glare and tried to focus on the view in front of him.

"I didn't think…" Kalen uttered in awe, staring at the vast panorama that stretched out below them, "… it would be this big!"

"Impressive, isn't it?" Jorge said, smiling.

Jorge walked to the edge of the terrace and stood by the barrier, motioning to the others to join him. Sunlight blazed mercilessly through the transparent roof of the crater's dome far overhead, bathing everything in an unnatural brilliance.

"I should have warned you about the light." Jorge took a pair of sunglasses from his pocket and put them on. "The artificial and natural lights haven't been balanced yet. It won't be comfortable until more filters are installed in the roof."

Kalen rested his arm on the top of the barrier and gazed out at the crater's interior. Taidor's sun was directly overhead and there were few shadows.

They were standing halfway up the side of the crater, two thousand metres above the ground. Below, the floor of the crater extended forty kilometres to its far side and was etched with straight dark lines. *Those must be the foundations for the new city*, Kalen thought. In the distance, he could see the tiny figures of the construction teams moving up and down, shaping the embryonic buildings. To the north, part of the structure of the shuttle port stuck out from the side of the crater, and immediately below them, the terraces were in various stages of completion.

The dry description in Kalen's briefing notes hadn't conveyed the sheer scale of the project. No wonder Taidor's Governing Council wanted to avoid delays. This would be Taidor's showpiece; the city would be the envy of colonists everywhere.

"See over there? That's where the main administrative centre will be, near the shuttle port." Jorge pointed northwards with a short movement, and then dropped his hand to his side. "There'll also be a transport link to the other craters."

"It's far larger than I imagined," Kalen admitted, slitting his eyes against the sunshine.

"Everyone says that." Dan chuckled. He had come to stand next to Kalen, his unprotected eyes squinting at the view. "The amount of space takes some getting used to."

"This is going to be the biggest development on Taidor," Jorge said proudly. "This is only one of three craters. When it's finished, the city will be three times this size."

"Will the port be enlarged?" Kalen asked, imagining the thriving metropolis it would become.

"There are plans to install an interplanetary port. The shuttle bay is only temporary and won't be large enough to serve the city. It's going to be the largest city on Taidor and probably the largest in this planetary system."

Kalen looked across at Sera who stood silently screwing up her eyes and fidgeting with her hands. She had trailed behind them all morning looking sulky, hardly saying anything or volunteering any information. When he'd caught her arm earlier to stop her falling, she had jerked away from him with a sullen expression. He wondered what was bothering her. His eyes were now streaming without sunglasses.

"Okay, I've seen enough," Kalen said. He could always return another time when he was properly equipped.

Jorge nodded and turned to go. "We'll go to the forty-sixth level now, where one of the accidents happened. After that I'll take you down to the new workings on forty-seven."

Jorge re-entered the tunnel and led them down a flight of stairs. Black spots danced before Kalen's eyes, and the shadows in the crevices seemed to move about. After climbing down several levels, Jorge turned off the stairwell and into another passageway lit by dim wall lights. At the far end, the ear-splitting sound of the drills assaulted Kalen as they emerged into the massive complex of the forty-sixth.

They stood in a huge cavern, the centre an empty expanse, while miners, drills, and machinery worked at the sides. Driverless, bucket-shaped metal containers two or three metres long glided a few centimetres above the ground across the gallery. As they got nearer, Kalen saw they were filled with rubble. They appeared to be moving between drilling machinery on one side of the chamber and shafts on the other.

Jorge pointed at the trucks and yelled, "All the rock we dig up is used for building on the crater floor. The trucks are filled automatically, and programmed to take their loads to the shafts for transport. They have sensors to stop them colliding with anything."

"Their sensors also control their speed," Dan added, as a truck moved silently past them.

"Wasn't one of those involved in the accident?" Kalen asked, watching the hovering rubble trucks.

"That's correct." Jorge raised his voice above the din. "It suddenly shot across the floor with a full load and flew at one of the main wall supports. It nearly hit a man."

"It stayed near the ground, but it ignored its sensors and directional programming," Dan expanded. "Afterwards we couldn't find anything wrong with it."

"Have you got any theories, Dan?" Kalen asked.

"There was a power failure about an hour before it happened. It's possible that when the power came back on, there was a surge that messed up the truck's programming."

"There have been a lot of accidents," Sera volunteered, biting off the last word. She scowled and the line between her eyes deepened.

So, she has a voice after all, Kalen thought. He pondered for a moment. Whatever was happening here should be mirrored in the U-Zone.

He turned to Jorge. "Did both of the accidents with the drill and the truck happen on your shift?"

Jorge shook his head. "No, the first accident with the drill happened in the U-Zone. I just read the reports later. The accident with the rubble truck happened on my shift, but I didn't see it."

"What about other incidents? I've heard about rock-falls as well?"

"We've had a few but no one has been hurt yet. Automatic supports have also collapsed several times but we can't find the cause. They're designed to stay rigid even if the power is disconnected."

"What about the location of the rock-falls? Is there any pattern?" The number of incidents puzzled Kalen.

"No, except we've had more than usual below level thirty."

Without warning, a vivid image of the terrified faces of the crew at Area Nine flashed into Kalen's mind and he heard screaming. *This isn't real; I'm not there*, he thought wildly. *I need another Narquum.* Fighting to clear the images from his mind, he coughed and concentrated on Jorge's voice.

Jorge glanced towards him. "It is dusty in here. We'll pick up the breathing tubes in a minute."

Jorge began moving again, leading them in a direction similar to the route that the rubble trucks used and towards the hammering of machinery. Kalen suppressed his instinctive reaction to step to one side when a rubble truck swung into view, and bore down on him loaded top heavy with dark chunks of rock. It glided gracefully past, only gently stirring the cloudy air.

"We'll use air tubes below," Jorge told him as they walked. "We've already got the suction equipment running in the main section to clean up the dust, but the oxygen will be too thin to breathe."

They reached the far side of the cavern where an exit had been rough-hewn in the granite. Beyond, Kalen could see another faintly lit corridor and stairwell. Just before the exit, Jorge stopped at a locker fixed on the wall and opened it. He pulled out four sets of breathing apparatus including masks and breathing tubes and handed them out. Kalen took out a breathing tube and an air canister and put the rest of the equipment in his pack. The others did the same.

"All ready?" Jorge asked, adjusting his breathing tube to fit near the corner of his mouth. "Then we'll go down to the forty-seventh."

Jorge led them out of the cavern and down the faintly lit stairwell. Multitudes of dust motes hung in the thin air around them and the sound of the drills increased as they descended. Jorge moved down the stairwell for several minutes and then turned off into another corridor and paused.

"We're at the forty-seventh now," Jorge shouted over the noise. "I'm taking you to the main site. Stay close to me."

Jorge guided them along the corridor, ignoring smaller corridors that branched off on either side, until they reached the entrance to another vast chamber, where he paused again. In the dim light, Kalen gazed at the panoply of activity in front of him and momentarily felt overwhelmed by the noise. He estimated that a full crew was working on this level and that the excavations extended two hundred metres or more in one direction and approximately half of that in the other. Mouths of dark passageways ran off the gallery and a number of rubble trucks crisscrossed the floor.

He watched the activity from the entrance with the others, while Jorge spoke to a foreman. Riders on mobile drills supplemented the work of the huge primary drills that pounded mercilessly at the sides of the cavern. The giant drills remained stationary while they pummelled the rock face and then crawled forward as it gave way, automatically inserting support struts behind them. *The drills look like they're working okay*, Kalen assessed. He turned his attention to the steady stream of rubble trucks that hovered smoothly backwards and forwards across the site. Nothing unusual about them either.

The bitter smell of the drills combined with the noise of machinery, would make this environment uncomfortable for someone unused to it, Kalen mused. Like Halle. He couldn't recall her visiting the construction sites. She only travelled to Morten where she had another office.

Jorge turned back towards them and shouted, "This way!" He waved at them to follow him along the side of the gallery, pausing halfway down. "Sera, I want you to show Kalen where you've been working."

"Okay." Sera moved ahead and disappeared into one of the side tunnels.

Kalen barely heard the exchange over the hubbub, but he followed her into a dusty corridor, where the temporary lighting cast weird shadows over the walls and ceiling. Inside, the noise of the drilling subsided although Kalen could still feel the drumming through the soles of his boots. Further down, the passageway widened, but leading off it were a number of roughly hewn narrow tunnels cleaved into the rock.

Sera paused at the entrance to one of the small tunnels. "These are the survey conduits. I take mineral samples from each section and then liaise with the surveyor about the layout."

Kalen peered into one of the narrow apertures, but with no lighting inside, he couldn't see anything. Sera walked a few metres further and then stopped again opposite a narrow crevice in the rock wall.

She gestured to the hole. "This is where I found the strange crystalline deposits."

"In there?" Kalen asked doubtfully. The gap looked little more than a crack, barely wide enough for someone to slide into.

Sera took out her torch and directed the beam into the hole. "The deposits are some way in."

"What's unusual about them?"

"The stones look like little pointy blue crystals. I've never seen anything like them before." Sera's voice rose slightly. "My initial view is that they're of an unknown composition."

Kalen glanced at Sera's face. She had become animated, excited even. This was clearly her passion; she loved her work.

"That's interesting." He waited for her to expand on the subject but she didn't go on. "Will they affect the building plans?"

"I don't know." Her face returned to a slightly sullen expression.

"When will you be able to give an opinion?" he asked, trying to keep the irritation out of his voice.

"After I've done a full analysis."

Perhaps she would have a view once she had done her analysis. He wouldn't push her on the first morning, but later he'd press her for the information he needed. The rock exposed inside the entrance to the fissure looked normal.

"Do you want to take a look inside? You can use my flashlight." She held her torch out towards him.

The hole looked too small for him to get into. He thought about asking her to crawl inside the crevice herself and bring out a fresh sample, but he decided that would be childish.

The other two were listening to the exchange, Jorge with a wry smile and Dan with an amused twinkle in his eyes.

"No, I don't think there's any point at this stage. I can always come back later if I need to see for myself. How long will your analysis take?"

"I don't know. I hoped to work on the samples this morning."

Jorge stepped forward. "We can let Sera go now, unless you want her for anything else?"

"Nothing I can think of right now. But I'll want to see the results of Sera's tests when they're ready."

She gave him a cold look and then left them, walking back in the direction they had come from. Kalen heard Dan chuckling behind him.

"Don't worry, she's always like that."

"I'll bear that in mind," Kalen replied.

Jorge ignored the remark. "Let's get on. I want to show you the rest of this level before we break for lunch."

Jorge led them into another tunnel and the air grew thinner, as they walked farther away from the main site. Kalen drew in another mouthful of oxygen from his breathing tube and tried to avoid inhaling dust. He listened as Jorge pointed out the smaller survey conduits and the places where the primary drills and supports would be placed, and described the proposed layout of the section. At this stage, the tunnels seemed to him to be a confusing labyrinth.

"We don't need to retrace our steps," Jorge said, after they had walked some distance. "We can get back to the main site another way."

As they went back through winding passageways, Kalen judged their distance from the main gallery by the increasing noise of the drills and machinery. After several twists and turns, they emerged into a wide corridor, where the air was visibly cleaner. Here the drills reverberated sharply and the ground vibrated. The walk had given him an appetite and he was ready for lunch.

"Not much further," Jorge said.

"Thanks for the tour. Is there anywhere to get lunch on this level?"

"No, we'll have to go up top. I'm getting hungry myself."

Their footsteps cracked harshly on the hard rock floor in a discordant clatter that seemed amplified in the confines of the tunnel. *Our footsteps sound loud*, Kalen thought. He'd never noticed that before. Something was different. He looked around him. Beside him, Dan had slowed his pace and was looking around as well. They looked at each other. Ahead, Jorge had stopped walking and appeared to be standing, listening. Realisation suddenly dawned in Dan's eyes.

"The drills have stopped! I can't hear the drills!" Dan exclaimed.

"You're right." Jorge turned to them, perplexed. "Something's happened. The drills never stop."

***

In her laboratory, Sera stared at the small blue crystals. They varied in colour from a shade of cornflower to a deeper blue and were shaped like tiny pyramids, each ending in a point. She had run all the standard preliminary tests but she hadn't been able to identify the stones. *These aren't crystals*, she thought, reading the test results again. *There's nothing useful here*. The readout gave no indication of the stones' age, composition, or structural integrity. She placed one of her samples under a microscope. The tiny stone appeared perfectly symmetrical with beautiful facets that glittered when the light caught it, like a finely cut gem.

The rock face had been grooved between the crystals and she had a nagging feeling that she had read about a similar formation before, but she couldn't recall the reference. Turning to her computer, she programmed it to search for comparisons. If a similar mineral had already been discovered, there would be a record of it somewhere.

She decided to conduct a sophisticated test that would analyse the crystals' composition. After setting up her equipment, she placed one of the tiny pyramids in a cylindrical container and adjusted the settings. The crystal glittered where the light caught it. Putting on goggles to protect her eyes, she turned the machine on and bright light immediately bathed the stone. After ten seconds, the machine's display lit up showing a line of zeros. *Another blank*, she thought with frustration.

She changed the settings to cut into the tiny blue stone. This time the beam would physically penetrate the outer layers, possibly slicing the pyramid in two. Standing clear, she switched the laser on. With a blinding flash and a sharp crack, the stone shattered into a myriad of tiny shards that bounced violently off the sides of the container. A brilliant flare erupted within the cylinder and then died, leaving nothing but a heap of tiny flecks that looked like sand. Nothing was left of the sample now, apart from a small amount of dull grit. She resisted the temptation to pick up the container and shake it, to get the glitter back.

The machine began to display the results.

"That's strange," she said aloud, staring at the reading. The stones were fragile and couldn't withstand pressure, but their constituent elements were unknown.

Out of the corner of her eye, she saw something move and swung around. A small scanner lay at the end of the workbench where she had put it, after turning it off, but now its display blinked with red figures. Measurements for rock density appeared and disappeared randomly on its display for several moments, and then faded out. *That's odd,* she thought, *perhaps it's broken.*

The results of Sera's computer search came back and she read them with growing excitement. There was no recorded reference to similar mineral deposits. As she had suspected, the stones weren't crystals, but a new type of mineral. She flicked to the charts on her computer screen and then labelled the small blue stones 'Uveid' in accordance with the Division's geological classification system.

Chapter Seven

They entered the main site at a run, Jorge pounding ahead followed closely by Kalen and Dan. One of the miners was running towards them.

"There's been an accident, someone's been killed!" the miner shouted hoarsely.

Jorge started towards the miner, who stopped to catch his breath.

"A man's gone under one of the primary drills. He's fallen under the strut."

"My God man, where?" Jorge demanded.

"Up there, at the end," the miner replied, pointing towards the far end of the chamber.

Jorge nodded at the man and sprinted across the central construction area. Kalen followed him at a jog.

In the main area work had stopped. The primary drills stood idle, the dull heartbeat of their continuous booming silenced. Instead, Kalen heard the sound of raised voices, shouting and arguing, and a woman's wailing. The voices were coming from the far end of the site where a crowd of miners had gathered. The near end of the site was nearly empty of workers and no one was riding the mobile drills. There was little movement except for the rubble trucks that continued to skim backwards and forwards across the floor.

"What the hell!" Jorge exclaimed and ran towards the crowd.

Kalen caught up with him as they reached the throng that surrounded one of the large primary drills.

With Kalen at his shoulder, Jorge pushed his way into the sea of backs shouting, "Let me through!" repeatedly. His voice was drowned in the babble, but as men turned and recognised him, they parted so he could get by and fell silent as he passed.

A hush rippled across the miners as Jorge and Kalen emerged at the front of the crowd. In the lull, the sound of a woman crying hysterically and another woman sobbing some way off was clearly audible. The voices of two miners arguing loudly also carried across the site, but they abruptly fell silent a few seconds after the shouting stopped. The expressions on the faces of the men standing around the drill ranged from dispassionate interest to wide-eyed horror.

Kalen took in the scene in front of him. The massive primary drill had been switched off and stood motionless. The body of a man lay face up underneath the overhang at the rear of the drill. A strut had struck the man in the centre of his torso, smashing his lower ribs and spine, pinning him to the ground. The strut was cylindrical, about twenty centimetres in diameter, and looked very heavy. It was one of the struts that the machine inserted behind it, when it moved forward after breaking new ground. Bone jutted from the entry wound and the man's innards spilled out of the hole in a bloody tangle. A hard hat lay several feet away. The man was bald, stout, and middle aged.

"How the…?" Kalen uttered involuntarily and then stopped himself from saying more. He must let Jorge deal with this. These were his men.

Kalen's stomach lurched and he thought he was going to throw up. He turned his head away and suppressed the violent urge to vomit. Jorge stiffened beside him. There was blood everywhere and a sickly smelling mess oozed from lesions in the man's intestines that spread across the ground. Kalen put his hand to his mouth and tried to ignore the smell. The man's face was turned to one side so he rested on his cheek and one of his eyes stared blankly up at the drill above him. A film of dust already coated it. With a shock, Kalen saw that the man was dressed in civilian clothes. *Who the hell was he and how did he get under the drill?*

"Stand back and give us room!" Jorge bellowed at the men. "Who saw what happened? Where's the drill operator?"

"I'm the operator," a man nearby stammered nervously. He looked scared and his face was pallid. "I don't know what happened. There was a scream and then I saw him under the strut. I don't know where he came from. I just shut the drill down straight away."

Jorge glared at the operator, turned to the crowd, and yelled at them, "All of you get back to work, except for the drill team. I said get back to work. Don't just stand there, move!"

The crowd dispersed except for the drill operator and a handful of men. Jorge stared stonily at them.

"What do you mean you don't know what happened?" Jorge rounded on the operator. "Your job is to keep an eye on the drill. He must have come from somewhere!"

"There was no one near the drill, then all of a sudden, the man was under it," the operator gulped out miserably.

"Anyone else? Someone must have seen something?" Jorge's eyes scoured the group. "I'm away for a couple of hours and you can't be trusted to keep people clear of the drill!" The men avoided Jorge's glare in guilty silence. "Who is he anyway?"

"He's a tourist," one of the miners said at last, meeting Jorge's eyes. "His tour group is over there. The foreman is with them."

The miner pointed towards a group of people at the side of the gallery. Kalen hadn't noticed them before. Seven or eight people, three of them women, stood huddled miserably next to the wall. They all wore hard hats, jackets, and trousers, in various colours. A young man stood in front of them talking to the foreman and another miner.

Of the party, a mature plump lady was crying into the shoulder of a man who had his arm around her, while another woman sobbed noisily. One of the other men was vomiting into the corner and another was staring towards the drill with a frozen look of disbelief. A third woman with dark hair stood slightly apart from the others. She looked younger than the rest and watched the activity with a keen interest.

"My God, there's going to be some explaining to do!" Jorge shouted. "A civilian, dead on my shift!"

"Tourists? Here?" Kalen asked incredulously. He could feel his own anger mounting. *I can't believe this*, he thought. *What are tourists doing here? How could they have got near the drill?*

"I'm afraid so. I put in an objection weeks ago. The U-Zone stopped their tours, but not our lot. This was the last tour." Jorge's mouth twisted in disgust. "They shouldn't be on this level anyway."

"Did anyone see the tourists before the accident?" Jorge turned his attention back to the men. Dan had joined them, and stood quietly staring at the drill and shaking his head.

Another miner stepped forward and said, "I was checking out the programme for the trucks. I looked up and saw them coming in from the back, over there." He pointed towards a dark corner of the hall, about forty feet away from the drill. "They were just at the corner and then I heard a scream. I didn't see them near the drill."

"Why didn't you stop them? They shouldn't have been down here!" Jorge raged.

"There wasn't time, it happened too quickly," the man stuttered.

"Did anyone see anything else?" Jorge demanded. "Was anyone working over there?"

"I don't think anybody was near them," another man timidly volunteered.

The foreman came up and pushed his way through the little group. "Security are here and the site commander's been called. The medics are on their way. The tour guide says he got lost and came onto this level by mistake."

"How did he get in?"

"He says he came in through the entrance in the corner." The foreman pointed towards one of the tunnels at the rear of the gallery. "He says they were trying to get back to the upper levels."

"He can explain that to the commander. The medics aren't going to be able to do a lot for this man!" Jorge snapped, glancing over at the crumpled body of the man that still lay under the machine. "We'll have to wait for the commander before we can move him. He'll want to speak to you all."

"As soon as the commander gives the okay, we'll retract the strut," Dan said.

"Then we'll need to take the drill apart, to make sure there isn't a fault," Kalen added bitterly. "It means more delay."

"We can get onto it as soon as the medics remove the body." Dan shook his head sadly. "What a way to go."

"Is there anything else you can think of?" Jorge asked Kalen.

Kalen gestured towards the tunnel in the corner. "Where does the tunnel go?"

"It's a survey tunnel."

"Let's take a look," Kalen said.

"Dan, you take charge here," Jorge directed. "We'll be back in a few minutes."

They left the team by the drill and skirted around the machine to the corner of the gallery, keeping wide of the rubble trucks that continued to hover across the floor. The corner had been roughly hewn out and was dimly lit. Rubble and boulders were strewn across the ground and Kalen had to keep checking his footing to avoid stumbling. The walls were rough and pitted, and in places, several vertical fissures ran down their length casting strange shadows across the ground. There was no machinery here, but a tunnel led out into a narrow passageway.

Kalen stopped at the mouth of the tunnel and looked back over the main site. They were a considerable distance from the primary drill but it was clearly visible. He could see that it had been excavating the wall to his left, and the length of the wall between where he stood and the drill was in shadow. *If the tourists had walked along the side of the wall no one might have seen them,* he pondered. Dusty air and dim lighting decreased visibility further. But why would someone walk into a drill?

Kalen turned and peered into the tunnel. "What's through there?"

"There are more survey conduits. They were only dug out a few days ago."

Kalen entered the tunnel but it was very similar to the corridors they had walked through that morning. He adjusted his breathing tube. The muggy air and his suppressed anger were beginning to make him feel light-headed. Jorge followed him into a wide corridor from which other tunnels branched off.

"There are no elevators on this side?" Kalen asked.

"No, they're all on the other side."

"Could the tourists have got over here without crossing the main gallery?"

"Yes. Near the lift shafts, there's an entrance to a corridor that runs adjacent to the main gallery. There's also a stairwell on this side. They didn't need to come across the main floor."

"I can't see any reason why they would be over here."

"Or on this level," Jorge added cynically.

They spent some time exploring the tunnels that branched off and after ten minutes emerged into the main site again from another entrance. A number of security guards were milling around and several medics were bunched together near the drill. A few metres away, the site commander stood talking to Dan.

"It's out of our hands now," Jorge said. "The Mining Division has no jurisdiction when a civilian is involved."

"I know, but I should get the results of the commander's investigation," Kalen replied, as they walked towards Dan and the commander.

***

Later that day, Kalen sat in his office in the central hub, reading the reports obtained by Security. The light on his console blinked on and he switched on the screen.

Halle's face appeared, frowning. She looked pale with faint blue rings underneath her eyes. "I've heard there's been an accident."

"Yes, it's bad. I'm just reading the reports. I was going to call you."

"I've been told that a civilian was killed? That he was found under a drill?"

"Yes, a tourist, on the forty-seventh."

"There was a tour group at Three-Craters?"

"Yes. According to the reports they'd just come from Area Eighteen and had permission to see the main crater and some of the upper levels at Three-Craters."

"What happened? How did they get to the forty-seventh?"

"A foreman left them on the terraces to make their own way back to the upper levels." Kalen grimaced. "Apparently the guide got lost trying to find the way back up."

"They were left alone?" Halle looked surprised. "I didn't think that was standard practice. Why didn't the foreman stay with them to make sure they got back to the elevators?"

"I don't know. Civilians are always accompanied on site. They're trying to trace the foreman to find out why he left them."

"I still don't understand how they would end up on the forty-seventh if they were supposed to be going back up?"

"The guide said he went down a stairwell trying to find the exit. I expect he was exploring. Tourists are always curious." Kalen shrugged. "They'd already been to Area Eighteen so the guide should have been familiar with this sort of site."

"Didn't anyone notice them? I mean, why didn't someone stop them?" Halle began to get agitated. "There must have been a lot of people working down there."

"They took a wrong turn and ended up at the corner of the main floor. No one saw them. It's pretty dark at that end. The guide stuck to the wall because he was frightened of the rubble trucks. The operator heard a woman scream and saw the man under the drill. The deceased is listed as Palum Kingston, aged forty-five. He teaches astrophysics at one of the universities and was travelling alone."

"Did the woman who screamed see what happened?"

"She says that the guide led them along the wall until they were about three metres from the drill. She thought she saw something move near the drill and looked around to see Palum Kingston under the strut. The other tourists say the same thing."

"So the man got sucked into the drill?" Halle's eyes grew wide as if she was imagining the scene.

"He couldn't have. There's no mechanism that would suck anyone in. He would have had to walk right into it."

"I don't understand?" Halle looked perplexed.

"You can approach the drill quite safely to within about a metre from the sides and the back also has an overhang of about a metre. No one in their right mind would get closer than that, unless they were suicidal. These are pretty large machines, so he must have walked into it."

"Why would he do that?"

"I don't know. I suppose it's possible he tried to get a closer look and fell. The light isn't good there. Or perhaps he was getting ill? Hallucinating?" Kalen suggested wryly.

Halle scowled at him. "It would be best if you kept that theory to yourself!"

"I know," he replied sardonically. "Anyway, we're going to check over the drill. There's probably nothing wrong with it, but we won't know for sure until we take it apart. We did a cursory inspection this afternoon, but we couldn't see any visible faults. Luther and the engineering team in the U-Zone will start dismantling the drill this evening, and tomorrow I'll continue the job with Dan. If there is a fault with the drill, we'll find it."

"I don't like this, Kalen. We've never had these sorts of problems before. If there's anything wrong with the drill and it caused that man's death, the Division is going to look bad. The Division will punish whoever was responsible, probably the engineers on site. Let me know the minute you find out anything."

"Will do. It could just be a fluke accident, but we'll know more later."

Halle terminated the call and Kalen stared at the blank screen for a moment, visualising Kingston's body, and then dismissed the image from his mind and returned to the reports.

Chapter Eight

Kalen entered the crowded mess hall and looked about for Jorge but he couldn't see him. He went over to the food dispensers, selected a dish of soya stew and vegetable cubes, and found a place at a table to eat. Around him, the miners and site personnel chatted noisily over their meals. He overheard snatches of their conversations and most of them were talking about the accident. A sense of deep disquiet pervaded their talk and more than once he heard someone referring to the 'curse' of the site.

The tourists sat by themselves at a table a few metres away from him. Their number was depleted. Kalen counted only five of them, the three single men, the tour leader, and the dark-haired girl that he had noticed before. They appeared subdued and sat in silence, ignored by everyone else. Only the girl looked as if she was interested in the other people in the canteen. Every now and again, she turned her head to stare at someone, and when she did that, her long black hair shone in the light.

As Kalen sat eating, he saw Jorge come in and make his way across the mess hall to the bar and lounge at the far end. A few minutes later, Dan joined him and they stood chatting near the bar. Kalen finished his meal and walked over to them.

"Any news?" Jorge asked.

"I've spoken to the Division. They know we're investigating," Kalen replied.

"This has been a bad day," Jorge said. "Haven't we got enough problems without having tourists thrown at us? We've got a schedule to keep and we're falling behind."

Dan made a face. "We got the strut out of him easily, but it wasn't pretty. He was a mess. The medics took him away."

"The initial checks on the drill didn't turn up anything," Kalen confirmed. "But we have to do a full inspection, just to be sure."

He had taken another Narquum to mute his anger but he still had a rising sense of frustration. It would take days to go over the whole drill, dismantling parts and then reassembling it, and they would probably find nothing. It would be logged as another unexplained accident to add to the growing list and would push the work even further behind.

"The man must have had a death wish, to get that close," Dan said. "He went in from the side."

"I doubt we'll ever know." Jorge took another sip of his drink.

"But how did he get under the drill?" Dan frowned, drawing his dark brows together. "It's the timing that gets me. If he'd fallen he would normally have hit the side of the strut, not ended up under it."

"What's the excavation rate on that machine?" Kalen asked. "How often does it put down the struts?"

"The rate is set depending on the sort of rock," Dan replied. "On forty-seven it's set to eat rock at half a metre an hour. The struts go down every two metres."

"Could there have been something wrong with the timing?"

"I doubt it. The operator would have noticed if the timing were out. I've already checked the programme and it was set correctly. The records don't show any deviation."

"The four-hour interval gives us plenty of time to put in the permanent structural supports behind the machine, before we remove the temporary struts," Jorge said.

"He was just unlucky," Dan remarked.

"The commander will conduct a full investigation, but the heat is on me," Jorge said irritably. "My men should have spotted the tourists and got them out of there before anything happened."

"The engineers are worried that they're going to get the blame, but that drill is maintained by the book." Dan turned to Kalen. "At least if you're involved in the inspection, there won't be any question about the results."

Kalen left Jorge and Dan, to get a drink at the bar. He had a disquieting feeling that he was being swept along by something that he couldn't control, as if he was on a ride that he couldn't get off. Everything was happening too fast. Involuntarily, he pictured the body with its rope of guts hanging out, lying under the strut. He needed a drink. Pushing his way through the crowd in front of the bar, he found himself face to face with the young female tourist that he had seen at supper. He prepared to go by her, but she stood in his way.

"Weren't you in the mine this morning?" she asked in a soft and melodious voice. "I thought I saw you talking to the commander after the accident?"

"Yes, I was," Kalen replied, seeing her close up for the first time. She had large green eyes, red lips, a pointy chin, and long, glossy black hair that tumbled down her back, shimmering in the lights when she moved. Overall, the effect was lovely. "You're with the tour group aren't you? I'm very sorry about what happened."

"It was horrible. He was such a nice man," she said, giving him a long look.

"Did you know Mr. Kingston well?" Kalen hoped that she didn't. Grief wasn't an emotion that he wanted to deal with that evening.

"No, I only met him on the tour, but he was good fun. I can't believe what happened. I'm Taily Newman." She extended her hand to Kalen. He took it and lightly squeezed her cool palm, brushing her slim fingers with his own. She held his gaze boldly and gave him a sweet smile, and he found himself smiling back.

Kalen's first instinct had been to make an excuse and move on, but now he reassessed the situation. She was very attractive. She wore a tiny skirt that showed off her long slender legs to advantage and a low-cut top that exposed the swell of creamy white breasts. A pendant on a gold chain nestled between them. It glowed with a yellow light that emphasised her cleavage and partially lit up the thin material of her top so that it was almost transparent. The effect fascinated him and he had to consciously drag his gaze away from her chest.

She looked at Kalen expectantly. Her eyes held an invitation that Kalen found hard to ignore. The Narquum he had taken earlier made him feel good. There would be no harm in talking to her for a few minutes. An image of Halle's face crossed his mind, accompanied by a twinge of guilt. Her possessiveness weighed on him and he tried to shrug it off. As the chief engineer on site, he couldn't be criticised for speaking to one of the tourists, to reassure her after the trauma of the day. Indeed, he should speak to her—she might know something about the accident. He concentrated on the girl in front of him. The smell of her spicy perfume enticed him.

"I'm Kalen, Kalen Trinneer. You must be shaken by what happened this morning."

"It was so sudden. I'm still shocked. I haven't been able to get the sight of Palum out of my mind. Do accidents like that happen a lot?" She tilted her head to one side and looked up at him with an expression of deep concern.

"Not often. It was a nasty thing for you to see."

"I only saw him afterwards, I mean after it happened. We were all standing together and then he was gone." A brief expression of horror passed across her face before she regained her composure.

"We don't know why he left the group and walked over to the drill."

"Didn't one of the workers call him over?" Taily asked.

"What do you mean?" He tried to make the question sound casual. She had his full attention now. There was nothing about this in the reports.

"Just before it happened, Palum said something about, 'he wants us to go over there,' and then he was gone." Taily took a mouthful of her drink.

"That still doesn't explain why he got so close to the drill."

"He was looking towards the machine when he said it."

"Did you see the worker that called him over?"

"No, it was quite dark. I was waiting for the guide to tell us where to go. The next thing I knew, Palum was in the machine. I told Security all this." She had turned pale.

"Perhaps he imagined it. The light can play tricks with your eyes down there. Are you sure you want to talk about this? Are you all right?" He would check it out tomorrow. He was being insensitive questioning her like this.

"Yes, I'm fine. It was just such a shock, you know." The crowd near the bar had grown dense and they were surrounded by people. She moved closer to him when someone brushed past her.

He changed the subject. "Tell me about your tour? Where have you been?"

"We've been to Central, Morton, and another construction site. We were due to see the observatory at the pole before going back to Central."

"Is that where you live?"

"No, I live in Lavoar where I work as an administrator in a sports complex. I came to Taidor six months ago from a planet called Drieve. I came on the tour because I wanted to see a bit more of Taidor. What about you? Have you always worked at the building sites?"

"Afraid so, but whenever I can, I go back to Central."

"Your job must be very dangerous." Taily's green eyes shone.

"I'm an engineer. Sometimes things happen and you just have to deal with it. How long will you be at Three-Craters?"

A man pushed behind Taily and Kalen put his arm around her back and drew her towards him. Her body felt firm under the silky material of her clothes and he felt the heat of her bare thigh when she brushed her leg against his. He imagined touching the silky strands of her sleek jet hair and watching it dapple where the light played on it, and stroking the soft curvature of her breasts above the flimsy top. He stepped slightly back so that he wasn't pressing against her.

"We're going back tomorrow. The tour has been cut short." She rested a delicate hand on his arm, and looked up at him, eyes glittering. "I would have liked to have done more."

"That's a shame." Her pupils were large and black in the midst of emerald green and he found himself locked in their gaze.

So, she would be leaving the next day. His interest increased. Her gaze was inviting and her hand rested lightly on his arm. He wondered whether he had a chance with her or if he was mistaken. Surely the day had left her too shaken to take things to an intimate level? He could do with the distraction to get his mind off the accident, but could she? He might never see her again after she left and Halle would never know.

The crowd around them started to thin out and men stared admiringly at Taily as they walked past. Jorge gave Kalen a brief nod as he left with Dan and the mess hall quickly began to empty. When the first siren of day end sounded, Kalen put his arm around Taily's waist and began to guide her towards the exit.

"Would you like to go somewhere else?" Kalen asked.

"Yes, I don't feel like going back to my room yet," she replied.

"You should make the most of your last night."

"Is there anywhere else to go? I thought everything closed at day end."

"I'm sure there's something open. Would you like a tour of the accommodation levels?"

"I would prefer another bar. I want to forget what happened today."

"I think I can find you one."

She peered at him doubtfully. "You're joking with me now."

"You don't trust me, do you? Are you staying in the staff quarters? Which level?"

"I don't know if they're for staff or not. I think we're on the seventh."

"You've probably got one of the guest suites. They're usually reserved for visits by senior personnel."

"I didn't see a bar on that level."

"That's because it's on another floor," he said, grinning.

They left the mess hall and she linked her arm in his, walking gracefully beside him in heeled shoes that made her just a few inches shorter than him. Her tiny skirt barely covered her bottom and was held up by a shiny belt that had little bells on it that tinkled as she moved. He caught a glimpse of white thighs beneath it and pictured himself running his hands up her legs and caressing her pert behind. She had pushed her heavy hair off her shoulders and it rippled down her back exposing the flawless ivory skin of her neck. The glow from the pendant resting above her bosom softly lit her face.

"There's a zone lounge on the eighth, we can go there," Kalen suggested. Perhaps later he could take her to her room.

"I'd like to do that." She gave him a hesitant smile. "This is all new to me."

"You've got lovely hair," he murmured. She didn't strike him as the kind of woman who would respond to superfluous compliments, but the beauty of her hair couldn't be denied. He pictured burying his face in it, smelling it and stroking it with his fingers.

"Thank you. I've been told that it's my best feature."

They walked through a Gate, leaving the central hub, and took lifts to level eight, arriving just as the final siren for day end sounded. In the corridors of the Ea-Zone block, the noise ricocheted discordantly across the walls. Kalen smiled when Taily made a face.

"I'm not used to hearing it in a place like this," she explained.

The sirens stopped and the booming of the drills far below became audible again. He heard voices up ahead and, rounding a bend in the corridor, they came to a small lounge crowded with people. They stopped at the entrance and he took hold of Taily's hand. The majority of the people in the lounge were men, but there were a few women in the throng. Kalen recognised the big miner that he'd seen earlier that day at breakfast standing in the middle of the room staring over the crowd. He followed the miner's gaze and saw Sera pushing her way through the crush of people towards the exit. She glanced towards the big man and then he lost sight of her.

"There isn't much room in there. Stay close to me," he said.

At that moment, Sera suddenly emerged from the crowd. She had a strained expression on her face that changed to surprise when she saw Kalen. She paused and glanced briefly at Taily.

Kalen said, "Good evening."

"Good night," she replied sharply before walking hastily down the corridor.

"Who was that?" Taily asked. "She seemed a bit put out."

"She works here. I expect she heard about the accident—everyone's had a bad day."

They made their way through the crowd to the bar and found a corner to stand in with their drinks. Around them miners and construction workers told crude stories and laughed raucously. People constantly buffeted them and Kalen drew Taily further into the corner. He put his arm around her and she leaned into him. Each time someone bumped her from behind, she pressed closer to him. Kalen could hardly hear what she was saying, but when he experimentally ran his hand down to her behind and rested it there, she made no attempt to remove it. They chatted for several minutes, but the bar became increasingly busy as more people arrived.

"It's getting a bit crowded in here now. Are you okay?" he asked her.

"I'm getting a bit hot," Taily admitted.

"Do you want to leave?"

"Yes, I've had enough."

"Come on then." He steered her towards the door and into the cool air of the corridor. "It was a little noisy in there."

"But it was fun. I don't often go to bars." She pulled at the rim of her top and a fastening came undone. Underneath, small beads of perspiration glistened on her flushed skin.

"I'll take you back to your room." Kalen put his arm about her shoulders and she snuggled close to him.

"Yes, it's been a long day and I have an early start tomorrow. But I've enjoyed myself."

"I've enjoyed the evening as well." So she planned to turn in, he thought, disappointed. He didn't want to bring the evening to a close so soon. He imagined her breasts glistening with perspiration underneath her thin top and the thought inflamed him. Perhaps she would change her mind.

He took her up to the seventh level and let her direct him to one of the guest suites. They paused outside the door.

"I suppose I leave you here?" he whispered, leaning over her so that his mouth was very nearly on hers.

"Yes, I'm very tired after what happened today." She reached out and pressed the keypad on the wall by the door.

He still had his arm around her and he drew her back to him as the door slid open, catching her around the waist with his other hand, so that she was very close to him, and kissed her. She parted her lips slightly and he kissed her deeply, breathing in her scent, and his mouth lingered on hers for several seconds before she broke off the embrace.

"Good night," she said, her dark eyes studying his.

He held her hands and asked, "Will you be all right?" There was something vulnerable about her, he decided. Now he wished she wasn't leaving the next day; he wouldn't get another chance with her.

"I ought to…" she started to reply and then paused as if coming to a decision. "But I don't want to be alone tonight, not after what happened today. Please stay."

"If you're sure," he replied, kissing her lightly.

"Yes, I'm sure." She turned and he followed her into the room.

Her things were strewn about the large comfortably furnished room and she led him to a sofa and pulled him down beside her. He put his arms around her and kissed her slowly while he stroked her long black hair. He let strands of her hair trickle through his fingers, and then kissed her neck, inhaling her exotic perfume. The pendant she wore glowed from within, casting golden shadows in the low light. Her top was partially undone and it had slipped down a fraction, so that he could just see the outline of hard nipples underneath.

She wriggled to lie across him and her skirt rode up to expose the bare flesh of her thighs. He caressed the soft skin above her leggings and the little bells on her belt tinkled as she squirmed with pleasure. He shrugged out of his jacket and dropped it on the floor. He now ached with excitement and when she slipped a hand beneath his shirt, her touch scorched his chest. She massaged him in tiny circular movements, first exploring his chest, and then his stomach. He kissed her gently, enjoying the softness of her smooth skin. His pulse raced, her touch sending a tingling to his core where he burned for her.

Suddenly she pulled away from him. Playfully, she planted both of her delicate hands on his chest and pushed him backwards. He caught hold of her so that she tumbled on top of him. She squirmed about and then bent her head and began covering his stomach with tiny butterfly kisses, using her hands to guide her mouth. Tiny fluttering sensations that stung his flesh, as her dainty hands and moist tongue moved downwards. He lay back and gave himself up to her.

Chapter Nine

The morning siren sounded and Sera left her quarters to go to her laboratory. The corridors were full of miners making their way to breakfast and she joined a line that had formed in front of the nearest Gate to her quarters. Once in the central hub, she ignored the elevators where clusters of workers waited and found a stairwell instead, climbing several levels until she reached the floor where her laboratory was situated. Going straight to her desk, she switched on her desk screen, flicking the pages until she found her Duplicate's report, and began reading it eagerly.

"He's got the same results as me," she said to herself.

They both agreed that the Uveid broke up easily under pressure and was unsuitable to build on. She noted that his analysis of the constituent elements was also inconclusive but his results indicated that the Uveid was not comprised of the same material throughout and he recommended further tests to establish the Uveid's exact composition. She would have to speak to the surveyor about another complete survey of the site. This was going to cause problems with the building programme; they'd have to change the plans to avoid the weak seams.

Sera decided to examine the Uveid in situ again and took the elevator down to the forty-seventh level. She found the passageway and the chasm easily. The air was thick with dust and the corridor was deserted. Stopping in front of the fissure, she exchanged her breathing tube for a facemask and secured a spare torch to her belt before crawling in. Now aware of the depth of the crevice, she crawled forward carefully until she saw twinkling blue crystals in the beam of her flashlight. The tiny blue pyramids gleamed in the torchlight like so many fairy lights and their radiance seemed to touch her soul.

Using a small laser, she detached several samples of the Uveid, feeling a strange reluctance to damage the tiny stones that nestled in the crevices with an alien beauty. When she had finished, she wriggled back out into the corridor, collected her equipment and began walking towards the main gallery. The boom of the drills pervaded the passageways and the ground vibrated in unison beneath her boots. She found a narrow access tunnel and turned into it to take a short cut to the main site. Inside the tunnel, there was no fixed lighting and Sera used her torch, but murky dust hung heavily in the air making it difficult for her to see. After several minutes, the dust cleared and when Sera played the beam of her flashlight across the walls, their serrated contours threw off confusing elongated shadows. The weight of the rock around her muffled the sound of the drills, but in the quietness, Sera became aware of a soft rustling sound that reminded her of whispering voices. She decided that it had to be an effect caused by the machinery. Then the tunnel widened and she emerged into a well-lit corridor noisy with the drumming of the drills.

Sera heard a heavy footstep behind her and suddenly two large hands caught her shoulders and spun her around. She found herself staring into the face of Lars. He towered over her with a malicious grin that exposed wolfish teeth. Without saying anything, he gave her a violent shove and pushed her back into the side tunnel. He yanked her helmet off and threw it onto the ground. It hit the hard surface with a loud crack and rolled away. His fingers dug into her shoulders, forcing her backwards until she was trapped against a wall.

"Get off me," she screamed, trying to push him away, but his iron grip didn't budge. Fear shot through her and her heart thudded in her chest.

"Don't be like that," he said. "You haven't thanked me properly for saving you yesterday. You were rude to me last night."

His large face contorted into an expression of mock anger and his eyes gleamed under bushy dark eyebrows. Getting hold of both of her upper arms, he leaned into her until his face was near hers and pressed his body against her. His clothes were coated in dust and he smelled sweaty. He must have come straight from the rock-face, she thought. He must have spotted her when he was working and followed her down here. He bent his thick bull neck and attempted to kiss her but she turned her face away and he slobbered against her cheek.

"Get away from me! Let me go!" She struggled to free herself.

He leered at her. "Shy, are we?"

She screamed as loud as she could and kicked out at him, but he was ready for her and avoided her feet easily. He caught both of her wrists in one of his large hands and pinned them above her head. Reaching down with his other hand, he began to yank at her top. With the weight of his body against her, she couldn't move. She screamed again and struggled, but his grip tightened with her movements.

"Lively aren't you? You won't get away from me this time."

"Get off me, you pig! Get off me!"

"So you want to play games, do you?" He chuckled hoarsely. "You've been leading me on. I know your sort, you really want me."

***

Kalen took the elevator to the forty-seventh level where Dan and his team waited for him at the large primary drill. The mining crew laboured silently, the men throwing him tense glances as he walked across the main gallery to the far end where the partially dismantled drill stood motionless. Dan and four engineers were inspecting the side of the drill when Kalen arrived.

"The U-Zone took the side wing off," Dan said. "They didn't find any faults but we've got a long way to go before we can say we're in the clear. Where do you want to start?"

"Let's start at the top and work our way down."

Dan nodded in agreement. "Okay. It's as good a place as any to start."

"It might be easier if we climb up the back. We can't get up the side with the wing off and we'll have to take the other wing off later."

Kalen turned towards the back of the drill. Rubble that had been ejected through the rear vents still lay strewn beneath the overhang and Kalen carefully picked his way over it until he could grasp a handhold on the machine and haul himself up. Dan and his team climbed up after him. At the top, nearly seven metres above the ground, Kalen looked back over the main gallery. Some of the miners had stopped work to watch them. He recalled the snatches of conversations he'd overheard throughout the day, short bleak observations from men weary and suspicious of accidents without an obvious cause.

He worked with Dan for several hours, inspecting control panels, testing programming and dismantling parts. *There's nothing here*, Kalen thought. *This is pointless. We're just wasting time.*

"I'm going to have a look at the side wing again," he called to Dan who sat straddled over a girder while reaching down to undo an access panel. "You don't need me here to dismantle the laser array."

Dan looked up. "Okay. I'll let you know if we find anything."

He climbed down the remaining wing of the machine, committing its structure and operating parts to memory, shining his torch along its flank to illuminate it clearly. The fore part of the machine had burrowed several metres into the rock and its full depth was partially obscured.

At ground level, he walked down the wingless side of the drill towards the rock face that it had been excavating. Out of the corner of his eye, he got the impression of someone standing halfway along the wall, but when he looked again there was no one there. In the half light, shadows flickered along the wall and long cracks and fissures created vertical black stripes down its face.

He turned to follow the wall towards the corner and saw something metallic glinting in the beam of his torch. A small piece of metal tubing had lodged behind a crevice and only part of it was exposed above the dust. He picked it up and examined it. It was about ten centimetres long, with horizontal lines indented along its metal casing. One end felt rough, as if it had broken off a larger part, and when Kalen looked closely, he discovered that it was not hollow throughout. He suspected that it had broken off one of the machines, but he couldn't identify it.

He put the piece of tubing in his pocket and turned to go. Suddenly he heard a faint scream in the distance that sounded like a woman's voice. He stopped and listened and the first scream was quickly followed by another. Definitely a woman, he decided. The sound was dulled by the surrounding rock but seemed to be coming from one of the ancillary passageways off the main corridor. He headed in the direction of the cries until he reached the place where he thought the sound was coming from. The passageway looked empty except for a helmet lying on the ground and an equipment case lying discarded on its side, but he could hear scraping sounds and a deep voice coming from one of the access tunnels that led from it. He took a large wrench from his belt and approached cautiously.

Kalen took in the scene in an instant. He recognised the big miner that he'd seen in the mess hall. The man held both of Sera's wrists with one large hand, pinning her against the wall, and with the other, was tearing at the fastenings of her shirt, while she struggled to get free. Anger surged through him.

"Get off her!" Kalen shouted. The miner turned his head but kept his grip on Sera. Kalen lunged at the man, hitting him hard against his upper arm with the wrench. Rage exploded inside him. The man was a brute and a disgrace to the Division. "Let her go!"

Surprised and off guard, the man released his grip on Sera and staggered backwards under the force of the blow. Kalen followed through, using the wrench to deliver another blow that caught the man's shoulder and nearly knocked him over. The miner recovered his balance quickly and came up to swing a punch that Kalen dodged. He glared at Kalen and then raised his fists and took a step forwards. His eyes shifted towards the insignia on Kalen's uniform and he hesitated. The miner appeared to make a decision and lowered his fists, wary of further attack.

"We were only having a bit of fun," the miner protested, with an attempt at a laugh. "Sera here knows how to give a man a good time."

"That's not what it looked like from where I'm standing." Kalen's voice strained with fury. Sera had fallen backwards and he could hear her sobbing.

"Then you got it wrong. You asked me here, didn't you Sera?" the man sneered, watching Kalen.

"He attacked me," Sera gulped.

Kalen stared stonily at the man and didn't take his eyes off his face. The miner's gaze flicked to and fro between Kalen's face and the wrench in Kalen's hand. The miner was taller and bulkier than he was and would win in a straight fight. He must try to diffuse the situation. There were too many problems on site already. He would report the incident and let the Division sort it out later. It wasn't his call to flay the man, although he would very much like to. He stifled the urge to hit the man again with the wrench.

"Get out of here!" Kalen shouted.

The miner needed no further invitation and, with a brief glance at Sera, strode off.

"Are you okay?" Kalen asked Sera, gently.

She was leaning against the wall, dishevelled and trembling, her face drained of colour. There were bright red marks on her wrists and neck and the top of her jacket was torn. She looked shocked and seemed to be fighting to compose herself.

She straightened her shoulders and said firmly, "I'll be all right. Thank you for getting him off me."

"What got into him? Why did he attack you?" *Had she led him on and then rejected him?*

"I don't know." Her eyes were bright with anger. "He's been following me around. He's just a bastard that can't take no for an answer."

Her eyes darkened and Kalen read a steely determination there.

"He'll pay for this," she said under her breath.

"I'll report this and you can make a complaint. I'll see you back to the main site. Come on." Kalen picked up her things.

She followed him without further comment. He doubted that she would make an official complaint; it would make working at Three-Craters very difficult for her. Incidents like this happened from time to time and the women who worked in the mines usually took this sort of thing in their stride. They were a tough lot. He would log the incident but he didn't want to get involved any further. He had enough problems to deal with already.

***

That evening, Kalen discussed the investigation with Halle.

His encounter with Taily was still vividly etched across his mind and guilt trickled down his spine like cold dripping water, as he spoke to Halle.

"One of the witnesses, Miss Newman, said that the dead man thought someone near the drill was calling them over," he explained.

"There's no reference to it in Miss Newman's statement to Security," Halle replied.

"I know, but that's what she says. She told me that she'd reported it."

"Well, it isn't in her statement. She probably just made it up."

"She sounded convincing to me." He found it difficult to meet Halle's eyes when he spoke about Taily. He hoped that she didn't notice. "Perhaps she just forgot to tell Security?"

"I don't think it matters. There was no one near the drill anyway."

"I'll put it in my own report. Perhaps my Duplicate, Luther, will find something that I didn't."

Halle gave him a sharp look. "I don't think that's a good idea. You don't know if it's true. Repeating it could affect your credibility."

"If it is true, it's highly relevant."

"Or nonsense. If you report it, she'll have to be contacted to confirm it. If she did make it up you'll look like a fool and so will I."

Kalen stared at Halle in surprise.

"It's just that I know how important this investigation is for your career. I don't want you to do anything that would jeopardise it."

"I understand, Halle, but Miss Newman could repeat her story and say that I knew."

"I'll have to discuss your report with the director before it's sent to our Duplicates."

"If there's anything that the director doesn't want the U-Zone to see, I'm sure it will be edited out," Kalen said.

"That isn't official policy. Have you had a chance to read the latest geology report?"

"I've just got Sera Ethern's preliminary report on the new mineral she's discovered. It appears from her initial tests that the Uveid can't take the weight of parts of the construction and it could be the cause of the rock-falls we've been having. She's running more tests, but it looks like we're going to have to revise the building plans to avoid areas where there are heavy deposits."

"Will that delay the programme?"

"It means a bit of delay but we'll also look at strengthening the areas near any known deposits to compensate for weakness in the strata."

"What's she like?" Halle asked suddenly.

"Who?" Kalen asked, thinking of Taily.

"What's Sera Ethern like? Do you think she's up to the job?"

"She seems competent enough." An image of Sera standing in the tunnel, pale and shaking with large eyes, flashed through his mind.

"Let me know straight away if she doesn't pull her weight. Have you spent much time with her?"

"Halle, I've been busy. I've hardly seen her!"

"Well, have you?" She searched his face meaningfully, her blue eyes ingenuous. "I know you, Kalen, you're hiding something. You don't fancy her, do you?"

"Don't be ridiculous. I've barely seen her." Kalen gave a short laugh. Halle intuitively knew that he'd been unfaithful but had hit on the wrong target. Was it so obvious? God, she was wearying. "There's been an incident with one of the miners, someone called Lars Mason. I found him forcing himself on her. He'd probably come on to her and got rejected—the usual stuff. I got him off her and filed a report with Security, so it's in the commander's hands now."

"So that's it. You seemed distant. It made me think there might be someone else."

"You know there's no one else. I'll see you when I get back."

Chapter Ten

Kalen surveyed the end section of the large gallery. A high steel skeleton stood mangled and warped, charred black, its beams protruding like ribs from the rock floor. Behind it, Kalen could just see the outline of one of the large equipment rooms, now nothing but burnt debris. The sharp smell of burning still lingered in the air and blankets of black soot lay over beams and girders, specks spinning into the air to settle on his overalls as his footfalls stirred it up. He put a breathing mask over his mouth and nose and blinked to clear his smarting eyes of the burnt flecks that floated about.

The men are right, this site is cursed, he thought angrily. He had been on site for four weeks now and the accidents were still happening. And he still didn't know what was causing them. Luther hadn't come up with anything either. After the tourist was killed, both zones had inspected the drill. They'd taken it apart but they'd found nothing wrong with it. Miners continued to get ill but the site doctor couldn't find the cause. Then there was the problem with the Uveid. Sera insisted the mineral deposits were unstable. He recalled the incident with Lars Mason. She had never reported it, so far as he was aware. And now this fire on level forty-two; they had to find something soon.

He touched one of the misshapen struts with his gloved hand. It was still hot to the touch and flakes of charred material came away on his glove. Acrid fumes that smelt of burnt plastic stuck in his throat despite his breathing mask.

The construction foreman looked at him questioningly. "What do you make of it?"

According to Kalen's brief, the foreman was a veteran of the sites, with many years' experience. No longer in his prime, his bushy brows and beard were grey, but he had the physique of a man who physically toiled for many hours every day. Now the foreman's eyes expressed suspicion and fear.

Kalen looked at the scorch marks that rose high on the walls. "A cable could have shorted. Doesn't the conduit for the cabling feed into the equipment room?"

"Yes, but we run cables all over the place. There's no reason for a short. I've see accidents before but nothing like this."

"The Mining Team broke a new level yesterday. A change in demand on the circuits could have caused a power surge."

The foreman shook his head. "If you say so, but I don't like it. This sort of thing has been happening for months. The men are getting sick of risking their necks every day."

"I'll find out what caused it."

"When will you know?" the foreman asked.

"I should have something in twenty-four hours."

"I'll be on the level below if you need me."

The foreman left him and Kalen prepared to trace the route of the cabling into the equipment room. At least, if he could pinpoint where the fire had started that would be something. He reached into his pocket for a Narquum and swallowed it dry. He then picked his way through the warped metal labyrinth, stepping over horizontal struts that lay across the floor and ducking to avoid girders at head height.

Poking through the charred girders and wreckage, he found nothing that could explain why the fire had started. The fire had begun in the U-Zone and he had read Luther's report, but it was thin and incomplete and only summarised the incident without giving substantive details. Date and place, personnel directly involved, and a theory that there had been a short in the main cabling. Not enough to support a thorough investigation and unlike Luther. There was nothing more for him to see here, he decided. He needed to speak to Halle. This assignment was different from the others that he'd worked on and perhaps he needed a different approach.

***

Kalen returned to his office and called Halle.

"Has Luther's report been edited?"

She looked at him with astonishment. "Why do you say that?"

"There's nothing in it! No details, no recommendations!"

"I believe there wasn't much information available about the fire."

"Well, has it been edited?" Kalen challenged her.

She glowered at him. "Not that I know of; that's the way the report reached the Ea-Zone. The reporting procedure between the zones is fully automated. It's conducted at a much higher level than me. Both zones submit their reports through the official channels but there's no liaison and no way to check if anything they send us has been edited. Why are you accusing me like this?"

"I'm not accusing you. It's just that I know Luther. I've worked with him for years and he always prepares full reports. This doesn't look like it comes from him. He's better than this."

"So far as I know, that's his report and it hasn't been edited. In any case, why would anyone want to change it?"

"I don't know, Halle. But I need to know why the fire started on the forty-second if I'm going to make any progress."

"I thought it was a power surge?"

"That's the easy explanation, but I don't buy it. There are power surges the whole time and they don't usually lead to a fire."

"You've inspected the area yourself. You've got all the information there is."

"No, I haven't," Kalen said carefully. "I want the U-Zone's complete records about the fire, including the security report and witness statements."

Halle's eyes widened. "You know that isn't usual."

"But I am entitled to make an official request for them."

"That's not a course I would recommend you take," Halle said stonily.

"Why not?"

"The U-Zone might see it as a sign of distrust, a sign of doubt about the reports that have been provided."

"How do I make the request?"

"They won't release them, even if you make an official request. So there's no point asking."

"I want to ask for them anyway. I'll put my request in writing."

"You're wasting your time," Halle snapped.

"I might be, but I still want to ask."

After Halle's face disappeared from the screen, he pondered over her reaction. She was too dismissive. Luther's report was so thin that it must have been edited, and she must know that. She wouldn't support his request, but he would ask for the U-Zone's complete records anyway. He needed the full facts. He couldn't make any headway without them. He wished that he could speak to Luther directly but the system automatically barred any calls or email. There had to be a way. He just needed to find it.

***

Kalen paused outside his office door and speculated about what he would find that morning. It was now a week since his request to see the U-Zone's fire records had been refused, and in the days that followed, Luther had started to leave things in the office they shared. Kalen had recognised these as small tools from Luther's personal pack that he should have taken with him at the end of his shift. He'd never done that before and it was in breach of the Zoning Regulations.

The first thing Kalen had found was a small sonic measure lying on the desk next to the desk screen. It still displayed a measurement but Kalen couldn't work out what it related to. On another day he'd found a handheld temperature gauge hidden at the back of a shelf, its display set on a reading that didn't make any sense. They shared larger equipment, but anything from personal packs would normally be removed by Security in the search at day end.

The tools worked perfectly, so Luther hadn't thrown them away, Kalen reasoned. He'd simply left them in such a way that Security had overlooked them. Possibly Security thought they were for joint use.

Kalen had left the tools where he found them and by his next shift they would be gone.

He pressed the keypad and the door slid open. At first glance, the office looked normal. Scanning the shelves and worktops, nothing looked out of the ordinary, except that his chair had been tucked under the desk. This was a new arrangement and he pulled the chair out. A button watch lay on the seat. He picked it up and checked its display. It had stopped at eight forty-five in the morning, Luther's morning, and he imagined the U-Zone at that time. The first crews descending to the lower levels and very few people on level forty-two. Did the fire start at that time?

Could Luther be trying to give him a message? Did Luther have information that he was prevented from passing on? He tried to imagine what Luther was like. Other than his engineering competence, Kalen had been told very little about him. His Duplicate was like a ghost, present but unseen; a twin that he'd never met.

Turning on his desk screen, Kalen brought up the Zoning Regulations and flicked through the pages until he came to the part he wanted. Reading the procedure, he memorised it and switched to a different page. He entered his request, detailing all the departments correctly, pressed the send button and smiled. He had asked to meet Luther personally. Now the ghost would become real, a real person who could give him the answers that he needed. He had followed the procedure to the letter and his official request couldn't be ignored.

***

Kalen still had the little metal tube that he had found after Palum Kingston's accident, and he turned it over in his hands studying it, while he waited to report to Halle. It was an unusual bit of piping and the lines on its side didn't relate to any scale of measurement or identification that he could think of. Aside from the markings, the barrel was smooth with a rough end where it had become detached from something.

He had been back to the place where he had found it and searched the area thoroughly but he hadn't found any other pieces or anything that it might have broken off. He had taken to carrying it around with him to see if he could match it to any of the machinery on site but so far hadn't identified anything that it could have come from.

The console bleeped and Halle came on screen, looking annoyed.

Halle came straight to the point. "Your request to see Luther has been turned down. The Division doesn't like direct contact with the U-Zone."

"You know why I made the request," Kalen replied, trying to hide his disappointment. "I need to speak to him."

"Only the members of each zone's Colonial Councils have personal contact when Taidor's Governing Council meets. Even I don't get to speak directly to my Duplicate, Javed Durton," Halle retorted.

"Don't they understand that we're not getting the whole story from the U-Zone?"

"Since you were assigned to Three-Craters there have been disputes with the U-Zone about general policy. There's probably more going on here than we're both aware of. We're told what they want us to hear. It's best not to stick your neck out."

He tried to reason with her. "If I can't speak to Luther it's going to be difficult to make any progress. I'm no nearer to finding the cause of most of the problems than when I first arrived here."

"A pessimistic attitude will get you nowhere. Your job is to fix the problems, not make excuses for failure. I need your full report and recommendations. I'm being pressed by the Division for it."

"I understand but I can't file my full report yet," Kalen said. "I still haven't got to the source of the problems. I can only let you have another interim report at this stage."

"What's the position with regard to the areas of weak rock?"

"Going forward, new plans have been drawn up to avoid the areas of Uveid and we're looking at strengthening the areas where construction has already started."

"What about the power failures?"

"I haven't found the cause yet. The machinery is still malfunctioning but I can't find any common link."

"Can't you attribute the power failures to normal fluctuations? Doesn't the system shut off sections when there's excessive demand? It's a remote site and it must be difficult to keep the power source stable there."

"I don't think that's the root cause," Kalen said wearily.

"But it's possible, isn't it?" Halle insisted. "When the power fails the machinery malfunctions and there are accidents. Anything else could be co-incidence. You can explain nearly everything."

"I don't think we can say that yet," Kalen said, keeping his face impassive. This wasn't Halle talking. She sounded rehearsed. "It's all too tenuous."

"But you could say it? I'm being pushed for something definite that would explain what's going on there. The Division is getting pressure from the U-Zone who is accusing us of delays. We have to wrap this one up now."

"Then what happens if there's another accident?"

"Some sites are naturally riskier to develop than others," Halle replied briskly. "You do want that promotion don't you? I need your report."

"Give me a few more days." This was a change in direction. He'd been sent to Three-Craters to find the cause of the problems but now Halle was pushing him to let it go. Could she be right? He didn't think so. A combination of factors couldn't explain all the incidents at Three Craters. "I'll go over all of the findings again. I'm not sure that we can write off the problems at Three-Craters like this, but I'll give it some thought."

"You've heard about the riots on Srietta? There's been a lot of damage and several people were killed, first in the U-Zone and then in the Ea-Zone?"

"It was on the news. People are always complaining about over-crowding."

"It's been a long time since it's been this bad. People are reaching boiling point. There's hardly any room for people to live normally in some of the colonies, which is why the building programme is so important. We have to do everything we can to get construction finished as soon as possible."

"I know that, Halle, but safety has to be a priority."

"I've finally got the report about your fight with Lars Mason." Halle changed the subject. "He says he was chatting to Sera Ethern and you picked a fight with him. Security spoke to her shortly afterwards but she didn't want to make a formal complaint. She wouldn't say very much, only that there was some kind of misunderstanding."

"That's her prerogative. The women on these sites don't want to cause trouble."

"Apparently Lars Mason has been spreading it about that you attacked him. You shouldn't have got involved."

"He overstepped the mark and I stopped him. What was I supposed to do?"

"It just puts you in a very bad light. You shouldn't have reported it unless Sera Ethern wanted to take it further."

"I'll bear that in mind next time I see a woman being attacked. I'm not usually popular at these sites anyway so it really doesn't make any difference."

"Everything makes a difference. You can't afford to give people any grounds to discredit you."

"Well there's nothing I can do about it now. It's over as far as I'm concerned."

"Don't be so sure. The Division is getting concerned about your lack of progress and this business with Lars makes it worse. They're starting to question whether you're the right man for the job."

"Lars is an irritation, nothing more. I haven't got to the bottom of what's going on here yet."

"And I don't think that you ever will. Don't waste any more time. Things have changed since you were sent there and I need your final report now. Recommend that the power supply is increased, the unstable sections are strengthened and leave it at that. The Division doesn't want any more delays at Three-Craters. You'll get promotion and I promise you that your next assignment will be easy compared to this one. Do your report and let's move on."

Halle terminated the call and a sense of disquiet settled over him. He wasn't ready to prepare his final report. Although the Uveid might have caused the rock-falls, he hadn't found the answer to the rest of the problems. For an instant, he remembered the face of the mining captain at

Area Nine. He shoved the memory forcibly away. The guilt that kept pulling him back to Area Nine now tied him to Three-Craters. He didn't want to leave until he found out what was going on.

But what if he was wrong? Was he wasting his time searching for answers that might not be here? If Halle was right, why waste more time at Three-Craters? He wanted to believe her. He wanted to take the easy route, prepare his report and leave Three-Craters. There was nothing here but trouble.

He took a Narquum and sat back, letting the drug relax him. The thought crossed his mind that when the Narquum wore off, he wouldn't be able to think until he took another. His days seemed to be structured around taking Narquum and it was affecting his judgement. Should he give up on Three-Craters now? What else could he do? Luther had to know what was going on. A tiny germ of an idea started to form in his mind. Perhaps there was something that he could do after all.

Chapter Eleven

Kalen stood by the food station on the forty-seventh level watching the miners working around him. Men on mobile drills attacked the rock surface throwing up clouds of dust that were quickly suctioned off by the air supply system, while the sounds of the continual grinding of the large primary drills came from the distant reaches of the hall. The discordant hammering and grinding noise of the drills contrasted with the grace of the soundless rubble trucks that floated about the cavern.

Occasionally one of the miners threw him a suspicious glance, but for the most part they ignored him. His thoughts turned to Sera Ethern's latest report on the Uveid. She had discovered that it was much weaker than originally believed and couldn't withstand heavy loads. The normal measures for dealing with a weak sort of rock wouldn't be enough. They would have to rebuild in places to avoid the Uveid seams and that was going to cause more delay. He decided to take another Narquum and got a coffee from the dispenser to wash it down, absentmindedly putting the packet of Narquum on the counter. A voice behind him abruptly interrupted his thoughts.

"Got a headache, have you?" Lars said. He snatched up the packet to read the label and then held it in the palm of his hand, smirking at Kalen.

"I'll have those back." Kalen reached for the packet and fixed Lars with a steely glare. Two of the miners nearby had stopped working to watch.

"Got to be some headache, I've never heard of Narquum before. I must look it up." Lars turned the packet over in his hand but made no effort to return it.

"I'll have those now," Kalen repeated in an icy voice. He was used to dealing with men like Lars; the construction sites were full of them. Around them, several miners had become aware of the altercation and an audience was building. Lars appeared to be enjoying the attention, but Kalen saw indecision in his face, as if he was thinking about the consequences of taking things further.

"Now!" Kalen barked and held out his hand again to take the packet.

"Sure thing, Chief." Lars handed him back the packet with deliberate slowness.

Kalen put it in his pocket. "Do you want something?" Kalen asked pointedly.

"No, I'm just on a break," Lars sneered.

Kalen casually turned away from him, leaned back against the side of the food station and took another swig of his coffee. He heard Lars stamp off towards another section of the gallery. Had Lars recognised Narquum as a narcotic? A chill went through him. One word from Lars and his world would be blown apart. He had been involved in a fatal accident already—if he were caught taking drugs on site now, the Division would show no leniency. The penalty would be imprisonment or worse, and he would be humiliated and disgraced.

No one would understand the pain that he had endured for weeks after the accident, only relieved by the Narquum that he was given in hospital; or the guilt, that was in some ways worse than the pain, that threatened to overwhelm him each time he remembered the faces of the men that died.

The effect of the Narquum kicked in, like a warm comforting blanket that dissolved the tension in his muscles, and the faces faded. It brought relief that chased the horror of Area Nine away, made it distant and unimportant. He continued to sip his coffee and bathed in the warm glow of the drug. Everything around him looked sharper and clearer and he thought about the problems at Three-Craters. The power failures had become more frequent and the illness persisted. More men had got sick and the figure was increasing every day. The crazy idea surfaced again; a simple, but dangerous way to find out what was going on. One step that he could take before accepting that Three Craters had defeated him. An illegal, outrageous idea, he admitted to himself, but it might work.

***

Kalen waited in his office for day end and thought over what he was going to do. It was nearing twenty hundred hours and he should have left by now. He still had time to change his mind. No, he would go through with it, ignore the siren and get into the U-Zone. See Luther and find out what was going on. He had never tried to go out of time before; it was a violation of everything that he'd been taught from birth to respect. The only people who defied the siren deliberately were either stupid or criminals. So what did that make him? *A drug addict*, the answer bounced swiftly into his mind. He should leave now and get back to the safety of the Ea-Zone, but if he did, he would never find out the truth.

Snatches of the Government's frequent broadcasts ran through Kalen's mind: "zoning for the good of all;" "stay in time and be well;" "happiness is living in our zone." What if he got caught? Penalties for breaching the Zoning Regulations ranged from on the spot warnings for a first offence, to trial and imprisonment for repeat offenders, or so he had heard. He couldn't think of anybody that he knew who'd been caught out of time.

Kalen considered the layout of the site. At Three-Craters, each zone presently only had ten Gates from their respective accommodation blocks into the shared central hub. In front of the body scanners, there were heavy metal doors that were closed and locked when the Gates were closed. He had observed that the Gates to his own zone were only manned in daytime when they were open, and the U-Zone Gates were shut and locked but had no guard. If the same system applied in the U-Zone, there would be no guards at his own Gates to stop him getting back if he could unlock the doors.

He had surreptitiously studied the locking system of the Gate nearest to his office. It had a code but he could disable the mechanism with the right tools. It seemed a flimsy barrier to keep people out.

A few minutes before twenty hundred hours, Kalen left his office and walked casually towards a large storeroom in a nearby corridor. He passed a number of people heading towards the Gates, and by the time he stopped in front of the door to the large storage closet, he was alone in the corridor. The first siren of zone change sounded. He quickly let himself in and closed the door behind him. The sensors in the storeroom brought the lights on automatically and they shone on a row of tall lockers that lined the walls, each large enough for a man to hide in.

Technically, he was still in time to leave the shared hub and return to the Ea-Zone. Even if he were caught now, he could still make an excuse for being in the storage room, but he pushed all thoughts of leaving aside: he had to speak to Luther. He opened a locker door. It contained the environment suits that Luther and he used occasionally when they needed to inspect dangerous areas where gas or other hazards were present. The suits dangled from hangers above helmets and other equipment nestling on the floor. After pushing the suits to one side, he clambered into the rear of the locker and pulled the suits back in front of him.

Reaching around, he searched for the switch to close the door and discovered it was on the outside. He took off his belt and laid it across the bottom of the doorway. Stretching forward, he found the switch on the outside and pressed it. The door slid across and jammed against his belt, leaving a tiny crack just wide enough to get his fingers around the edge. A sliver of light from the slit pierced the darkness inside and then blinked out as the sensors no longer detected movement in the room. Kalen shuffled behind the suits and rearranged the equipment boxes in front of him until he was completely hidden from view.

Squatting in the dark recess of the cabinet, Kalen heard the final siren signalling zone change. There was no going back now—he would have to see this through. He thought about the multitude of people on Taidor going through the Gates at that moment—either returning to their zone blocks or entering the hub to start their day. Their lives were ruled by the siren because there wasn't enough space. And things were getting worse. The rioting on Srietta might be quickly put down by both zones, but there would be more violence in other colonies as space ran out. What would it be like to live on a planet without zoning? He found it difficult to imagine. No siren and the freedom to stay in the city all of the time. Apart from Earth, he could only think of a handful of non-zoned planets and transfer to them was prohibited.

The division of the population was no longer just physical, he mused. Many of his subordinates worked without liaison with their Duplicates, depending on the nature of their job. He had heard that this situation was mirrored throughout the colonies. Many people didn't talk about the other zone at all, as if they had blocked it out of their thoughts.

People tried not to acknowledge that their reality relied only on social conditioning, something that was so frail that if they examined it too closely, it would break and they would never be able to live comfortably in their world again. If they thought about it, they would see everything differently; notice the petty restrictions and the unfairness of it all. The siren was their only reminder of the other half, the faceless others who took up half of their space. And now he was going to break through that barrier, that taboo, and see the other half for himself.

After several minutes, the locker became hot and stuffy. He listened for sounds, but after hearing an initial burst of footsteps in the corridor, it had grown quiet. Now everyone had gone, Security will come through to search, he thought. If he kept still they would miss him. Then he could emerge into the U-Zone and go back to his office to wait for Luther's arrival.

What would Luther be like? How would Luther react when he met him? An image of a man surprised and perhaps frightened flashed through his mind, and he quickly dismissed it. No, Luther wouldn't call Security; he would accept Kalen's presence calmly and listen to what Kalen had to say.

Suddenly Kalen heard the sound of heavy footsteps and doors opening and closing in the passageway outside. The noise came nearer and then he heard men's voices outside the storeroom.

"Better check in here," a man said.

"Okay but let's make it quick, Tom," another man replied.

Kalen heard the storeroom door slide open and a slice of light came through the crack in the locker door. He could hear movement in the storeroom.

"Look at this, Mart. That door's not closed. What's the matter with it?"

A shadow fell across the slice of light, partially blotting it out. Kalen's heart hammered so loudly, he thought that they must hear it.

"Leave it," the man called Mart said. "The door must be faulty. If we touch it we'll have to report it and deal with administration. It's not our job."

The shadow backed off but he heard a locker door open near him.

In the distance a voice shouted, "Clear! Clear!"

Kalen tried to concentrate on keeping still, but one of his legs had cramped up and he shifted his position slightly to relieve the pain. Immediately, he heard the voices again nearby.

"What was that? I thought I heard a noise."

"Come on Tom, you're imagining things. We haven't got time to mess about."

"I'm sure I heard something. I think it came from that locker. I'd better take a look."

Kalen shrank back behind the cartons. The door slid open with a hiss, flooding the locker with light and the belt fell to the floor. The beam of a torch played briefly above Kalen's head and he held his breath, trying not to move.

"You're right," the guard called Tom said. "There's nothing here, only equipment. I must have imagined it."

"Like I said."

The door hissed closed again, but stopped short when it hit the tip of the belt that still lay in its path and Kalen heard Tom's voice.

"Look, it's done it again! I think we should check this out."

Kalen heard one of them playing with the lock and the door hissed open again. He heard someone pick up the belt.

Tom's voice said, "What's this?"

"It looks like a belt, just a minute."

The guards fell silent and then Kalen heard a rustling sound. Suddenly the suits were pulled aside and he saw a tall thin man with a narrow face and close-set eyes staring at him in surprise.

"What are you doing in there? Get out!" the man barked. Kalen identified him by his voice as the one called Mart. The guard took hold of the suits and threw them onto the floor behind him, and then pulled out the boxes so that Kalen was totally exposed. The second guard was shorter than his companion and they were both staring at him with expressions of disbelief.

Kalen straightened up and stepped out of the locker. He should have expected this; his plan had been too simple. Of course the guards would search the lockers. He still had his uniform on and he assumed an air of authority.

"I was checking your security, it's part of my job," Kalen said.

"In a cupboard?" Mart exclaimed.

"That can't be true. We would have been told," the second guard added.

"Show us your I.D," Mart demanded.

"Here's my Division badge. I'm investigating problems on site." If they didn't believe his story it didn't matter, so long as they chose not to dispute it.

Mart studied Kalen's badge and his expression became respectful.

"We've been told nothing about a security check, sir. Finding you here is unusual. We'll escort you out, but we'll have to report this. Please come with us."

They ushered him into the corridor and positioned themselves on each side of him.

"What were you going to do if we hadn't found you?" Mart asked curiously. "I mean it is day end. It's a funny time to do a security check."

"Once you'd left I would have made myself known."

"To who? The U-Zone? Unity's security?"

"That would be a bit reckless," Tom chuckled. "You would have had to face the Gate!"

"You're lucky that we found you. Were you planning to go through the Gate?" Mart laughed as if they were sharing some private joke.

"Yes, I know the code to get out."

"You were planning to go through the Gate out of time? Do you know how it works?"

"I don't think he does," Tom snorted. "The door has a code, the Gate doesn't!"

"If you did, there's no way you would have tried to stay out of time," Mart told Kalen. "It isn't advertised because the Government doesn't want people to feel coerced into complying with zoning. There's a standing joke that once you've been through the Gate out of time, you never breach zoning again!"

Kalen didn't reply. He had been a fool—it was never going to be so easy to get into the U-Zone. He should have known that, but what were the guards talking about?

They had reached one of the exits to get into the Ea-Zone accommodation, a Gate that Kalen had used many times already.

"I want to show you something." Mart stepped into the Gate and beckoned Kalen to come forward.

The metal framework of the Gate rose like an arch up the walls of the corridor and over the ceiling, extending along the passageway to a depth of about two metres.

"We're now in the Gate itself and it's scanning us," Mart said, leading the way through the length of the Gate and stepping out into the Ea-Zone corridor where he stopped. Mart pointed back towards the open exit into the central hub behind them on the other side of the Gate. "Now my colleague will demonstrate how we close the Gate to keep the U-Zone out!"

Tom pressed a switch on the wall and a door on the far side of the Gate slid across closing off the central hub from view.

"Now, I want you to look at this." Mart indicated the metal archway of the Gate they had just come through.

"So? It's a security scanner," Kalen said. What were they getting at?

"It's only a scanner when we're in time. Out of time, it's a barrier. Now stand back. Show him." Mart nodded to Tom.

"Watch!" Tom opened a small control panel on the wall and began flicking switches. Suddenly the archway burst into life, lighting up in a stunning blaze of electricity, sizzling and crackling ominously. "This is how the Gate works!"

Kalen stared in surprise. In an instant, the corridor had changed into a swirling frightening maelstrom, a hellish furnace of electricity thrown in sheets from wall to wall, exploding in ferocious bolts that bounced off floor, walls, and ceiling. Powerful electric charges ran along the length and breadth of the corridor inside the archway, darting backwards and forwards off the metal framework in sparking crackling flares. Sizzling with heat, the temperature in the corridor became noticeably warmer. Inside the maelstrom, the air wavered in a heat shimmer as the tongues of electricity sparked and shot across the space. Kalen doubted that anyone could survive even briefly inside it.

"You wouldn't want to walk through that," Mart said with relish. "We can set the level from mild electric shock to fatal. Right now, it's set to be agonising. It won't kill you if you're fit. Most people could just about crawl through and come out with a few burns."

"People are made to walk through it?"

"Oh, we don't make them walk through it!" Mart chortled. "If you're caught in Unity, they throw you out. They open the door from the other side and push you out of their space! They don't like intruders! They'd push you right out and you'd have to crawl through the Gate to get back into Early!"

"But we set the intensity level of our Gates," Tom said. "And they do the same with their Gates."

"Neither side likes deserters," Mart added. "If we find any of their lot we send them straight back as well!"

"What happens if someone goes out of time by mistake?"

"Unity will still push them out. They don't know whether we've set the Gate to a mild shock or fatal. They don't care. They take the view that the offender is from the

Ea-Zone and it's up to each zone to decide how to deal with their own people," Mart explained. "The only exception is children who are lost. They get handed back at day end."

"I've never seen it activated like this." Kalen stared at the light show in front of him. How could he have walked through the Gate every day and not known?

"That's not surprising," Mart said. "The Gate is hidden behind another door that's locked from our side. If anyone made it to the door, they can call for help and if it's one of our lot we can let them in."

Mart indicated a section of the wall and pressed a switch, and a door slid across the corridor hiding the Gate and the furnace behind it. He punched buttons on a panel to set the lock.

"I thought first offenders got a warning?" Kalen asked. Had everything he had been taught about the Gate been a lie?

"They do. The Gate is the warning." Mart burst out laughing. "They get the Gate and they don't stray again if they know what's good for them. What were you really doing hiding in that locker?"

"I told you, it was a security check." Provided he didn't admit to anything and stuck to his story, he might be let off with a reprimand. He should have done some research and been better prepared.

"Well have it your way, but it seems crazy that you'd want to get into Unity. But we still have to report that we found you."

The guards left him to make his own way back to his quarters and he listened to them chatting and laughing as they walked away from him. For them it was probably a first, he thought. He would be the subject of discussion for days to come: the crazy engineer who tried to get into the U-Zone. He should have thought of a better plan. Had it been the Narquum that had given him the idea? He had to get off the stuff before he did anything like that again. Now he faced reprimand by the Division and Halle's wrath.

Chapter Twelve

Summoned to the site commander's office, Kalen paused at the doorway and contemplated the dressing down he was likely to receive. On a day to day basis, Kalen had little to do with the site commander, but he expected to be treated leniently in deference to his rank. He had decided to say that he was checking equipment; taking a pro-active approach to his job.

The commander didn't rise from behind his desk when Kalen entered his office, but merely nodded his head in recognition with a hangdog expression that exuded slight curiosity and weariness. He had greying hair and a spreading middle that strained at the front fastenings of his jacket, giving him an untidy look that was augmented by his hat lying casually on a table in the corner. *He's probably sick and tired of all the trouble on site*, Kalen thought, *and I'm adding to his problems. He'll have to record my arrest in his log.*

"Come in, Chief Trinneer, and sit down," the commander said, sighing heavily. "I've been told that you were found hiding in an equipment locker at day end. What were you doing?" The commander fixed him with tired eyes.

"I was checking the equipment. I regularly inspect the environment suits," Kalen replied crisply. He had rehearsed this speech and kept his face expressionless.

The commander looked at him sceptically, fiddling with one of the fastenings on the front of his jacket that threatened to burst apart. "That's not what the guards say. They say they caught you hiding and that you told them that you were checking security."

"I wasn't hiding. You know I'm here to investigate the problems on site and sometimes that means I have to do things that appear strange without giving an explanation."

The commander looked unconvinced. "It certainly does sound strange! A chief engineer hiding in the back of a cupboard! You were lucky that the guards found you. The U-Zone isn't known for being very tolerant of aliens."

"It's all a mistake. I was checking equipment and forgot the time. The guards jumped to the wrong conclusion. I was going to return to the zone."

The commander sighed again. "Have it your way but you realise that I have to treat this formally? It's an infraction of the Zoning Regulations?"

"Yes, I do. I repeat that I had no intention of breaching zoning and in fact did not breach zoning because I left with the guards."

"I have a duty to enforce security at this base for the safety of all personnel. A report will be sent to the Colonisation Division and your superiors will decide whether to take any further action. You can tell it to them."

"I understand," Kalen said. Hopefully it wouldn't lead to more than a reprimand.

The commander looked at him thoughtfully. "You don't look well. Perhaps you should get yourself checked out at the infirmary? You might be able to blame this whole thing on your health."

"I'm fine. Just a little tired."

The commander gave him a sharp look. "If you say so," he said, dismissing him.

***

Kalen's interview with Halle was not going smoothly. He had been required to submit a written explanation for the zoning breach and she had not taken it well. Now she was in a rage.

"How could you be so stupid, Kalen?" Halle shouted, her pretty mouth distorted in anger. "What were you doing?"

"I was checking the equipment. I have to check it regularly."

"At day end?" Halle shrieked. "The guards say they found you hiding in the back of a locker!" Red angry blotches stained her cheeks contrasting with the bright topaz blue of her eyes.

"I wasn't hiding, I was looking for something at the back," Kalen repeated patiently. She glared at him with disbelief.

"Don't lie to me. I know you too well."

"The Division wants an explanation and that's my statement. I don't want to argue with you anymore."

"If you insist on sticking to your story there's nothing I can do! I'll have to let it stand, but it sounds ridiculous! No one's going to believe that you missed the siren! What were you really doing, Kalen? Off the record."

"Off the record?" Would it matter if he admitted it to her?

"Yes, I just want to know." She still glared at him, but her face had softened a little and he recognised the signs that indicated her anger was nearly spent. He gazed at her saying nothing.

"I just want to know, it's such an odd thing to do."

No more lying, he would tell her the truth. "I wanted to speak to my Duplicate."

"Are you mad? You've already been refused permission!" Her voice rose again in agitation.

"I thought if I could speak to Luther I could get some answers."

"Answers about what? You already know everything you need to know. In any case, he's been re-assigned. Give it up, Kalen!"

"What? He's been re-assigned? Why wasn't I told?" Had he risked everything for nothing?

"What has that got to do with it? You tried to breach the Zoning Regulations. Don't you realise how much trouble you're in?"

"Why wasn't I told about Luther?"

"I didn't know that he'd gone until yesterday. I'm still waiting to be officially told the name of your new Duplicate. What difference does it make?"

"It makes a lot of difference to me," Kalen shot back angrily.

He didn't believe her. She must have been told earlier that Luther had gone but why had she kept it from him and why was she lying to him now? *There is an irony in this*, he thought. *I lie to her and she lies to me, but can I really blame her? She gets her orders from above.*

"We're getting away from the point which is that you breached zoning. There'll be a hearing and you could be dismissed."

"Technically I didn't. I came out with the guards."

"You need to be more convincing about the equipment check if you want to ride this out and things would go better for you if you filed your final report. I've told you already that I need it. I've got your last report and I'm not happy with it."

"What's wrong with it?"

"I think that you've overstated the weakness of the Uveid deposits. They should be treated in the normal way. We always find weak mineral seams at the construction sites and the Uveid is no different from the sort of weaker rock that we've found before. Where the seam can't be avoided, strengthen the levels in the same way that you deal with weaker areas at other sites."

"We can't treat the Uveid in the normal way," Kalen replied, feeling irritated. He shouldn't have to explain the obvious to her. "It's too fragile to withstand the weight of some parts of the construction. We have to build around it, even if it means changing all of the plans. Where we've already built on a Uveid seam, strengthening the level may not be enough. We may have to change the layout of those levels and rebuild."

"Rebuilding would cause tremendous delays," Halle snapped. "Sera Ethern's data has been sent to Central and the geologists there don't agree with her opinion on the permissible loads that the Uveid can take. We should be able to simply strengthen the levels where the construction is complete without rebuilding."

"Sera Ethern is a trained professional and as she is the geologist on site I can't ignore her recommendations."

"The Division's senior geologists at Central dispute her opinion and believe that simply strengthening the levels should be enough. The Division doesn't want to delay the building programme any longer over this. You should know that the U-Zone is pressing for Early's proposals to get things back on track."

Kalen tried again. "Where we've already built on Uveid, it could be dangerous to only strengthen it. The whole level could give way in the future or at the least, there could be a serious rock-fall. We should be planning to rebuild those parts of the development where we know the Uveid seams run through the level."

"The Division would never sanction that," Halle said firmly. "You must apologise formally to the Division for the zoning breach and submit your final report. Recommend that the plans are altered so that future building avoids the Uveid where possible and where that isn't possible, that the area is strengthened to compensate. Drop all reference to changing the layout and rebuilding. Recommend that the power supply is increased to stop the power failures and conclude that the rest of the problems at Three-Craters are a combination of variables found at any large site."

"I'm not sure I can do that. Simply strengthening the areas where there are weak seams isn't enough. I still don't know what's causing the power failures or what's affecting the machinery, and I really don't agree that the problems are a combination of normal factors."

Why were Sera's findings being dismissed by the Division? He didn't like Sera but surely her professional opinion shouldn't be ignored? Why was he being pushed to condone a building programme that could be unsafe?

"You must do it, Kalen, if you want to have a future with the Division. There have been too many delays with the work at Three-Craters already and the Division simply won't accept any recommendations that will cause any more delay. They'll use the zoning breach as an excuse to suspend you instead and probably dismiss you from the service altogether." She paused and gave him a hard look. "But if you submit a report recommending that the Uveid is dealt with in the normal way, I can get you reassigned immediately. Once you're out of there, the zoning breach will have less significance and the Division won't pursue it. Let's face it, you're not making any progress anyway. Three-Craters is just one of those sites where there are problems for a variety of reasons."

"I'll think about it." Could he really walk away from Three-Craters now? He had done all he could to find the answers and there was nowhere left to look. He could write his report emphasising the weakness of the Uveid and leave it up to the Division to decide how to deal with strengthening procedures. Perhaps it was time to let it go? He wanted promotion.

"What is there to think about? If you report now, the Division will be pleased that you've found the cause of the problems. I promise you that the zoning infraction will be forgotten," Halle said and smiled.

A nasty feeling of guilt washed over him. Disjointed images of the mining captain's face, rubble hurtling down, and black dust flashed into his mind, and then he heard the screaming voices of the trapped men at Area Nine. The blackness and the crushing rocks and the crow were there again and something else that he couldn't quite remember. Pain, terror, and death—it took him over in an instant and he felt his throat close. He mustn't give in; he mustn't let Halle see. He shook his head to clear the images and took a deep breath.

Could he risk that happening again? Leave Three-Craters knowing that there could be another tragedy like that?

"I need more time."

"Please Kalen! Don't shake your head at me!" Halle pleaded. "I shouldn't be telling you this, but there's a storm brewing. Unity is blaming Early for the delays and pushing for a resolution. I'm under tremendous pressure to go back to the Division with the answers. We have to show that we're doing everything possible to get the building completed on time."

"I want to go over the data again."

"How can I make you understand? If you don't submit your final report soon, the Division will just replace you! You'll be recalled for breaching the Zoning Regulations and replaced by another engineer who will agree that the problems there are caused by a mixture of factors."

"I'll give you an answer soon."

"Why are you being so stubborn? If you submit your final report now and close the case, you'll be promoted. The Division rewards loyalty."

Kalen excused himself and then sat for a few minutes thinking. Why was he being asked to cover up the problems at Three-Craters? He didn't buy the delay excuse; the Division always made safety a priority even if it delayed work. Perhaps the Uveid wasn't as weak as Sera thought but why take the risk? Halle had never asked him to do something like this before but she was right, the Division would simply replace him and another engineer would put his name to the report. The Division must want to close the investigation at Three-Craters and had ordered Halle to pull him out.

He knew Halle to be a consummate actress, who had played him throughout their relationship to get what she wanted, and sometimes he had questioned whether she really loved him. But today he had sensed something behind the façade, a real concern for him. Perhaps she did love him in her own way. Perhaps the way she sought to possess him, control him, simply reflected her own insecurities. Whatever her feelings for him, he had a decision to make. Why destroy his career for nothing? He had asked for more time, but would he learn anything new? Could he walk away? Should he walk away?

***

The construction reports made uncomfortable reading. Several incidents had hampered work, each one more bizarre than the last. Kalen groaned as he went through them: failures in the lighting system on level fifty-one; a primary drill stalling for no reason on level fifty-four; and an unofficial memorandum about more miners getting sick. One man had hallucinated that he was drowning in a pool of water after his breathing mask slipped off. The last report was unusual. Why would a miner think of water? It was a scarce commodity on Taidor and there were no public pools or baths.

There seemed to be nothing to connect the incidents or explain the sickness. He had checked the ventilation system and it appeared to be working properly. Should he write his final report now? He had to make a decision soon. Unless he could find something else, the sensible course would be to cut his losses and leave. But he was responsible for what happened here. If he left now, he could be condemning Three-Craters to a continuing catalogue of accidents and rock-falls. He wasn't ready to ignore his conscience, despite Halle's constant urging.

Now, he had a meeting with Jorge on the lower levels to discuss opening up the fifty-fifth floor. Despite all the problems, construction had continued at a reasonable pace and the large digging machines had punched down to a vast natural cavern that would become the fifty-fifth level. Switching off his desk screen, he left his office to take the elevator below.

He found Jorge waiting for him near the lifts on the fifty-fourth level, standing by a water cooler.

"We're still only a few weeks behind schedule, despite everything," Jorge said wryly, taking a sip of water from a cup. "Found anything lately?"

"Nothing new. I'm going to have another look at the ventilation system. That might turn up something."

Jorge shrugged. "There may be nothing wrong with the ventilation system. It's possible that the power failures are affecting the air supply. If the Division agreed to increase the overall power supply to the site, most of the problems would probably disappear, including the weird sickness. I'm surprised you're still here."

Kalen shook his head. "It isn't that simple. Even if the Division agreed to increase the power supply I don't think it would cure all of the problems."

"If it cured the sickness, the commander could avoid declaring quarantine. The men need some kind of resolution."

Kalen gave Jorge a sharp look. Even Jorge wanted him out. "You wanted to discuss level fifty-five?"

"You've seen the plans? The floor extends into another large cave to the west, through a narrow opening. The plans call for the west cave to be enlarged by several hundred metres. Tomorrow we've got to move one of the primary drills on the fifty-fifth from the east side to the west cave. I'd appreciate your help." Jorge looked down into his cup.

"Is there a problem with it?" Normally he wouldn't be involved moving the drills. "Won't you be supervising Dan and his team?"

"There isn't a problem as such but we've got to move the drill quite a distance and get it through an opening into the west cave. Dan's going to have to programme the direction controls on each side of the drill with the exact route it will take, and I'm going to have to walk ahead and monitor it to make sure that it doesn't deviate from the route by even a metre. I'd appreciate your help with that. I'm unhappy about the geography."

"What's the matter with the layout?"

"The gap into the west cave is very narrow; it's going to be tight." Jorge frowned. "With the number of accidents that we've had, I'd welcome all the help I can get." He threw his cup irritably into the disposal bin and the cooler began to purr as it sucked the cup down for recycling.

"Okay. I'll come and give you a hand."

"See you tomorrow then." Jorge nodded his head and left.

Chapter Thirteen

The next morning, Kalen made his way down to the fifty-fourth level. A number of the mining crew were still working on the level and the sound of the mobile drills tore at Kalen's ears when he moved away from the elevators. He found a locker and collected a full set of breathing apparatus, helmet, and a radio headset. After putting the helmet and headset on, he walked to the end of the gallery where markers ringed a shaft that had been sunk to the floor below. Several men were working at the top of the shaft, running cables down, and shouting through their radios into the well. Kalen recognised the foreman, a burly man with a loud voice. He approached unnoticed and peered over the rim.

The hole had a diameter of eight metres and a drop of over thirty metres with a narrow metal ladder running down one side. Poor lighting and dusty air made it difficult to see the bottom. On the other side, two miners hung a third of the way down the well, suspended on cables, fixing electronics and tracks inside the shaft, and liaising with the men at the top by radio and hand gestures. Kalen strapped his pack onto his back and swung his facemask around his neck, ready to descend.

The foreman looked up. "Come to take a look, Chief?"

"I'm meeting Jorge below, how's it going?"

"We've just finished setting up the first auto-lift." The foreman indicated the set of tracks running down the shaft. "We'll be using it until the main elevators are in place."

On the opposite side to the ladder, a pair of rails had been run down the shaft with a shallow platform between them, just deep enough for someone to stand on. The platform had a handrail set at waist height adjacent to the wall. A few metres away from the first set of tracks, more rails had been run down the side, with a larger gap between them and a wider shelf. An equipment lift, Kalen thought.

"Has the large machinery already gone down on the tunnelling worms?"

"That's right," the foreman replied. "The crews working below have been using the ladders down the shafts on the far side or riding down in the large machinery. We've only got the light stuff left to send down now. We're planning to sink twenty or more auto-lifts in this area. They'll be used until the main lifts are up and running and then left in place in case of emergencies."

"Is the auto-lift ready to use?" Kalen eyed the narrow platform. "I'd rather give the ladder a miss."

"We're just about to try it out. Would you like the first ride?" the foreman asked with a look of amusement.

"So long as you take it slowly," Kalen replied, smiling. He recalled that the auto-lifts could be precarious until they were properly adjusted and it was a standing joke amongst the crews that only the foolish went first.

He walked around the edge until he came to the lift dock, pulled on his breathing mask, and stepped onto the platform, facing the wall. Taking hold of the rail, he gave a nod to the foreman, who pressed the release and the lift started to descend slowly. After a short distance, he was fully below the rim and the two workers inside the hole were above him. The lift crawled slowly downwards and then suddenly shuddered and stopped.

He heard the foreman's voice through his radio. "Don't worry. We'll get it moving again in a moment. It usually takes a few runs to get the speed calibrated properly."

Kalen began to regret agreeing to test the lift. The ladder would have been safer but it was out of reach now, and the controls on the auto-lift had been set to remote until it was declared safe. He estimated he had travelled only seven or eight metres. It was a large drop and he wasn't wearing a safety harness if he fell. He tightened his grip on the handrail and reminded himself not to step backwards.

"You okay down there?" the foreman asked.

He looked up and saw the foreman peering down at him. "Yes, I'm fine. I just wish you'd get this thing moving."

"I'm just about to start it up again. Make sure you're holding on. Are you ready?"

"Yes, I'm ready."

The lift began moving again, slowly at first. Then it suddenly jolted and hurtled downwards. The motion jerked Kalen backwards and nearly threw him off the platform. He gripped the handrail tightly and his stomach flipped into his mouth as the tunnel walls whipped past him in a dark blur. He braced himself for the impact and the thought flashed through his mind that he might die, but the lift braked abruptly just before it hit the floor and came to a stop. Kalen breathed a sigh of relief and stepped off shakily.

To his left, there was an exit from the well into a dark corridor. He pressed the auto-release and watched the lift ascend back up the shaft to the foreman and his team. A question came to mind. Had the lift really run out of control, or were they trying to scare him?

***

Kalen emerged from the corridor onto the main floor of the fifty-fifth level. There were few workers in the immediate vicinity and the cavern stretched wide and bare, apart from the drilling machines at the walls. Bad lighting, thick dust, and deafening noise from the drills made it an uncomfortable environment. Kalen couldn't see very far up the cavern and could only make out the blurred shapes of the large drills in the murky atmosphere. He began walking towards the eastern end of the cavern and then paused to adjust his radio to reduce the noise of the drills. Eventually, the outline of the giant drill that had to be moved came into view and he walked quickly up to it.

Dan had climbed up the side of the machine and was giving instructions to several men further up who were adjusting controls and levers, whilst Jorge stood in front of it talking to Sera. Kalen was annoyed. What was she doing here? She was bound to get in the way; she caused problems and had a bad attitude. He tried to think of a way to get rid of her, but couldn't find an excuse.

Two other men stood near the drill, one of them holding a portable console.

Jorge turned towards him. "Glad you could make it. We need to move the drill in a line down the centre of the floor, through the opening at the end to the far wall of the west cave. I've been discussing with Sera where we're going to place it once we've got it down there."

"We're going to have to turn it first," Kalen remarked. "I see one of the men has got a remote control."

"That's only for back up. Dan's programming it for the turn now. Once it's made the turn, he'll re-programme it for a straight run to the west wall. He's going to ride it with some of the crew and control it from there."

Dan had opened a panel to make adjustments to the direction controls for one side of the machine and was giving instructions to the two men above him who were working on the main drill unit.

"How are you doing? Have you turned off the drill function?"

"Yeah, we've shut the lasers off," one of the men replied.

Kalen couldn't see the last man clearly, only a bulky outline, but there was something familiar about him. The man's face was obscured by his breathing mask and for a moment Kalen thought that he didn't know him. Then he recognised him. Lars! A combination of Lars and Sera must spell trouble, he thought. He didn't want either of them here, but it was too late to do anything about it.

Kalen studied the drill they were going to move. It was the basic model used on the construction sites. On the front face of the drill, there was a series of cylindrical outlets for the highly powered pulsed lasers that were used to pound the rock face until the shock waves tore it apart. The laser emitters were arranged in a bank of eight rows with ten in each row and were capable of obliterating anything in their path. The machine had vents at the front and rear to suck in and discharge the resulting rubble. Kalen walked around the drill and shone his flashlight into the vents until he was satisfied that they were unobstructed.

Dan was conducting safety checks with his team on the drill.

"Let's go through them," Dan called. "Laser one?"

"Off," Lars called back.

"Laser two?"

"Off."

"Laser three?"

"Off."

Over several minutes, Dan ran through each laser in turn.

"Laser eighty?"

"Off, that's the last," Lars confirmed.

"Okay, what rate is the drill set at?" Dan called up to Lars.

"Still set at half a metre per hour with a pressure of eighty-four per cent," Lars replied.

"Okay. Leave it at that. It makes no difference to the move. We'll recalibrate it when we have it in position at the west wall."

Dan noticed Kalen and waved to him. "I've just programmed the on-board computer and set the direction controls on this side for the initial reverse. I've sent one of my men, Ryan, to set the unit on the other side."

"If you give me the readings I'll check on him." Kalen got a small hand terminal from his pack. "I'll come up and link in to the on-board computer."

Kalen climbed up the huge drill to Dan's position and studied the instrument panel, keying in the coordinates to his hand terminal.

"We're programming every metre it will travel into the direction units," Dan explained. "But initially we're only programming the turn. We have to move this baby in stages."

Taking a note of the readings, Kalen climbed back down and walked to the far side of the drill. Ryan was halfway up its side. Kalen hauled himself level with him and began checking the direction settings Ryan had entered into the unit.

"We're ready on this side," Kalen said. He clambered down and walked over to Jorge and Sera who both held hand terminals.

"All personnel except those directly involved in the move have been ordered to leave the area," Jorge said. "We'll drive the machine on its rollers. Dan and Ryan will ride on each side of the drill to control the direction units, and Lars and Rajid will ride on the mid-section. I'll walk in front of the drill to check that it doesn't deviate from the programmed coordinates and as a backup, I suggest that you walk at the side and do the same. Sera will walk on the other side. Okay?"

"That's okay with me," Kalen said.

Sera nodded mutely, peering down at the display on her hand terminal.

Jorge called to Dan, "We're all set down here."

The drill lit up and vibrated as its power units came on. The roar of its heavy engines echoed around the gallery.

Jorge gave the order, "Okay. Go!"

Dan took the controls and the massive machine slowly reversed towards the centre of the cavern, its rollers grinding heavily across the floor and throwing up clouds of dust. When the drill reached the turning point, it ground to a halt, and Dan adjusted its settings. Giving Jorge a signal to stand clear, Dan started the drill again and turned the gigantic machine until it faced due west. He powered down the machine and reprogrammed the direction settings.

"We're ready for the run to the west cave," Dan confirmed.

"Stand clear," Jorge shouted. "Go!"

The drill began to trundle slowly forward, travelling westward across the gallery, its rollers shaking the rock floor and throwing up dirt and dust. Kalen walked to one side of the drill, constantly checking his small hand terminal, while Jorge walked in front of it and Sera walked on the other side. Glancing behind him, Kalen couldn't see the men aboard the drill, but he could hear Jorge and Dan speaking over his headset. The huge machine gradually crawled up the length of the east cave until it finally reached the narrow opening in the far wall. In this section of the cave, the walls closed in, leaving a space barely wide enough for the drill to pass through.

"The passageway eventually opens out in a funnel effect into a wide gallery on the other side," Sera explained through his headset. "The survey shows that an Uveid seam runs down the north side of the passageway. We can't chance breaching the seam in case we destabilise the area."

"So we've used the robot worms to create the narrow gap into the west cave until the exact location of the seam can be established," Jorge added.

"The gap's hardly wider than the drill," Kalen replied.

"I need to check the coordinates of the final position with Sera again," Jorge said. "Kalen, can you take over from me while I do that?"

"No problem." Kalen took up position in front of the drill.

"Sera, you're with me." Jorge motioned to Sera and they walked rapidly ahead.

Kalen walked ahead of the drill, continuously watching its coordinates and scanning the ground for any obstacles that the clearance teams might have missed. In the narrow passageway, the drill rolled no more than ten metres behind him, its wings almost brushing the rock-face on each side. Now Kalen could see nothing behind him but the massive bulk of the drill, its lights twinkling in the dim illumination. Ahead, the western cavern was faintly lit, but the drill kicked up dust that swirled about Kalen like a thick fog. He had lost sight of Jorge and Sera and from his position at the front, he couldn't see Dan or Ryan riding on the machine.

"Everything okay Dan?" Kalen asked.

"Yes, it's going well. We'll be out of here in no time."

Kalen walked on. He couldn't see anyone in the gloom and he didn't like it. His instincts told him that something was wrong, but he couldn't pin it down. He pushed the thought aside. It had to be the Narquum wearing off, making him paranoid.

The power units in the drill heated up the atmosphere around it and Kalen began to get hot and sticky. The grit kicked up by the drill enveloped and obscured everything, making it difficult for him to see ahead. He walked farther on, deliberately widening the distance between the drill and himself. He wondered if Jorge was within radio range.

"Jorge, can you hear me?"

He got no reply. Dan and the crew on the drill should have picked up his voice.

"Dan, can you hear me?"

The radio only crackled with static. He recalled that the radio headsets only had a short range. Perhaps he had walked too far away from the drill? He slowed his pace, feeling uneasy. Suddenly a bright, harsh light illuminated everything around him. Through the veil of dust, he could see the black crevices in the tunnel walls and the mouth of the tunnel ahead. Momentarily stunned, he turned and stared at the machine. The top row of the laser bank had come on. Blinded, he put up his arm to shield his eyes from the dazzling light. Then the second row flashed on.

"The lasers have come on! Turn them off!" he shouted into his headset, but his voice was cut off by a loud roar as the drill suddenly lurched forward.

"Shut it down!" he shouted, but the machine kept on coming.

The tunnel walls hemmed him in. He was right in the drill's path and it would soon be on him. He had to get out of its way. A surge of adrenaline coursed through him and he ran. The drill picked up speed behind him. The third row of lasers blinked on and the machine gathered speed. It was nearly on him. He mustered all of his energy to outpace it. The fourth row lit up the cave. He was still under the lasers' trajectory. He gasped for breath and his chest burned. Sweat trickled down his back.

He propelled himself forward in one final burst of energy. The fifth row of lasers blazed and white light flashed above his head. The lasers would hit him soon. The sixth row burst into life. The tunnel mouth was ahead, but his legs ached and shook. If he could run a few more metres, he would be safe. The seventh row flared. Then the walls fell back and he threw himself headlong to one side, out of the path of the drill. The ground vibrated as the drill rolled past him and another brilliant flare erupted. That must be the final row of lasers, he thought. Then he heard a terrible thundering noise and the walls of the cavern collapsed around him.

Chapter Fourteen

Sera had been standing with Jorge at the far end of the western cavern, when the drill became active. The lasers had missed them, playing along the wall, destabilising it. Jorge had pushed her to a safer position and run towards the neck of the tunnel frantically shouting to his men to turn the drill off. There had been no response. Sera had watched in horror as the lasers came alive, and the western wall began to crumble. She had heard the rage of the machine as it exploded with full power and tore forward, and then she smelled burning through her breathing mask. She had watched the blaze of light intensify, lighting up the entrance to the tunnel that gradually widened into the west cave.

A figure had run out of the dust cloud, the drill nearly on top of him before it suddenly lurched away, deflecting its array onto the tunnel wall. The drill had then hit an overhang, which it bore into for several metres before it stopped and its lasers shut down. There were men on the drill but she had lost sight of them when it went into the overhang. A thunderous roll had then boomed across the gallery and the tunnel mouth had caved in, blanketing everything in a hail of rocks and stones.

The lighting hadn't failed, and Sera could still see in the gloom of the dust-laden atmosphere. Everything had occurred so quickly. She didn't understand what had happened, but she stood still and waited for the groaning of the rocks to die away as the stone settled. When the noise stopped she judged it safe to move, but her whole body shook and her legs had gone weak, as if they might buckle under her. The sound of screaming invaded her headset and then she became aware that she was making the noise herself. She tried to stop by closing her mouth, but the shock and fear inside her demanded an outlet and she reverted to hysterical sobbing. Her legs gave way and she sank onto her knees.

Someone shook her arm.

"Sera! Pull yourself together!" Jorge shouted urgently. "Are you hurt?"

He looked unscathed but his jacket was covered in grit. He peered at her anxiously through his facemask.

"Are you hurt? You look all right. Stop crying." He took hold of her arm and pulled her to her feet, planted both hands on her shoulders, and shook her gently again. "Listen to me. You're going to be okay. You're just in shock right now."

She stared at his face. "What happened?" She couldn't make sense of it. One minute the drill had been in the tunnel and then it was gone. Everything was gone, the tunnel, the drill, and the men on it. The pictures in her head were wrong.

"There's been an accident. The drill ran out of control and now there are men buried under the rubble. We've got to get them out as quickly as possible. This is no time to fall apart. Take a minute and then come and help me."

He let go of her and strode away towards the place where the drill had been. She tried to marshal her thoughts and focused on the scene in front of her. Through the murky atmosphere, she could see Jorge climbing up a large mound of rubble. *The drill is underneath the rubble*, she thought. It didn't seem possible; there had been miners on the drill. They were in the rubble and she had to help. Her legs were only trembling a little now. She willed her legs to work and started to run towards Jorge.

As she got nearer, she heard Jorge calling for survivors over his radio. Heat still radiated off the drill and walls and the atmosphere was full of acrid fumes. Nearly all of the drill was submerged under the rock-fall apart from a piece of its side section. Jorge had climbed onto the rubble and was bent over frantically lifting rocks with his hands. From the base of the mound, she couldn't see anyone else. Jorge suddenly straightened and turned as if listening to something.

"I think someone's up there." Jorge pointed farther up the hill of rubble. Sweat dripped off his forehead and he ran his hand across it, leaving a grey smudge. "I heard something on my headset."

He clambered farther up the boulders, stopped, and began digging again. She had heard nothing through her radio except for his voice.

"I think it's Dan," Jorge exclaimed, continuing to dig. "If I can get to him there may be a chance."

"What about the others?" She pictured the team earlier that morning, preparing to move the drill.

"The other side and mid-sections are completely buried. They must be under this lot." He strained to drag a heavy boulder aside. "We'll search for them."

The horror of the accident welled up inside her again and she tried to swallow back her tears. *This can't be happening*, she thought. But it had happened. She was here, alive, and Jorge was digging in the rubble. She remembered a running man. That must have been Chief Trinneer. He hadn't been riding on the drill.

"Someone was running in front of the drill. Was that Chief Trinneer? Where is he?"

"The drill probably hit him. He couldn't have survived," Jorge said brusquely, pulling another boulder away.

"I thought he got away."

She looked around her at the huge piles of rock and gravel banked against the machine and blocking the tunnel mouth. Fixed lighting illuminated the west cave, but it seemed to have grown dimmer.

"Do you know how long the lights will last?" she asked.

"They'll last for a couple of hours at the most on emergency power." Jorge scrabbled in the rubble, hurling the smaller pieces down the side of the hillock.

"Someone might have been thrown off the drill before it hit the wall. I'm going to search at ground level before we lose the light."

"Okay," Jorge replied and carried on digging.

The dust had thickened and she could hardly see into the hollows and crevices, the subdued lights creating an eerie twilight. Switching on her flashlight, she played the beam over the debris at the base of the hillock, sweeping outwards in circles, waving the beam in an arc over the uneven floor and working towards the point where she had last seen the running man.

Next, she shone the beam carefully along the walls. No access tunnels had been created in this section yet and the rock-fall completely blocked the exit into the east cave. Part of the west and north walls had been destroyed by the lasers and had crumbled in places, leaving large deposits of rubble. She couldn't see a way out.

She picked her way methodically over boulders, shining her torch into the dark shadows, and turning over stones that could hide a hand or leg. She heard a noise through her radio that sounded like a man groaning. Someone was alive. He had to be near her. Sweeping her flashlight over the ground, she moved towards the sound. She heard the noise again. It was coming from an area to the rear of the drill where the rock-fall had been lighter. She climbed onto a pile of rocks and saw a man lying in the hollow on the other side.

Rocks and scree engulfed the man except for his head and one hand that stuck out starkly against the dark debris. He still wore his facemask, a smattering of grit covered part of it, and rubble covered his back. Switching her radio to maximum range, she called Jorge but got no reply. She clambered down to the man and saw it was Chief Trinneer.

"Can you hear me?" she asked, playing the beam of her torch over him. A thick layer of stones and debris covered him. "I'll get this off you."

"I'm trapped, I can't move," he groaned.

"Just hold on. I'll get Jorge."

"No, there's no time, I can hardly breathe," he gasped painfully. "The rocks… the rocks on my back… they're crushing me."

She dismissed the idea of going back to Jorge for help. It would take too long. Switching off her torch to conserve its power, she tucked it into her belt, bent her knees, and began to move rocks off his back as quickly as possible. The sharp stones cut into her hands and she put her gloves on. He moaned and winced as she lifted the rocks off him.

"Don't worry. I'll get this off you soon."

She continued to dig him out, scooping up handfuls of scree, flinging it aside, and throwing the larger rocks away individually until she had uncovered his back and torso. He had saved her from Lars. Now it was her turn to help him. She questioned how she would feel if this had been Lars. Would she be so keen to help? She wasn't sure.

"Can you breathe now?"

"Yes, that's better but I can't move my arm." He grimaced in pain.

Both of his arms were still trapped under a blanket of debris. He lay twisted to the right, so that his right arm and shoulder were completely buried and, except for his hand, his other arm was invisible beneath the stones. Sera took several minutes to uncover his left arm and shoulder and then started on his right side. His legs were trapped by a mound of rocks and stones that looked as if it had fallen from a larger bank behind him. If he had been a few metres farther away, he would have escaped the rock-fall, she reckoned. She finally got most of the rocks off him so that only a smattering of scree remained. He stretched a leg out of the layer of grit and pushed himself up into a sitting position. He began rubbing his right arm with his left hand.

"Can you bend it?" she asked.

He flexed his arm and gingerly bent his elbow.

"It's sore, but it seems to work." He winced with pain.

"What about your back?"

"It feels okay, just bruised. But my chest hurts like hell."

"Can you move your legs?"

"I think so," he said, moving each leg in turn and reaching down to massage them. "I'm pretty stiff but I should be okay as soon as I get the circulation back into them. It's my chest that hurts. I'm pretty battered." He rubbed his hands over his ribs, grimacing. "I don't think anything's broken though."

"Can you breathe okay?"

He inhaled deeply and flinched. "It hurts a lot but I can still breathe. I think it's only bruising." He looked around. "Where are the others? What happened?"

"The drill ran out of control. It crashed—over there." She pointed towards the hillock, but the light had nearly gone and there were only shadows. "Jorge's looking for the others." She aimed the beam from her flashlight in the direction of the drill.

He started to get up and stumbled.

She reached forward to help him. "Can you stand?"

"I think so."

He got to his feet, swaying slightly, adjusted his facemask, and then unclasped his torch from his belt, shining the beam over the ground around him.

"What a mess!" he muttered under his breath. "Where's my backpack? It got ripped off when the roof came down."

The beam of his torch picked out his pack lying a short distance away. Its straps were torn and it had burst open, spewing its contents across the ground. He made his way stiffly towards it.

She helped him gather up the contents. He tied a knot in the straps and turned to stare towards the drill.

Although shock was etched on his face, he appeared controlled. "Where's the drill?"

"It's over there. Where that rise is."

"I can't see it? You mean the whole drill's buried? What about the crew, where are they?" he asked, disbelief in his voice.

"They're under there as well," she replied quietly, tears stinging her eyes.

"They can't be." He shook his head. "They just can't be." The shock on his face slowly turned to acceptance. "We have to do something. We have to get them out."

"Jorge's already digging for them."

"We must help him," he said.

***

Kalen began to walk towards the drill, making his way carefully across the rocks that were strewn everywhere, using his torch to guide him. He could hear Sera following and see the beam of her flashlight as it flitted across the alien landscape littered with mounds of rock and debris. Where the drill had pulverised the outer layers of the walls, it had left striated surfaces, with deep vertical ridges that soared upwards into the darkness and cast long twisted shadows across the ground. The air was thick with tiny floating particles that were settling in a fine powder over everything.

Dust had got in his mouth, and he spat it out and used the grimy sleeve of his jacket to wipe his face. His chest hurt, his back hurt, his elbow throbbed, and every time he breathed, he got a sharp stabbing pain in his chest. He fought to stay upright but his right leg ached from his old injury and every time he took a step, he suffered a twinge of pain. Reaching into his pocket for the packet of Narquum, he recalled that it was in his backpack. He would wait and take one later.

At least three of us are still alive, he thought. He remembered the drill and throwing himself to one side of it, and then the walls collapsing. Pummelled by boulders, he had been pinned down, unable to move, and he had found himself back in the black pit of Area Nine again. The crow had sat heavily on his back, a dead weight crushing the air out of his lungs, its claws jabbing his shoulders while it pushed him further and further down into the pit. Everything had gone black and the next thing he could remember was seeing a light and hearing a woman's voice. He had felt the touch of gentle hands and the crow had raked its claws across his back one final time before it lost its grip.

He approached the bank of rubble that covered the drill. From the position of the drill, it looked as if it had swerved away from him at the last minute, he decided. If it hadn't, he would have been hit by its laser array. But how had the accident happened? Dan had been on the drill with access to the primary speed and direction controls, but the laser array was another matter. The lasers were on a different circuit regulated by a power unit situated towards the mid-section where Lars had been riding. If the lasers had been switched on while the machine was being moved, the drill function would sense no resistance and that could have affected its speed. Dan's controls could have been overridden.

Nearing the rise, he saw that the drill had been totally swallowed up by the rock-fall, except for a side wing sticking out. The thick rectangular metal wing looked out of place jutting from between the rocks and detritus that covered the drill. Unless Dan and the others had jumped, they were underneath it all. A cold stone grew in the pit of his stomach. Three-Craters had claimed more victims. *The site is cursed,* he thought. *Or am I cursed? Does death follow me around?*

Chapter Fifteen

A man's voice came through Kalen's headset but the words were indistinct.

"Jorge, is that you?"

"Yes. Is that you Trinneer? I thought we'd lost you. I think I've found Dan. I'm trying to dig him out now."

"How is he?"

"Unconscious, but alive." Jorge's voice sounded hoarse from exertion.

"Where are you?" Kalen directed the beam of his torch across the rise but couldn't see him.

"I'm on the drill, near the top."

Sera had stopped to listen and she pointed up at the side of the slope. "I think he's up there."

Kalen looked up but couldn't see Jorge on the mountain of dark boulders and gravel. The beam of his torch picked out jagged pieces of stone that had hurtled down in the rock-fall and the outline of the drill underneath it all. A flurry of stones suddenly spattered down the side of the slope, and the beam of a flashlight came out of the gloom.

"Jorge, are you up there?"

"Yes, I'm directly above you. Come on up."

Kalen began to climb up, but each time he took a step, loose scree gave way beneath his boots and he slid backwards. He looked around for an easier way up. The side wing of the machine peeked out from beneath the layer of stone and the boulders above it were slightly larger than the rest. They must have sheered straight off the roof, he thought. If he climbed up above the wing, the larger stones would give more purchase, he decided. Sera stood mutely at the base of the machine, watching him. He gestured to her to follow and started to climb, reaching to grasp the grey metal girder and haul himself up. He extended an arm to Sera and pulled her up after him; then continued upwards stepping carefully on the bigger rocks, avoiding the loose rubble between them. His leg throbbed and he gritted his teeth against the pain.

"Don't get too near me, in case I fall," Kalen said, glancing over his shoulder at Sera.

She was frowning in concentration as she clambered up, sending scree clattering down to the ground below. Stones had cracked away leaving edges as sharp as a knife. Kalen winced from time to time, as he nicked his hands on them and cursed himself for not putting his gloves on before he started the climb. Pausing, he swung his pack off his back, and rummaged for them while Sera waited. They were only a few feet away from Jorge now, and he could hear his panting as he laboured to free Dan.

Jorge looked up. "Can you get above me and dig him out from there? Sera, can you get to the other side? I've nearly got him out."

Dan lay unconscious half buried in the scree, the visible parts of his body covered in blood and grit, his face with a grey pallor beneath his breathing mask. He had lost his helmet and there was blood seeping through his hair. Jorge had freed an arm and a leg but each time he scooped the rubble away, more scree from the slope above slithered down to replace it. Kalen carefully climbed around Jorge but each step he took sent scree clattering down the slope.

"Careful there," Jorge exclaimed. "This whole section is unstable."

Kalen eventually got himself into position above Dan and began scooping the scree away while Sera picked her way sideways across the slope and crouched near Dan's head. Dan's arm dangled at an unusual angle and he was barely breathing. He won't survive, Kalen thought. Rage swept over him. *Why had this happened? Had someone deliberately sabotaged the drill and caused this?*

"We have to get him out," Jorge said desperately. "He's my best man."

Kalen ignored his aching body and concentrated on clearing the rubble, using his anger to propel his efforts, hurling the larger stones down the slope.

"Have you found anyone else?" Jorge asked in a ragged voice.

"I searched around the drill but didn't see anybody else," Sera replied tearfully.

"The rest must be buried under here." Jorge's mouth formed an angry line.

"We'll do another search, just to make sure," Kalen said.

"Let's get Dan out first."

They dug for several minutes until they had uncovered Dan but he remained unconscious. Blood seeped through his clothes and one of his legs had broken, the femur jutting out from the skin on his thigh.

"Help me carry him down," Jorge said.

Kalen took hold of Dan's legs while Jorge held him under his arms, and together they manoeuvred him down the slope, sliding every few metres when the scree gave way beneath their boots. Finally, they got to the base of the rubble and rested Dan on a flat piece of ground.

"I don't know what we can do for him," Kalen said. His rage hadn't left him. He had to find out how this had happened.

"He has to hold out until we're rescued." Grief briefly passed across Jorge's face, then it settled into an unreadable mask. "Sera, stay with Dan and do what you can, while we search the area."

They left Sera and Dan while they carried out a search around the base of the drill. The cave was silent apart from their footsteps and Kalen couldn't hear the pounding of the drills from the main site. That worried him. There had to be a lot of rock cutting them off from the east cave. How long was the passageway? Even if the commander mustered a rescue team immediately, their largest drill set at maximum would only cut a metre an hour in this terrain. If the cave-in extended a hundred metres or more, a rescue team might not reach them for days. Their air wouldn't last that long. They had to find another way out or they would suffocate.

***

Sera sat next to Dan, in front of the huge mound that towered behind them, listening to his shallow breathing. He hadn't regained consciousness and looked badly hurt. He could die, she thought. She felt her eyes well up but remembered Jorge's admonishment to pull herself together, and sniffed back the flow of tears that threatened to overwhelm her. The main lights in the cavern were growing dimmer. She switched on her flashlight and in the arc of light created by its beam, got out her handheld scanner, which incorporated a compass and range-finder.

"Let's see," she muttered, aiming her scanner at the place where the passageway between the east and west caves had been.

The passageway had been over two hundred metres long, but her scanner only gave a reading up to seventy-five metres. Would the blockage be that extensive?

"No, it's impossible," she mouthed, staring at the results. There was only rock where the passageway had been. They couldn't get out that way.

She recalled that the main crater lay to the north west of their position. The survey of the terrain between the west cave and the crater's edge had indicated that it was comprised mostly of granite interspersed with the Uveid seams. The west wall had been damaged by the lasers, but her scanner confirmed that there was only solid rock behind it. The area to the south hadn't been fully surveyed, but there wasn't anywhere for them to go in that direction.

A cold fear began to grow from deep within her that spread from her tummy and upwards into her chest, and she felt herself shaking. They were trapped unless she could find a way out, and in a short time, their oxygen would fail. Perhaps the others would think of something. They would need a miracle to get out of here. She remembered her mother. She had believed in miracles, believed in God and the power of prayer. *Mother had unshakeable faith, but all of Mother's prayers didn't stop Father dying. That was my turning point*, Sera thought. *I knew then that all the faith in the world couldn't stop my father dying.*

Now she was sitting in a cold cave with no way out. Would there be any harm in saying a prayer? It couldn't hurt, things couldn't be much worse. She didn't want to die.

Suddenly Sera heard a scraping sound behind her from the direction of the drill. She stood up and aimed her flashlight towards the machine but couldn't see anyone.

"Who's there?" she shouted, but there was no reply.

She shone her light on Dan who was still mute and unconscious and her spine prickled. They had searched this area already. There couldn't be animals down here. She must have imagined the noise. She remained standing, facing the direction the noise had come from, and then she heard the rasping sound again.

"Is anyone there?" she asked again.

If someone had survived, they would reply. She would hear them through her headset, so why the silence? Perhaps their radio had broken, she thought. She looked down at Dan. There was nothing she could do for him. She put her equipment away and placed her pack beside Dan, and climbed over to the drill. The noise seemed to be coming from under the steel girder of the wing that protruded from the drill two metres above her. Immediately under it, there was movement—small stones clattering down the bank. Suddenly, a pair of hands emerged from the rubble, scraping away the stones, and Lars's head appeared. He used a hand to wipe the front of his mask and looked around.

"Well, aren't you going to help me?" he demanded. "Why are you just standing there?"

"Yes, of course," Sera stuttered. She loathed and despised this man. Why had he survived instead of those who were more worthwhile? Perhaps there was a reason. She must put her feelings aside if she was going to survive this crisis. "What do you want me to do?"

"Can you get up here, and pull me out?"

She fastened her torch to her belt and climbed up the rubble until she was parallel to the girder. Bracing herself against its side, she reached over to Lars.

"Get hold of my hands," he commanded.

Sera took hold and pulled. He wriggled and then slowly his shoulders emerged.

"Just a bit more," he grunted. "I'm nearly out."

Sera heaved again, and he slid free to his waist.

"I can take it from here."

She stood back and watched as he used his hands to dig his lower body free.

"Why didn't you answer me?" Sera asked. "How did you get under there?"

"My radio must be off because I didn't hear anything. When the drill went out of control, I dived under the girder and hung on. There's a space under there."

He shrugged his shoulders to shake off bits of debris and then placed his hands firmly against part of the metal girder and pushed himself up. He slithered out, twisting his body around until he could grab hold of a panel to lever himself free. Sera held onto the girder, watching, as Lars gained his footing.

"Are you coming down?" he asked, turning to climb to the ground.

Sera remained where she was and waited for him to get down. His jacket was torn and his rough hands were covered in little cuts. Severe bruising around his eyes and on one cheek darkened his face and he kept rubbing one of his wrists.

"Suit yourself. Where's everyone else? Or are we alone?"

"Jorge and Chief Trinneer are searching. Dan's badly injured." She tried to keep the loathing out of her voice. She hated this man and now she was trapped in a cave with him.

Lars started to descend but the scree gave way under his weight and he grabbed hold of the girder to support himself, before picking his way carefully to the ground. Once he was at the bottom, Sera cautiously climbed down after him. There would be no escape from him here. The crunch of Lars's footsteps echoed loudly, and her lighter footfalls were just as audible. He disappeared into the haze, out of the range of her flashlight, and she didn't follow him. She had to get back to Dan.

***

Kalen methodically searched the area around the tunnel mouth but didn't find anyone else. He re-joined Jorge and they circled around to search the area on the far side of the drill, running the beams of their flashlights over the fractured walls to throw variegated shadows across the ground. They scoured the surface, pulling aside large rocks and jagged metal pieces that had been sheared off the drill in the final seconds of its run. A large part of the roller housing had been torn away and lay several metres from the drill's final resting place. The big piece of metal had warped from the impact. They partially moved it, careful of its sharp edges, to check underneath, and found Rajid's body. He lay in a crumpled heap, clothes sticky with blood, and his arm nearly severed at the shoulder. His facemask had been dislodged and dust covered his face and stuck to his open staring eyes.

"He must have been thrown from the drill before the crash," Kalen said. His stomach lurched and his mouth watered as if he was going to gag. He looked away.

"He was a good man. Help me get the rest of the panel off him," Jorge replied.

"We should leave him here. There's nothing we can do for him."

"I know. But we can use his equipment."

The main lights had nearly gone and Kalen couldn't see Jorge's face in the gloom. The idea of stripping anything from Rajid's body repulsed him, but Jorge was right, they might need the equipment. He heard footsteps behind him.

"Who's that?" Jorge called out.

"It's Lars, boss. Need any help?"

Lars came out of the darkness. The bruising on his face was clearly visible and he seemed to have lost some of his former swagger. *How had the man survived?* Dark thoughts raced through Kalen's mind. *Did Lars turn the lasers on? Was the crash deliberate? The drills had so many safety features it was virtually impossible for the lasers to come on accidentally. Could it have been sabotage? No one in their right mind would do that.* It had to be the paranoia of the Narquum getting to him again.

"Where did you come from?" Jorge asked. "I thought you were dead."

"I got under the axle housing."

"What about the other men? Did you see what happened to them?" Jorge demanded.

"There was no time. I just dived under the housing." Lars caught sight of Rajid and shrugged his shoulders. "Guess I was lucky, the poor bugger. What about the others?"

Jorge grimaced. "I found Dan, but there's no sign of the rest. Can you help us get this off him?"

"Sure thing."

Lars took hold of the end of the metal casing and together they lifted the panel clear of Rajid's body. Jorge bent down to remove his equipment including his breathing apparatus, clinically rolling Rajid to one side to retrieve his pack.

When he had finished, Kalen swung his flashlight in a wide sweep across the area. "I think we've searched everywhere."

"I agree. I don't think we're going to find anyone else," Jorge replied.

Kalen turned to speak to Lars. "What happened on the drill Lars? Who switched the lasers on?"

"I don't know what happened. I didn't touch them."

"But you were at the controls?" Kalen persisted.

"No, once the lasers were disengaged, the unit was closed. I rode further down."

"Did you see anyone else near them?"

"There was no one at the lasers. Why would anyone turn the lasers on?"

That was a good point. The obvious answer was to fry him, but the machine had run out of control as well.

"Why didn't someone turn the power off?"

Lars glared at him. "I don't know. Are you accusing me of something?"

"No, but if it wasn't you, who was it? There must have been someone at those controls."

"Look, what do you take me for, an idiot? If I'd seen anybody at the laser controls, I would have jumped on them immediately. Do you think I want to get myself killed?"

"Okay, I believe you," Kalen conceded. "Perhaps there was something wrong with the drill's programme."

"There's no way we can resolve this standing here," Jorge said sharply. "We'll have to deal with it later. Right now we've got to find a way out."

Chapter Sixteen

Sera sat beside Dan, bending down to check on him every few minutes. She had covered him with her jacket, but he remained unresponsive. Her face mask was grimy so she wiped some of it away and then checked her oxygen supply. Despite the spare oxygen cartridge in her pack, she estimated that her supply would only last for a few hours. Trying her radio, she couldn't pick up anyone from the main site. That didn't surprise her. The signal probably couldn't penetrate the layers of rock cutting them off.

The sound of voices came over her headset and she looked up to see the others coming towards her.

"How is he?" Jorge asked, crouching down beside Dan. He felt for a pulse and put his ear to Dan's mouth. "He's hardly breathing."

"He hasn't come round at all," she replied.

Chief Trinneer remained standing, looking about them. "We have to find a way out of here."

"Can't we get out through the tunnel?" Lars asked.

"It looks like it's blocked off," Chief Trinneer said. "Sera, have you taken any readings?"

"My scanner shows that the rock-fall is solid for at least seventy-five metres."

"Won't the rescue team dig us out?" Lars asked.

"It will take them too long," Chief Trinneer replied. "Even using our fastest drills, it will take them days to reach us and our air won't last that long."

Lars didn't appear convinced. "If they can't get to us through the rock-fall, can't they drill down to us from the level above?"

"That's not possible," Jorge explained. "This section isn't directly under level fifty-four. We're further south. There's nothing but solid rock above us."

Chief Trinneer shone his flashlight towards the west wall. "Sera, is there another way out of here?"

They were all looking at her. "There aren't any access tunnels in this section yet. The main crater is northwest of us. The area in between hasn't been excavated so far and it's mostly solid granite. There's no way through. That only leaves south, but there's nothing there."

Jorge appeared thoughtful. "What's the terrain like to the south?"

"The initial survey suggested cave systems running through that area." Surely he wasn't going to suggest that they go south? It could take years to find a way through the cave systems that ran in that area.

"How far are we from the rim of the main crater?" Chief Trinneer asked.

She rummaged in her pack for her hand terminal, set it to display a map of the area, and pointed to their position. "We're at one of the farthest points from the rim; it's about six kilometres away."

Chief Trinneer frowned. "Even if we could get through, we'd never make it. It's too far."

"How much oxygen and water have we got between us?" Jorge asked.

"Including Rajid's supplies, I estimate that we can last up to twelve hours with what we've got, and a few hours more if we can get to the equipment on the drill," Chief Trinneer said. "We have to look for another way out."

"I have an idea." Jorge reached over to the small display screen and ran his finger down the map to indicate a spot southwest of their location, a little over three kilometres away. "If we can get to this point, then we can get out."

"But there's nothing there," Sera repeated, confused. They had to have a destination.

"There is something there. There's a fourth crater. It stretches for over thirty kilometres and is already enclosed with a breathable atmosphere. Its existence is classified but there should be a base there. If we can reach it, we can get out."

"Are you sure? I've never heard of it," Chief Trinneer queried.

"Neither have I," Sera said, glancing at Jorge in surprise. Technically Chief Trinneer was senior to Jorge. How did Jorge know about it and not Chief Trinneer? She wanted to believe Jorge even if it sounded unlikely.

"I worked there before Three-Craters and I'm pretty sure of its location. I think it's our best shot."

"How are you sure of its location? It isn't marked on any surveys I've seen," she asked.

"Believe me, I know it's there. I worked there for months. Is there any way we can get to it from here?"

Sera considered for a moment. "It looks like there's a cave system running down here." She indicated a line on the map. "But there's no guarantee we can get all the way through."

"I think we've run out of other options. I think we should try and get to the fourth crater through the cave system," Jorge said.

Chief Trinneer peered at the map. "I don't think we've got much of a choice. We'll run out of air if we stay here."

"I can't tell how extensive the cave system is from my instruments," Sera said. "We could get half-way there and find we're trapped."

Jorge looked around at them all. "I think it's our only option, unless anyone has a better suggestion?"

"Okay, let's give it a try. We can't stay here and wait for rescue. We'll run out of air long before anyone can reach us," Chief Trinneer said. "At least going through the caves gives us a chance."

"Okay by me," Lars agreed.

Jorge nodded. "It's not going to be easy, but if we can take lasers, we may be able to blast a way through if there are obstructions."

Lars gestured towards Dan. "What are we going to do about him?"

"We'll have to make a decision," Jorge said.

"We can't leave him here. His air will run out before the rescue teams arrive," Sera protested.

Jorge stared at Dan's unconscious form. "It will be difficult to carry him through the caves. It could get rough."

"We don't have to make a decision yet," Chief Trinneer said. "We need to salvage what we can from the drill first. There should be hand lasers, breathing apparatus, and emergency supplies in the equipment lockers. If we can get to them, we've got a better chance of getting out. Jorge, why don't you and Sera try and find a way into the caves, while Lars and I get the gear from the drill?"

"Agreed." Jorge prepared to leave.

The drill had finally cooled and the temperature had plummeted. Sera's jacket still lay across Dan's body, which was now covered in dust, and she shivered violently. Without a word, Chief Trinneer reached down, drew her jacket off Dan, and handed it to her. Surely he wasn't going to let Dan freeze? She opened her mouth to object, but before she could say anything, he had shrugged out of his own jacket and put it over Dan. She had misjudged him.

"I can manage without it for a while," he said, and turned towards the drill.

"Thank you," she said, but he had already gone and Jorge stood waiting for her.

She shook her jacket out and put it on, glad of its warmth. Chief Trinneer was right, they couldn't stay here. She looked down at Dan and tears welled up in her eyes again. A layer of grey dust had coated his face mask and she could hardly see his chalky white face underneath. They couldn't leave him here, alone and unconscious. A rescue attempt could take days and he wouldn't last that long.

***

Kalen stared up at the drill.

"The top locker will be the most accessible," he said to Lars. "Up there, above the side wing." He pointed to the top of the rise, above the metal girder that protruded from the rubble.

"We can climb up the side wing," Kalen continued. "Let's find something to dig with first." He flashed his torch over the debris until its beam illuminated a short piece of metal with a flat end. "That will make a good spade."

He picked up the piece of metal and chucked it over to Lars who caught it easily, and then looked around until he found a similar piece for himself.

"Let's go." Kalen began to climb up to the girder. "Don't get too close while we're climbing."

"Whatever you say." Lars followed him, keeping a short distance behind.

Each step Kalen took sent scree slithering down the slope, but he continued to scramble over it until he could get hold of the girder to haul himself up. The rubble above the girder provided slightly better footing and he carried on going until he judged he had reached the site of the locker. Over his headset, he heard Lars grunting and puffing behind him. He didn't like having Lars at his rear, he didn't trust him.

Kalen pointed to the rubble when Lars reached him. "The locker is probably half a metre beneath this lot, but we should be able to get to it if we work together."

"Just tell me where to dig."

"Here, right here." Kalen pointed to the spot in front of him and began digging.

After a few minutes, sweat began trickling down Kalen's back and he started to shake. He hadn't taken a

Narquum since that morning. The packet had been in his backpack but it wasn't there now. It must be lying in the dust somewhere. If any of the others noticed his shaking, he hoped they would put it down to shock. He was still sore from his earlier battering and his leg ached painfully. Only adrenaline and anger kept him going as he balanced on the side of the drill, digging with Lars in continuous motion. If they could reach the locker, they would have extra supplies and that could make the difference between life and death.

They fell into a rhythm, digging alternately, each scooping out a spade full of rocks to throw down the slope while the other dug into the hole. The rocks and gravel bounced down the side of the hillock in rivulets, clattering down to form a small mound below. The sound of their digging echoed around the cave like a slightly irregular heartbeat. Lars set the pace and Kalen found it difficult to keep up with him. His chest was giving him sharp spikes of pain and his arms ached.

"We should reach the locker soon," Kalen said.

"How far down do you think it is?"

"We must be nearly there, but I can't see the markings yet."

"What if we're not digging in the right place?"

"I'm pretty certain it's here. Just keep going."

Kalen scooped another load of stones away and caught a glimpse of shiny metal underneath. He quickened his pace until a patch of metal was exposed, but he couldn't see any markings.

"I can't see the locker yet. We need to widen this area but I'm sure we're digging at the right spot."

Lars grunted and carried on until they gradually expanded the patch of exposed metal.

Kalen swept the beam of his flashlight over the smooth surface. At the edge of the cleared patch, he saw a mark on the metal.

"Just a minute, I need to check this." Taking his makeshift spade, Kalen carefully cleared the debris away from the edge until he could see part of an arrow symbol. "It's here. We just need to dig further over."

They changed position slightly and continued digging until they had extended the hole enough to expose the locker cover. There were deep scratches on the metal and a large indentation near one edge. Below the arrow symbol, there was a small keypad. Kalen bent down, brushed the last pieces of scree away, and then pressed the keypad. Nothing happened and he tried again but the cover did not move.

Kalen stared at the keypad. "The opening mechanism must be damaged."

"There should be a manual handle at the edge."

Kalen found the handle and turned it firmly, but the cover did not budge. "It's locked solid."

"It's broken, isn't it? What are you going to do?" Lars remarked sardonically, watching him.

"We need a crowbar."

"Let me have a go."

"Okay." Kalen stepped aside.

Lars bent over and pressed the keypad but the locker still didn't open. Next, he tried the handle, twisting it until the muscles in his neck bulged. He continued pulling at the lever forcefully but the cover still refused to move.

"Let me try something else," Lars said, picking up his pack and taking out a long metal wrench.

Carefully aiming his swing, Lars struck the locking mechanism hard with the wrench and made a shallow dent. Varying his position slightly, he continued striking the lock until the metal finally caved in around it, and then reached down and tried the handle again. This time there was movement and with a final tug, he wrenched the cover open.

The locker contained extra breathing apparatus and oxygen cartridges, food, water, hand lasers, tools, and a medical kit. Kalen calculated that together with the supplies they already had, the emergency rations would provide the group with enough air and water for nearly eighteen hours each. He found two packets of Narquum in the medical kit and palmed one of them for his own use.

Kalen contemplated the supplies. "We're going to have to make do with this. There are two more lockers on the drill but I don't think we can get to them. One is on the side that hit the wall and the other is deep inside the casing. Let's take this lot and get back to the others."

Kalen handed half of the extra supplies to Lars and then began climbing down the side of the slope. The scree gave way under his feet and he nearly tumbled over twice. *I can't afford to fall now*, he thought, desperately trying to retrieve his footing. Behind him, Lars stumbled heavily, sending rocks and scree skittering past Kalen.

"Watch it!" Kalen snapped.

Lars made no reply and Kalen carried on scrambling down. Below him, he could see the beams from Sera and Jorge's flashlights, moving towards the base of the drill. He had switched on his helmet light and its beam cut into the darkness haphazardly with the motion of his head. Nearing the base of the slope, he saw that Jorge and Sera had reached Dan, who still lay inert where they had left him. *He won't make it*, he thought again. They couldn't carry him and he wasn't going to survive long enough for the rescue teams to reach him in time. He made his way carefully over the debris, towards them.

"We got into the locker," Kalen said, rifling through the supplies and pulling out one of the foil emergency blankets. "Dan could use this."

Sera took the foil blanket from him and carefully covered Dan with it. A pack lay next to Dan, and Jorge bent down and began going through its contents.

"Dan still had his pack on when we found him," Jorge explained. "I'd say he's got enough air and water to last for at least twelve hours, but he hasn't shown any sign of coming round."

"Let's sort this stuff out first and then we'll deal with him." Kalen divided the supplies into four piles and they each took a share.

"We need to discuss what we're going to do, but not in front of Dan. Let's go over there to talk." Jorge nodded towards the other side of the drill.

"Okay," Kalen said, fastening his pack and hoisting it on his back. "Come on, Sera." He helped her with the straps of her pack. It looked too heavy for her now.

Jorge walked along the side of the drill until they were some distance from Dan, and stopped by the wall.

"Switch off your radios. We need to discuss what we're going to do with him. We can't take him with us," Jorge said.

"What do you mean? If we leave him here, he'll die. We have to take him with us!" Sera exclaimed.

Kalen shook his head. "He'll probably die anyway if he's moved. He's badly injured and we don't know how long it's going to take us to get out."

"But he has no chance if we leave him. At least he has a chance if we take him with us," Sera pleaded.

"I don't think he'll survive if we move him but if that's what everyone wants to do, I'll take my turn carrying him, but I don't think it's a good idea," Kalen replied.

"Trying to carry him isn't realistic, he'll slow us down too much," Jorge said.

"We're going to have to cover some rough ground. It would be very difficult to carry someone through it," Kalen added.

Jorge took a deep breath. "He's better off if we leave him here; he's got over twelve hours of air."

"We can't just leave him alone with only a few hours of air." Sera's voice quavered. "At least we have to leave him an extra air cartridge and more water."

Kalen gave Jorge a sharp look and their eyes met. Those supplies would be wasted on a dead man.

"We can't leave him extra air. We need the water and air for ourselves," Jorge explained patiently. "We would be sacrificing four of us for him, and he's probably going to die anyway."

"What if he wakes up and finds himself alone?"

Sera's face contorted and she began to cry. *She isn't being realistic*, Kalen thought. They couldn't carry Dan—if they tried, they would never get out alive. She was going to be a problem unless she accepted what was happening. To have any chance they all had to pull together as a team. He moved nearer to her and gently touched her upper arm but she ignored him.

"I'm going to check on him again, and then we can take a vote if you want," Jorge said. He strode off in Dan's direction, the beam of his flashlight bobbing in the darkness.

"If we leave him like this, I'll feel guilty," Sera snuffled. "I'm sorry, but this is horrible."

"If you were lying there and not him, I bet he would leave you," Lars commented.

"We all feel bad about this but Dan wouldn't want us to sacrifice ourselves for him," Kalen said reasonably. "He would understand why we had to go on without him."

"I just can't get it out of my mind how terrible it would be if he came round and found us gone," she sobbed.

A few minutes later, Kalen heard footsteps and Jorge gradually emerged out of the darkness carrying an extra pack.

Jorge was frowning. "The decision has been made for us. I'm sorry, but when I got back, I found that Dan had stopped breathing. He's dead."

"Please God, no!" Sera let out a sob, and tears coursed down her cheeks making her face mask wet.

Kalen stared at him in disbelief. The timing was too perfect. "How?"

"When I got there he looked very pale so I checked and he wasn't breathing," Jorge replied, slinging the extra pack over his shoulder. He also had Dan's jacket and blanket over his arm. "He won't need these now. Has anyone space in their packs to carry these? We need everything we can use and Dan wouldn't have minded. Between us, we now have nearly twenty-one hours of air each. I've left his personal identification on him for the rescue unit to find. If you're ready we should leave."

"Just a minute," Kalen said. "I think I left my gloves near Dan. I need to get them."

He turned around and walked swiftly towards Dan before Jorge could stop him. Sera's sobbing faded in the distance and Jorge and Lars's voices grew quieter. Dan was lying in the same position they had left him in and Kalen bent down to check his pulse and breathing. He also looked for any sign that his death had been hastened, but found nothing suspicious. After sweeping his flashlight over the area again, he walked back to join the others.

"We should get going," Jorge said when he returned.

"Okay. I've got everything."

Jorge turned on his heel and strode off into the darkness towards the south wall and the others followed.

Chapter Seventeen

At the south wall, Jorge stopped in front of a deep crevice. The fissure was high and wide enough for a man to walk through but the walls were rough and jagged edges of stone jutted from the sides.

"Sera and I found this. It looks like the best way through," Jorge said, stepping into the crack.

The glow from Jorge's flashlight briefly lit up the hole before Sera and Lars followed him in. With one final look behind him, Kalen stepped into the fissure after them. The narrow corridor twisted and turned and in places, he had to stoop. He caught his jacket on the rough walls and hit his head several times until he got used to the hazards. In front of him, Lars stumbled along clumsily, frequently hitting his shoulders against the sides of the walls, his frame almost blocking the width of the corridor. Perhaps walking behind him hadn't been such a good idea after all.

The narrow corridor broadened into a large gallery with oddly shaped sides. His torch lit up long elongated structures that lined the walls like contorted columns, etched with circular and oval patterns that were repeated across the hard rock floor. The dust cleared, and ahead, Jorge stopped to confer with Sera who used her scanner to take readings. She guided them to a circular hole about a metre in diameter, situated at waist level in the far wall. Jorge shone his torch inside it to reveal smooth sides. It reminded Kalen of one of the access tunnels.

Jorge turned towards the group. "We're going through there. Sera thinks that it's about twenty metres long, but it should be wide enough."

If it's a metre wide all the way through then we shouldn't have a problem, Kalen thought. *But what if it narrows?*

"Lars, would you like to bring up the rear for a while?" Kalen asked.

"If you think that's best." Lars dropped back behind him.

Jorge swung himself into the tunnel and helped Sera in behind him. Kalen switched his helmet light on and climbed in after them. He heard Lars behind him, his heavy breathing audible through his headset. The tunnel was dark and claustrophobic. Cold clawed at him through his jacket while he crawled forward, keeping his head low and eyes focused on the tunnel in front of him. Sera's bottom bobbed up and down in the beam of his helmet light.

The beams from their lights bounced off the smooth walls. Kalen scraped his shoulder against the side of the tunnel and shifted his position to centre, but then scraped his other shoulder. Although he tried to keep his head down, the top of his helmet brushed against the ceiling. He studied Sera again. Her body nearly filled the entire space now. Something jabbed his thigh and he remembered that the bit of tubing he'd found after the tourist had died was still in his pocket. Behind him, he heard Lars scuffling and grunting.

"Stop for a moment," Jorge said. Ahead of him, Sera stopped crawling.

"Do we go down there, Sera?" Jorge asked.

"We carry straight on," Sera replied.

Jorge started moving forward again and the beam of Kalen's light picked out an obsidian crevice cut into the tunnel wall, its darkness impenetrable. He passed by it, following the others, his knees sore.

After a few more metres, Jorge stopped again. "Are you sure we're still going in the right direction?"

"I've gone over the coordinates and we're going due south at the moment. My scanner shows that this tunnel carries on a bit farther then runs into a large cave. There's definitely a large cavity ahead," Sera confirmed.

"Okay, but it's getting narrow."

"According to my readings it's our best route, but I can't get an exact reading on the width of the tunnel."

After a few metres, the roof suddenly dropped so that the tunnel ended in a wall intersected only by a horizontal crack about half a metre high. Jorge's light suddenly winked out and in front of Kalen, Sera dropped to her stomach, ducked her head under the overhang, and shuffled forward. He wriggled into the hole after her, keeping his head down, and used his arms to pull himself forward under the low ceiling. The floor became rough and tore at his gloves but the width of the crevice extended metres into the darkness on each side, the roof falling to a few centimetres high in some places.

Something glistened in the beam of Kalen's light and he paused to look. In the crevice to his right, thousands of tiny blue stones glittered, lighting up the hollow like blue fire.

Kalen heard Lars shuffling behind him.

"Don't stop, Chief!" Lars called out.

"Okay." He continued shuffling forward.

The material of his jacket and trousers caught on the rough surfaces, chaffing his skin when he moved, and he began to feel lightheaded and dizzy. Perhaps his oxygen was getting low. He checked his air gauge but it indicated that there was still oxygen in the cartridge. In the bobbing torchlight, he imagined shapes jumping out at him from the shadows. At first, they were tiny wisps of light that danced in front of his eyes, gone before he could make out their form. Then fluid shapes moved across his field of vision, floating like balloons that elongated, narrowed, and then reformed into bubbles. He tried to study one, but it evaporated before he could see it properly. He blinked the shapes away and concentrated on following Sera's feet until she stopped suddenly.

"Hold on everyone. I think we've got a problem," Jorge's voice came over his radio.

Only Sera's feet and legs were visible to Kalen. He lay stretched out in the tunnel, with very little clearance under the roof and he felt as if the walls and roof were pressing in on him. *This is not the time to get claustrophobic,* he told himself. The shapes had gone, but he ached all over and still felt lightheaded. He wished he could get up and run, to be able to do anything but lie motionless in the darkness. He heard Jorge moving up ahead.

"What is it?" Kalen asked.

"We've reached the end of the tunnel. We're half-way up a cliff with a sheer drop," Jorge said. "I can't see a way down."

"It'll take us too long to go back and we haven't got enough air. What about up? Can you see anything above the tunnel? Is there anything further up?" Kalen asked.

"I don't know," Jorge replied. "Sera, get hold of my feet. I'm going to get out as far as possible so I can take a good look. Be ready to drag me back in if I start to fall."

"I'll hold your feet as well, Sera," Kalen said. He took off his gloves and reached in the gloom for her ankles, encircling them with his hands, under her trousers. He shifted forward a little to get a better grip and moved his hands up her legs. Her bare skin felt pleasantly smooth under his fingers. She twitched one of her legs and he moved them back to her ankles.

"Sorry, just trying to get a better grip." He was disappointed that she had noticed. He didn't like her, but she had nice legs, he admitted to himself.

He heard the sound of scuffling ahead and then Jorge's voice. "There's a large cave. It's pretty high and I can't see the roof or the end of it. There's a sheer drop immediately below and I can't see a way down. Hang on, I'm going to try and get a better look."

Kalen tightened his grip on Sera's ankles. She tensed briefly to take Jorge's weight and then relaxed when Jorge pulled himself back into the crevice.

"There's a ledge about five metres below us just to the right. It's about a third of the way down. If we can get to it, we might be able to climb from there," Jorge said.

"How big is it?" Lars asked.

"Just about big enough for us all to stand on."

"But how are we going to get onto it?" Sera asked. "We haven't got any climbing equipment. Can we burn handholds with our lasers?"

"That's too dangerous—we could bring the cliff down. We can use our belts. If we fasten them together, we can use them like a rope. They should hold," Kalen suggested.

"There's nothing to tie them onto," Sera pointed out.

"We can lower each other down," Kalen said. "The rope won't be long enough to abseil."

"Let's do it," Jorge said briskly. "I've also got Dan and Rajid's belts in my pack."

"You took them off their bodies?" Sera asked, in surprise.

"They weren't going to use them."

"How's Lars going to get down, if he's the last?" Sera asked.

"We'll think of something," Jorge said tersely. "It isn't as if we've got much choice, we can't go back."

Kalen took his belt off and fastened it to the belt that Lars proffered from behind him and then to Sera's belt, in turn.

"Pass the end of the belts up to me, Sera, and I'll fasten them to mine. I'll put my belt around my chest," Jorge explained. "Then you can lower me down."

Kalen wished that Sera wasn't in front of him, but there was no room to get past her.

"Sera, I have to get forward as much as possible, otherwise you'll be the only one taking Jorge's weight at the end," Kalen said.

"There isn't much room," Sera replied doubtfully.

"I know but I'm going to have to come forward and reach over you. It's going to be a tight squeeze. Lars, you must do the same."

"You're not really my type. You should have let me go first. I wouldn't mind snuggling up to little Sera there," Lars sniggered.

"Let me know when you're ready. Once I'm down there, I'll send the rope back up for Sera," Jorge said.

"Sera, I'm going to lie over you, as far as your waist," Kalen said. "It may be a bit uncomfortable but there's nothing I can do about that. There's no other way."

Kalen shuffled over Sera's legs until he lay flat on top of her, with his upper chest reaching her hips while his body covered her legs. She felt warm underneath him and he could feel the rhythm of her breathing.

"You're squashing me," she objected.

"Sorry, it won't be for long. Remember, that once Jorge is out, we have to move forward to the rim."

She squirmed under him, and he twisted to one side to relieve her of some of his weight, resting his head on her back. Her breathing had quickened and she had begun to tremble. Kalen felt Lars move up behind him.

"Ready?" Jorge said. "Here goes."

Chapter Eighteen

Kalen watched Jorge wriggle forward and swing his legs over the edge and drop, so that he gripped the shelf with his arms and elbows facing inwards while his trunk hung over the void. By the torchlight, Jorge's head, arms, and shoulders were silhouetted in the mouth of the tunnel.

"Get forwards, Sera," Kalen directed, pushing her towards the lip of the tunnel.

"I'm going to drop down now. You've got the rope?" Jorge asked.

"Yes, we have you. Don't worry," Kalen replied.

"Okay, hold on to it," Jorge said and his head disappeared.

Peering over Sera's head, Kalen could see that Jorge was gripping the edge with his fingers, the strap tight around his chest. He heard Jorge kicking the side of the rock-face and the rope swivelled in his hands.

"It's no good," Jorge panted. "The cliff is nearly sheer and I can't get a foothold. You'll have to lower me down."

"We'll hold on to you," Kalen called out.

"Ready? Here goes." Jorge let go of the lip.

The strap jerked viciously and went taut and Kalen hoped the belts would hold. He gripped the strap firmly with both hands and hung on, trying to relieve Sera of the strain, and with Lars behind him, they took most of the weight. A knife-like pain in his ribs made him gasp but Lars wedged him down solidly and he couldn't move. The rope jerked in spasms as Jorge dangled precariously just underneath the tunnel mouth, twisting around until he steadied himself against the rock-face.

"Okay. Lower me gently," Jorge shouted.

"We're going to let out the rope slowly," Kalen explained. "Just feed it out steadily, Sera."

They began to play the strap out gradually, lowering Jorge slowly down the cliff face. The tension on the straps increased, the further Jorge dropped.

"We're nearly out of rope, Chief," Lars said.

"How much left?" Kalen asked.

"We've got another metre at the most."

"Hold on. Jorge, are you nearly down?"

"I've got another couple of metres to go."

"Okay, Lars, give me the end of the rope." Kalen braced himself and there was a jolt when Lars released the end of the strap.

"Jorge, are you near the ledge?" Kalen asked.

"I'm nearly there. Can you give me some more rope?"

Carefully, Kalen fed out a short piece of the strap until he held the end of the last belt.

"Lars, get back and hold onto my ankles. I'm going to try and move forward a bit more," Kalen said. "The roof is slightly higher at the mouth of the tunnel so there might be enough clearance for me to lie over Sera. Sorry Sera, but we're running out of rope and you can't take Jorge's weight by yourself."

Lars shuffled backwards and took hold of Kalen's ankles. Holding firmly onto the strap, Kalen used the tension on it to haul himself forward over Sera until he rested on top of her back. His torso covered her body, and he lowered his head until his head was nearly touching hers.

"You're crushing me!" she protested and wriggled about.

"Sorry, but the rope isn't long enough." He lay sprawled over her with his hands in front clutching the strap, her body warm beneath him. He edged forward until he could see over the lip. Jorge hung down the side of the cliff suspended by the belt under his arms and he was trying to swivel around to a ledge just below and to one side of his position.

"Get to the wall, Jorge," Kalen shouted. "The ledge is below you to your left as you face the wall. You need to climb over to it."

Jorge swung himself around until he grabbed hold of the wall. Without footholds, Jorge's feet scraped uselessly against the wall but he used his hands to claw his way sideways. Kalen played out the last of the strap but Jorge still hadn't reached the ledge. He hung about a metre above and just to one side of it.

"There's no more rope," Kalen shouted.

"I can see the ledge. If I can get above it, I can jump," Jorge replied.

In one movement, Jorge hurled himself sideways, stretching his left arm and leg outwards towards the ledge, while he released the clasp of his belt with his right hand. Suddenly, the strap went slack. Jorge landed half on the ledge, hitting the floor with his shoulder, leaving his legs hanging over the side. *He's not going to make it*, Kalen thought. Then Jorge twisted around onto his stomach and hauled himself up with his arms until he got his legs on the ledge. He sat still for a moment and Kalen heard him panting while he recovered his breath.

"Are you okay?" Kalen asked.

"Yes, I'm fine." Jorge stood up and shone his flashlight around him.

From Jorge's perch, his flashlight illuminated more of the cavern. The cave was vast and the beam of the flashlight could not reach its roof and walls. The ledge that Jorge stood on protruded from the side of the cliff about ten metres above the floor of a cave.

"We'll send Sera down now," Kalen said.

He wriggled off her and immediately felt the loss of her body heat. Mourning the loss of Sera's warm body squirming under him, he pulled up the strap, made a loop, and slipped it over her head.

"Fasten it around your chest and under your arms," Kalen told her.

"I know what to do," she snapped. Her hands were trembling and she fumbled with the belt in jerky movements.

"There's nothing to worry about. Lars and I are strong enough to lower you down, and Jorge will catch you. When you're ready, get over the rim and lower yourself until you're holding on with your hands. Here, let me check that." He reached forward and tightened the fastenings on the belt.

After an initial hesitation, Sera swivelled around at the mouth of the tunnel so that she lay on her stomach facing inwards with her legs hanging over the edge.

"Just a bit further," Kalen said.

Looking afraid, she pushed herself a little bit further out and then stopped so that she hung by her elbows.

"One more push, then hold onto the edge with your hands. I'll tell you when to let go."

"I can't do it!" she exclaimed shrilly, her eyes wide with fear. "I just can't!"

She tried to scramble back inside the tunnel but only managed to haul the top half of her body inside, leaving her hips and legs dangling over the side.

"Come on Sera," Kalen said in a calm voice that he hoped would soothe her. "You can do it. Just look at me and drop down. You won't fall. Lars and I have got hold of you."

"I can't! I'll fall!" she shrieked. "It's too high!"

"You're wasting time!" Jorge shouted angrily from beneath them. "Just get yourself over the side and drop down. Stop messing about!"

"You must trust me. We're not going to let you fall, just keep your eyes on me and drop down. You'll be all right."

She pushed herself back a fraction, her face white. "I hate heights," she cried. "I don't want to die like this!"

"You're not going to die. You'll be down in a couple of seconds. That's right, just push yourself back and take the weight on your elbows, then hold on with your hands."

She manoeuvred herself over the rim and hesitated.

"Go on, you're nearly there. We're holding you."

She took a deep breath and dropped down until she hung from the edge by her hands.

"Okay, I want you to let go now."

She gripped the edge tighter and didn't move. "I can't! I'm going to fall, I know I'm going to fall!" she screamed, staring at him with huge eyes.

"Try letting go just one hand at a time," Kalen coaxed her.

She took her left hand off the rim, so she hung by one hand only.

"That's right, now let go of the other one. Use your hands to steady yourself against the wall. We've got you."

She let go with a small scream. Kalen had braced himself against the tug on the strap but she wasn't heavy compared to Jorge. For a few seconds she dangled precariously below the tunnel mouth and then they lowered her slowly until Jorge caught hold of her legs and pulled her over the ledge. Jorge held her legs while she unfastened the belt around her chest before dropping down onto the shelf.

Kalen pulled the strap back up and prepared to go next. He would be dependent on Lars to lower him down. Would Lars be able to take his weight? Could he trust him? Lars could easily let him fall and make it look like an accident. He pushed his suspicions aside; there was no other way down.

"Lower me as quickly as you can, Lars. That way you won't have to hold me for too long."

"Just tell me what to do."

Kalen fastened the belt underneath his arms. "Are you ready?"

"Yes, go on," Lars said.

Kalen swivelled himself around so that he faced inwards at the tunnel entrance and then levered himself over the rim until he was half-way out of the tunnel, taking his weight on his elbows and arms. With a deft movement, he dropped below the tunnel mouth and let go of the rim, gritting his teeth against the pain as the belt gripped his chest, but Lars took his weight and the belt held. He dropped steadily, bumping against the vertical rock face, but suddenly the strap gave way and for an instant, he was falling and banging his elbows and knees against the wall. *This is it, I'm going to fall*, he thought. Then the strap jerked up short and he bounced against the wall.

"Sorry," Lars voice floated from above. "I lost my grip for a moment."

Had he heard a snigger in Lars's voice? How much resentment did Lars carry towards him for the incident with Sera? Suddenly he felt Jorge's hands on his legs.

"I've got you," Jorge shouted.

Kalen quickly released the clasp on the strap and dropped down onto the ledge. The ledge was narrow, barely wide enough for them all to stand on, and above, the beam of Lars's flashlight shone out of the black cavity high in the wall.

"We have to find a way to get Lars down," Jorge said.

"Lars, keep hold of the rope while we work out how to get you down," Kalen shouted.

"Can't you use the hand lasers on the cliff to make footholds?" Lars asked.

"No, it could bring the whole wall down and the ledge with it," Jorge replied.

"I don't know, looks like a long way down to me. There's nothing up here to tie the end of the rope to."

Kalen had an idea. "Fix the belt around your chest, Lars, then throw the end to us."

Lars tied the belt around him and threw the tail of it down. Kalen caught it easily.

"What now?" Lars asked.

"When I say so, climb out and hold onto the edge with your hands," Kalen shouted.

"Sera, hold onto the end of the belt," Kalen instructed. "Jorge, if I can climb onto your shoulders, I should be able to reach Lars's feet. Do you think you can take the weight?"

"I should be able to for a few minutes, but won't you overbalance?"

"I know it's a risk but it's all I can think of."

Jorge knelt so that Kalen could climb onto his shoulders, facing the wall, and then straightened up. Carefully, using the wall to balance himself, Kalen stood on Jorge's shoulders and Jorge grasped his feet and ankles to steady him.

"Now Lars, quickly," Kalen shouted. "Drop down but keep hold of the rim."

Lars heaved his bulk out of the tunnel. The beam of the light fixed to his helmet arced over the gallery, lighting up hidden corners as he emerged from the cavity. He pushed himself around until he was on his stomach half in and half out of the tunnel with his legs swinging freely over the edge. Then he shuffled backwards, the tips of his boots unsuccessfully trying to find purchase in the rock until he hung by his elbows.

"Just a little bit more," Kalen shouted.

With one final movement, Lars slipped back until he hung by his fingers.

"That's enough." Kalen reached up and gripped Lars's ankles.

"Stand on me," Kalen said, guiding Lars's feet to his shoulders. When he took Lars's weight, his bruised body ached. "Now very carefully lean into the wall and push yourself slightly to your left."

Lars gingerly let go of the rim and used the flats of his hands to manoeuvre himself sideways until he had aligned himself directly above Kalen.

"Hold on," Jorge said. "I'm going to lower you. Sera, steady him."

Below them, Jorge carefully lowered himself into a kneeling position with Sera's help, his muscles trembling under their joint weight.

Jorge moved back slightly from the wall. "Now step off me."

Sera and Jorge helped him step down and lower Lars and suddenly Lars's weight lifted. Relieved of the burden, Kalen slumped down against the wall to catch his breath, his shoulders and back aching and his head throbbing. He checked his air gauge. He had already used up half an air cartridge and it had taken them over five hours to get this far. They needed to make better time.

Kalen shone his flashlight over the side of the ledge and played it over the cave. They were still high above the floor of the cavern but the wall underneath the ledge was pitted with small cracks and crevices. The ground below looked smooth, and to the west of their position the cave narrowed into a gorge, while to the south the cavern stretched out of the range of his flashlight, into darkness. The edges of his vision blurred but he put that down to an effect of the light.

"I think we should get down and check where we are," Jorge said.

"We're still going in the right direction," Sera said. "We need to start bearing west, over there."

She gestured with her hand into the darkness. She looked ethereal in the torchlight and Kalen caught a wisp of her perspiration, a soft female scent overlaid by fear. Despite himself, he felt aroused when he remembered her warm body beneath his. She turned and glanced towards him and looked away again, out into the cavern. He was still gazing at her when a wave of dizziness suddenly washed over him.

The figures had come back. They danced in front of him, visible now in shining hues of red, blue, and gold. The colours swirled into each other as the forms rotated and mutated into fluid shapes that multiplied as they moved in front of his eyes. They danced in the void, in the blackness, danced around his head, filling his vision with yellow and orange lights. They glided, glowing in the blackness, surrounding him with light, and he felt himself sucked in amongst them. He wanted to join them and be a part of them, and then the darkness dissolved and all he could see was a golden light, with the figures moving through it.

"Hey, what's wrong with you? Where are you going?" A strong hand shook his shoulder. "Snap out of it!" Jorge's voice echoed from outside.

Then a hand on his other shoulder was shaking him roughly, wrenching him from the golden world, bringing him back. *It must be the Narquum*, he thought. He screwed his eyes together and then opened them again to clear his vision. He had moved to the rim of the ledge and had his arms outstretched in front of him as if he were reaching for something in the void. He couldn't remember walking to the edge or reaching out. All he could remember were the strange fuzzy dream shapes.

"I thought I saw something." Kalen mustered all of his strength to sound normal.

"There's nothing there." Jorge gave him a hard look and shrugged, turning away to peer at the cliff underneath them.

"It must have been the shadows playing tricks."

"Then let's get going. It should be an easy climb down," Jorge said, scrambling over the edge.

Chapter Nineteen

At ground level they walked due west, following the line of the cave into the gorge. Kalen aimed the beam of his flashlight upwards, but the roof of the cave was out of view in the darkness, somewhere high above him. As they walked deeper into the gorge, the cold began to eat into his jacket and his torch beam could not penetrate the shadows. Eventually, the roof lowered and he found himself walking in a tunnel along the side of a dry canal. In places, the banks were steep and the bottom of the canal would be three metres or more below them but in other places, the banks were shallow.

"It could have been an old riverbed that carried water or some other liquid a long time ago," Sera explained, while scanning the rocks around her. "This is the best route I can find."

They walked for over six hours and Kalen's leg began to play up from his old injury. Every step gave him shooting pains and the rest of his body began to throb from the battering he had taken in the rock-fall. He was relieved when Jorge called a break and he suspected that Sera was tired too. For the last hour, he'd watched her dragging her feet and stumbling frequently.

"There's a bit of even ground over there where we can sit," Jorge said, taking off his pack and sitting down.

Kalen took the emergency blanket out of his pack, wrapped it around his shoulders, and sat down. Rifling through his pack, he found the rations from the locker and opened a food bar to eat. A few metres away, Lars gulped from his water bottle, and nearby Sera sank to the ground and sat with her back against the wall.

Jorge checked his air gauge. "We've made good time but I calculate we've used up half of our oxygen supplies already. We're only going to have enough to reach the fourth crater if we don't have any setbacks."

"It's going to be close," Kalen said. Dizziness swept over him again and he shut his eyes. Throughout the walk, he had sensed something following him, but whenever he'd looked around, there had been nothing except shadows that moved in the beam of his torch.

"We'll make it," Jorge said optimistically. "The crater has air."

"What's in the crater?" Kalen asked bluntly, opening his eyes to look at Jorge.

Jorge paused for a moment as if considering what to say. "I'm not sure. I worked on the site before any building took place. As soon as the basic mining was finished, I was pulled out. I was told, at the time, that some kind of military base was going to be built there."

Kalen adjusted his mask and took a sip from his water bottle to try to alleviate the dizziness. It must be exhaustion, he reasoned. He had taken another Narquum and changed his air cartridge, but it hadn't made him feel any better. He stared into the black recesses of the cave around him and saw the shapes again. Vividly coloured spheres and oval shapes floated in front of him, glistening and bright. Red, blue, green, silver, and golden images filled his vision in a kaleidoscope of colour. He wanted to step into the swirling mass and join them but they faded into greyness and he fell asleep.

Sounds of the others moving about woke him up and he opened his eyes to find that he had slept propped with his head on his backpack, and his water bottle lay beside him. He pondered the strange shapes he had seen. *I'm hallucinating, I must have the miners' sickness*, he thought. He had to fight it. He stood up stiffly and slung his pack onto his back.

"Sera's worked out a route that will take us further along the canal," Jorge said.

"The canal starts to bear south from now on. We can follow it until we're nearly at the crater," she confirmed. "Then we have to continue west through another cave system to reach the rim."

Jorge led the way along a ridge above the canal. The sound of their footsteps echoed around Kalen, magnified in the confined space. A scuffed boot, or the rattle of the equipment they were carrying, became a symphony of sound that filled every tiny crack and crevice of the variegated stone landscape they walked through. The sudden crack of metal against rock made Kalen flinch involuntarily and his own breathing rasped loudly in his ears. Without the constant heartbeat of the drills, the caves seemed dead and distinctly alien. His world had shrunk to the circle of light from their torches and outside the light, nothing else existed.

Uneven ground forced Kalen to look down constantly and when Jorge finally paused, he swept the beam of his torch around him. They stood at the top of a shallow incline that led down several metres into the channel below.

"We can walk in the canal," Jorge said, scrambling down the slope to the dry stream bed.

Kalen followed the others down into the canal. It was wide enough for two or three people to walk abreast, but they continued to walk in single file. Ahead of him, Jorge swung the beam of his torch as he walked, lighting up the path before them, and the sides of the canal. The surface of the stream bed was smooth but the banks that rose on each side were riddled with potholes, some small while others were wide enough for a man to climb into.

"At one time this channel must have been a raging river," Sera said. "It must have drained liquid from the surrounding area."

"I've only seen rivers on film," Kalen said. "I can't imagine it."

Sera switched on her range-finder and studied the readings. "I think this goes into a tunnel then fans out again.

We can follow it to the end and then adjust our heading a few degrees southwards to intersect the crater."

As they walked on, the canal began to narrow and Kalen noticed that the banks were getting steeper. The roof began to drop until they were walking in a tunnel and Kalen found himself stooping under overhangs. The ground and walls became smooth and the channel curved about, so that the beam from his torch only lit up the canal as far as the next twist in it. Sera used her instruments to guide their direction and Kalen plodded on, following in the wake of the torchlight that bobbed about as they walked.

Several times throughout the next few hours, Kalen glimpsed movement out of the corner of his eye, but when he looked, there was nothing but shadows. His arms and shoulders ached and his leg hurt. Ahead of him, Jorge stopped at a wall that ran across the riverbed, effectively damming it, save for a wide low hole at its base. Jorge shone his torch into the cavity and Kalen could see that inside it narrowed.

Jorge turned to Sera. "That's too small for us to get through. What does your scanner say?"

"The tunnel carries on under the rock for eight metres, then widens into a large cave."

"So you're saying that this wall is solid rock?"

"That's right," Sera said. "What are we going to do?"

"What about blasting our way through?" Lars suggested.

"We can't widen the hole like that, it would probably just cave in," Kalen said.

"What about the surrounding walls?" Jorge asked.

"I can scan them. I may be able to find a weak point into another cave, but we'd have to work our way around to bypass this section," Sera replied.

Jorge nodded. "If you can find a weak point we may be able to cut through."

"It might be possible so long as we're careful," Kalen agreed.

"Then try and find a weak point," Jorge said.

Sera adjusted the settings on her scanner and walked back the way they had come, running the scanner over the walls on each side of them. After a short distance, she stopped and studied her readings, adjusted the scanner again and pointed it at a section of the tunnel wall.

"It looks as if it's less than a metre thick here. I read a hollow on the other side."

"Any idea where it leads?" Jorge asked.

"I'm not sure, but it looks like there's another cave behind the wall. If we can get through to it, we might find a way back to the channel."

"What do you think?" Jorge turned to Kalen.

"It's worth a try, but we might bring the whole tunnel down."

"Sera can you mark the spot?" Jorge asked.

Sera took an electronic marker out of her bag and carefully traced a pattern in the rock.

"This is the centre of the most fragile part," she said. "The rock is thin around this point, then thickens substantially again. There is also a narrow band of weaker material running across the face that intersects it. If you aim here, you should be able to collapse the wall to give us a way through."

"I'll use my laser," Jorge said. "It has a long range but the tunnel twists too much to get a clear line of sight. I'm going to have to fire from much nearer so I suggest that the rest of you get as far down the tunnel as you can. There's no sense in us all risking our necks."

Kalen led Sera and Lars back along the tunnel for over fifteen metres and stopped.

"Is this far enough?" Sera asked.

"Probably, but firing in an enclosed space is always risky," Kalen replied. "I've seen a hand laser fired into a thin wall for a bet. Instead of creating a hole, the complete section collapsed."

Kalen crouched down and pulled Sera down beside him. Moments passed before an echoing boom hit his eardrums with excruciating pressure. Pain shot through his head, and he swallowed hard to try to alleviate it. A billowing cloud of dust swept through the tunnel and the air went opaque around him. He put his hands over his ears and rubbed them until the pain subsided, but his ears were still ringing when he heard Lars's voice through his headset.

"Guess he's done it then," Lars said.

Lars stood up and disappeared into the haze. Grit had settled on Kalen's breathing mask and he took a moment to rub it off, leaving dirty black smears across the surface. He turned and helped Sera to her feet.

He found Jorge and Lars inspecting a large fracture in the wall. Jagged edges around its perimeter bore witness to the way that the laser had torn out its heart, but the wall had survived. Rubble covered the floor of the passageway and blocked the lower half of the hole leaving a space that was just large enough to crawl through. Jorge shone his flashlight into it and in the beam, Kalen could see a small cave beyond. *We've still got a chance*, he thought.

"Let's get out of here," Jorge said. "This might come down at any minute."

Jorge bent into the gap and began to crawl across the rubble.

Kalen stood to one side and motioned to Sera. "You go first."

She got onto her knees and crawled after Jorge, into the gap. After switching on his helmet light, Kalen crouched down and crawled through, the sharp edges of the rocks cutting into his hands and knees. Ignoring the scratches, he gingerly crawled forward until he could stand up in the next cave. Looking around, he saw that the cave was small, but Jorge and Sera were already disappearing through a gap in the wall ahead. Kalen quickly followed them and found himself in an enormous gallery.

"According to my readings, there's a series of large interconnecting caves," Sera explained, pointing at the west wall. "We need to go that way to join up with the main channel again."

"Is there a route through?" Kalen asked.

"So far as I can tell, it intersects the main channel farther ahead."

They began walking across the cavern towards the far wall. Kalen could hear Lars's footfalls behind him. He shone his torch around the cavern. Indentations in the walls created patterns as if they had been scored into the rock-face—oblongs, circles, cones, and ovals glowed green and red in the beam of his torch. High up on the walls, spidery rock formations stretched across corners that glistened as the light caught them. Small round pebbles covered the ground and clattered away in a noisy rattle when Kalen stepped on them.

The cave led through to another cavern that was larger than the first. Kalen began to think about Halle. Would he ever see her again? Her jealousy and possessiveness seemed irrelevant in the inky darkness. He wondered what she was thinking now. Was she worried about him or did she think he was dead?

Suddenly there was movement in the periphery of his vision, a flicker in the light of his torch, but when he looked, he only saw another obsidian vertical crevice. He was imagining things. Walking on, he rounded a bend and saw a form and this time he was sure. It hovered just out of range of his torchlight, a glowing figure that flowed towards him in the restricted light and paused, too far away for him to see its features. There were other shapes behind it and around it that moved and merged in a chaos of colours. Then they were everywhere, crowding in and surrounding him. He was hallucinating again. He screwed his eyes up and then opened them, focusing on Sera.

"I think we should take a break," he called out.

Sera stopped walking. "That's a good idea."

Jorge circled back and threw his pack on the ground. "Let's take ten then."

Kalen sat down and stared into the darkness. Images came into his mind of moving shapes across a golden landscape, liquid forms that swam in front of his eyes blotting out everything and filling his consciousness. They hung in front of him now, all colours, no longer flickering insubstantial shadows, but solid forms that had detail. People? No, not people, but they were transforming. He could see their outlines and feel their presence as they surrounded him. He was amongst them now and consumed by an irresistible desire to join them and become part of them.

Suddenly the beam of a torch played across the barren cavern and the shapes scattered. He became aware of the hard floor and his weariness returned making his body feel so heavy that he could hardly move. A tiny spec darted across his field of vision and he focused on it until he could make out its shape. Then the other shapes crowded in and surrounded him again, lifting him up, and the pains and dead weight of his body were gone and he floated amongst them.

Memories of his life spun through his mind in quick succession—he saw himself grow from child to adult and watched his parents get older. Images of joshing with his brother, being disciplined by his father, his schooling, the academy, Area Nine, and making love to Halle, all hurtled through his thoughts. Then the pictures disappeared and the balloon shapes came again, floating, playing, and changing colours as their fluid movements intermingled about him. They floated away and above him and he drifted upwards towards them, but they remained out of his reach.

He floated upwards until he was nearly amongst them, and then he was overwhelmed by a familiar feeling. He tried to identify it and found himself taken back to a time before his memories, before his birth, to a state of existence that felt so profoundly real that in an instant he understood. This was the reality. Life was the counterfeit—a dreamlike excursion where memories were built, but this was his natural state, his true condition.

Images from his past and future stretched out on each side of him like a mirrored repetition into infinity. In this form of existence, time had no meaning. Past, present and future existed simultaneously. Time was to do with the other state, the counterfeit life. Curiously, he tried to peer into the images of his future but the first few frames were confusing. He saw people that he didn't recognise and dark streets and then the frames shrank too small for him to see.

As he rose upwards, he felt as if his consciousness was stretching out into the atmosphere around him, becoming part of everything, yet still separate. He had nearly reached the shapes when they pushed him away and down. He had to go back. He couldn't join them. If he tried, he would cease to exist in corporeal form.

He came round to the sound of Jorge's voice, and sat for a minute trying to recall where he was. Had he been dreaming or had it been real? Was this life the illusion and the other the reality? What was reality? It had to be the miner's sickness, he decided. He had been hallucinating. He felt the hard, cold ground beneath him. It was real, and his body ached in a very real way. He began to get up and resolved to shake the hallucinations off. He had a long walk ahead.

Chapter Twenty

Sera sat down and took a quick sip of water from her bottle. After a few minutes, the icy chill of the floor had penetrated her clothes and she decided to get up. Although she couldn't see Chief Trinneer's face properly, he sounded as if he was muttering in his sleep and she caught the words "Area Nine" a couple of times. Jorge sat a little way apart, inspecting the contents of his pack, and only Lars sat near her. She stood up carefully, flexing her stiff legs, and reached a hand up to massage the kink out of her neck. One of her legs had a cramp, but as she stretched it, she strained a muscle. The pain was excruciating and she massaged the leg vigorously before jumping up and skipping around to try to restore circulation. Lars watched her with a smirk on his face.

"What are you doing? Your morning exercises? Now that's something I could watch all day."

"We need to get going," Jorge interrupted, standing up as well. "How much air have you got left?"

She glared at Lars and checked the gauge on her breathing tube. "Under three hours."

Chief Trinneer stirred. "I've got about three as well."

"Same here," Lars said. "Have we got much farther to go?"

Sera took out her monitor and studied the map. "According to my calculations we're just under a kilometre away from the crater. We should re-join the main channel soon and then branch off when we're nearly at the rim."

"We're going to be tight on air," Jorge said, putting his pack on his back. "It could easily take us an hour just to find the canal again."

"Do you think we're going to make it? Two hours will be enough, won't it?" she asked him.

"If we get going now and keep up a good pace, then we might make it, but it's going to be very close. Just don't hold us up again!"

Sera smarted at the rebuke, remembering her hysteria at the cliff, but neither of the others commented.

Jorge took the lead and Lars brought up the rear. She walked ahead of Chief Trinneer who said very little. They made their way through a labyrinth of caves. At times, she had to clamber over boulders in chambers where the roof was so high that it was out of her view, and at other times, she had to squeeze through small crevices. She worried that she would be blamed if they were lost and constantly called for stops to check their direction. Eventually, much to her relief, they found the main canal again and Jorge strode forward along a narrow strip that ran above its banks. In parts, the path petered out and they were forced to scramble down the bank to the dry riverbed below, before climbing back up to return to the path.

Ahead of her, Jorge slowed his pace and turned. "This doesn't feel right to me. Let's check the direction again."

Sera checked her compass. "I'm sure we're going the right way but we'll have to leave the canal soon. Here, take a look." She held out the compass for him to see.

Jorge glanced at it briefly and then continued walking, his jaw set in a determined line. Sera trudged in the tail of his flashlight, concentrating on her footing and the compass. They had to be near the crater. She switched on her scanner but it didn't detect a large void. It would be hard to miss if they were near it. They needed to find it soon, before the air ran out. She said a silent prayer. If God saved them now, she would never doubt him again.

The canal narrowed until it disappeared under a rocky overhang and their path became blocked again.

"I think this is the point where we turn off," Sera said.

Jorge swept the beam of his flashlight over the walls until he found an opening. "Through here?"

She checked her scanner. "That's the right direction, there's a large cave behind."

Jorge squeezed sideways through the opening and Sera followed him into a large gallery. The beam of her torch did not extend far enough to illuminate the walls and roof, and the stone columns soared upwards into the darkness. Jorge set off into the blackness between the monoliths on the heading that she had given him. Behind her, Chief Trinneer and Lars walked quietly, their flashlights lighting up the sides of the gallery as they passed by. Some of the columns were several metres thick in diameter and she reached out to touch one of them. It was smooth, cold, and dusty. Directing her torch at her feet, she saw that the ground was dusty too. Eventually Jorge stopped at the foot of one of the columns.

"I'm nearly out of air. I've probably got about fifteen minutes left," Jorge said.

"Have we used all the reserves?" Chief Trinneer asked.

"Yes, that's it."

"What now?" Lars asked.

"Now we have to find the crater," Jorge said. "We must be near it."

"And then what?" Sera asked, her voice rising with fear. "If it's airtight, how are we going to get in? There's hardly going to be a door that we can just walk through."

"Let's find it first," Jorge said evenly. "If there's a problem we'll deal with it when we get there. What does the compass say?"

"If the location you gave me is correct, then it's adjacent to the west end of this cave," she replied. "We should have heard machinery or seen lights by now."

"Not necessarily, we could be nearly on it, and we wouldn't know," Chief Trinneer said.

Jorge began walking again. "Let's get going. Look for anything manmade."

In the beam of Jorge's flashlight, Sera could see nothing ahead except the stone monoliths standing silently in the darkness. Jorge strode between them, sweeping his flashlight across the floor and walls, searching every crevice. She joined him, directing the beam of her torch methodically over the walls. Her lungs felt uncomfortable and she took a deep breath but it didn't help. *I can't be running out of air already*, she thought. She checked her scanner again. It indicated a void ahead. Was it registering the crater or another large cave? She said another prayer.

"Ahead. My scanner registers a large void ahead."

"I can't see anything," Lars said.

Chief Trinneer pointed the beam of his torch towards the far wall. "Keep looking. It may not be at ground level."

"We must be nearly on it, we'll see it soon," Jorge added.

At the far end, the roof dropped and the cave narrowed into a wide tunnel. Sera began to get breathless and checked her oxygen canister. It was nearly empty. She tried to take shallow breaths but her lungs objected and she felt even more uncomfortable. This was hopeless. There was nothing here and they were all going to die. Jorge disappeared around a bend in the passageway in front of her until all she could see was the glow from his torch. She followed him around the corner and then stopped. A grey barrier blocked their path and it looked manmade.

Sera stared at the smooth surface of the grey wall and relief washed over her, quickly followed by anxiety when she saw that the barrier completely shut off the passageway. It had a sheen that reflected the light from their torches, and when she touched it, she discovered that it was warm and made of a strong plastic. They shone their flashlights over it, searching for a door or lever, anything that would allow access, but found nothing. There were no gaps or windows and she couldn't hear any noise from the other side.

"What is it?" she asked.

"It's a boundary panel, designed to seal the crater," Jorge said, pressing the wall. "It's strong."

She watched him trying another area with his hands, but the barrier didn't buckle. "How are we going to get in?"

"We're going to have to burn an entry," Chief Trinneer replied.

"How long will that take? I'm running low on air." Sera's voice rasped with each breath.

"We can get in quickly but I don't know what's behind it. There's only one way to find out. Stand back," Jorge said, taking his laser out of his jacket pocket. He adjusted it and aimed at the centre of the barrier.

"Wait!" Chief Trinneer shouted. "We'll need to seal the hole behind us. We have to cut out a small panel that we can reattach afterwards."

"Why?" Lars asked. "Why does it matter if there's a hole in the wall? We need to get in, otherwise we'll all suffocate."

"The perimeter controls may pick up a breach and automatically turn off the oxygen. We can't take that chance."

"You're right. I'll cut an outline first that we can seal back in place," Jorge said.

Sera stepped back and watched Jorge run his laser vertically up the wall and around in an oval pattern. A thin yellow line appeared on the surface that glowed orange hot as the plastic melted, giving off acrid fumes that clawed at Sera's throat when she inhaled, despite her breathing apparatus. She silently thanked God for bringing them to the crater but she wished Jorge would hurry up.

Jorge traced a hole with his laser just large enough for a man to crawl through. When he had finished, he placed the palm of his hand in the centre of the patch and pushed, but some of the edges stuck where they were still hot. Jorge waited a few moments, then adjusted the setting on his laser, and burnt away the remaining bits until he could push the whole panel out, leaving a gaping black hole. He stepped through into the darkness beyond.

"Is there anything there?" Sera asked impatiently.

"Come and see for yourself," Jorge replied, his voice muted.

She quickly stepped through the hole and found herself in a confined space about three metres wide, facing another grey barrier.

"I don't understand, I thought we'd get into the crater?"

"It's a double skin to ensure that the structure is airtight and contains any leaks." The chief's voice came from behind her. "If there's a breach in the inner wall the air leaks out into the cavity between the two walls, which is partitioned off in sections. That way very little of the oxygen escapes and the atmosphere inside the crater is maintained until the wall can be repaired."

She took her breathing mask off and tried the air but there was no oxygen and the empty mouthful made her lungs ache.

"Don't do that!" Chief Trinneer snapped, grabbing hold of her mask and placing it over her nose and mouth. "We have to get through the next wall before there's any air."

Lars had clambered through the gap as well and stood waiting.

Chief Trinneer spoke to Jorge. "We have to seal the outer barrier behind us before opening up the next wall. There should be air on the other side, but we can't risk an uncontained leak. The sensors would shut down the supply to this section until it's repaired."

He picked up the loose piece of panel that Jorge had cut out and fitted it back into the hole. Taking out his laser, he aimed at the edges until they melted and then pressed them together to create a join. Jorge moved forward and carefully took aim at the lower portion, to repeat the process.

"I think I've probably got about five minutes of air left," Chief Trinneer said. "If we've all got the same then we have to act quickly, but this could take a while. It's going to be close so no unnecessary talking. There's only enough room for Jorge and me to do this, so I suggest the two of you stand back."

Sera watched Jorge and Chief Trinneer slowly reinstate the piece of wall panelling, testing the join in each segment before moving on to the next part. The bright white light of the lasers made spots on Sera's vision and she could taste the bitter fumes from the burning plastic. She could hardly breathe and her chest was tightening with each breath. *I can't have much oxygen left*, she thought. Jorge worked with focused concentration, his face betraying nothing, but Chief Trinneer laboured to breathe as he worked. Lars had sat down and intermittently gave out noisy gasps.

Jorge and Chief Trinneer continued to melt and join the edges of the panelling section by section until there were only two small areas at the sides left to join. Sera's chest ached and she gulped into her facemask, her frantic gasps sounding loud in her ears. Panting, she slumped to the ground as Lars started to make loud barking noises.

"They can't breathe," Chief Trinneer muttered.

"Ignore them," Jorge said.

Lars barked again.

"Stop that, stay calm," Jorge said sharply, his voice hoarse.

She closed her eyes and then opened them again. Jorge and Chief Trinneer were inspecting each section of the join now, trying it with their hands and running over bits with the lasers until it held. Finally, Chief Trinneer stepped back, coughing into his facemask, while Jorge made a final inspection. *Soon*, Sera thought, *we must get air soon*. Once they were through the barrier, they would be safe. There would be people. She shut her eyes again, drowsiness overcoming her, her chest hurting.

"No time," Chief Trinneer whispered.

She forced her eyes open and saw Chief Trinneer aim his laser at the second wall. He swayed as he fired at the centre of the inner wall and it exploded in an orange fireball, the plastic dissolving and peeling away to leave a black gap that air rushed through.

Chapter Twenty-One

Kalen ripped his mask off and breathed in the clean air that rushed out of the hole, only faintly tainted by the plastic residue from their work. His mind had gradually cleared during the walk and now he felt almost normal. The shapes had gone although from time to time he suspected that they hovered just outside his conscious perception. He peered into the black gap but no light or sound came from the other side. He turned on his radio, setting it to the distress signal and his personal identification code.

"We'll have to let the wall cool before we can take a look," he said. "It'll take a few minutes. I'll try and raise someone on my radio."

"Are you getting anything?" Sera asked.

Kalen shook his head. "I'm getting nothing. There's probably machinery interfering with the signal or the range is too short. I'll try again once we're inside."

"Perhaps someone will notice the damage to the barrier and come and investigate?" she suggested.

"Not for a while," Kalen replied. "It depends on how big the installation is. If it's a large installation, everything might be automated at the outer perimeter and it could be several days before someone is sent out to check an air leak. There's still a possibility that when the leak is detected the supply will be cut, so it isn't a good idea for us to hang around. We don't know what failsafe systems they've put in place."

Kalen got up and shone his torch into the hole, and stepped through into a long narrow passageway where the floor and sides gleamed dully metallic and his footsteps echoed on the smooth surface. Sensor arrays and machinery lined the sides and cabling ran along the walls and ceiling. In the distance, he could hear a low hum that got louder as he walked forward. Ahead he could just make out the outline of an exit from the corridor, silhouetted against a deep grey light. He walked on until he was level with the exit and cautiously shone his torch into the gloom.

Outside the corridor, it was still very dark, and his flashlight could pick up very little except their immediate surroundings. The exit from the corridor was blocked by a large piece of inert machinery that Kalen did not recognise and the humming was coming from beyond it. The machine had a rectangular framework formed by uprights that rose up several metres and a solid midsection. There was a gap between the outer frame and midsection just large enough for him to squeeze through if he turned sideways. Gesturing to the others to wait, he took off his backpack and edged through the gap. A pleasant smell that he couldn't identify permeated the air and the temperature seemed warmer. He could hear nothing apart from the humming.

He emerged between two long rows of troughs, which stood nearly two metres high on each side of him with a space between the rows just wide enough for a man to walk down. A metal rail ran along the ground midway between the rows of troughs matched by another rail that was suspended directly above it, several metres over Kalen's head. The two rows of containers stretched out in a neat line as far as he could see. Behind him, the machine rested under huge tanks that were fixed to the wall, which soared upwards out of the range of his flashlight. Pipes ran down from the tanks, into a web of ducting that snaked along a network of metal tracks suspended high above the rows of troughs. Kalen could see foliage growing out of the troughs, its colour drained by the lack of light. A grey glow came from above, but it was still too dark to see the roof. He tried his radio again, but got no response.

"What's there?" Jorge called to him.

"It's okay, you can come through. I'm not sure where we are but it looks like some kind of farm. I still can't get anyone on the radio."

The others joined him and they stood silently looking around them. The outline of bushes was visible in the troughs but Kalen didn't recognise the plants, which gave off a strange earthy aroma. He looked around for a way out. The lines of troughs were unbroken with pipes and equipment filling the space beneath them and there was no room to squeeze in front of the machine at the end of the row behind them.

"Where are we, Chief?" Lars asked. "Where are the people?"

"We must be right at the edge of the crater. The radio range is too short to be of use. It looks like they're using this bit for cultivation."

"It's a plantation," Sera said, excited. "Look at all those bushes!"

"Jorge, do you remember any of this?" Kalen asked.

"I was transferred before this was installed. I was only involved in the initial stages of construction."

"Has anyone any idea what sort of bushes those are? What are they growing?" Kalen asked.

"I've no idea," Jorge admitted. "But it looks like some kind of crop."

"It's a kind of vegetable," Sera said, pointing to small red globular masses that protruded out of the plants' stalks. "Look at it all! Isn't this wonderful? I've never been in a farm before. I think those round parts must be edible but I don't know if they're ripe yet."

"We're going to need something to eat soon," Lars said.

"Why is it so dark in here?" Sera asked. "Surely if we're in the crater, there should be light?"

"It's getting brighter, so this could be natural light, before the dawn," Kalen said.

"Dawn?" Sera queried. "I don't understand."

"You'd usually only see it if you were outside the colonies," Kalen explained. "All of the cities are run on the twenty-four-hour continuous lighting system so that both zones can share the natural and artificial light equally, so you wouldn't ever see the dawn. The artificial lighting is usually still operational and compensating when the sun comes up and it's the same at sunset."

"I suppose the farms are different," Sera said. "Plants must need the real daylight and darkness at night."

"That's interesting, but we have to find a way out of here, and work out where we are," Jorge said. "The Security base should be at the south end of the crater, and if we've come in at the north side it could be over thirty kilometres away. There might be an installation in between, or at least a speak station we can use to call for help. We have to get out of these plants first."

"It doesn't look like we can get around the machinery at this end of the row," Kalen said. "There's no route down the side of the wall."

"Then we'll have to see what's at the other end of the row," Jorge said. He gave the machine a final glance and then began walking briskly down the row.

Kalen hesitated for a moment and then followed Jorge and the others who had also begun walking. In the dim light, the rows of troughs stretched out interminably in front of him with no end in sight. The humming sound radiated from the distance and he wondered what was causing it. It was getting louder with the dawn. The stillness of the plants in the grey light, the strange smell, and the odd humming tore at his nerves.

He walked silently with the others between the lines of containers. Gradually, the light brightened until he could see the true colours of the plants. As the sun rose, the leaves of the bushes transformed from a greyish green to a deep emerald and under the leaves, deep pinkish globes hung from long yellow stems. Farther on, the plants changed and he saw that some of the troughs also contained clusters of purple pear-shaped vegetables nestled amongst tendrils growing thickly around frames. Kalen switched his flashlight off, but the end of the row was still too far away to see. He looked up at the same time as Sera.

"Oh look! The sun!" she exclaimed.

High above them the transparent roof of the dome arced in a vast curve a kilometre or more above the surface of the crater. Low on the horizon, the first beams of the early dawn seared through it, burning reddish orange as if thrown from a fireball. The rays from the orange disc reflected off hexagonal facets in the dome roof, creating spots of dazzling brightness. Kalen instinctively turned his face towards the sun, luxuriating in the warmth on his cheeks after the coldness of the caves. Sera did the same, while Lars stood with a smile on his face and Jorge watched impassively.

"Why isn't the roof smooth?" Sera asked. "I've never seen a dome like that."

"It's been designed to maximise the heat from the sun," Kalen said. "We can also tell our direction from the sun now."

"Maybe, but I think I'll continue to rely on my navigation kit," Sera replied, laughing.

"Now we've got a bit of daylight, I'll try and get a better view," Kalen said, pulling himself up the side of the nearest trough and clambering onto it.

"We're in the middle of a huge plantation," he reported, standing up amongst the bushes. "There are hundreds of rows of plants and I can't see the end of them. The rows aren't all the same. Some of the containers are different shapes and in the distance, I can see larger bushes. The rows nearest to us have rectangular troughs arranged in straight lines."

The troughs were filled with damp earth and Kalen bent down to rub a little of the soil between his fingers and sniffed it. There was a sharp sour edge to the earthy smell and his hands began to sting and redden. He rubbed the soil off his hands and dabbed them with water from his pack before climbing down.

They continued walking between the troughs but Kalen had a nagging sense of anxiety and he tried to work out what was making him uneasy. He'd seen no access points for people and when he looked around, he couldn't see any walkways or other structures for the maintenance crews. There were only the troughs in rows and even the gap they walked along had the rail running down its centre, protruding from the ground, which he constantly tripped over.

The sun still hung low in the sky, like a giant golden orb. Above the dome's roof, the sky was clear blue and Kalen could see no sign of the dust storms that usually made it hazy. The troughs and plants around him stood motionless in the thick atmosphere and there was a heavy silence only broken by the humming that was getting louder.

"Can you hear that noise?" Kalen said. "It's getting closer."

"Best keep going then," Jorge replied.

"Just a moment, let me have a look."

Kalen turned towards the direction the sound was coming from, climbed up the side of one of the containers again, and stood upright. He went cold. In the distance, row upon row of vegetation moved about haphazardly. Branches, leaves, and stems shook and trembled in disturbed vibrations and, as Kalen watched, another quiescent row suddenly erupted into twitching violence. He caught a glimpse of something large moving quickly between the rows of bushes. He estimated it wouldn't be long before it reached them.

"We've got a problem. There's some kind of machine going down the rows and it's coming towards us. We're going to be right in its path."

"How far away is it?" Jorge asked.

"I think we've got a few minutes, but we need to get out of here. Run!" Kalen swung himself over the container's lip and jumped down.

For a brief moment, the others stared at him, as if they hadn't understood what he had said, and then they began running. Kalen ran after them, catching Sera up easily, the pervasive humming filling his ears. He looked about for somewhere to go but the troughs stood in a continuous line, and the end of the row was still out of sight.

Ahead, a huge machine suddenly came into view gliding towards them. Skimming effortlessly on the metal rail that ran along the ground, its massive rectangular frame filled the whole width of the gap between the tubs. A thick strut rose out of the machine to intersect a cross bar that swung over the troughs of plants. Huge tanks rested on the crossbar, secured to tracks running high above the lines of containers. Strong jets of liquid squirted from the arms onto the vegetation sending it into a quiver of frenzied movement.

Sera screamed, "It's going to crush us."

She turned back towards Kalen, but tripped on the central rail and started to fall. He caught her in his arms and spun her around. Holding her by her waist, he lifted her up the side of the nearest trough.

"Get into the trough," he shouted. "Under the bushes!"

She grabbed hold of the lip while he propelled her upwards and then she was over the top. He threw himself at the side of the container, pulling himself up and found a bush to crouch under.

A few metres away, the machine moved rapidly along the row towards them, working with inhuman efficiency. The arms swung backwards and forwards, spraying a yellowish liquid that saturated the vegetation beneath. Close up, it generated terrific heat, and the air around Kalen became stifling. His eyes smarted and his nose and throat stung when he inhaled. He glanced towards the others. Lars was crouching between two bushes, watching the machine approach.

"Cover yourselves!" Kalen shouted, frantically reaching into his pack.

"Why all the fuss? It's just a watering system," Lars shouted above the noise of the oncoming machine.

"That's not water!"

The machine was nearly on them now. Kalen pulled on his gloves, crouched as low as possible beneath the thickest part of the bush, and held his pack over his head. The noise from the machine became overwhelming and then its arms were directly overhead. The foliage around him erupted into a frantic dance as the jets of liquid hit it. Streams of fluid, ejected at pressure, saturated the plants sending them shaking and twisting as they were bathed in bitter nutrients. The air became acid vapour and Kalen choked as he tried to draw a breath. He placed one hand over his mouth and nose and tried not to inhale as acid rain pounded him, the liquid burning into the outer layer of his clothing. Needles of hot acid burned the exposed skin at his wrists and the back of his neck as he bent his head under the chemical shower.

Then the machine moved on, leaving the bushes dripping with the toxic mixture. The noise diminished until it was a faint hum in the distance. Kalen stood up, carefully avoiding the branches around him. His wrists and the back of his neck were raw where the fertiliser had splashed him. Sera emerged from the foliage looking pale and shocked.

"Are you okay?" Kalen asked her.

"My legs feel like jelly but I'm all right."

"That was close," Jorge said, standing up and looking around him. "I don't want to go through that again."

Lars still crouched under a bush, which gave his bulk little cover. He had no gloves on and his hands were red and bleeding. On his forehead a mass of red blisters had erupted, oozing puss that trickled down the sides of his face, and there were burns on his neck.

"Be careful not to touch any of the plants, they're covered in that stuff," Kalen cautioned him, as Lars started to get up, brushing the leaves aside with his hands. "You look burned."

"Thanks for noticing. I'm a bit sore, but I'll live."

"We have to get away from the plants. The machine might come back at any minute. We have no idea how often they run down these rows," Kalen said.

"It will take us too long to climb over the troughs," Jorge pointed out. "We're going to have to keep on going and try and find a way around at the end." He jumped down and continued walking in their original direction.

"But that's where the machine came from," Sera objected.

"It's behind us now, so we shouldn't have a problem with it," Jorge said.

"It's the only way we can go," Kalen agreed. "We can't climb across the middle of the farm, and there's no way out behind us, so we have to go forward. We also need to get some more water."

"Surely they water the plants? They can't just feed them fertiliser?" Sera asked.

"I expect there's some kind of watering system," Kalen said. "If we can find it, we can fill our bottles."

Jorge began walking quickly again and Sera went after him, leaving Kalen to follow behind her. As they walked, he noticed that Sera's bottom swung slightly from side to side in the same enticing way that it had bobbed up and down in front of him when they crawled through the caves. She had taken her hat off and her brown hair had a glossy sheen despite her ordeal. *She doesn't weigh much*, he thought, remembering lifting her up into the tub. She was only slight. A spark of desire went through him and then he dismissed the idea. He had enough problems with Halle already without complicating things further.

Chapter Twenty-Two

Sera worried about the irrigation machine while she walked. It had gone but it could come back at any moment, and that made her nervous. Once they got to the end of the row, perhaps they would find a way out, or even find a speak station. They could be at the base in less than an hour. She imagined washing and changing her clothes, and eating a hot meal. Yellow, thick-skinned globes dangled temptingly from the bushes above her and she pictured picking one of them and biting into it.

Stumbling from time to time, Sera struggled to keep up with Jorge, the straps of her pack biting into her shoulders. She had a strange sensation that Chief Trinneer was staring at her back. She told herself that she was imagining it, but she could almost feel his eyes boring into her. She remembered the way he had lifted her into the trough and felt a tingle of excitement. He had stood right behind her and lifted her in one effortless movement. But that didn't change anything, she reminded herself, picturing him with the black-haired tourist. He was a man who probably used women and she must remember that. But she had to admit to herself that she was warming towards him. He made her feel safe.

The track continued relentlessly with no sign of the end, but Jorge kept going. After another hour, Sera's legs ached and she couldn't catch her breath. The gap between Jorge and herself had widened.

"Let's stop. We need a rest," Chief Trinneer shouted.

Jorge stopped and turned around. "Okay, but let's make it short."

Sera sat down on the ground and took a few deep breaths. Her chest and throat hurt and she rasped when she inhaled.

"You sound very hoarse," Chief Trinneer said.

"I got a mouthful of that stuff the machine was spraying."

"You should swallow some water to wash it out."

"I haven't got much left."

"Don't worry, we'll find some soon. Be careful about touching anything. Our clothes and the plants are covered in that acid, so keep your gloves on."

Before she could reply, he had moved on and was speaking to Jorge. "Can you see the end yet?"

"Not quite, but if you look at the roof of the crater it's already started to curve down to the edge, so I don't think we've got far to go."

Chief Trinneer came back to her. "Are you ready to move on?"

"I'm okay now." She wondered what she should call him. A lot had happened since the accident. "Thank you, Chief Trinneer."

He stared at her for a moment and then laughed. "Call me Kalen."

She felt herself reddening and dropped her eyes.

"You walk in front of me. It might be safer if the machine comes back," he said, moving aside.

Ahead, Jorge began walking again and Kalen fell into step behind her.

While they walked, Sera concentrated on her footing, and with the tall troughs on each side and Jorge in front of her, she had a limited view. She kept listening for the machine but the humming was distant.

Suddenly Jorge shouted, "I can see the end now!"

"Any sign of an exit?" Kalen asked from behind her.

"Not yet. I can't see. We're not close enough," Jorge replied, quickening his pace.

The row ended at the wall of the crater where huge storage tanks hung from high vertical supports, connected to a network of rails and to pipes, tubing, and cabling that ran outward along the tracks suspended above the vegetation. Below the tanks, there was an empty space about the same size as the machine they had encountered. Above the docking station, an elevated walkway with a mesh floor and railings ran along the side of the crater wall in both directions.

"There's a walkway," Jorge said, making his way over to a vertical metal ladder on one side of the docking station.

Jorge climbed the ladder first and Sera followed him unsteadily, keeping her eyes on the rungs in front of her. At the top, Jorge helped her onto the walkway and she clambered onto it gratefully. The walkway was three or four metres wide with a pair of parallel rails running along its centre, but there were no vehicles in sight.

Beside her, Jorge gestured towards the parallel rails. "They must have some kind of transport system. It's probably used at harvest or to carry equipment."

"But we're going to have to walk," Kalen said, joining them. "I can't see a speak station either."

"Before we go any farther, let's check where we are," Jorge replied.

Sera took out her compass. "We're on the west side of the crater now."

"We can use the walkway to circle south. Going around the edge of the crater means a longer walk but there isn't another safe route," Jorge said.

Lars took out his water bottle and shook it. "I'm getting very low on water. Do you think there's water in one of those tanks?"

"I expect so," Kalen said.

Sera had been studying the tanks and the pipes that ran between them. There were two large tanks that fed into the docking station and another above them. She reasoned that any one of them could contain water but she didn't know which. Below her, the farm spread out to the horizon, and in the distance, tiny irrigation machines moved up and down amongst the rows.

Humming close by caught her attention. The bushes below began to twitch and then the fertiliser machine came into view, skimming along its rail towards them. She shuddered at the thought of another run in with the machine. Thank God, they were above the plants now.

She returned her attention to the storage tanks. The tank nearest to her had writing on the side, but the lettering made no sense.

"Here, let me take a look," Kalen said. He had come up beside her, and was peering at the markings.

"These are chemicals, but that one could be water." He pointed to another tank farther away. "We need to trace its pipes."

Below them, the sprayer had slid almost noiselessly into its booth where automated systems locked it in place and began to fill its tanks.

"I bet it goes out again, with water this time," Lars remarked.

Jorge said, "Let's find the water and get going. We've still got a long way to go."

Sera's throat hurt and she still had a bitter taste of chemicals in her mouth. She leaned against the railings and watched Kalen trace the pipes to a tangle of flexible tubing that ran near them and aim his laser at it.

"Now we'll see." He held his water bottle ready in his other hand.

The tubing glowed briefly where the laser beam hit it, and then the rubber disintegrated and water squirted out. Kalen ran a finger under it and cautiously put his finger to his mouth.

"It's water," Kalen said, pressing his bottle to the gash and then passing the tube to Jorge.

They filled their bottles quickly and Kalen taped up the hole in the tube. The machine had finished refilling and glided away down the row, squirting out liquid from powerful jets that sent up a cooling mist, soaking each of the bushes in turn. In the adjoining rows, other machines moved between the troughs, irrigating the foliage in an organised sequence.

"Why couldn't we have got the water run?" Lars muttered and shook his head.

Sera said a quick prayer of thanks to God for getting them this far and then joined the others walking south.

***

The day remained clear and the sun rose until it was directly overhead, shining warmly through the roof of the dome. Kalen walked with the others for several hours along the walkway, but he saw no sign of people or the base. He tried his radio regularly but got no response. They took intermittent breaks, sitting on the mesh floor above the plantation that stretched out below them. As they walked, the plants they passed changed from time to time, although Kalen couldn't name them. Eventually the bushes and smaller plants gave way to large fruit trees in long troughs.

The orchard was separated from the rest of the plantation by a barrier of fine netting that extended across the width of the crater and high above the tops of the trees, totally enclosing the wooded area. The entrance to the enclosure was through a mesh door, and inside, the walkway continued along the side of the crater, above the trees. Just before the door, a steel staircase led upwards to another walkway that ran outside the netting, several metres above the one they were on. Jorge reached the door first and opened it.

"I think we should use the lower walkway. The upper walkway might be for roof maintenance," Jorge said.

"I'm not sure. There's netting around this bit," Kalen said.

"Perhaps they need to look after fruit trees differently," Sera suggested. "Aren't they beautiful? I want to stay down here. This is all new to me."

"It is pretty isn't it?" Kalen agreed. "Okay, we might as well stay on this path. At least we can see where it goes."

"I knew there were plantations, but I never imagined that they looked like this," Sera said.

They went into the enclosure through the mesh door and closed it behind them. The branches of the trees were covered with thick leaves. Red, green, yellow, and purple fruit nestled amongst them. The lower walkway ran along the side of the crater wall above the orchard and beneath them the trees stood in lines, immobile, and laden with fruit. Except for their footsteps on the metal platform, there were no other sounds. The air was moist and comfortably warm.

Kalen stared at the trees below them. "It's nearly a forest."

"I can smell the leaves from here. Can't we stop for a while?" Sera asked.

"Only five minutes," Kalen said. "Jorge?"

Jorge nodded. "We can have a longer break later."

Kalen took off his pack and sat down. Using the railings as a backrest, he watched Sera shrug out of her jacket. Underneath, her shirt clung to her where she had been perspiring. He admired the outline of her breasts for a few moments and then shifted his eyes away from her. Taking off his own jacket, he shoved it in his pack, closed his eyes, and put his face up to the sun. The temperature was almost tropical in this part of the dome, and a pervasive laziness came over him.

"That's enough." Jorge's voice broke the silence. "We should get going."

Walking on, they passed through several enclosures separated from each other by netting and mesh gates, all containing trees strewn with bright colourful fruit. At intervals, they passed ladders running up the side of the crater wall. The sun remained warm but had started to dip by the time the walkway began to descend gradually towards another mesh door. On the other side of the door, the walkway continued just above the treetops.

"Look! The trees aren't growing in tubs! It looks like a real wood," Sera exclaimed.

"They've covered this whole area with some kind of artificial earth and planted the trees in that," Kalen said, looking at the ground between the evenly spaced trees. "I expect there's an irrigation system buried underneath."

Kalen stared at the branches thick with fruit and his mouth watered. He could almost reach out from the walkway and pick the fruit. Further along the walkway, a ladder ran down to the orchard below where there was a gap between two plots of woodland.

"Please, can we stop?" Sera asked. "We could go down and pick some fruit."

"Provided everything isn't covered in that fertiliser," Jorge replied.

"Okay," Kalen said. "I can't see any machinery and it looks safe enough. But let's be sure. Wait here."

Kalen climbed down the ladder, ran a finger carefully across a leaf on the nearest tree, then reached up, and rubbed one of the fruit. He walked on a few metres and repeated the process at another tree.

Satisfied, he shouted to the others, "No fertiliser, but wash anything you eat. You can come down."

At ground level the orchard was dense, but sunshine lit up the path between the plots. Some of the fruit had fallen and lay rotting on the ground, and the fresh smell of leaves and a sweeter scent from the fruit permeated the air. Kalen reached up and picked a ripe apple from one of the trees, carefully washed it and took a bite. It had a delicious sweet flavour so he picked a couple more and several smaller purplish fruit, and then settled himself with his back against a tree trunk.

"This is like paradise," Sera said, spreading a blanket across the ground and sitting down. "There are no people or noise."

Lars snorted. "You don't say. We can't get anyone on our radios."

"There could be something interfering with the signal," Jorge said.

"I've never been anywhere so quiet before," Sera went on. "I can't even hear the irrigation machines."

"I know what you mean," Kalen agreed, looking over at her. "I sometimes go up to the water tanks above Central to get away from the noise and the people."

Sera lounged on the blanket, propped up by her elbows. Then she rolled over on her back and started eating small yellow fruits, dropping them into her mouth one by one.

"Do you know what that fruit is?" Kalen asked.

"No, but they taste a bit like apricots."

"Don't you think you're taking a risk eating something you don't know? They might not be ripe."

"What are those purple ones you're eating?" she asked.

"I've no idea," he said, smiling. "But they look good."

Sera laughed and continued eating. The trees cast long shadows as the sun dipped lower on the horizon, its rays slanting through the roof of the dome. Jorge sat at one side of the glade, staring at the ground in front of him and frowning as he bit into an orange fruit. Lars was out of Kalen's sight.

"We're going to lose the light soon," Kalen said. "We must get back to the walkway before then."

"We can stay down here for a bit longer, can't we?" Sera asked.

"Ten minutes, and then we have to get moving."

Kalen reclined against the tree and stretched out his legs. The air was heavy with scent and some of the trees had beautiful white and pink berries hanging from their branches. The purple fruit were juicy with a slightly bitter flavour and he took another bite. Sera was now lying flat on her back, with eyes closed and mouth slightly open, singing softly to herself. She was smiling and the crease between her eyebrows had disappeared, giving her face a beauty that he hadn't noticed before.

He considered asking if he could join her on the blanket but decided that she would probably say no. Although she seemed to have thawed a bit towards him, he doubted whether she'd melted that far. He imagined lying beside her under the trees in the last of the day's golden light. They had left the machines far behind and the stillness and silence was only broken by the sounds of their own breathing and a gentle rustle in the trees. He studied a cluster of small pink berries dangling from a branch above his head. They were ringed by leaves, rich green in the fading light of the afternoon. The cluster hung still as dusk approached. He gazed at another tree nearby, its leaves and fruit hanging motionless. He sat up with a jolt.

Sera heard his sudden movement. "What's the matter?"

"Can you hear that sound, as if the leaves are rustling?"

"Yes, it's lovely," she murmured, settling back down and closing her eyes.

"Nothing's ruffling around us."

"So? It's coming from farther away."

"But there's no wind. If there was a breeze, the leaves would be moving and they're not."

"It's probably the irrigation system," Sera said.

"I don't think it's machinery. Whatever it is, I don't like the sound of it."

"Perhaps there's a breeze farther away," Sera said lazily, yawning.

Kalen looked around. Jorge had already got to his feet and was staring in the direction of the noise with a puzzled look on his face. Lars was farther away, lying asleep under a tree trunk. Half-eaten fruit and cores littered the ground around him. Dark, pink juice stained his hands and clothes and ringed his mouth, contrasting with the blisters on his forehead that still looked raw and sore. The noise was getting louder and now Kalen could discern a strange underlying whine.

"I can't place that noise." Kalen glanced towards Jorge. "I think we should leave."

Jorge began closing his pack. "Come on, Sera."

She still lay prone with her eyes closed. "Do we have to? Can't we just stay a bit longer?"

"Get up, Sera," Jorge commanded sharply. "We have to get out of here. Can't you hear that noise? We don't know what it is!"

"Oh, all right," she said grumpily and opened her eyes. She sat up, put on her jacket, and started to collect her things together.

The noise was becoming more distinctive; underneath the rustling the whining sounded stronger, wavering in pitch and volume, like discordant singing. Kalen searched his memory but he couldn't find a reference. It didn't sound like a machine. It sounded like something else. His heart began hammering and all of his senses became acute. He had an overwhelming urge to run before whatever was causing the noise reached them. Of the others, only Jorge had sensed the danger. Lars was still asleep and Sera was only making half-hearted efforts to get up.

Jorge turned to leave. "Lars, get up! We're going. Something's coming and we have to go!"

Lars stirred groggily and opened his eyes. "What is it?"

"For God's sake Lars, get up!" Jorge shouted at him. "Can't you hear it? We have to leave." Jorge started towards the steps.

"What is that whining?" Sera asked, looking in the direction of the noise.

Kalen took two strides towards her, grabbed her arm, and pulled her to her feet.

"We have to go now!" he snapped, pulling her behind him towards the steps. The drone had become a shrill buzzing sound. "There's something coming."

"It isn't another machine?" Sera asked, alarmed.

"Not this time!"

At that moment, the edge of the glade changed colour as a large swarm of bright red insects burst from between the trees. They were two inches long with bodies that tapered to a pointed tail and buzzing angrily. Thousands of them filled the clearing in an aggressive scarlet cloud. They veered around in a curve, moving as if they were one, their translucent wings glistening in the last rays of the sun. The buzzing became high pitched as the glade turned red.

The swarm dipped to the ground to devour a handful of rotting purple fruit before soaring up again and then down once more. Jorge had discarded several apple cores and the swarm found them easily, swooping down to consume them, the pitch of their buzzing oscillating while they ate. Lars stood frozen with a surprised look on his face, half eaten fruit scattered around his feet, and Sera screamed.

"Run!" Kalen yelled at Sera, pulling her behind him as he raced for the ladder.

Chapter Twenty-Three

Kalen pushed Sera in front of him, propelling her towards the ladder. Lars didn't follow. The swarm was in Lars's path to the steps and, after hesitating, he turned to run in the other direction. He only took two steps before the swarm attacked him, targeting the open sores on his face and the juice on his skin. Thousands of insects engulfed him, buzzing around his head and tearing into his skin and the sticky parts of his clothes. More settled at his feet where he had discarded half-eaten fruit. Kalen saw him put up his hands to protect himself, but the insects tore into them, gorging themselves on his flesh.

"Don't look back!" Kalen shouted at Sera, as they ran for the ladder several metres away.

Ahead of them, Jorge had already reached the ladder and was scrambling up its rungs. Behind them, the buzzing had become louder and Lars was screaming. Kalen glanced back.

The swarm was boring through Lars's clothes in a feeding frenzy. Blood had seeped through his jacket and trousers creating dark patches that intermingled with the fruit stains. A cloud of insects encircled his head, biting at his face and mouth. Lars still had his hands over his face, but the insects attacked him relentlessly, flying into his gaping mouth when he opened it to scream. Kalen saw him fall to the ground still holding his face in his hands, his screams choked off. In the middle of the red cloud, his body twitched and writhed in agony.

At the base of the ladder, Kalen pushed Sera before him and then bounded up it after her. Several stray insects buzzed viciously about his head and he swatted at them ineffectually with his hand. One of them darted at his neck and bit him, drawing blood, while another stung his arm when he swiped at it.

"If you've got any fruit on you, get rid of it," he shouted.

He fished in his pocket for a ripe pear and threw it as far as he could into the trees. Jorge had begun sprinting along the walkway towards the nearest gate a hundred metres away and they ran after him. They had lost the stray insects but the sound of the swarm behind them had changed. The oscillations in the noise had become less pronounced, and the whine had settled into the alternating pitch and volume that they had heard earlier before the attack. Kalen risked breaking pace and looked back. The red cloud was hovering at the foot of the stairs, devouring the last of the fruit they had thrown away, and then it started to rise up to the walkway.

He heard buzzing close to his ear. Then the buzzing was duplicated and amplified. Several of the insects buzzed around Sera's head and she slowed down, still screaming, and tried to swat them.

"Keep going," he shouted, grabbing her hand and pulling her after him. "We're nearly there!"

The door was a few metres ahead but the air around them was turning red. Jorge reached the door and punched the opening mechanism but nothing happened. He pulled out his laser and fired a short burst at the lock. The door slid open and Jorge launched himself through it. Kalen pushed Sera after him, before flinging himself through the opening. Jorge wrenched the door shut behind them, but a cluster of the insects had got through and buzzed furiously around their heads. Behind them, tubing ran along the wall to various tanks, and in one deft movement, Jorge tore the tubing from its brackets.

"Stand back!" he shouted, as he fired at the tube, severing it.

An acidic liquid squirted at high pressure out of the break. Sera screamed and Kalen pulled her out of the way. Jorge grabbed one end of the tube and sprayed the scarlet cloud with the liquid. The insects buzzed ferociously, then shrivelled and dropped to the floor, where they twitched for a few seconds before dying. On the other side of the door, the swarm had massed. High whining reverberated across the walkway as the insects tried to burrow through the mesh gate. Jorge swung around and sprayed them through the mesh and after a few seconds, the red cloud began to thin and return to the trees. Kalen's heart still raced and he was out of breath. He bent over, put his hands on his knees, and breathed in deeply. Beside him, Sera sat on the mesh platform crying hysterically, making loud hiccupping noises.

"What was that?" Jorge murmured.

"They must use them in the plantations. Part of the artificial ecosystem, I suppose," Kalen replied, standing up. He bent to put a hand on Sera's arm but she twisted away from him. "It's over now, they're gone. It's going to be all right."

Sera continued crying and Kalen caught Jorge's eyes over her head. Jorge raised his eyebrows and glanced towards the netting. Kalen nodded and looked up. Above them, the overhead walkway was still visible outside the netting.

"Come on," Kalen said, helping Sera up. "We have to carry on and then once we're out of here, we'll stop for a while."

"Lars… it was horrible. I can't believe what happened to him," she sobbed. "Why? Why did it happen? They ate him! They ate him!" Her voice rose in a hysterical wail and she looked up at Kalen with dark terrified eyes.

"You mustn't think about it. It's over now. Put it out of your mind."

Jorge cut in tersely, "Come on, we don't have time for this. We have to get up to the other walkway."

"Sera, we must get out of here as quickly as possible," Kalen said patiently. "It's going to be dark soon, and we need to get onto the upper walkway before then."

He took hold of her arm to guide her forward and her crying began to subside as she walked. A short distance ahead, a ladder ran up the side of the crater wall to a metal hatch that exited the netting and Jorge stopped at the foot of it. Kalen judged the hatch to be about ten metres above them and the upper walkway ten metres above that.

"I think we should try it. We can't risk staying in here," Kalen said.

Jorge studied the ladder. "Wait here while I go up. If the hatch is locked, I might have to use my laser."

Jorge climbed nimbly up the ladder to the hatch and pressed a keypad on its underside and the hatch slid open. He disappeared through it but after a few seconds, his face appeared in the opening.

"You can come up. There's another platform up here."

"Sera, you go first," Kalen said, pushing her towards the ladder.

She stared at him numbly. "It's too high."

"No it isn't, just don't look down. You'll be up there in a few seconds."

"I don't want to go up there," she said stubbornly.

"We can't stay down here. There might be another swarm of insects in this enclosure."

Without another word, Sera turned and began scrambling up the ladder.

Climbing quickly after her, he followed her through the hatch onto a narrow platform about fifteen metres long, bounded by a handrail that was intersected by metal posts. The platform was level with the netting that stretched over the trees below them and Kalen guessed initially that it might be a viewing platform. When he looked over the edge, he discovered that his first impression was mistaken. A number of boxes about a metre square were suspended immediately in front of and below the platform, arranged so they jutted out in a row along its length. The upper side of the boxes was level with the netting but the rest of the boxes hung below, inside the wooded enclosure.

A number of similar platforms, positioned several metres apart, overlooked the orchard. The undersides of the boxes were open to the enclosure below them, but the tops had mesh lids on them. Kalen peered into one and saw that it was hollow inside. At first glance, the lids looked as if they were part of the netting, but when he inspected them closely, he saw that they were designed to open and were attached to control panels fixed to the posts on the platform. A tangle of machinery and pipe-work above the platform and metal arms with tubing hung over each box. It reminded Kalen of the irrigation system used to feed the plants. The control panel nearest to him showed a green light.

It was nearly dark and Kalen looked for a way off the platform. Above them, there was more netting. Nearby, another ladder ran up to a hatch that exited the netting to the upper walkway. A loud clicking noise and bubbling sounds suddenly drew his attention to the metal arms above the boxes. The lights on the control panels blinked red and the metal arms started to descend. Then with a loud clank, the mesh lids of the boxes began to retract. An overpowering sweet smell came from the tubing over the boxes and with a start, Kalen realised where they were.

"My God, we've got to get out of here! Get up the ladder!" he shouted.

Jorge was already at the foot of the ladder and he didn't hesitate. Sera looked bewildered and Kalen got hold of her and pushed her up.

"Climb!" Kalen shouted, climbing after her. "Quickly, we're at the hives! Just go!"

He heard a distant roar, like the sound of a strong wind blowing up a storm. The noise became louder, the sound of millions of insects. Then the collective droning became an overwhelming high-pitched whine that drowned out the noise of the machinery and Sera stopped on the ladder in front of him. Above her, Jorge fiddled with the lock of the hatch, while below, the vanguard of the red swarm had entered the enclosure.

Clouds of red insects swarmed below them, engulfing the nests and feeding tubes. The swarm grew as more insects poured into the chamber through the feeding boxes. The discordant whine of their buzzing blocked out all other sound and the lower rungs of the ladder disappeared in the red mass. Gradually the red cloud rose up towards them. A needle sting pricked Kalen's ankle and then another and then the insects began darting at his hands. Above him, the hatch suddenly slid open and Jorge launched himself through it. Jorge half turned, grabbed Sera's arm, and pulled her up. Kalen threw himself after her, sprawling onto the deck as Jorge leapt forward to close the hatch.

"We should be safe here, as long as there are no breaks in the mesh," Kalen panted.

Sera covered her face with her hands. She still sat on the floor where Jorge had thrown her and she began to shake. Bringing her knees up, she put her head down until she was curled into a ball. She started to rock from side to side. She didn't look at the others and began to mutter something under her breath that Kalen couldn't catch. In the last of the light, she was no more than a silhouette in the dusk.

Jorge stood up and looked about them. "I think we're okay. This bit looks as if it was designed to run outside the enclosures, but it's getting so dark it's difficult to see."

"I don't like being above the hives. I think we ought to keep moving until we're out of this area and then try and find somewhere to stop for the night," Kalen said.

"We might have to walk several kilometres to get clear of the hive platforms. They look like they run right along the length of the orchards. We'll have to use our torches and we're not going to be able to see much."

"I still think we should move. We don't know how often they maintain the barriers. If there's any kind of break in the membrane then we're in trouble."

At that moment, Sera whimpered and Jorge glowered at her. "You've got to toughen up, Sera. Stop crying. We're leaving now."

Kalen reached for Sera's arm to help her up. "We're nearly back. We only have a few more kilometres to go before we get to the base. The worst is behind us."

She raised her head and stared at him. He could hardly see her in the twilight, but her face shone ghostly white in the last of the light.

"I'm all right," she murmured in a tearful voice. She took a deep breath and then continued, "Really, I'll be all right. I just want to get out of here. I want to go home."

She stood up shakily and took another deep breath.

"I'm ready to leave," she said in a flat voice, staring into the distance.

Chapter Twenty-Four

Darkness descended quickly. There were no lights in the crater and they used their torches. The temperature had dropped considerably when they lost the sun and Sera pulled her jacket around her. Nothing seemed real anymore. She was living in a nightmare that she couldn't escape. The images wouldn't go away and they played over and over again in her mind. She had looked back when they ran for the stairs. She saw Lars screaming in the middle of a swirling red mass and then he had fallen over. For a brief moment, she had seen what was left of his face.

Then she was running up the stairs and along the walkway; running for her life. The insects would get her next. She had known it; she had known that she was going to die like Lars. Then they had got to the door, but they weren't safe. She had to run again and the swarm came back. She'd known that this time she was really going to die. She had asked God to save her and when she thought she was dead, the universal God-force had protected her and they had found safety. But Lars was dead. He was a despicable man and God had punished him.

While Sera walked, she thought about the tenets of Cinall her mother had taught her. Growing up, she had believed in the Almighty and the power of the God-force, but when Father died, she had become disillusioned and embraced science instead. Now she understood that the God-force had always been there, protecting her, and she had been blind not to see it. She must have faith and know that God would keep her safe.

She walked in silence repeating a short prayer in her head and focusing on the slice of the walkway that she could see in the beam of her flashlight. Despite her prayers, they didn't find any speak stations or any sign of the base. After they had walked some distance, the walkway descended to a lower level, and so far as she could see, they were no longer above the netted enclosures. The plants were in rows of troughs again and appeared to be smaller bush varieties.

She was glad when the others decided to stop. She was tired and needed to sleep but she wondered what she was going to sleep on. She had left her pack and blanket in the orchard when the swarm came and had nothing with her except the clothes she wore and the equipment on her belt. She watched Jorge spread out his blanket and prepare to lie down.

"Here, you can use my blanket," Kalen said, shaking out his blanket on the floor in front of her.

"But what about you? It's too cold to sleep without something."

"I can use my jacket, it's quite thick."

His offer was tempting. "I can't let you do that—the floor is too cold."

"I'll tell you what. I'll put my blanket down and we can both lie on it. We can use Rajid and Dan's jackets to cover ourselves. They're in the packs."

She hesitated. It was a good offer but she would have to lie next to him all night. But what was the alternative? She told herself to be practical. This was no time to worry about niceties. "Okay, thank you."

She was beginning to like him. She remembered how he had held her hand and pulled her away from the insects, but she didn't want to think about it again and pictured his smile instead, his dark hair and eyes. Was he smiling now? His voice carried a smile but she couldn't see his face in the dark. He was an attractive man and women probably threw themselves at him. *I mustn't fall for him*, she thought. But that thought was followed quickly by another. *Why not?*

He handed her a jacket and she lay down and tried to cover herself with it, and he joined her, stretching out with the other jacket over his shoulders. He turned away from her and within moments his breathing had dropped into a regular rhythm, and she knew that he was asleep. She tried to find a comfortable position but her arms and legs ached. Tiredness quickly overwhelmed her and she fell into a deep sleep.

***

Morning came with a grey light illuminating the dawn. Kalen awoke to find himself lying against Sera who appeared to be soundly asleep. He savoured the moment and he would have liked to remain like that for a little longer, but she stirred, so he gently disentangled himself and got up. Jorge was already moving about and gradually their surroundings became distinct in the daylight. They were still on the walkway but at a lower level, with bushes beneath them. The end of the plantation was not yet in view but the roof of the dome had started to curve downwards.

They collected their things together and started walking again.

A storm above the dome had obscured the sun, making the sky an iron grey. The vibrant colours of the day before had gone, leaving everything looking dull and drab. The rows of bushes continued for some time and then the plantation ended abruptly. Beyond the last line of troughs, a massive structure, over two hundred metres high, loomed over the bushes. A wall had been built around the base of the structure but behind it, the installation was not solid. It was comprised of thick metal girders encompassing a mass of noisy machinery with two tall towers rising out of its central parts. As they neared, Kalen could also hear the sound of humming and a deep regular pounding sound.

Sera stopped walking and stared. "What is it? Is that the base you were talking about? Where are the people?"

"That isn't the base," Jorge said. "But there might be someone about."

"Let's hope so. At least we're out of the plantation," Kalen added.

The structure rose up in front of them, filling the horizon. Kalen couldn't see any people or lights, only gantries and moving machinery above its high walls. A network of stairs, ladders, and platforms ran amongst the machinery, but it looked deserted. The walkway sloped downwards and then became a track at ground level that led up to the installation and around its sides. Lower down, the walls around the installation blocked off Kalen's view of the inside. The track ran along the front of the building but Kalen couldn't see any maintenance vehicles.

"Everything looks automated, same as the plantation. Are you sure there's a manned base in the crater?" he asked Jorge.

"That's what I was told. We're not at the end of the crater yet and it was being built on the south side so it can't be far from here."

"Do you really think so?" Sera's voice betrayed her excitement. "I want to get back. We must see someone soon!"

"We can't be far from the base, Sera," Kalen said. "We just need to keep going a little bit longer and we'll find it."

They had got to the front of the building but Kalen could not see an entrance.

"We need to go around the building," Jorge said. "We're not going to find anyone in this place." He turned and started to walk away.

There was a renewed energy in Jorge's step and Kalen followed him with a feeling of anticipation. They had to see the base soon. The track ran in front of the installation and then curved around a corner to run due south along its side. The pounding sound got louder as they walked along the side of the building but at the halfway point, the track ended in a low wall. Just before reaching the wall, a narrower path branched off to a door set into the side of the installation.

Beyond the low wall, Kalen saw that the ground appeared to have a smooth, slate grey surface that stretched out towards the edge of the crater, empty of any buildings or other structures. The surface had sheen and resembled a vast expanse of silver. It reflected the weak sunlight causing streaks of glimmer to run across it. In places, it had a dull metallic look, dark and foreboding, and spread southwards over the crater's surface.

"What is it? Where are the buildings?" Sera asked anxiously.

"I'm not sure," Kalen replied.

"Can we walk across it?"

"We'll soon find out."

"Is it some kind of metal? What's it for?" she asked again.

"I've never seen this sort of thing before," Kalen admitted. "Jorge, didn't you hear anything about this place when you worked here?"

"Not really. I worked mostly at the other side of the crater."

The pounding had become muffled and deeper, as if someone was hitting a base drum in regular rhythm, and the air had become cooler. When they reached the wall, Kalen looked out over the metallic grey expanse. It met the sheer cliffs marking the southern edge of the crater, over two kilometres away. To his immediate left, the building jutted out another half a kilometre over the slate surface, obscuring the crater to the east. Kalen couldn't see past its retaining walls, but he could hear the sound of the machinery working in low thumps accompanied by swishing sounds that he couldn't identify. In the distance, on the other side of the silver shield, there were faint twinkling lights halfway up the cliff face.

Kalen pointed over the grey plane. "Can you see those lights over there? It must be the base."

"At last, I was beginning to think we'd never find it."

"Is it really? Show me, I can't see it," Sera said.

"Can you see the lights half-way up the cliff? There must be a building there."

"Yes! I can see it now. How far is it? Can we walk there?" she asked and then reached down to touch the grey surface behind the wall and her hand went through it. "Water?"

"It can't be, not in these quantities," Kalen said.

He took off his glove and tentatively reached down to touch the surface behind the wall. The water was cold and wet. He waggled his hand about rippling the surface, and little eddies spun out in circular patterns. He couldn't see how deep it was. Sera laughed and twirled her hand about, playfully splashing Kalen's arm, and then her face dropped.

"How are we going to get over it?" she asked.

"Just a minute." Kalen rolled up his sleeve and put his arm further in. "I can't feel the bottom."

"I can't see the bottom either," Jorge said, peering into it. "It's probably very deep, so we can't walk through it. We'll have to find another way over to the base."

"We need a boat, that's what they're called. To go on the water," Sera said. "Perhaps there's one inside the building?"

"We can take a look." Kalen straightened up. "Come on." He led the others down the path to the side door.

The thick metal door had been set into the wall and had a keypad beside it. Kalen tried the entry switch but the door was locked.

Kalen turned to Jorge. "Can you remember any of the security codes here?"

"I can try a couple I used when I worked here, but they were changed regularly." Jorge stepped up and pressed several buttons on the keypad but nothing happened.

He pressed the keypad again, but the door didn't open. "I'm not having any luck."

"I can try and dismantle it," Kalen said, taking out his laser. "I'll have to break the outer panel to get to the control box. Stand back."

He adjusted his laser and fired it at the top of the keypad.

"Careful," Jorge cautioned. "Don't burn the controls."

The surface of the keypad gave off a noxious whiff of smoke and melted, glowing orange before turning black. Sera coughed and covered her mouth, but Kalen ignored the smell. He checked that the material had cooled and then broke off the covering to expose the electronics underneath it. After studying the wiring, he spent several minutes separating and detaching the wires.

"That should do it," Kalen announced, carefully twisting a wire.

The door slid open. Behind it, the path wound into the structure between metal struts and pylons and a maze of moving machinery intersected by ladders and trellis platforms. High above the installation, the two towers soared into the air and to the south side the structure extended into the water where giant machines laboured mercilessly. Kalen followed the path through the tangle of machinery until they came out at the water's edge.

Huge girders rose a hundred metres or more out of the water and between the girders several giant wheels turned, each at least a hundred metres in diameter and thirty metres thick. The sides of the wheels were solid, encompassing a number of spokes, but the interior was hollow and divided into pockets. Kalen stared at them in fascination. Near the wheels, several other large machines churned the water. Each of these had a central horizontal bar with wings on both sides that moved up and down in a swinging motion, plunging into the water on the down turn to push it away in violent currents and then rising up again, before repeating the process. Beneath the machines, the water swirled and eddied dangerously, black and forbidding, a ferocious whirlpool generating massive power.

Chapter Twenty-Five

"I can't see anything that could be a boat," Kalen said, watching the massive machines turning and rocking. "I can't see anywhere they'd dock a boat either."

"Let's keep looking," Jorge replied. "Parts of the station jut out over the water so we might find a boat."

They explored the installation near the water's edge but did not find a boat and eventually took a path that branched inwards. The station had a framework of thick metal pylons and posts, intersected with platforms and struts, and unusual machinery that Kalen was unfamiliar with. Sheets of metal panelling closed off sections that contained moving parts, and circuitry and pipe-work were interlaced with stairwells and equipment. Near the middle of the installation, one of the towers rose up above the machinery. It had a platform at the top. Steep steps led up to the lower levels of the installation where there was a network of walkways. Further up, vertical ladders ascended to various parts of the machinery and to the base of the tower.

Jorge stopped and looked up. "We should get a better view from up there. We might be able to see a way over to the other side."

"I don't want to go up there," Sera protested.

"It should be safe if we stick to the obvious routes. We'll be able to see if there are any boats," Kalen said.

Jorge started to climb and Kalen ushered Sera in front of him.

The lower steps and the walkways in the main section had handrails, but narrow mesh walkways without handrails branched off to give access to adjacent machinery. They quickly gained height but the drops were steep and their route became less secure with fewer handholds, the higher they climbed. Soon they were high above the bulk of the installation, and could look over the water towards the wheels and butterfly machines, and beneath them to a labyrinth of twisted metal and moving parts. They continued to climb until they were at the base of the tower, which ascended to a small platform at the midway point and higher up to an observation deck. In front of them, a narrow walkway ran above the machinery and out over the water to the first of the butterfly machines.

Sera looked nervously up at the tower. "We're not going up the tower, are we?"

"It's the best vantage point," Kalen explained. "We'll be able to see everything for kilometres from the top."

"It looks as if we can get onto that swinging machine from here," Jorge said, staring at the butterfly machine. "Why don't we go to the end of it and have a look first before we try the tower? Sera can stay here and wait for us."

"I don't think we should separate," Kalen said.

Jorge laughed. "Sera will be all right here, won't you, Sera? We won't be long. Nothing's going to happen to her if she waits here for us."

"I'd prefer to wait here. I really don't like steep drops. I'd probably just slow you down."

"We'll only be a few minutes."

"Okay, but Sera, stay here and don't go off exploring on your own," Kalen instructed. "If you fell we would never find you. We'll be back soon."

The walkway had handrails but was only wide enough for them to walk singly. Kalen let Jorge lead and soon they were over the water's edge. A narrow bridge connected the installation to the spine of the nearest butterfly machine, which had a horizontal metal bar with wings on each side of it that waved up and down in sequence, churning the water. The roar of the water mingling with the sound of the machines was all encompassing, and fine spray billowed up in clouds, making the air damp.

The spine of the machine was just over a hundred metres long and less than two metres wide and Kalen followed Jorge onto it. The spine did not move with the wings but it had no handrails and a smooth metal surface that was wet from the spray. At the edges, there was a short metal lip, and below the lip, the wings stretched out on each side, ribbed with rough and smooth alternating vertical panels, like the wings of a giant moth. They dipped and soared in unison, shaking the water off their tips on the upturn, and churning it when they plunged into it on the downturn. The crosspiece they walked along vibrated from the machinery below their feet.

"Let's go to the end, we should be able to see from there," Jorge said, walking ahead.

Kalen found it difficult to see past the huge machines that laboured farther out. His view to the sides was obscured by the retaining walls of the installation and the giant wheels that turned relentlessly.

"I'm not sure there's much point going any farther," he shouted. "We need to be higher up to see anything."

"We might as well go to the end, we're nearly there," Jorge shouted back.

One of Kalen's boots slipped on the wet surface and he slowed down. "Jorge, this is dangerous. We need magnetic boots to walk along here. We haven't got the right equipment, let's go back."

Jorge ignored him and carried on walking until he reached the end of the spine and then stood with his back to Kalen, looking out over the water. Kalen slowly made his way forwards and when he had nearly reached him, Jorge half turned with an intense expression on his face. He gestured in the direction of the base.

"I can't see any boats or any way over there. We've come all this way for nothing," Jorge said bitterly.

"There might be a road around the crater's edge."

"If there is, I can't see it from here. It looks like we're stuck here."

Kalen turned around and looked back towards the power station, scanning the waterfront. A pier jutted out from the far end of one of the retaining walls that bounded the water machines. Putting his hand up to shield his eyes, he squinted into the distance, but the pier looked empty. Below him, the water made whooshing sounds as it threw up clouds of cold mist that saturated his clothes and hair. The air had a fresh clean smell but he was damp and uncomfortable.

Kalen pointed to the pier. "There's a dock over there but it's empty. Let's get back. We might see something from the tower."

He began to walk back towards the station. The fine spray had coated the surface of the spine making it as slippery as glass and he took a couple of careful steps but then his boot slid and he fell forward. He flung his hands out to break his fall, but at that moment, a searing pain erupted in his left shoulder, crumpling his left arm, and he hit the ground heavily.

He heard Jorge moving behind him and tried to push himself up with his right arm. He glanced around. Jorge stood over him, pointing a laser at his head. Instinctively he twisted his body to one side and rolled over just before another searing blast hit the metal floor beside him.

"Why?" he shouted, trying to scramble to his feet.

"Nothing personal," Jorge said in a flat voice, hard eyes betraying no emotion.

Jorge trained the laser at Kalen's head, swivelling around to aim another shot at him. He fired again but Kalen had his footing and dodged the beam. It narrowly missed him and scorched the deck behind him in a burst of sparks. In an instant, Jorge was upon him. He threw himself at Kalen, his eyes dark, and rammed him towards the edge. Kalen staggered backwards, the pain in his shoulder excruciating.

His old injury caused his right leg to buckle under him and his cheek exploded in pain as Jorge landed a punch. He fought to regain his balance and then fell to the deck but Jorge sprung at him again.

Jorge thudded into him, giving him a violent push. Kalen fell, sprawling half over the lip of the deck, an arm and leg dangling over the abyss. The lip gave him purchase, and he reached up, grabbed Jorge's ankle with one hand, and pulled. Caught by surprise, Jorge pitched backwards and dropped the laser.

Kalen heaved himself back onto the deck and fell on Jorge, punching him hard in the stomach and head. Jorge twisted under the blows and fastened his hands around Kalen's neck. Kalen struggled in the vicelike grip, coughing as Jorge squeezed his throat until he managed to get hold of Jorge's wrists and prise his hands away from him.

Jorge fell back again and before he could recover, Kalen used all of his strength to shove him towards the edge. Hanging backwards over the rim, Jorge grappled with Kalen's arms but Kalen was too quick for him. He drew his right fist back, smashed it into Jorge's face, and followed it up with another blow. Jorge grabbed the front of Kalen's jacket with both hands, but Kalen punched him again and again in the head until he released his grip and fell back stunned. Kalen pushed him again until his torso hung over the edge and then gave one final shove.

Jorge flailed his arms wildly, grabbing at thin air as he toppled over the side. He screamed as he hit the wing, which was completing its upturn. For a brief instant, he seemed to be suspended on its ribbing, but then it plunged downwards, sending him slithering towards the water. He thrashed his arms and legs about as his body bumped and bounced down the striated surface like a rag doll, until he disappeared from view, swallowed in the roiling depths, and then the wing rose gracefully again, continuing its tireless motion without a pause.

***

Sera found a place to sit and wait for the others to come back. She had soon lost sight of them as they walked towards the butterfly machines and their footsteps faded away. Leaning against a trellis, she sat listening to the pounding rhythm of the machines beating the water and the hum of the machinery and closed her eyes. She thought about the God-force and prayed that Kalen and Jorge would find a way to get to the base. Even at this height, the water nearby freshened the air, and the day had started to warm up, with a bright sun peeking through clouds above the dome. She relaxed and had begun to doze when she heard footsteps.

She opened her eyes and saw Kalen in the distance. He walked unsteadily, his left shoulder hunched. He held his left arm across his chest, using only his right hand to hold onto the railings along the walkway. When he got nearer, she could see that there were burn marks in the shoulder of his jacket and the rest of his clothes were wet and torn in places. He had a grim expression and his eyes blazed with anger.

She stood up, suddenly afraid. "What happened? Where's Jorge?"

"There was an accident," he replied tersely, looking away from her.

"Where is he? Is he hurt?" she asked shrilly.

For a moment Kalen said nothing, staring silently at something beyond her; then he met her gaze and said in measured tones in a half whisper, "He won't be coming back."

"What do you mean?" she demanded, searching his face.

"He's dead," he replied, eyes dark with controlled rage.

"How? How can he be dead? You were only going to the machine and coming back again." Icy fear ran through her. Jorge dead? It didn't seem possible; they had only been gone for a few minutes.

Kalen pursed his mouth. "He slipped and fell into the water. I'm sorry Sera."

"Couldn't he have got out? I don't understand."

"No—he went under immediately. The currents are very strong."

Kalen sat down and leaned his back against a strut. The shoulder of his jacket had burned through and underneath, his scorched skin was red and blistered. It looked like a laser burn, she decided. Something had happened, something terrible.

"You're burnt? How did it happen?"

He grimaced. "I got too near a power line, it's nothing."

She wanted to believe him, but it didn't ring true.

"Is that why Jorge slipped? Did he get near the power line as well?"

"We both got too near."

His words echoed in her mind and despair gripped her. Her eyes welled up and she began sobbing into her hands. Another death. How could it have happened? Why had it happened? She couldn't believe she would never see Jorge again. She looked over to the walkway leading to the butterfly machine and imagined that she saw him there. Surely he would return? Surely he had escaped somehow?

"There was nothing I could do," Kalen said gently beside her. "I'm sorry Sera, but there was nothing I could do." He sounded weary and dispirited, his anger leaking away.

"I don't understand. First it was Dan, then Lars, and now Jorge. Why would God take them all? Jorge was a good man."

Kalen sighed. "Sometimes things happen and there doesn't seem any reason for it. The important thing is that we have to carry on."

She studied him, trying to swallow her tears. He sat hunched over, his face dark, and holding his left arm with his right hand. He was all she had now and if anything happened to him, she would be alone in this strange place. She wiped her face with her sleeve and sniffed back her tears. He was right; whatever God's reason for taking Jorge, they had to carry on. She said a quiet prayer for Jorge, committing his life force to the eternal and dismissed his face from her mind.

"Take your jacket off and I'll have a look at your shoulder. You shouldn't leave it like that."

He took off his jacket and slid his shirt back to expose the burn. It wasn't deep and she cleaned and sprayed a dressing on it from the emergency medical supplies that he had in his pack. He sat quietly, as if deep in thought, while she tended to him, occasionally taking sharp intakes of breath when she touched his injuries. Had he fought with Jorge, but why? Nothing made sense but she decided not to press him. If he wanted her to know, he would tell her. For now, she had to forget Jorge and concentrate on getting to the base.

"You'll live," she said, finishing up. "Are you hurt anywhere else?"

"No, it's just the shoulder."

"You need to sit for a while." She handed him some water, got a meal bar out of the pack, and gave it to him. "Here, eat this." She thought about having one herself, but she didn't feel hungry. She sat beside him listening to him munching on the bar.

After several minutes, she asked, "Did you see any boats?"

Kalen shook his head. "No, there's a pier farther out but it's empty. All the boats are probably moored at the base."

Surely Jorge didn't die for nothing, she thought. There had to be another way to get to the base. "Won't they come over here to check the machinery? Can't we just wait here until a maintenance team arrives?"

"This place is fully automated and they might not come over for days or weeks. There's no way of knowing." Kalen shrugged.

"Couldn't we sabotage something so that they would have to come and repair it?" she asked hopefully.

"Technically that's possible." Kalen took a deep breath and continued, "But we would have to do a lot of damage to prompt an immediate visit and that would be difficult. Most of the systems are designed to either self-repair, or the circuits re-route pending repair, so that the maintenance teams don't have to come out too often. When the maintenance teams do come, they'll do repairs right across the facility. The visits could be as infrequent as months apart."

"So we could be stranded here for months? What are we going to do?"

He roused himself and looked directly at her. "You have to go up the tower. I can't climb with my shoulder like this, but you can. From the top you'll be able to see most of the crater and whether there's a route around the edge to the base."

"I can't do that! I can't climb up that ladder. It's too high and there's a sheer drop. I'll slip and fall like Jorge," she jabbered.

"Of course you can do it. There's nothing to it. You'll be up there in no time."

Sera stared at the tower. A ladder ran vertically up the side of it, with rungs that were spaced widely apart and it disappeared far above her into a rectangular hole cut into the first platform. Above that, the tower narrowed into a single metal support with a ladder running up another fifty metres or so, to the observation deck at the top. She imagined herself on the ladder with nothing between her and the sheer drops and her legs started to shake. She felt dizzy already.

"I don't know if I can do it. Really, I'll get dizzy and fall."

"No you won't. You've done lots of climbing already. Once you get up there you'll see how easy it is."

"If there's a path, wouldn't we be able to see it from here?"

"You'll get a much better view from the top. There might be a path to the base or you might be able to see another exit from the crater."

She began to reply, the argument ready on her lips. Then an inner voice told her that she was being a coward. God would protect her. "Okay, I'll try but I don't know how far I'll get. Do I need to take anything with me?"

"Take some water. It will get hot up there."

"Anything else?" Her legs already felt weak and the shaking had got worse. Now her stomach churned and she felt queasy. "What if I'm sick on the ladder?"

"You don't need anything else and if you feel sick, drink some water. You'll be fine. Just climb the ladder and don't look down while you're on it. After you reach the first platform, carry on going right to the top. Here's my radio. Try it when you get to the top." He fished out his radio and gave it to her.

"Okay." Now she was shaking all over, but she had to do this.

"Promise you won't stop half-way? You might be able to see something from the top that you can't see from lower down."

"I promise."

Chapter Twenty-Six

Sera stood at the bottom of the ladder and put her foot on the first rung. Her legs shook and the palms of her hands were clammy but she gripped the ladder tightly and began to climb. Keeping her eyes on the rungs in front of her, she lifted one foot at a time, ignoring her quickening heartbeat and the dizziness that had swept over her. The ladder slithered underneath her wet palms and her stomach churned. Fighting down her panic, she concentrated on climbing as quickly as possible, but she kept on seeing Jorge's face and hearing Kalen's voice, "he slipped… Jorge's dead." She didn't want to die like Jorge; she didn't want to fall from the ladder and crash down onto the metal framework below. Not here. Not like this.

The void beneath her seemed to suck at her feet when she lifted them and her whole body felt heavy. If she stopped for even a moment, she was sure she would pitch to the side, lose her grip on the ladder, and fall. Nausea rose in her throat and the acid taste filled her mouth. She had to keep going; she had promised Kalen. The sun had got hotter and her forehead began to burn, but she kept going. Only a few more rungs, she told herself. Suddenly her forehead cooled and a shadow fell across her. She looked up to see the first platform directly overhead, with an access hatch seven or eight rungs further up. Focusing on the hatch, she climbed until she could put her hands on the edges and clamber onto the deck.

A barrier about waist height ran around the platform and she crawled over to it and gingerly stood up. Grasping the barrier firmly, she peered across the water to the other side of the crater. Beyond the wheels and butterfly machines, the base was visible. It had been built into the side of the cliff and protruded out over the reservoir but she couldn't make out any detail. There was no track around the edge of the crater to the base, so far as she could see.

She turned around so that she was looking over the power station. To the east, she could see the other tower, which looked more substantial than the one she stood on, with enclosed sections. It might have a stairwell or elevator, she thought. Below her, there was the mass of machinery and walkways, and to the north was the plantation. Even from that height, she couldn't see the end of it, or any exits from the crater. It seemed pointless to go higher but she had promised Kalen. Steeling herself for the next climb, she walked shakily to the foot of the ladder that ascended vertically up the centre post.

Staring up the ladder that ran to the top platform, her sense of balance seemed to desert her and she felt herself swaying sideways. She took hold of the ladder with both hands and put her foot on the first rung. *God will protect me,* she thought. *God has sent me here for a purpose and I must do this.* She took a deep breath and started to climb, willing herself upwards, careful not to look down. With each step, her legs felt heavier and her shaking increased. Her heart thumped and her hands slipped about on the rails. *I have to keep going,* she repeated to herself. *I promised.*

If I let go of the ladder for a moment, I'll fall, she thought. *I'll plunge downwards and fly through the air. What will that be like? Flying free but knowing I'll be dead in a second? Don't think about it,* she told herself. *Just keep going and don't look down. I won't faint if I keep going. I'm not going to be sick. I'll make it; God is with me. God will keep me safe. I'll get up there and coming down will be easy. I'll see Kalen again and we'll get to the base together. Everything will be normal again. So just keep going.*

She began to count the rungs as she climbed them. She started at one hundred and fifty to allow for the ones up to the lower platform: one hundred and fifty-one, fifty-two, fifty-three. She let the numbers fill her mind; squeeze out the thoughts of falling. Two hundred and seventy, seventy-one, seventy-two. How many more were there, she wondered. She glanced upwards. She was close. There were maybe thirty or forty more until she reached the upper platform. It was smaller than the first and she didn't feel its shadow until she was immediately under its rim. Clutching at the lip of the hatch, she scrambled thankfully onto the deck. She sat for a moment until her trembling subsided and tried Kalen's radio but couldn't get a response.

She crawled to the edge of the platform and stood up, clinging to the railings that bordered the deck. The reservoir looked the same to her, flat and grey. No boats or even a ripple to indicate traffic. She still couldn't see any detail of the base. Changing her viewpoint, she looked back over the plantation. Although she could see a little farther this time, she still couldn't see the end of the crater, or any exits. The only movement she could see were the tiny machines skimming up and down the rows of troughs.

The platform was about three metres wide, and she half-walked, half-crawled to the other side and peeked out over the power station. She found that she was looking down onto the roof of the second tower that comprised a large circular platform. She could make out something on its roof. She changed her position to get a better view. *It can't be,* she thought. She peered harder. No, she wasn't mistaken. She had to tell Kalen. He'd been right; she could see more from the top. She stepped to the hatch, swung herself around, and began quickly climbing down, her legs feeling steady once more.

***

Kalen sat alone, thinking about Jorge in a cold rage. Jorge must have sabotaged the drill but he probably only intended to kill him, and not the others. He couldn't remember seeing the man with the remote console once the drill began moving. What had happened to him? Had Jorge used the remote in some way to override Dan's controls?

Someone in the Division wanted to silence him. There was something going on at Three-Craters that they didn't want him to find. It was something important enough for Jorge to be ordered to kill him. Palum Kingston suddenly came to mind. Did someone have instructions to kill him as well? His death had never been explained. For the first time, he questioned the reception that he would receive when he got back.

Sera had been gone for about thirty minutes. He had watched her climb steadily upwards to the first platform and then he had lost sight of her for a few minutes, before she reappeared higher up on the ladder, climbing to the top. Now she was coming back down and moving quickly. He watched her for a few moments and then his thoughts drifted to Halle.

Did Halle know what was going on? *Possibly*, he thought, remembering the way that she had urged him to whitewash the problems at Three Craters. Halle had to know something, but did she know about the plot to kill him? How could he ever trust her again? He heard a noise and looked up. Sera was nearly down. He got to his feet and waited while she climbed down the last few rungs. She hopped lightly off the ladder with a big smile on her face.

"There's something on top of the second tower, she said excitedly. "I think it's a shuttle."

"Are you sure? What does it look like?"

"It's black and oval shaped with a transparent screen at the front and not very big, but I couldn't see any wings."

"Did you see anything else when you were at the top, like a boat?"

"No. The plantation stretches for kilometres and the water goes right up to the sides of the crater so there's no way round. The base is too far away to see properly. But if there's a shuttle we'll be able to fly over there, won't we?"

"I know how to pilot a shuttle but I need to take a look at it first. The other tower should be easy to reach—if we get down to ground level we can follow one of the walkways through the power station."

"I took a reading with my compass and marked the co-ordinates. The tower is nearly due east of us."

"Okay, let's go then," Kalen said, picking up his pack. "If we hurry we might be able to get to the base before it gets dark."

***

Kalen led Sera back along the walkway to the top of a steep ladder and climbed down it onto another walkway that ran towards the centre of the installation. He guided Sera along a series of gangways and down ladders until they reached a large machine. Pausing, he tried to remember their route. A walkway wound around the machine to a flight of metal treads that went to ground level. He thought that was the direction they'd come in. He took Sera that way, carefully retracing their steps until they were on one of the central paths, and then set off to follow a route through the machinery towards the second tower. He passed shiny panelling screening off machinery that made chugging noises and a large junction box that hummed loudly. He could hear pumps working near the waterfront and the hiss and sizzle of electricity.

"Be careful, don't touch anything. A shock from one of those circuits can kill you," he warned Sera.

The corridor they were following petered out and terminated in a small open area that was bordered on one side by another junction box about three metres high, and on the other side by a mass of tangled pipes and a narrow ladder rising to a small platform about three metres above them. The platform did not lead anywhere and Kalen couldn't see an easy way through. There should be maintenance tracks he thought, but he couldn't see any.

"Stay here while I have a look. Don't move and I'll be back in a minute."

He took off his pack, left it at Sera's feet, and squeezed through a gap at the side of the junction box. Behind it, a lattice of thick pipes ran in all directions and thick plastic tubes of cabling criss-crossed the area leading to pieces of equipment and machinery that vibrated and hummed. The network of pipes extended into the interior of the installation for twenty metres or so and he couldn't see what was behind it. He shuffled sideways back through the gap to the clearing where Sera was waiting.

"There's enough room between the pipes for us to get through. I don't know where it leads but it's worth a try."

Sera followed him past the junction box and into the maze of pipes and cables. For several metres, they were able to make their way forward, ducking under some pipes and climbing over others. In places, electric cabling snaked through the pipes to connect with smaller junction boxes that hissed ominously and Kalen gave those a wide berth. In other places, they passed vertical ladders that led to equipment at the upper levels but he could see the tower ahead, its solid structure rising above the machinery. He heard a gasp from behind him and turned to see that the arm of Sera's jacket had snagged on a piece of protruding metal and she was struggling to free it.

"Don't move. Stand still and I'll get it." Her head was centimetres from an electric cable that was wired into a box above her. He quickly untangled the jacket but the fabric had torn. "Never mind, we'll be back soon and you can get another jacket."

"Are we nearly out of here? How much farther have we got to go?"

"The tower is just over there, but there's more machinery in our way and we'll have to get around it."

He gestured towards a large square structure in front of them that thrummed and crackled, and took hold of her hand and led her forward until they were standing about a metre away from it.

"This is where it gets interesting. We mustn't get any closer to the machine because it's too dangerous. I think we're going to have to start climbing."

"I can see the tower." Sera pointed beyond the huge machine. "That's the way we want to go."

The machine was box-shaped with solid side panels higher than Kalen, encasing its engines and circuitry. Metal arms and cabling grew out of it to connect with adjacent junction boxes and apparatus. A trellis of thick pipes converged at the bottom of the panelling and wound up the side of the machine. It coiled across its top before disappearing into a web of metalwork farther on.

Kalen stepped onto the pipes. "Come on, we'll go up here. Follow me."

"But there's nothing to hold on to," Sera objected.

"It'll be okay. The pipes are wide enough to walk on. Just keep your hands in and don't touch anything. There's a lot of live cabling about."

He began walking along the top of the pipes, keeping his arms crooked and elbows in. Below him, the engine throbbed and hummed and he continued walking farther into the labyrinth until the pipes branched off in different directions. At the fork, he stopped and considered their route. He thought it would be foolish to try to climb the pipes any farther, but ahead he could just see the end of a girder that looked wide enough to walk along. Metal struts, pylons, and pipes obscured his view of anything else. If he climbed across one of the pipes and levered himself beneath another, he thought he could jump down onto the girder.

Checking that Sera was still behind him, he slung his leg over the nearest pipe and swung down under the next, holding on with both arms until he found his footing on the girder below. After making sure that he was standing securely, he motioned to Sera to follow and helped her onto the steel girder. She slithered down and he found himself squashed up against her in the confined space. For a moment, he held her close and then let her go and stepped back. Holding onto a strut, he looked around and immediately regretted his decision to come that way.

Chapter Twenty-Seven

Kalen studied the machinery in front of them. A row of giant pumps stood in a rectangular pool of black water, about ten metres wide and thirty metres long, supported by a network of girders. Each pump had an upright about seven metres tall on the top of which a long metal bar pivoted, pitching diagonally down into the well, plunging in and out of the water in a regular motion. The pumps were working in unison and made a loud booming sound. Two horizontal crosspieces were attached to the base of the upright of each pump. When the bars thrust downwards, the crosspieces swung out ninety degrees in a synchronised motion, sweeping a wide deck on each side of the well, at the height of Kalen's knees.

"If we can get to the other side of the well, we'll probably find an access for the maintenance crews," Kalen said.

"How are we going to get past the beams?" Sera asked, staring at the crosspieces swinging over the deck. "They'll hit us. Can we crawl under them?"

Kalen spied a small junction box nearby. "I've got a better idea. Stay put."

He carefully edged along the steel girder they stood on, until he reached the junction box. Using his laser, he aimed at the casing of the box and fired until it burnt through, and then fired at the wiring inside. After the wiring caught alight and blackened, he traced the cables that ran from the box to the pumps, and burned through them also.

Shuffling back towards Sera, he repeated the process on another junction box near her, and then isolated more cabling and burned through it. He saw another box a few metres away and attacked that as well, burning through the cabling that connected it to the pumps.

All of the pumps suddenly stopped and went quiet with the metal bars tipped downwards and fully extended into the well. The horizontal crosspieces had swung out to their farthest reach and were now stationary across the width of the deck.

"Come on!" Kalen shouted.

"Are you sure it's safe?"

"Yes, it won't start running again for some time."

He began to walk along the right side of the well, stepping over the first crosspiece and heading towards the next. "Watch your boots on the surface, it's slippery."

He could hear the sound of gurgling water sloshing about under the station and his clothes had become damp again from the spray churned up by the pumps. A glaze of moisture covered the deck and his boots slid as he walked across it. To his left side the well dropped into blackness and the motionless pumps dipped down in a stricken posture. A tremor suddenly ran through the deck and he heard a power cell start to hum.

Beside him, Sera paused. "What's that? I thought you said that you'd turned this thing off?"

"Don't worry, just keep on going," he replied, walking faster.

The deck trembled beneath his boots and the uprights and girders around him started to vibrate. It can't be coming on, he thought. He'd disabled all the pumps. Had he forgotten something? Lights suddenly flickered on along the length of the well, illuminating a series of robotic arms attached to posts set apart at regular intervals. He saw movement out of the corner of his eye and glanced to his right. A giant metal arm with pincers on the end was swinging towards his head.

"Get down!" he shouted, ducking behind a crosspiece.

Sera threw herself onto her stomach behind him. "What is it?" she screamed.

"It's designed to repair the machine. It must have detected the damage to the junction boxes."

"Then why is it attacking us?" Sera shrieked as he pulled her under the crosspiece after him.

"It must be programmed to destroy anything that shouldn't be here."

She huddled against him under the crosspiece. "Will it shoot us?"

"Keep still! It detects movement. It won't use lasers to avoid damaging the equipment."

The arm swept the area behind the crosspiece and then partially withdrew and became inert. Along the row of posts, more robot arms had flexed.

"What are we going to do? Please tell me you know what to do!" Sera cried hysterically.

"It's all right; I know how these things work. I'll get us out of here but you must stay calm and do exactly what I tell you. Okay?"

"I thought that thing was going to kill us."

"There's a robot arm opposite the end of each beam but we're safe when we're under them. We're going to run for the next one. When I say go, I want you to run as fast as you can to the next bar. I'll be right behind you. Keep an eye out for the arm and be ready to duck if it comes out."

"Okay."

He took off his belt. "Are you ready?"

She nodded her head.

He bunched up the belt in his fist and tossed it out to his right. "Go!"

Sera sprinted towards the next crosspiece and he followed her. The mechanical arm darted out and plucked up the belt in its pincers, paused briefly, and incinerated it in a whiff of smoke. It struck out again at Kalen, pincers snapping empty space where his head had been a moment before, as he rolled under the crosspiece. The arm hesitated momentarily, and then pulled back, pincers swivelling.

"That was close," Kalen gasped, breathing hard. "Those things are adaptable. We might be able to fool it for another run, but after that, it will learn to go for us first and ignore anything I throw. We're the bigger targets and therefore the bigger threat to the machine."

"Can't you just blast the arms?"

"There's too many of them. We wouldn't be able to get a clear shot before one of them got us. Give me your laser. I've got another idea but it'll use all the juice we've got."

She gave him her laser and he adjusted the settings on it to maximum and did the same with his own. Taking both lasers, he shuffled on his stomach along the underside of the crosspiece to the end. A post supporting a robot arm stood about a metre away from him and he aimed his laser at a control box fixed halfway up it. The white laser beam tore into the metal covering of the box, exposing the wiring inside.

Kalen crawled out from under the crosspiece and bounded to the post. He reached up to the box just as an adjacent robot arm swung towards him. He was within its radius and he flung himself sideways to dodge it. Working quickly, he opened up the lasers and began connecting them to the wiring in the box. The arm twitched and took another swipe. Holding onto the post, Kalen twisted behind it, and the arm shot past his ear. The arm darted out at him again, pincers snapping on nothing, and then withdrew, sensors clicking as it tried to get another fix on him. After waiting for a few seconds, he edged back to the control box to complete wiring the lasers to it.

The robot arm shot out at him again. He ducked and finished setting the time delay on the lasers. The arm got another fix on him and streaked towards him, its pincers snapping and whirring. It caught the sleeve of his jacket but he wrenched his arm away, jumped onto the deck and dived under the crosspiece. The pincers snapped, narrowly missing his feet and ankles but latched onto his boot. He kicked out with all of his strength, his foot meeting hard metal and then he was free. He shuffled back along the underside of the crosspiece to where Sera crouched.

"Watch this! I've wired the lasers to send a charge down the main circuit to blow the control boxes."

A few seconds passed and then a bright flare erupted from the first control box and it burst into flames with a loud cracking sound. Within a second, another control box exploded in a shower of sparks, and then one by one each of the control boxes fixed to the row of posts exploded in quick succession and the robotic arms went limp. The smell of burning plastic and smoke wafted through the machinery.

"Okay, I think that's done it." Kalen scrambled out from under the crosspiece.

Sera scrambled after him and he helped her to her feet. Taking her hand, he led her across the deck, negotiating the crosspieces as they came to them. The robot arms hung limply, frozen sentinels now blind to the unauthorised intrusion. Behind the row of arms, lights winked, and Kalen wondered vaguely if they were being watched. At the end of the well, a platform stretched across its width, accessible by a short flight of stairs.

"This should lead to a way out," Kalen told Sera, climbing the stairs.

Standing on the platform, Kalen could see a path winding through the machinery to the second tower, twenty or thirty metres away, and a ramp leading to its entrance.

***

The door of the second tower slid open and circular overhead lights blinked on automatically when they stepped inside. Sera saw the elevator opposite the door and in her mind said a prayer to thank the God-force. At last, they were out of the machinery. At one point, she had doubted they would get out, but she had been wrong to doubt God. The God-force had kept them safe and they could leave this horrible place now. She followed Kalen into the elevator, wondering about the shuttle on the roof. Would it fly? Could they leave tonight?

The elevator took them to the roof. The sun had sunk nearly to the horizon and purple and orange streaks coloured the sky. High above the power station, the small shuttle sat alone in the middle of the roof, its glossy exterior reflecting the gold of the setting sun. It had doors on each side, and when Kalen tried one, it opened easily, letting out a rush of warm air. Inside there was seating for the pilot and three passengers.

Kalen climbed into the pilot's seat and began studying the console. "I've never flown this model before, but I should be able to work it out. It's baking hot in here."

Sera leaned into the cockpit. The inside of the shuttle was dim and she could just make out the console with a confusing array of switches and buttons. Kalen flicked a switch and the interior lights came on.

"Don't get too excited yet, I have to make it work first. I don't know if it will fly. Get in the other side," he said.

She walked around the shuttle and climbed into the front passenger seat. "But it must work, if it's parked up here?"

"It could have been left here because it needed repair. They may be bringing parts for it the next time they come over." Kalen tried switches on the console in front of him and the doors slid shut with a click.

"I need to go through each of the systems and double check that there isn't a fault. There's no room for error because we're so high up. If I try to take off and make a mistake we'll crash."

Outside the sun began to dip below the horizon and the golden tint of the dome roof started to fade to grey.

"I'm sorry Sera, but I think it's too dark to leave now. I haven't got the co-ordinates of the base to programme into the navigation equipment. That means that I'll have to fly this manually, and I need the light to do that. We're going to have to wait until the morning."

"But that's hours away. Why can't we fly in the dark? Hasn't the shuttle got lights?"

"We won't be able to find the base in the dark. Even if it's lit up, I won't be able to see it until we're almost on top of it."

"Please, can't we try? I don't want to stay here all night. We're so high up that it really scares me," she pleaded.

"It's too risky. In the daylight, I would be willing to chance flying without the proper co-ordinates but in the dark, it could go terribly wrong. It's safer to stay here for a few hours. We'll be all right in the shuttle."

"Isn't there a radio in here? Can't we call for help?"

"No, whatever band they usually use, it isn't working. We're going to have to wait for the light. Why don't you get some sleep in the back while I check out the controls?"

She nodded her head in agreement but she didn't want to sleep. Her mind still whirled with the events of the day: Jorge's death, the climb up the tower, and the way Kalen had saved her from the machines. The God-force had been with them, but Kalen had saved her. She felt safe with him and she liked being with him, she admitted to herself.

Kalen switched off the main lights and she watched him as he continued trying the switches and dials on the console. He had stubble on his cheeks but she decided that didn't distract from his attractiveness. It was stifling hot in the craft and he had taken his jacket off. Now his body was silhouetted in the light from the control panel and she could see the outline of his muscles under his shirt when he moved. He must work out, she thought. His body was tightly honed and his muscles rippled when he stretched to turn a dial or flick a switch. She could smell his perspiration, and thoughts and images tumbled through her mind unbidden. What would it be like to touch him? To snuggle close to him and have him hold her in his arms and kiss her? He was different from any of the men she had known.

"How's your shoulder?" she asked.

"Still sore," he muttered, continuing to work.

"Would you like me to take a look at it? It wouldn't do any harm to change the dressing."

"Okay, thanks, in a minute. I'll just finish checking this."

He made a final inspection of the instruments and swivelled round to face her. "I'm all yours."

She reached into his pack for the medical kit. "Take your shirt off and turn around."

"If you say so." He gave her a quick grin then faced the other way.

He took off his shirt and underneath his back glistened with perspiration. He sat facing away from her, his back and broad shoulders pale in the near darkness. The dressing on his left shoulder stood out white against his skin and she gently peeled it away. When she touched him, she felt the heat of his skin through her fingertips.

"It looks as if it's healing okay. I'll put some salve on and another dressing." She found the tube of salve and sprayed it over the burn, and sprayed another plastic dressing over it.

"Thank you. That feels better."

He bent forward to retrieve his shirt and she brushed her fingertips across his other shoulder. She was so close to him that he must feel her breath on his bare skin.

"Does it hurt anywhere else?" she asked quietly, skimming her hand softly down his back.

He turned around with a quizzical look. "Do you want to check?" he asked, smiling.

She blushed and lowered her eyes briefly before meeting his gaze. For a moment he studied her face and then he gently pulled her towards him. He kissed her slowly, drawing her to him so that he held her against his naked chest. His lips were soft against hers and he wrapped his arms around her. He ran his hands under her shirt, caressing her, and she returned his kisses, clasping him to her, feeling his hard muscles under the sticky heat of his skin.

He stroked her gently and kissed her neck, his breath warm against her. His unshaven cheeks rubbed and tickled her and she reached up to the nape of his neck and ruffled his thick dark hair with her fingers. She tingled with each of his kisses and felt herself melting within his embrace. He pulled away slightly and stared into her eyes, as if he was seeing into her soul.

"You're beautiful," he whispered.

He kissed her again and then started to ease away from her, dropping his hands to her waist where he continued to hold her lightly.

She reached up and clasped his neck and kissed him, and then leaned backwards onto the seats, pulling him on top of her. In the warm light of the console, his eyes seemed to hold a question, which she answered with a deep steady gaze.

"Don't stop," she murmured. "Don't stop."

***

Kalen was in a deep dreamless sleep when he was woken up by a cold rush of air and a bright light. He opened his eyes. The door of the shuttle was open and a flashlight blinded him.

"Get out!" a voice shouted. "Hands up where I can see them!"

"What?" Kalen said, still half-asleep.

"You're under arrest! You're not authorised to be in this sector," the voice screamed.

Hands took hold of his arms and dragged him out of the cabin, and flung him violently onto the hard surface of the platform. The air was cold and he didn't have his jacket on. Several soldiers wearing black uniforms and berets surrounded him and they pulled Sera out of the shuttle after him. She had wrapped herself in a blanket and they pushed her towards him. One of the soldiers had retrieved their jackets and was perfunctorily searching them. He found their Division badges and passed them to an officer, then threw their jackets at them.

"Who are you? Why did you sabotage the pumps?" the officer demanded.

"We're from Three-Craters," Kalen said, getting to his feet. "We got trapped in an accident and were trying to get to the base."

"How did you get here?" the officer barked.

"We came through the caves," Kalen said.

"Names?"

"Kalen Trinneer and Sera Ethern."

"Come with us," the officer ordered.

They were handcuffed and pushed across the platform to the elevator. Inky blackness surrounded them. There was no moon and the only lights were those carried by the soldiers. When they reached ground level, they were marched to a boat moored at the end of the pier and pushed into it. Kalen sat beside Sera as the boat manoeuvred past the giant wheels and butterfly machines. From time to time, it got caught in the pull of the current and suddenly lurched to one side but once they had cleared the machines, it sped across the water effortlessly, skimming towards the base that hung from the cliff face, its lights blazing above the obsidian depths.

Chapter Twenty-Eight

At the base, they were taken to a room that was bare except for a table and chairs and left there, still handcuffed. A plaque about twenty centimetres high stood on the table with the word 'Unity' emblazoned on it in gold lettering. Kalen noticed another plaque, larger than the first, hanging on one wall with the words 'Unity is Freedom' written across it. Beside him, Sera sat white faced.

"Don't worry, they're just verifying our identity," Kalen tried to re-assure her. "Once they confirm who we are, things will be okay."

"We're not in the Ea-Zone are we?" she asked plaintively.

"No, I think we're in the U-Zone."

"If we were in the Ea-Zone they wouldn't treat us like this."

"They'll find out that we're missing, and send us back," Kalen said with more confidence than he felt. Someone wanted him dead and until he was back in Central, his life was in danger, and possibly Sera's too. Whoever wanted to kill him wouldn't want witnesses.

The door opened and two soldiers came into the room. They each wore a gold triangular brooch on the left breast of their black jackets. The brooches had the number five on them.

"Kalen Trinneer, the commander wants to see you," an officer behind them barked at him.

The officer wore a peaked hat and gloves and also had a brooch in the shape of a triangle pinned to his jacket. He waited while the soldiers removed Kalen's handcuffs.

"Stand up and come with me," the officer ordered, and the soldiers stood aside and then fell in behind Kalen.

Kalen followed the officer along corridors with burnished alloy floors that muffled the sound of their footsteps, and bright strip lights that ran along the centre of the ceilings. The walls had been painted a subtle shade of blue. Kalen supposed the military also colour coded their floors. The officer stopped in front of a door, paused to request access and then went in.

"Kalen Trinneer, sir," the officer announced.

The soldiers ushered Kalen into the room where the commander sat behind a desk. He was a young man with fair hair and eyebrows, light eyes, and a sharp chin.

The officer stepped back and positioned himself near the door while the soldiers didn't enter. There was no seat for Kalen to sit on and he remained standing in front of the commander.

"So you're Kalen Trinneer? I've been told that you got here from Three-Craters?" the commander enquired, one of his eyelids twitching rapidly giving him the look of a nervous ferret.

"That's correct," Kalen replied.

"I've read the accident report. A primary drill ran out of control and several people are missing. What happened?"

Kalen described the accident and the journey through the cave system, leaving nothing out except his fight with Jorge. The commander interrupted him several times to ask questions until he eventually appeared satisfied.

"Why did you destroy the pumps?"

"We were trying to get to the tower. We got trapped."

The commander laughed suddenly. "The power station wasn't built for visitors!"

"We were trying to get out."

"So you say. That's all very well, but you did a lot of damage. And Jorge Narve was with you until you reached the station?"

"Yes, but he slipped and fell from one of the machines," Kalen repeated, trying to keep his voice level.

"I see." The commander looked thoughtful. "And you, how did you get that injury?"

"I brushed my shoulder against a live power circuit."

The commander looked sceptical. He stared at Kalen for several seconds, drumming his fingers against the desk, as if deciding what to do with him.

He doesn't believe me, Kalen thought. *He knows I killed Jorge.*

Finally, the commander seemed to make a decision. "You'll be taken to Central as soon as transport can be arranged."

"What about Miss Ethern?"

"What about her?"

"Will she be coming to Central as well?"

"She's none of your concern."

"This is the U-Zone isn't it? Aren't you going to wait for the Ea-Zone and hand us over at day end? I thought that was the usual procedure." Kalen remembered the Gate and shuddered inwardly.

The commander laughed again. "I think not. The usual procedure is the Gate! But don't worry, I'm not going to send you through it."

The commander nodded and the officer came forward to escort Kalen from the room. The soldiers were waiting outside and they fell into step behind him as the officer led him to a small room where he was left by himself. After the door slid closed he tried the catch, but it was locked so he sat down to wait. Thoughts crowded his mind. If someone wanted to kill him they would do it here. Everyone would think he had died in the caves. Why would they send him back to Central? Why separate him from Sera? Suddenly the door opened and two soldiers appeared.

"Come with us," one of the soldiers said.

The soldiers took him to an elevator and along endless corridors, until they reached a large hangar containing several shuttle craft. Most of the craft were planetary shuttles, designed to carry a dozen or more passengers, and capable of withstanding the harsh atmosphere on the planet's surface. The soldiers steered him towards one of the shuttles that had its doors open. The pilot had already started the craft and the soldiers ordered him aboard and climbed in after him.

Kalen's sense of foreboding increased. He was in the U-Zone but normal protocol demanded that they wait for Ea-Zone transport at day end. U-Zone military should take over the central hub of the base at twenty hundred hours. Why weren't they waiting to hand him over then?

Before he could think about it any further, the doors closed and the shuttle began to ascend. Kalen heard the roof slide open above them and then the shuttle broke free and they were flying in the planet's atmosphere. It was another clear day, and the bright yellow sun blazed out of an unbroken blue sky.

The shuttle had twelve seats but Kalen and the two soldiers were the only passengers, so he sat by a window. Below them, the landscape was barren and there was no sign of Three-Craters. They were flying over a wide, bare sandy plain towards a range of sharp peaked mountains. From the position of the sun, he worked out that they were flying south, but he recalled that Central was to the east of Three-Craters.

The craft descended as it approached the mountains and then wove through a narrow pass, flying within metres of the vertical rock faces on either side. Kalen peered out at the nooks and crannies in the rocky crags, occasionally catching a glance of the dry and inhospitable ground below. After a few minutes, the pass opened out into a small valley, ringed by mountains. Kalen could see a low metallic looking building in the centre of the valley with a landing platform beside it.

The shuttle headed for the low building and came down slowly to settle on the landing platform. The pilot turned the engine off and sat waiting, saying nothing. No one had spoken throughout the journey and Kalen now looked at the soldiers expectantly. One of the guards sat at his side and the other immediately behind him and both of them stared straight ahead, avoiding eye contact with him. Were they going to kill him here? Fear crept through his innards.

Kalen heard a clank and then a hissing noise. Thank the Planets, he thought. He began to relax and think about Sera. He hadn't meant to start an affair with her, but her hidden passion had been surprising and he would never have guessed that she could be so sensual. He began to worry about her. Why were they sending him to Central without her? There was another loud clank and the shuttle shuddered as the refuelling mechanism detached itself. Without a word, the pilot powered up the engine again and the craft rose up and wound its way back through the pass to resume its journey heading east, once it had cleared the mountain range.

***

The shuttle docked at Central in a military facility that Kalen was unfamiliar with. Looking around, Kalen saw that the rest of the docking bays were empty. They appeared to be in a holding area, detached from the main base. There were no other craft within view and he tried to calculate the time. Taking into account the length of the journey, it was past twenty hundred hours in the U-Zone and day end. The Ea-Zone should have control of the city and the military terminal.

The soldiers escorted him off the craft and into a building where another officer, wearing a triangular badge, waited to meet him.

"We have arranged for the Ea-Zone to take custody of you," the officer said formally. "Follow me."

The officer led Kalen and the two soldiers escorting him down a short corridor that was blocked at the end by a large metal door. The officer pressed a control panel on the wall and the door slid aside to reveal the metal framework of a Gate. Behind it, crackling electricity fizzed within the scanner, sparking off the walls, floor, and ceiling, and bouncing off the thick metal archway. Flashes streaked across the corridor, between the sides of the arch, leaving tracers of bright white light. The officer pressed another button and the electric storm died. The door on the far side of the Gate remained closed.

"Proceed," the officer ordered and the soldiers pushed Kalen into the Gate.

He heard a noise and the door slid closed behind him. He was trapped in the Gate. *They'll kill me now*, he thought wildly. *Any moment now, they'll turn on the Gate and I'll fry.* The door at the end barred his exit. He began to walk towards it, fear weighing down every step. Another metre and he would be there. Suddenly he heard another noise and the door in front of him slid open, revealing the corridor beyond, where a soldier stood waiting for him.

***

Sun Hider, the Ea-Zone Divisional Director for the Colonisation Division, scowled at Kalen. He sat behind his desk, a solemn fat-faced man in late middle age with bushy eyebrows, fleshy jowls, and hair that had begun to recede and turn grey. The Military had handed Kalen over to civilian Security and they had brought Kalen straight to headquarters. Now Sun Hider was questioning him, his scowl growing darker with each of Kalen's answers.

Finally, Sun said, "You have a reputation for being unreliable and a troublemaker, and it was your neglect that caused the drill to run out of control. You're responsible for the accident and the deaths of those men."

Before Kalen could object he went on, "You'll be charged with gross negligence particularly as you have a history of this sort of thing. There was a cave-in at one of your previous assignments and that will be taken into account. There's also a note on your file that you tried to enter the U-Zone at Area Twenty."

"The accident wasn't my fault. There was nothing wrong with the drill," Kalen said tersely, fighting to control his anger.

"You'll get a chance to say what you want later. We'll see if Sera Ethern corroborates your story about Jorge Narve. Until formal charges are brought, you are suspended and forbidden to leave Central. See your Supervisor, Halle Rison, on the way out," Sun replied, dismissing him.

Kalen left Sun's office and found that the security guards had gone.

***

When Halle saw him in the doorway of her office, she stared at him speechless for a moment, then ran to him and entwined her arms around his neck.

"I thought you were dead. I thought I'd lost you. I can't believe you're back."

"I nearly didn't make it." He caught hold of her hands to remove them from his neck. "Not now." He continued to hold her hands to soften the effect of his actions.

She searched his eyes. "Do you still love me?"

"Of course," he replied, taken off balance. He wasn't sure what he felt anymore except for a deep rage about what had happened. He didn't love her, of that he was certain, but a tiny residue of feeling still remained. He didn't want to lie to her, but he needed her support. She had dressed to seduce, leaving the top of her jacket unfastened to give a glimpse of her breasts, and she was all soft curves and smelled of roses. "You look very nice."

"When I thought you were dead, I realised how much I loved you." She reached up to him again, pulled his face to hers, and kissed him.

He drew back. "Halle, a lot of things have happened in the last few days. Sun Hider is blaming me for the accident."

She stepped back from him and dropped her hands. "I know and we have to discuss it. They've replaced you at Three-Craters already. They've broken through the rock-fall and retrieved the bodies."

Kalen visualised Dan's body lying in the darkness and for a moment, he imagined himself lying there, in place of Dan, and then the screams of the miners rang in his ears and he was back in the rock-fall at Area Nine with the black crow pecking at his back. He mentally shook it off.

"You know about the charges?" he asked, unable to keep the anger out of his voice. She returned to her seat behind her desk and he sat down as well.

"I was told before you got here. You've changed, there's something different about you." She looked at him quizzically.

"Of course I've changed! I was nearly killed!" Kalen raised his voice. "Someone sabotaged the drill!"

Halle stared at him. "What do you mean?"

"The drill was sabotaged to make it run out of control," he said angrily.

Halle fixed him with a hard look and said firmly, "I've read the report. They're blaming you for the drill being faulty. Why would someone want to sabotage it?"

"Maybe they wanted to delay construction, but I know there was nothing wrong with the drill before we started to move it. Dan and his team ran a thorough check." He wouldn't tell her about Jorge yet. Not until he knew he could trust her.

"That's not what the report says. They've inspected the drill and its speed unit was faulty."

"That can't be right. Dan checked all that."

"Didn't you help him?"

"That's right. His team assisted as well."

"You were the senior engineer there. You were senior to Dan, which made it your responsibility to check that the drill was in running order, not his."

"It was in running order," Kalen insisted.

"Not according to the post-accident inspection."

"The unit must have been damaged in the accident."

"The report discounts that theory." Halle softened her voice. "Are you sure you didn't make a mistake?"

"There was a remote console for the drill," he explained. "If someone had used it they could have overridden the manual controls."

"The report makes no reference to a remote being used."

"One of Jorge's team was carrying it. I think it was used to sabotage the drill."

"Do you know the name of the person?"

"I didn't know the man. He was with another miner, but after the accident I don't know what happened to him."

Halle looked him straight in the eye. "You will be charged, Kalen. They want someone to blame for the accident."

"When they hear the evidence, I'll be cleared."

"No you won't and your career will be finished. I don't want that to happen." Her voice choked with emotion.

"I haven't seen the report yet. Can you get me a copy?"

"I haven't officially got a copy yet. I managed to get a look in advance but they have to provide it when they charge you."

"I'll dispute the findings. I'll demand another inspection of the drill."

"It will be too late then. Inspecting the drill won't do any good, and you have no witnesses. Dan and the other men who worked on it are dead."

"So they'll find me guilty?" He knew what she was going to say.

"They intend to make an example of you. The sentence is likely to be severe, probably a minimum of five years detention. There's pressure from the U-Zone to punish someone."

"So what do you suggest I do?" Kalen asked. His anger simmered and churned in his stomach.

"There is another way," Halle said, looking at him earnestly. "Make yourself useful to the Division and they won't charge you."

"How can I do that?"

"Complete your report on Three-Craters attributing the power failures to normal fluctuations and drop any reference to rebuilding where there's Uveid. Attribute the rest of the problems to human error and natural causes."

Kalen looked at her sharply. "Why do you want me to whitewash the problems there?"

"It isn't a whitewash. The professional opinion of the Division's geologists in Central is that the Uveid can be dealt with by normal measures, and everything points to the power supply being insufficient. The site is very important to Taidor and the Governing Council wants it completed as soon as possible."

"So they want to get rid of me to stop me talking?"

"Of course not." Halle looked offended. "If you make yourself important to the Division, they won't do anything to discredit you, although there'll still be an enquiry into the accident."

"And what do I say about the accident with the drill?" Kalen asked, curious to know what Halle would say next. She had it all worked out.

"You would accept that the speed unit malfunctioned and say that you can't explain it, but point out that Dan was riding at the drill's controls, and suggest that he must have missed something. You must blame Dan and say that perhaps he did something when he was at the controls that caused the problem."

He considered his options while he gazed into her innocent blue eyes and began to question her feelings for him. Did she really care for him or was she just using him? Was she playing and manipulating him to get what she wanted? He didn't trust her anymore. If he didn't co-operate he would be tried and sent off world, but if he fabricated a report there would be other accidents and other deaths at Three-Craters. He wasn't sure he could do that, but if he let Halle believe that he was going to acquiesce then it would give him more time to think it through.

"It doesn't look as if I've got much choice."

"You haven't. Let's put this behind us. Are you coming to my room tonight?" Halle asked.

"Do you think that's wise given the position that I'm in? If we're seen together it could damage your career. We should wait a few days until this is over."

Halle looked disappointed. "You're right but let's not wait too long. I've missed you a lot."

Chapter Twenty-Nine

Kalen learned that Sera had been taken to an Ea-Zone medical facility on the south side of Central to be treated for exhaustion. Since their night in the shuttle, he had thought about her constantly, remembering her dark eyes and smooth skin, and he wanted to see her again. This might be his last chance. The Division could arrest him without warning and he wanted to see her one final time. He had been back in Central for nearly two days and so far had put off writing the report, but pressure was mounting and he didn't have much time left.

Leaving his accommodation, he took the nearest Gate into the city, passing Ije who gave him a cheerful smile. In the city streets, throngs of people meandered about the shops and restaurants in the sunlight, vibrant in colourful clothes. Had there always been so many people in the city? After the emptiness of the plantation, the streets seemed overcrowded, and he became aware of the pervasive smell of cooking from the restaurants, as he pushed his way through the crowds.

He found the hospital easily, passing back through a Gate to enter the facility, and the reception gave him directions to Sera's room. He passed nurses in white uniforms and smelled antiseptic. At Sera's door, he paused and listened for the sounds of other visitors before pressing the entry button. Sera admitted him and the door slid aside to reveal a small neat room, with bed, table and chairs, and a combined entertainment and work console. Sera sat curled up in an easy chair, reading. She looked up when Kalen came in and began to smile, but the smile quickly died from her eyes and she adopted a closed expression. She looked drawn and tired.

"Hello, how are you feeling?" he asked.

"I'm fine. I'm just here for a rest," she said stiffly.

"I wanted to see that you were okay." He wondered what was wrong. This wasn't the Sera he knew.

"I was dehydrated, but I'm fine now."

"How long will you be here for?" Kalen asked, sitting down on the corner of the bed.

"Two more days," she said and paused before continuing. "I got a call from Halle Rison."

"Why did she call you?" So it was Halle; he should have guessed.

"She asked me about the accident and the trip through the caves."

"Did she say anything else?"

"Not really." Sera looked away from him uncomfortably.

"What is it Sera? Did Halle say something about me? It's all right, you can tell me."

Tears welled up in Sera's eyes and she stuttered, "She said… she said to keep away from you, that you were her partner."

"Oh Sera, you mustn't pay any attention to her. She's always been jealous of me ever since I started reporting to her." Kalen moved over to her chair and took hold of her hands. They were creamy pale and soft. "Now, don't be silly."

He bent over and kissed her and she didn't resist, her lips parting under his and her hands reaching up to him. Pulling her up into his arms, he kissed her again, this time slowly, and put his arms around her so that her head rested on his chest. She snuggled against him. Her body was soft beneath the thin silky material of her top and trousers and he held her even closer and kissed her again. He wished they were elsewhere—somewhere they wouldn't be interrupted, but this was a hospital and someone could come in at any moment. There were also things he needed to tell her and he didn't have much time.

"Can we see each other when I leave here?" Sera murmured in his ear.

"I hope so. But I need to talk to you. Here, let's sit on the bed."

He took her hand and she sat down next to him.

He said quietly, "I'm being blamed for the accident. They're going to charge me with negligence. I could get five years in prison."

"No! They can't do that!" Sera exclaimed, her face draining of colour. "Halle Rison didn't tell me that."

"I was involved in another cave-in before Three-Craters. They're going to bring that up as well."

"I don't understand. The accident was caused by the drill running out of control. Why are they blaming you? You weren't even on it."

"They're saying that it was faulty and I was the senior engineer, so it was my responsibility to check that it was running properly before we moved it. I know that there was nothing wrong with it. I helped Dan and his team with the inspection before it was moved."

"When I was brought back they asked me a lot of questions about what happened and I told them what I'd seen, but I don't know anything about machinery. What are you going to do?"

"Halle says that she can get me off the charges if I do a report playing down the problems at Three-Craters. Do you know if you're going to be sent back there?"

"I've been told that I'm going to be re-assigned in another couple of weeks and until then I'll be staying in Central."

"So you're not being sent back to Three-Craters?" Kalen probed.

"No, I've already been replaced. I have a new Duplicate as well."

"That's probably for the best. There were too many problems at that site."

"But I wanted to continue my tests on the Uveid, and now I won't be able to," Sera said earnestly. "The Division originally questioned my analysis of the strength of the Uveid seams and I'm sure they're wrong. I've been told that the Division are still looking at my results but I don't need to be involved anymore."

"Can't you continue your research anyway?"

Sera frowned. "No, I've been denied access to my records from Three-Craters and told that they're classified. I've been told that my replacement will take over my research there."

"Is that standard practice?" *So the Division was covering up her results*, he thought. He shouldn't have been surprised.

"No it isn't. Usually I would be given full access to my records from previous assignments so that I could carry on with any research that I needed to do. There's also something else." Sera hesitated, searching his face, as if deciding whether to tell him. "When I found the Uveid at Three-Craters I couldn't identify it from the official database. I thought I'd read about something similar, but I couldn't find any reference to it, so I registered it as a new mineral. Since I've been back in Central, I've searched the records again. I've found out that the Uveid had been discovered before, but for some reason it wasn't registered officially!"

"I think you should let it go. There will be other sites and other minerals to analyse," Kalen said, suddenly afraid for her.

"You don't understand. There was Uveid at Area Nine, where you were stationed." Sera met his eyes and he realised that she knew his secret.

"Why were you looking at the records for Area Nine?" he asked sharply.

Sera shuffled slightly. "You were muttering about Area Nine when you were asleep in the caves and I wanted to see where you'd been posted before Three-Craters. I didn't know you'd been involved in an accident but when I saw there'd been a rock-fall, professional curiosity got the better of me and I had to find out why it happened." Sera took a breath before continuing in a quieter voice. "I couldn't see anything that would explain why the roof would cave in like that, so I kept on looking. It took me hours of searching, but buried in the geologist's report is a reference to finding strange blue rocks with sharp and pointy ends. He describes the rocks as 'pyramid shaped' so he must have been referring to the Uveid. The geologist was killed in the accident and there's no other record of the blue rocks."

Kalen stared at her. "That still doesn't prove anything."

Sera gazed at him frankly. "Yes, it does—all the records show that the area had been stabilised and should have been structurally sound. The geologist found the Uveid in the level above the accident site and from its location, I'm sure that it must have caused the rock-fall—it was simply too fragile to support the structure."

Disbelief, relief, and anger swept over Kalen in quick succession. Why hadn't he been told before? Could she be mistaken? He stared into Sera's brown eyes, momentarily speechless.

"I thought you would want to know," she said, blushing, and looked away from him again. "I wasn't meaning to pry. You're not angry are you?"

"No, no—are you sure about all this? That the Uveid caused the rock-fall?"

"I read through all the reports and there's no reference to any analysis of the Uveid or that it's fragile, but it was found in a location that would have weakened the whole level."

"Thank you for telling me. I always thought I was responsible."

"You weren't to blame. The accident wasn't your fault."

Kalen laughed. "I feel as if a weight's been lifted off me! All this time, I've thought it was my fault, even though I've never been able to figure out what happened, and now you tell me that there was a weak seam running through the works! That makes sense but I think it's probably too late to clear my name."

"Do you think there's a cover up at Three-Craters?" she asked suddenly.

"At the beginning I wasn't sure but now I do."

"So are you going to write the report they've asked you to do?"

He took both of her hands in his. "I haven't completely made up my mind but no, I don't think so. I came to say goodbye in case I didn't see you again. I've possibly got another couple of days before they arrest me when they realise that I'm not going to co-operate."

"I'll tell them that the accident wasn't your fault and about the Uveid and that it caused the accident at Area Nine." She looked distraught. "They can't arrest you for something that you haven't done!"

"Come here." He gathered her in his arms so that her head was resting on his shoulder and her warm breath tickled his neck. "It's my problem and I don't want you to get involved. Don't worry about me, I can look after myself."

He kissed her gently, slipping his hands around her waist.

She gazed into his eyes. "I love you," she said.

He didn't reply, but held her close and kissed her again.

***

Back in his room in the Ea-Zone block, Kalen sat staring at the desk screen pondering whether to call Halle. What was he going to tell her? That the Uveid caused the accident at

Area Nine and that all this time there had been a mistake? That wouldn't make any difference to the problems that he had now. She was loyal to the Division and probably wouldn't do anything. His last Narquum had begun to wear off and he shook another pill out of the packet.

The small green pill lay in the palm of his hand and he looked at it thoughtfully. He had started taking Narquum after Area Nine but why was he still taking it? His leg ached occasionally but it was a long time since he'd needed a painkiller for his body. He took Narquum to numb his mind, he admitted to himself. Numb his mind from the guilt of Area Nine, to let him forget that he'd killed those men. But he knew now that he hadn't killed those men, so why did he need the Narquum? He didn't need to hide from himself anymore.

He could never be part of a conspiracy to cover up the problems at Three-Craters and on some level, he'd always known that. The consequences of his refusal to co-operate with the Division would never outweigh the guilt that he would suffer if he gave in. He flipped the pill over with his thumb and studied the pattern etched into it and remembered all the times that he'd agonised over the accident at Area Nine, asking himself again and again why it had happened, feeling crushing guilt at being responsible for it all. He'd hated himself for what happened but none of it had been his fault. He'd suffered all of that guilt and shame for a lie. He'd preferred to accept what others told him instead of trusting himself. He'd beaten himself up for nothing.

Anger gripped him. He stood up, threw the packet of Narquum at the wall, and pressed his fists to his temples. He was angry at the Division and angry at himself. He must never let the Division manipulate him again and the first thing he had to do was stop numbing his brain with drugs. Twenty-four hours, perhaps forty-eight, and the physical symptoms would be over; the sweating, trembling, and sickness would go. He could stay in his room; he had enough provisions to sit the withdrawal out. He could do it now that he knew the truth and when they came to arrest him, he would be free of the drugs and the guilt and be able to think clearly.

Chapter Thirty

Without warning, the door to Sera's hospital room slid open and two black clad soldiers appeared. She had been lounging in an easy chair and she looked up, startled, and screamed. In a flash, they grabbed her arms with gloved fingers that dug into her flesh and wrenched her up, holding her in a vicelike grip. A third soldier, an officer, strode in after them and planted himself in front of her. She struggled to free herself and opened her mouth to scream again, but the officer stepped forward and hit her across the face with the flat of his hand. The force of the blow jarred her head backwards.

"Bitch! Shut up!" he shouted.

The officer hit her again, this time harder across her cheek. It stung painfully and her eyes watered. She blinked the tears out of her eyes and tried to focus on him. He was dressed in a black uniform with three vertical gold stripes arranged just below the right shoulder of his jacket and wore a peaked hat that was similarly adorned with gold stripes. He glared at her, his tiny piggy eyes sparkling and the corners of his thin lips twisted into a smirk.

"You're under arrest for sedition," he barked.

"What? I haven't done anything," she cried. Her face had begun to throb from the blows and her neck ached.

"You heard me. We're taking you into detention," he sneered.

"This is a mistake! Why are you arresting me?"

"You are Sera Ethern aren't you?"

"Yes," she sobbed. This couldn't be happening; there had to be some mistake. She hadn't done anything.

"No mistake." He reached for a pair of handcuffs hanging on his belt.

"Please don't put those on me," she pleaded, a tear rolling down her cheek.

He hesitated and let go of the handcuffs. "Don't try anything."

The soldiers dragged her out of the room and along a corridor towards a closed door. There was no one else in the corridor and on the other side of the door, the passageways were silent and empty. Further on, she was propelled into a small lobby and pushed into an elevator that ascended for several seconds. The doors opened onto the roof of the building where more soldiers waited beside an empty monorail car. They bundled her into the car and climbed in after her so that she was surrounded. The doors closed and after a short pause, the monorail moved off, almost soundlessly.

"You're making a mistake. I've done nothing wrong," she repeated.

The officer fixed her with an icy stare but didn't reply. Sera looked out of the window. They were heading north across the city towards the transport terminals and interplanetary docks.

"Where are you taking me?" she asked.

"You'll find out."

"You said I was under arrest, but the detention centre is the other way."

The officer sneered. "That isn't where traitors go."

"I don't understand," she stammered and began to shake. "What are you talking about? I haven't done anything!" She said a silent prayer. She must trust in the power of the God-force if she was going to get through this.

They were nearing the edge of the city now, and ahead, Sera could see the shuttle bays and further on the massive structure of the docks for the interplanetary ships. Surely they weren't going to take her off world? If not, then they must still intend to take her out of the city.

The monorail crawled above the rooftops and veered off towards the shuttle terminal. It was mid-afternoon and below her, the streets teemed with people. She tried to collect her thoughts. If they took her out of the city, she wouldn't have access to anyone who could help her. The officer knew her name and had called her a traitor so her arrest wasn't a mistake. Nothing made sense, but if she didn't escape now she wouldn't get another chance. She had to stop them taking her out of the city. She looked around the car but she couldn't think of a way to escape while it was moving.

The monorail slowed as it approached the shuttle terminal and then slid along the rail behind the docking bays and into a dark industrial area. It travelled through a forest of huge machinery and emerged at the far side of the docking bays, near a building. In the distance, a shuttle rested on a docking platform and in front of it, people milled around a public concourse. The monorail stopped and the car doors opened, letting in the roar of a departing shuttle high above and the sound of loud machinery. The soldiers on each side of her gripped her arms again and pulled her out of the car. She didn't resist.

"It's okay, I'll come quietly," she said.

A soldier approached the monorail and saluted the officer.

"I have another one," the officer said.

The soldier nodded. "Bay ten, sir."

The soldiers marched her towards a building nearby. There was another shuttle dock behind it, obscured from public view, where a small military shuttle with Ea-Zone markings sat. She stared at the military shuttle. There was something odd about it, but she couldn't pin it down. A thunderous roar of engines suddenly drowned out all other sounds, and at the entrance to the building, another soldier waited.

Saluting the officer, the soldier shouted, "Better get inside sir, the public shuttle's just about to leave."

She was led into a waiting area with no windows, where a dishevelled looking man sat handcuffed to a bench by one of his wrists. He looked up hopefully as she was led in, but when he saw that she was also a prisoner, despair washed over his face and he slumped down again. The officer pushed her down next to him onto the bench and the other soldiers took up position at the door. After several minutes, the thunderous roar became louder for a few moments and then faded away.

In the quiet aftermath, she heard voices. "Can we board now? There's only these two."

"Not yet sir, there's another shuttle coming in."

While she waited, the other prisoner shuffled nervously and wriggled his handcuffed wrist several times as if unconvinced of the strength of the restraint. He tapped the fingers of his other hand intermittently on the bench. She glanced at him sideways and he caught her glance, and for an instant, his fearful eyes met hers. Until then her arrest had seemed unreal, something temporary that would soon be resolved, but his fear was contagious and she became aware of her thudding heart. Once she was on the military ship, they could take her anywhere and no one would ever know.

Sera heard the roar of another shuttle landing, and after the noise had subsided, soldiers came into the room and released the man from the bench, handcuffed his hands behind his back, and hauled him to his feet. Two other soldiers pulled Sera up and hustled her out of the building after him. Far off, on the other side of the concourse, the public shuttle had opened its doors and people were getting off.

The prisoner in front of her began to struggle and his captors dragged him forward by his arms. When he stumbled, they jerked him up violently, his legs gave way, and he sagged against them, forcing them to take his weight. As the guards tried to pull him up again, the man suddenly regained his footing and threw himself against one of them, knocking him off balance. The other guard fought to maintain his grip on him, but the man wrenched himself free. Using the full weight of his body, he rammed his shoulder into the first guard and sent him crashing down, and then turned and began to run.

At that moment, the guards holding her arms let go, and started forward after the running man. From behind her, she could already hear the sound of more soldiers running towards them, but for a brief moment, she was unrestrained. *This is my chance*, she thought, launching herself into a wild run towards the public concourse. If I can get to the people, I might be able to get away.

She heard shouting, "Stop! Stop, or we'll shoot!"

Sera carried on running as fast as she could, fighting to catch her breath, her chest aching with exertion. She heard more shouts and the thunder of boots, but she kept on going, using all of her strength to propel herself forwards. The people around the public shuttle were a hundred metres away across an open space. The soldiers sounded closer and she forced herself to increase her pace, focusing on the crowd ahead, but her legs ached and she was nearly out of breath. A stitch in her side stabbed sharply but she ignored it and kept on running. Behind her, the shouting got louder and a post to her left suddenly burst into flames. *That's a warning shot*, she thought. Next time they would aim at her. She put her head down and charged forward.

***

Sunlight created dappled patterns across the rooftop. Kalen stood near the edge of the flat roof, looking out over the buildings of Central and the streets far below. There were no other people on the roof. He had discovered this place by accident when he was called out to inspect the dome's thick metal safety roof after one of its wings would not retract. Looking down, he had seen the huge water tanks spread out across the flat roof, one of a handful of water installations dotted throughout the city.

The installation was situated high above the city's rooftops, nearly at the level of the rim of the crater, and accessed by a series of mesh gangways and steep steps. Kalen had not been put off by the restricted signs or the climb and had been rewarded with empty space and a good view over Central. He had fallen into the habit of climbing to the water tanks when he wanted to be alone and now he stared out over the rooftops towards the shuttle docks and watched a ship depart, ascending from the terminal on its docking platform.

"I have to leave Central," he said to himself. He had the means now, he thought, remembering the identity cards that he had stolen that morning.

It had been a hellish two days. He had gone through every stage of withdrawal, first the shaking, then the sweating and the vomiting, and burned hot and cold as if he had a fever. At times the black malevolence that had engulfed him at Area Nine had returned and he was back again in the churning depths of hell, but this time it had been different. This time he had shaken off the dark images, been able to rise above the dark depths and got free. He was whole, for the first time in a long while, he admitted to himself. He would never touch Narquum again, he didn't need it. Now he had a decision to make.

"Where can I go?" he said aloud.

The sunlight dazzled his eyes and he turned back towards one of the water tanks and sat down in its shade. He still had the small piece of piping from Three-Craters and he took it out of his pocket. It intrigued him and he twirled the tiny cylinder between his fingers, studying the markings on its side. Perhaps it didn't come from the machinery at Three-Craters? Perhaps Palum Kingston or one of the other tourists had dropped it? Why had Kingston died?

The sound of a footstep near him broke his reverie and he looked up to see Sera standing by one of the water tanks. She had a bright red mark running across her cheek and her eyes were pink and puffy. He got up and went to her.

"I remembered you telling me that you came to the water tanks." Her voice cracked and she began to sob. "I hoped you'd be here."

Kalen put his arms around her. "Are you all right? What happened?"

She rested her head on his chest. "They came to the hospital."

"Who came?" He stroked her hair tenderly.

"They were soldiers in black uniforms. One of them hit me across the face," she said numbly.

"Here, let me look." He gently put his hand under her chin, and studied the mark on her face. "You're just a little bruised. You'll be okay."

"They said I was under arrest."

"What for?" He was puzzled. Why would they arrest Sera?

"Sedition, and working against the interests of the Government. I told them that I didn't know what they were talking about." She buried her face in his jacket.

"Did they say any more than that?"

"No, but they knew my name." She choked back a sob. "They fired at me when I ran for it. Why did they arrest me? Why did they accuse me like that?"

He hugged her to him. "Here, don't cry. You're safe now."

"They took me to the shuttle docks but I got away from them. I ran until I was in the crowds at the shuttle terminal and managed to lose them. I didn't know what to do," she gulped.

"Did they say who ordered your arrest? The Division uses regular Security, not the Military." Was it possible that the Colonial Council was involved?

"No, they just said I was under arrest. They were going to put me on an Ea-Zone ship." Her sobbing began to subside.

"Why do you think it was an Ea-Zone ship?"

"It had 'Ea' on the side of it."

"That's strange."

"Why?"

"I've never seen any military vehicles actually zone marked. Both zones share the same craft and neither zone, so far as I know, is allowed to appropriate them for individual zone use. The other thing is that it means your arrest was either ordered or endorsed by the Ea-Zone."

"Perhaps the military don't share?"

"The military must share in the same way as the other Government departments. There are insufficient resources for single zone use. Come and sit in the shade." He led her into the shade of one of the tanks and sat down beside her.

"I don't understand," she said.

"I think the Division is hiding something at Three-Craters, but I don't know what it is. I think that it's connected to the problems they've been having there. I was told that they disputed your view on the pressures that the Uveid could withstand, but I think there's more to it than that. I think that your hospital room must have been bugged and they were listening to you telling me about the Uveid at Area Nine."

"I still don't understand. The Division can't ignore the weakness of the Uveid. If they try and build on the levels where there are Uveid seams, the levels won't take the weight and there could be rock-falls."

Kalen was silent for a moment, his gaze resting on the pools of light and shadow on the roof in front of him. "There's something important that the Division is trying to hide. I think the drill was sabotaged and that's why it crashed. There were two miners with a remote control and I think they used it to sabotage the drill, to try to kill me. Do you remember seeing them?"

"I remember seeing a miner holding a console when the drill was being turned. He was with another man, and after the turn, I didn't see them again. I thought they were walking behind the drill."

"I have to find out what's going on, but it isn't safe for either of us to stay in Central. Even if I co-operated with the Division, once they had no further use for me, they'd get rid of me anyway."

"They'll trace us if we try to leave," Sera pointed out.

"No they won't. I've stolen new identity cards for us," Kalen said. "I saw one of my neighbours on the terraces with his daughter, so I stole their identity cards from their rooms. He's elderly and hardly ever goes into Central so he won't miss the card. The daughter has young children and she'll think they've taken her card as a prank. They don't usually check age at the terminals unless there's some kind of query."

"How did you know I was coming with you?"

"I didn't, but I thought I'd take the other card in case it was useful and I sort of hoped I'd see you again," he said, smiling. He brushed her hair off her face and kissed her. "I've thought about you a lot over the last couple of days."

"I want to be with you," she said.

"Good," he said, taking out two cards and handing her one. "I'm Travis Reinhard and you are Natasha Reinhard."

"Where are we going?"

"We're going to Morten to get some answers."

***

A security guard stood on each side of the main entrance to the transport terminal and Kalen's heart sank when he saw them. *They're looking for us*, he thought. They had made it through the city but now they had to get past more guards. Beyond the entrance, the central concourse was filled with people, the hum of their voices carrying into the street outside. The guards' eyes scanned the constant flow of people passing by them and Kalen guessed there would be more guards inside. Ahead of him, a large party of workers walked together in a pack towards the entrance. Taking hold of Sera's hand, he swiftly walked forward and wormed his way into the middle of the group, who did not seem to notice them.

"Don't look at the guards," Kalen whispered to Sera and felt her hand tremble.

Beyond the entrance, hundreds of people moved about the concourse and security guards stood in the corners observing the crowd. Leaving the group of workers, Kalen found a line to buy tickets. Security cameras fixed to buildings and posts ringed the concourse, monitoring the lines of people. Nearby, a guard lolled against a wall, watching the queue.

Kalen turned his back to the guard and said to Sera, "Don't look at him and try not to let the cameras get a shot of your face. There's a transport to Morten that leaves tonight. We should be able to get tickets—it's still early. Don't worry, just act normally and pretend you're my wife."

He glanced over his shoulder but the guard had disappeared. The line moved slowly and it took several minutes for them to get to the booth. Kalen bought two tickets to Morten and paid using Travis Reinhard's card. The clerk checked the identity cards and Reinhard's credit and appeared to notice nothing unusual. Kalen thanked the Planets that the old boy had enough credit in his account.

"There you are, sir, two tickets to Morten. Have a good journey."

The clerk smiled and handed Kalen the cards and tickets. Kalen felt relieved. The theft hadn't been reported yet. But it would be, and when it was, the Division would trace the tickets and know that they'd gone to Morten. He took hold of Sera's hand again and they walked away from the ticket booth. Near the rear of the line, the guard was no longer lolling against the wall, but speaking to a man and woman about the same age as Sera and him.

"We can board early. We'll stay in our cabin until it leaves," Kalen said.

They made their way through the crowd and joined another line to go through the barriers. Kalen counted the minutes as they waited. If they were discovered now it would all be for nothing, he thought. They would be imprisoned and sent off world, at the very least. He restrained an impulse to look at two guards standing nearby and reminded himself that he didn't need Narquum now.

They were nearing the barrier and the inspector. Anxious questions ran through Kalen's mind. Once they were on the transport they would be safe until Morten, but would Sera go along with his plan? How would she react when she found out? His plan was risky but it was their only chance.

"Tickets and IDs please," the inspector said.

Kalen handed him the tickets and cards and waited. After a cursory glance, the inspector handed them back.

"Have a good journey," the inspector said, waving them through.

Chapter Thirty-One

As the transport entered Morten, Kalen stared out of the window, thinking about the risks they faced. The journey had been without incident, but by now the theft of the Reinhard cards would have been discovered and Security had probably traced their journey. Sera sat opposite him gazing at the buildings they were passing.

"We're nearly there. Remember, they'll be looking for us here, too," he told her.

Sera shuddered. "I thought we'd be safe once we got out of Central?"

"They probably know we're on this transport. We need to get off it quickly before they start searching."

The terminal came into view and the transport slowed to a stop. Kalen opened the compartment door to the passageway where people scuttled about gathering luggage. Motioning Sera to follow him, he squeezed through the throng and jumped down onto the platform. The only security guards he could see were at the far end of it. Taking Sera by the hand, he led her to the exit of the terminal, where he paused to survey the street.

"This looks even more crowded than Central," Sera said.

"It's Taidor's second city. It will be pretty busy."

"Hey, don't just stand there, you're in the way!" a passer-by shouted angrily, jostling him.

Kalen took Sera's arm and began to walk.

"Where are we going?" Sera asked.

"We're going to spend the day in the city, and then at day end we're going to the Division's offices."

Sera looked confused. "But I thought you'd been accused by the Division? You told me that you were called in by the Divisional Director, Sun Hider. His superior is the Divisional Commander and he's based in Central."

"The Division deals with a lot of work from Morten. We need to find someone in the Division who isn't part of the cover up at Three-Craters and I know someone who usually works here."

"The corruption might go right to the top," Sera said. "If it were that easy we could have gone to headquarters in Central."

"There's no one to help us in Central, but there might be someone here who can do something."

"Then why do we need to wait until day end?"

"He won't be back until then."

"Who?" Sera persisted.

"I think it would be best if I didn't tell you who it is just yet. If you're arrested you can truthfully say that I was simply taking you to the Division's offices to look for help. Right now, I think we should go and get some breakfast."

***

The Division's offices in Morten were located in the middle of the city and Kalen had no trouble finding the building. He had been there once before and had a clear memory of the large reception area. He thought he had timed their visit perfectly. It was now nearly day end, but the public lobby was still full of people, and he ushered Sera to the end of a line to use the public consoles at the rear of the room. While they were waiting, Kalen studied the overhead security cameras that monitored the hall.

"Keep your back to the cameras," Kalen said. "The Division won't be looking for us in here, but the monitors may still pick us up."

When it was Kalen's turn to use the console, he brought up a list of departments and personnel and memorised the information. Satisfied, he switched off the console and with Sera behind him, squeezed through the crowd to the far corner of the lobby, where they were obscured from the view of the cameras. The crowd began to thin and the lines at reception became shorter.

"What are we going to do?" Sera asked.

"Get your Division badge out, but don't show it to anyone yet," Kalen replied.

He glanced at his watch and then at the lines before reception as if he was considering whether he still had time to queue and finish his business that day. The first siren for day end sounded and the staff started to close their stations. Several more security guards appeared and stood watching as people began to leave and the lobby gradually emptied. A steady stream of workers began filing out of the staff doors at the far end of the lobby where a guard lingered.

"Now," Kalen said. "Follow me and use your badge."

"Won't they stop us when they see our names?"

"The guards aren't interested at day end—they haven't got time. They've got to start clearing the building so they won't bother us. Try to act as if it's normal for us to be here." He walked purposefully towards the staff doors and Sera followed him. A security guard stood in his path.

"Where are you going, sir? The exit is that way." The guard pointed towards the main doors.

Kalen flashed his badge. "We're working on an assignment and I need to collect something urgently for my team tomorrow. We'll only be a few minutes."

The guard glanced at Kalen's badge. "I haven't seen you here before, sir?"

"I'm usually on site and work out of Central," Kalen explained. "My colleague is working on the project with me."

Sera held up her badge and smiled at the guard. "We'll come straight back down. We've got a few minutes, haven't we?"

"Okay, but you need to be quick. We'll start clearing the floors in a few minutes and you need to be out before then."

The guard stood aside and they took the elevator to the fifth floor. Kalen chose a route through the network of empty corridors, by tracing numbers on doors until he found the office he was looking for. The door was locked. He punched a code into the keypad and it slid open.

"There's no one here," Sera said, peering into the empty office.

"Come inside. Quickly," Kalen whispered urgently, pulling her in. He locked the door behind them.

"What are you doing? The guards will find us," Sera said, alarmed.

"Halle told me that they don't search every single office at day end. If an office hasn't been used all day and the door is locked, they don't go in. They haven't got the codes for all the doors."

"Whose office is this? How did you know the code?"

"It's Halle's office. She's got two offices, one in Central and this one; although I don't think she comes to Morten very often. I know the door code for her office in Central and she once told me that the codes were the same for both offices."

Sera's face paled to a ghostly white and she took a step away from him. "She'll turn us in, she's one of them. Why?"

He caught hold of her hands and drew her towards him. "It's okay. We're not here to see her. So far as I know, she's still in Central."

The final siren sounded and moments later, he heard footsteps outside.

He put his index finger to his mouth. "Shush." The footsteps died away.

"Then why are we here?"

"We're waiting for Javed Durton, Halle's Duplicate. Halle told me that he usually works in Morton and he shares his office with her. If we can speak to Javed and tell him what's happened, we can ask the U-Zone to help us."

"What? We can't go to the U-Zone. They'll send us back and then we'll be punished for being out of time on top of everything else."

"We're already in trouble. I can tell Javed Durton what I know and ask him to help us. The U-Zone can insist that Early treats us fairly."

"This is crazy," Sera stuttered, eyes wide.

Kalen put his arms around her. "Don't worry, it will be all right. You'll see."

He stroked Sera's hair and waited. After several minutes, he heard more footsteps in the corridor.

"The U-Zone probably doesn't search locked offices either," he whispered. The footsteps paused outside the door and then moved on. "If Javed is anything like Halle he'll come in early but we can't guarantee it, so we could have a bit of a wait. You might as well sit down."

He pulled out a chair for Sera in front of the desk and looked around the office. It was similar to Halle's office in Central with the same layout and the same sort of desk and screen. He fancied that he could smell Halle's perfume lingering in the air and momentarily pictured her plump bust and golden hair. His eyes rested on Sera. She looked thin and her face had adopted sharp angles. She sat staring at him with large brown eyes, nervously fidgeting with her hands in her lap.

"What are you going to say to him?" she asked.

Before Kalen could reply, he heard a noise outside the door and stepped to one side of it.

"Come over here, so that he doesn't see you when he comes in," he whispered, beckoning to Sera.

The locking mechanism clicked and the door opened. A short, older man with a portly build walked into the room carrying a bag. He put his bag on the desk and took off his hat, revealing a bald pate. With hat in hand, he seemed to freeze for an instant, and then whirled around to face them with a startled expression. On the breast of his jacket, a triangular brooch gleamed in the light.

"Who are you?" the man demanded, his eyes fearful.

"Our names are Kalen Trinneer and Sera Ethern. We work for the Division," Kalen replied.

The man's eyes showed no sign of recognition. "How did you get in here? The office should have been locked." He began backing away towards the door.

"I already had the code so we let ourselves in to wait for you. I'm a chief engineer and Sera is a geologist. We wanted to speak to you."

"Why didn't you make an appointment? It's an offence to break into someone's office." The man glanced towards the exit. "Why shouldn't I call Security?"

"I usually work with Luther Stonway. He reports to you, doesn't he?"

"That's correct."

"I report to Halle Rison, your Duplicate."

The man glared at Kalen, a look of astonishment gradually washing over his face. "You're from the Ea-Zone? Are you insane? No wonder I didn't recognise your names. And you say you are a chief engineer, so why are you here, breaking zoning? It's a serious offence and I should call Security."

"You're Javed Durton, aren't you?" Kalen asked, eyeing the man's brooch. It had the number eleven set in the triangle.

"Yes, I am," Javed confirmed, still guarded.

"I'm Luther's Duplicate and I worked with Sera on site."

"So?"

"We both worked at Three-Craters and we were trapped in the rock-fall when the drill ran out of control on the fifty-fifth level. We need your help."

"Help? Why would you need my help?"

"I was ordered to write a report covering up the problems at Three-Craters," Kalen explained. "Miss Ethern discovered a very weak mineral called Uveid that can't take much weight but the Division disputed her findings. I was told to deal with the Uveid in the usual way, just by strengthening the areas where we couldn't avoid the seams. The Uveid can't be dealt with like that. It can't withstand heavy loads and can't be built on. I was also ordered to cover up problems with the power supply and illness on site."

"And did you?"

"No, I refused and then I was trapped in the rock-fall when the drill crashed. I believe the drill was sabotaged in an attempt to kill me."

"That's quite a story and a serious accusation! I know about the accident at Three-Craters, of course." Javed began to relax and took his chair behind the desk. "Even if there was a conspiracy to kill you and what you say is true, why have you come to me? Neither of you are even citizens of Unity!"

"We need someone important in the Division to support us."

"Go to Halle Rison." Javed folded his arms, scrutinising their faces.

"We can't. The Division is against us."

"The Division is not against you," Javed snapped and scowled. "Unity knows nothing of these matters."

"The Ea-Zone does," Kalen said.

"They tried to arrest me and said I was a traitor but I haven't done anything," Sera blurted out.

"Who tried to arrest you?"

"Government soldiers in black uniforms."

"The Government? You're suggesting that the Governing Council would frame someone? You're suggesting that Unity is involved?" Javed was scathing.

"Not Unity. The ship they tried to put me on was Ea-Zone."

"Why do you say that?" Javed swivelled his chair to face her and fixed her with a penetrating stare.

"It had Ea written on the side," she stammered.

Javed gave her a sharp look. "Are you sure?"

"Yes, I got a good look."

Javed frowned and fell silent, and then uncrossed his arms and addressed Kalen. "Sit, I'm listening."

"I've never found the cause of the problems at Three-Craters but I was told to write my final report blaming normal variables," Kalen said. "Reports were edited and information was withheld from me and I still haven't got the answers. When I got back to Central I was threatened with negligence charges unless I agreed to co-operate and cover up what was going on."

"The Division disputed my findings about the pressures the Uveid could withstand but their results didn't make sense," Sera added.

"That's right. I was ordered to treat the Uveid seams in the normal way in spite of the fact that it would leave the construction unsafe. I need to find out what's causing the problems at Three-Craters so that I can protect Sera and myself. I need to get some answers!"

Javed listened without interrupting, and when they had finished, he sat back and contemplated them.

"Our geologists also believe that the Uveid is very fragile and they have recommended that appropriate measures are taken to deal with it, but the Ea-Zone has disputed our results and rejected our recommendations on the basis that it would delay construction."

"Can't the U-Zone officially support Sera's findings and intervene on our behalf?" Kalen asked.

"All of this has already been put to the Ea-Zone and rejected. You've told me nothing new. I need something more from you, if you want the U-Zone to do anything."

"I think my reports were edited as well as Luther's reports," Kalen said.

"That's entirely possible. But our own staff came to much the same conclusions as you and considered everything you've covered," Javed replied.

"Do you know what's causing the problems at Three-Craters?"

"I've been advised that the rock-falls are caused by the Uveid and been given varying theories about the cause of the rest of the problems. If you've come to me looking for answers, you've come to the wrong place."

"I investigated the death of an Ea-Zone tourist, Palum Kingston. Were you advised about the accident on level forty-seven?" Kalen asked.

"Ahh… yes, it was a nasty accident involving a drill, I believe. He fell under one of the struts, didn't he? An unfortunate incident, but these things happen." Javed spread his hands.

"I still haven't found out the cause of the accident. I think the witness statements were edited. One of the tourists told me that Kingston thought that a man was waving him over to the drill, but there was no reference to it in the statements."

"That wouldn't surprise me. The Ea-Zone would be embarrassed by one of their workers causing the death of a tourist," Javed said.

"Even if he was waved over it still doesn't explain why he got so close to the drill."

"It isn't always possible to find the cause of an accident," Javed remarked.

Kalen remembered the bit of pipe that he had found. "When I searched the area after the accident, I found a little piece of tubing with marks on the side. It hadn't come off the drill so I didn't think that it was relevant at the time. I thought it must have broken off one of the smaller machines but I wasn't able to match it to any of the equipment on site. Someone must have dropped it and now I keep thinking that it must have been connected to the accident in some way."

Javed moved forward in his seat. "You found a piece of pipe that someone dropped?"

"I never found out where it came from, so I think someone must have dropped it."

"What did it look like?" Javed asked sharply.

"I kept it," Kalen said, taking the small cylinder out of his pocket. "Here, have a look."

"Is that it? Is that the bit you found?" Javed's fingers twitched on the desk surface.

"Yes, it's only a piece of broken pipe but it didn't come off any of the machines on level forty-seven."

"Please, may I have a look?" Javed asked, reaching forward to take it.

Kalen handed the cylinder to Javed who took it with shaking hands. He carefully examined it, turning the tube about and inspecting the ends with intense interest, a smile curling at the corners of his mouth.

"That's the piece I found at Three-Craters," Kalen said. Javed was now holding the tube up to the light to see it more clearly. "Do you think it's important?"

"You've had it all of this time? Luther found a similar piece near the accident site and it's possible that this part broke off it. I'll have to make enquiries. Please wait here."

Javed got up and hurried out of the room, taking the cylinder with him, and within minutes, Kalen heard marching footsteps that stopped outside the door.

***

Two hours later, the door opened and Javed came back into the room.

"I've made arrangements for you to be escorted back," Javed said, motioning towards two guards who appeared in the entrance.

"Wait! Can't you help us?" Kalen exclaimed.

"They'll take you to the nearest Gate and hand you over at day end. You'll be all right." Javed turned to leave.

"Please!" Kalen stood up. "Won't you help us?"

Javed hesitated. "How? Unity can't protect you in the Ea-Zone. We have no jurisdiction there."

"Then what are we going to do?" Sera asked. She was on her feet now, and they both stood staring at Javed who was looking at them impatiently.

"What do you want me to do?"

"We want the U-Zone to intervene on our behalf," Kalen replied.

"I've already told you, there's nothing I can do."

"You could support our case with the Division," Kalen insisted.

"Surely you can help us in some way?" Sera pleaded, her eyes watering.

Javed looked at Sera and his face softened. "Do you want to go back?"

"Of course I want to go back, I have family," Sera replied.

"You've been useful to Unity and there's a case for asylum if you ask for it. It's the only way I can help you."

"What do you mean?" Kalen asked. You were born in one zone, and lived and died there. People didn't transfer.

"You can ask the U-Zone for asylum and come and live here."

"I didn't think that was possible, no one is allowed to transfer," Kalen said.

"That's the position normally, but Unity will consider a request for asylum if there are grounds."

"We would be allowed to live here?" Sera asked.

"If your request is approved," Javed answered.

"But the Ea-Zone would never approve it," Kalen said. Halle would do everything she could to stop him leaving.

"Early wouldn't have any choice. You make your decision now and don't go back. You stay here. But if you do decide to stay, then we expect your full co-operation with the problems at Three Craters and the Uveid. You would have to be loyal to Unity and give up any ideas of returning to the Ea-Zone. But what has the Ea-Zone done for you? Do you really want to go back there after they tried to kill you? The fact that you came to us for help, will go greatly in your favour if you request asylum."

"But I'd never see my family or friends again. I would lose everyone," Sera said.

"You won't see them when you're in detention on a prison planet either," Javed said dryly. "If you came to the U-Zone you would be able to continue your research on the Uveid. And, we could use your expertise, Chief Trinneer, particularly about the problems at Three-Craters. But the decision is entirely yours. The U-Zone is sympathetic to your plight, but we don't need more people. Go back if you want."

"What would it involve?" Kalen asked.

"You would stay here and be assigned accommodation in the U-Zone blocks but you would keep your existing ranks and jobs in the Division. You can change your names if you want to but that isn't strictly necessary. We tell the Ea-Zone formally that you've defected and they record that you are no longer their citizens. They won't like it, of course, but there's nothing they can do about it."

"Would you be able to notify our families?" Sera asked.

"The Ea-Zone will notify them. From what you've told me, I think you'll be happier in Unity. We believe in honesty and core values and you'll be treated a lot better than you have been in Early."

Kalen looked at Sera. "Can you give us some time to discuss it?"

"I'll leave you here for half an hour, but I'll need your decision then. If you decide to leave I'll arrange for you to be escorted back." He left the room and the door closed behind him.

Chapter Thirty-Two

In the end, it hadn't been a hard decision to make, Sera recalled, as she sat in the monorail car travelling over Central. She had prayed for guidance and the answer had been simple. Stay, don't go back. Kalen sat beside her, and in front of her two security guards sat impassively, staring out of the window. Her only regret had been leaving her family. She wished that she'd had a chance to explain and say goodbye, but it was too late now.

Below her, steady streams of people moved along the street. They all walked in the same direction on one side of the street and the other way on the opposite side, the brooches pinned to their jackets twinkling gold in the sunlight. Rivers of people, Sera thought. The overcrowding was much better controlled here. People weren't lingering to talk to each other and getting in the way. It was like that in the U-Zone she mused. Everything was tightly controlled. When she walked in the street, she took care not to bump into other people and in turn, they didn't bump her. A refreshing change from the haphazard way the Ea-Zone operated.

"I'm glad we're here," she said.

"So am I," Kalen replied in a low voice.

"I mean, this is a wonderful opportunity to start a new life, a chance to start all over again."

"I know, and we're safe here."

She turned slightly and put her hand on his arm. He straightened up beside her, but said nothing, his jaw set in a hard line. He was wearing his formal uniform for the Allegiance Ceremony and he took his hat off and put it in his lap. His black hair sprung up in a disordered pattern, and he put a hand up and brushed it away from his forehead. *He's forgotten*, Sera thought. She was aware of her own hat, with small brim and neat band, which was still a novelty to wear. It was just another one of the things she would have to get used to, she supposed.

One of the guards sitting opposite gave Kalen a pointed look and said, "Hats are always worn in public."

She squeezed Kalen's arm and he quickly replaced his hat, saying nothing.

"You'll get used to our rules, they're for the good of everyone," the guard added.

"We're glad to be here after the way the Ea-Zone treated us," Sera replied.

"That's not surprising. I've heard they've got no morals. It's just a shame that we have to share the planet with them." The guard made a face as if he had a nasty taste in his mouth.

"You're right, but it wasn't our fault that we were born there," Sera agreed.

"If you work hard and obey the rules, you'll have a good life here," the guard said sympathetically.

"I'm sure we will, thank you."

"We're coming up to the administration building now. We'll take you to the hall where the Allegiance Ceremony will be held," the guard said.

The monorail crawled to a stop and they disembarked onto the roof of a large building. Inside, they were taken into a spacious room that had a table at one end with a handful of chairs set out in front of it. Sera recognised it as one of the meeting rooms, usually used by the Ea-Zone for informal work briefings. A sign hung on the wall behind the table, bearing the words 'Unity is Freedom.' On the table, there was a plaque with the word 'Unity' written on it and two brooches, each in the shape of a triangle.

"Those are our Divines!" Sera whispered to Kalen. "Isn't it exciting? This is the beginning of our new life."

He glanced towards her with a guarded smile but did not reply. There were already two people in the room, a man and a woman, both dressed in blue jackets and trousers, adorned only by triangular brooches pinned to the left side of their chests.

"The civilian administrator will arrive soon to take the ceremony and in the meantime you should sit here," the man said, indicating the chairs in front of the table. "We're the witnesses and we'll be standing behind you during the ceremony itself."

They sat down and waited for several minutes and then Sera heard the door at the rear of the room open.

The male witness hissed, "Stand!"

Sera stood up nervously at the same time as Kalen and a man in a dark blue uniform walked to the front and stood behind the desk.

"I'm the administrator and I'm here to conduct this ceremony of allegiance to the United Colonies Time System. Are you Kalen Trinneer and Sera Ethern?" he asked formally.

"Yes," Sera said.

A voice behind Sera hissed, "Sir!"

"Yes Sir, I mean," she said firmly.

"Yes Sir," Kalen said in a monotone beside her.

"Do you both understand that the declarations that you make today, shall be irrevocable and binding for the rest of your lives?"

"Yes Sir."

"Yes Sir."

"Kalen Trinneer and Sera Ethern, in front of these witnesses, do you now absolutely renounce your citizenship of the Early Colonial Time System and relinquish all rights of residence in that zone?"

"Yes Sir."

"Yes Sir."

"Do you absolutely relinquish all loyalty and connection with the Early Colonial Time System?"

***

While the administrator's voice droned on during the ceremony, Kalen's thoughts drifted to the events of the previous days. Once he had made the decision to join Unity, his rank had been confirmed and he had been debriefed about his experiences at Three-Craters. He had been told that he would be reporting to Javed, who had made it clear that he wanted his expertise on the problems at Three-Craters. Javed had asked him to come to Divisional headquarters in Central after the ceremony.

"We've matched the bit of tube you found with the piece we've got," Javed had said. "There's something I want to show you and I need your input. Come over when you're done with the administrator."

Kalen wondered what Javed had discovered. It seemed a long time since he'd found the cylinder after Kingston's death, but Javed spoke as if it had some kind of importance. He would find out as soon as he could get out of this place and see Javed, but for now, he stood in front of the administrator, repeating affirmations. Sera stood beside him, nodding fervently every time the administrator asked her a question and answering in a shrill voice.

"Do you now solemnly pledge allegiance to the United Colonies Time System and agree to be loyal citizens and abide by its laws, customs, and beliefs, so that from this time onwards all of your loyalties shall be owed to the United Colonies Time System and no other zone?" the administrator droned.

"Do you agree to take up residence in the United Colonies Time System and agree to instruction in the Divine and to uphold the values and moral conduct of the Divine?"

"Yes Sir," Sera said.

"Yes Sir," Kalen heard himself repeat, wondering what the administrator meant.

"Today, in front of these witnesses, you have affirmed your loyalty to the United Colonies Time System and renounced all other connections, and you are now granted citizenship of the United Colonies Time System." The administrator paused and picked up the brooches on the table in front of him. "As a citizen of Unity you are now entitled to wear the Divine and will wear it in all public places as a symbol of the true religion and your loyalty to Unity. Come forward."

The words washed over Kalen and he began thinking about Sera. She looked gaunt and had tied her hair back, but it hung lank and dull. Her eyes were bright and she appeared animated. They had only been in Unity a few days but she had changed in other ways as well. He had had no opportunity to be alone with her, but there was something different about her that he couldn't put his finger on. Her manner had subtly changed and she moved differently. The administrator had stopped talking and was staring at him with a scowl on his face. "I said, come forward."

Kalen took a step forward, and the administrator pinned one of the gold brooches on the breast of his jacket. It had a figure one in the middle of the triangle.

"Here is your Divine for you to wear with pride, and it is so marked to remind you that you are at the first stage of understanding. Instruction will be arranged, so that in time you will gain a greater understanding of the God-force and reach a higher stage of enlightenment. Step back."

Kalen watched while the administrator repeated the ceremony with Sera.

"Thank you," she trilled, her face flushing.

"Welcome to Unity," the administrator said.

Behind them, the witnesses began clapping.

***

Kalen was familiar with headquarters, but now it seemed different. Like the city, everything seemed muted and formal. The personnel that he passed in the corridors stared at him curiously. He wore full uniform but nobody recognised him and he wondered what they knew about him.

Their hard looks were almost hostile and from their stares, he guessed that they suspected he was from the Ea-Zone. No one chatted as they walked or laughed. Making the comparison, Kalen preferred the easy ways of the Ea-Zone but he was in Unity now and he couldn't go back.

There was another man with Javed when Kalen arrived at his office.

"This is Paul Neill, one of our top physicists. He's got something to show you. Remember the piping that you found? Well, we had a piece already that Luther found. It's a little bit different from yours—it's shaped like a 'V' but it has similar markings on the outside edges of the pipes. When I showed Paul the bit that you had, he was certain that it had broken off the other piece and he's fitted them together."

Paul held out a small trident. "On the piece we already had, there was a hole in the apex of the 'V' and I found that your piece of pipe slotted into it." He pointed to the indentations along the edges of the prongs. "It's a good fit and you'll see that the markings on the edges of the prongs are identical. There's no doubt that both pieces are part of the same object."

"It does look as if the bits go together," Kalen agreed. He recognised the piece of pipe that he'd carried around in his pocket. It fitted snugly into the fork of the other bit of tubing.

"I'm going to tell you something that you mustn't repeat outside this room," Javed said. "You need to keep an open mind about this. You wanted some answers, well, this is the start. We think that the trident is of alien origin. We can't identify the metal and we don't recognise the markings. We think it was uncovered by the drills and thrown up in the rubble."

"Are you serious? The Division hasn't discovered anything that could be connected to an alien civilisation in over a hundred years! The nearest we've come to discovering alien life is to find a form of bacteria," Kalen said. Had he really carried around an alien artefact without knowing?

"We're certain that it's alien because we can't identify the metal but it's the only artefact we've found so far. We haven't found anything like it at any of the other sites," Paul said.

Kalen stared at the object that Paul still held. "So what is it?"

"Paul's been working on it with his team and he's managed to activate it. We think it's a communications device or a musical instrument. If we can work out how to use it properly, we'll have access to an alien technology! A technology different or more advanced than ours would be of enormous value." Javed's eyes glinted.

"I can't see any mechanism."

"I'll show you how it works," Paul said.

Paul placed the flat of his hand on the end of the middle tube and pressed downwards. The device emitted a high-pitched squeal and then a series of loud clicking sounds that became a regular repetitive sequence.

Paul continued, "We think that the clicking noises are some kind of code and we've discovered that it emits more than one sequence. By applying pressure on each of the symbols in a particular way, we can vary the sequence."

Paul pressed the indentations on the side of the middle prong and then two or three of the markings on the sides of each of the outer prongs and waited. The little cylinders came to life and the device started to make clicking noises of varying length and volume that settled into a distinctive repetitive sequence.

"The clicking sounds coincide with the markings. So pressing a different sequence of markings creates a different sequence of sounds, which is why we think it could be a communication device." Paul pressed down on the end of the centre prong and the trident fell silent.

"So what is it saying?" Kalen asked. Why did they think it was for communication? The clicking could have a different purpose.

"We don't know yet," Paul replied.

"Then how do you know it's for communication?"

Javed coughed. "You're right, that's why we wanted your opinion. You're an engineer, so you're used to solving puzzles. You've been to Three-Craters and seen at first-hand what it's like so we thought you might have some ideas?"

"Even if it's designed for communication, it was damaged in the rubble when the prongs came apart, so it might not work properly anyway," Kalen pointed out.

Paul thought for a second. "That's true but we know there's a synchronicity between the input and the output in the device. With enough time, we might be able to translate the code but my initial attempts have been unsuccessful. I think the device is designed to give a message but I'm convinced that the clicking noises are not the message, just a warm up sequence to something else. Have you ever found anything similar to this at Three-Craters or any of the other sites you've worked at?"

"No, I haven't. When I first picked it up, I thought it was a piece that had broken off one of the machines."

"The device doesn't have any obvious power source but I have a theory about that," Paul said.

"You found the piece of piping near the primary drill on level forty-seven? I want you to show us exactly on the plans where you found it." Javed turned to his desk screen and pointed to the display.

Kalen studied the map on the screen and pointed to a position near the boundary of the level. "That's as near as I think I can get to it. The layout will have changed since I was there."

"We still haven't found the cause of the power failures and other problems at Three-Craters. We have certain theories but the Ea-Zone won't co-operate with us.

We know that they've been secretly conducting their own research and they won't share their results with us," Javed said.

"Why would the Ea-Zone do that? They don't want delays in the building programme." None of this made sense. They weren't telling him everything.

Javed exchanged a look with Paul, and said, "We've made valuable discoveries during the course of construction at Three-Craters that could be of enormous benefit to both zones, but the Ea-Zone wants to keep any benefits for themselves. They don't want to share the results of their research with us."

"The Ea-Zone has been going its own way for years. They don't want to share new technology with us," Paul added.

"I thought everything was duplicated and shared?"

"It hasn't been for a number of years. The U-Zone has been getting increasingly concerned by activities in Early. We think they're hoarding resources," Javed said.

"But they can't do that! Won't the central Earth Government intervene?"

"We're too far away for Earth to concern itself in internal politics. We also have to provide the proof and that's difficult. Now most of the colonised planets are zoned, Earth has started to lose its control."

"And Early has been sending scientists secretly to the new sites to conduct research," Paul said.

"You say that Early has been carrying out secret research? When I was at Three-Craters I wasn't aware of any scientists on site. I don't remember anyone like that coming in."

Javed let out a deep sigh. "Early has a policy of discreetly sending in their scientists to examine the excavations and collect samples, once work reaches the lower levels on these sites. In recent years, they have become very secretive. Our intelligence reports that they're building up an independent military presence. Even Miss Ethern confirmed that she saw an Ea-Zone shuttle when she was arrested. All shuttles should be shared vessels, but Early had commandeered it for their own use. We think they've amassed quite a fleet of vehicles and have them hidden."

"How could they hide them? There's nowhere for them to store them without Unity knowing."

"They've built secret bases in the mountains and they tried to keep the fourth crater secret from us, but it was too big a project. Unity now insists on keeping a full military complement there, which was lucky for you. When you turned up there with Miss Ethern, Unity ran a check and realised what had happened. If the U-Zone hadn't escorted you back to Central, the Ea-Zone would have quietly killed you both. You had become a nuisance to them."

"You knew that? Did you know the cave-in with the drill wasn't an accident?"

"We gather information from various sources and we found out afterwards that the drill had been rigged to kill you. I didn't recognise your names when you first came to me."

"The mining captain on site, Jorge Narve, tried to kill me at the power station. I think he must have arranged to sabotage the drill."

"He's one of Early's most senior men and they usually send him to the important sites."

"Have you had any feedback from the Ea-Zone about our defection?"

"They were informed through the official channels that neither of you were coming back. My Duplicate Halle Rison acknowledged the message and submitted a formal request that you be returned to the Ea-Zone to face charges. Of course we ignored it." Javed paused and smiled. "You know, she really had a thing for you! She did a lot to protect you after that business at Area Nine and she covered up your Narquum dependence. Don't look so surprised. She knew about it all along and it was only her superiors who didn't. She probably demanded your return because she wanted to see you again!" Javed laughed.

"You know? You know about the Narquum?" How could Javed know? Why hadn't he said anything before now?

"Of course we know. We get reports from our sources and even the pharmacist in Central has a Duplicate. The only reason it didn't reach the ears at the top of the Division was Halle Rison. She stopped the rumours going any further and she's quite influential in her own way. Sleeps with all the right people, you might say. I'm glad you've managed to kick the habit."

"I'm off it and I won't fall into that trap again," Kalen said tightly.

"That's good. Make sure you stay off it."

"I haven't thought about Halle since I've been here."

"Well you don't need to see her again—you can forget all that trouble in Early," Javed said jovially. "There's work for you do to here. Three-Craters is very important to both zones but the problems still have to be resolved before construction can be completed. You know the site and you know what we're up against. I'll need your help. I'll be going down there in a few days and I'd like you to come with me."

Chapter Thirty-Three

The streets of Central were crowded when Kalen set out to walk to the meeting room in one of the city precincts. He'd been told to attend instruction in the Divine and his attendance was compulsory. It would be the first of many sessions and he wasn't looking forward to it. He had no time for religious waffle but he supposed he had to obey. Be seen to fit in, as Sera put it. He shrugged mentally and wormed his way through the crowds of people all walking in his direction, being careful to match their pace and avoid touching anyone. *There's no room to break into a jog here,* he thought, looking around him. The majority of the people walked with purpose and no one stood idly in the street apart from the security guards.

He discovered that the meeting room that he'd been sent to was one of the smaller recreation rooms usually used in the Ea-Zone for gaming. A number of people, mostly young adults and children, were already waiting inside, although Kalen spotted a couple of older men amongst them. The men and women stood on opposite sides of the room from each other facing a dais at the front. Kalen joined the men and found a position beside the wall. There were no seats and most of the young people stood fidgeting and whispering to each other.

An elderly man dressed entirely in light blue entered the room. He wore a long jacket that reached to his knees, narrow trousers, and a square hat. The whispering died away as he strode up the aisle in the centre of the room and mounted the dais, and turned to face the crowd.

"Unity," the priest shouted, bringing his right arm up with palm facing the crowd in a salute, before putting his hands together in an aspect of prayer.

"Unity!" the crowd responded and copied his movements.

Kalen did the same and tried to appear interested. He sighed silently, remembering his orientation briefing. He might face years of instruction. There were daily sessions and he was expected to attend, but Javed had asked him to come with him to Three-Craters and he was leaving in the morning. Hopefully there wouldn't be any instruction there. Paul Neill was already on site and had discovered something important. He wondered what he had found, and then noticed Sera standing near the front with the women. She appeared to be engrossed in what the priest was saying.

The priest started propounding the tenets of Cinall, the first great philosopher. Kalen had heard of the tenets before and tried to remember what he knew about them. It was one of the old religions that had long since become outdated as science had evolved. He'd always thought that only a few sects in the more remote colonies still adhered to it and he was surprised to find it here. But the philosophies of Cinall were generally regarded as harmless and the Government had never banned them.

"God is all powerful and pervasive," the priest intoned. "God is the universal force that governs everything. Each and every one of us is born with the God-force and we all carry the God-force within us, if we open ourselves to God's power and will.

"We must fill ourselves with the God-force by embracing truth and purity, by rejecting evil and by accepting the power of God and adhering to God's will.

"We must pray to access God's power, to call upon the God-force that is part of us all and there for our use, and meditate to be one with God and be filled with the God-force of the whole.

"Those who are devout in their worship will be rewarded by stronger links with God and will be filled with the God-force so that they will become worthy.

"The more each of us pray, and the more each of us meditate, the more we contribute to the glorious universal force that is God.

"When we pray together in a group, God will yield greater power to us, so that we may use it to support our needs."

Kalen listened with a sinking heart while the priest continued with his theme, that on death a person's God-force merged with the universal God-force and on birth part of the God-force broke off and became an individual. To become filled with the God-force, daily prayer and meditation were mandatory, as was a clean and moral lifestyle. Kalen groaned silently to himself. The tenets were rather strict—to what extent did they enforce them? It didn't sound like a lot of fun and the sessions were going to be tedious. This wasn't for him but he would attend instruction for the sake of conformity and keep his views to himself.

***

When the session ended, Kalen went outside the building to meet Sera. While he was waiting, he watched the crowds of people walking by. A young woman moving towards him caught his eye; there was something familiar about her. Tall and slim, her long black hair was tied back in a ponytail but her face was a picture of misery. She walked with downcast eyes, but as she came level, she glanced towards him, as if sensing his gaze. For an instant, her striking green eyes met his. With a shock, he recognised Taily Newman. What was she doing here? Then she was gone into the crowd and at that moment, Sera came out of the building.

***

Sera saw Kalen waiting for her outside the building. He stood to one side of the entrance, his Divine golden against the burgundy of his jacket, his eyes searching the faces of people coming out of the hall. A shadow fell across his forehead where the sun hit the peak of his hat, and he squinted slightly from under it, ignoring the surreptitious glances of women passing by. She gave him a wide smile, then blushed and lowered her eyes. He walked towards her and tried to take her hand.

"Not here, we're in public." Hadn't he listened to any of the sermon?

He looked confused. "What do you mean?"

"They might think that we're in an immoral relationship."

"Okay, I forgot. I'll walk with you back to the accommodation block. It will be day end soon so we haven't got time to do anything else in the city."

They began walking and soon found themselves in the middle of several people headed towards the west side of the crater.

"Wasn't the sermon good?" Sera asked. "It took me back to my childhood. My parents used to take me to daily prayer meetings and I learned the tenets by heart." Suddenly, her mother's face came to mind and a deep feeling of sadness swept over her. Somewhere her mother would be grieving for her. She must have been told by now about her defection. She would never see her mother again. She'd lost both of her parents now. She felt her eyes well up.

"I didn't know that you were religious? I thought the tenets had been abandoned except in some of the very remote colonies," Kalen replied, his voice carrying an inflection of surprise.

She tried to remember if she'd ever mentioned her upbringing to Kalen. "I was brought up in a tiny settlement on Borle that I suppose you would call remote. Our group always followed the philosophies of Cinall although we were in the minority. I didn't have many friends growing up because my parents didn't want me to mix with unbelievers."

"Your parents must have been very strict. Weren't you lonely?"

"I don't remember feeling lonely. Everyone I knew followed Cinall so I didn't think my parents were strict. When we went to prayer meetings, I always felt as if I belonged to a special group. Until we came here, I hadn't felt like that for a long time. I'm so ashamed, Kalen." Tears rolled down her cheeks and she chided herself for being so weak. "When my father died I denied the God-force and joined the Division. That's when I came to Taidor and I stopped practising the tenets, but I always felt different."

"You've got nothing to feel ashamed about. No one follows the philosophies in the Ea-Zone," Kalen said reassuringly.

"Borle is a zoned planet but once I left Borle I didn't meet anyone who followed Cinall. I always felt different from everybody else and now I know why. The tenets are the true faith and I shouldn't have denied them. I've got a chance now to put that right. I feel as if I belong here. I feel as if I've come home."

"The important thing is that you're safe and happy. Come on, this is supposed to be a happy day." Kalen gently patted her arm.

She glanced towards him and he smiled at her, his eyes twinkling under the shadow of his peaked hat. She was glad she was with him, here amongst strangers. It was as if God had led him to her and both of them to Unity. She belonged here and with Kalen. It was as if God had had a plan for them both. Everything was fitting into place now. The crowd around them had thickened and they were coming up to a junction. They stopped along with the crowd for a few moments and then began walking again towards the U-Zone Gates.

"What about you? Were you brought up in a faith?" He had never talked about God or his beliefs to her. What did he really believe?

"I'm sorry to disappoint you but my family were very modern and their God was science. I was brought up to believe that science is everything so I'm rather new at all this." He smiled at her again, the corners of his mouth crinkling up into that little boy look that she loved so much.

"Oh, that's dreadful, Kalen. You've missed so much. Following the tenets gives you an incredible feeling of joy and a sense of who you really are. I wish I could explain it to you. When you've been to a few more meetings you'll begin to feel it and then you'll understand what I mean."

"I'm sure you're right, but I have to go to Three-Craters tomorrow."

"Tomorrow? So soon? I wanted to spend some time with you and there's another instruction meeting tomorrow." She was disappointed. They'd hardly had any time together and he was leaving Central already. She'd imagined going to the prayer sessions with him and explaining the things that he didn't understand and meeting the new community with him.

"I won't make that, I'm leaving in the morning."

"That's a shame. How long will you be away for?"

"Javed told me that it would only be for a few days so I'll be back soon. We can do something tonight if you want."

"We can eat together in the canteen in the block if you want."

***

The canteen was crowded when Kalen arrived but he spotted Sera easily. Although the place was nearly full, she had saved him a seat, and she smiled when she saw him, her eyes shining. He made his way over and sat down beside her, aware of the low hum of muted conversation around them. She gazed at him intently, her brown eyes large in her face. There were blue circles under her eyes and hollows under her cheekbones. The deep frown between her eyebrows seemed to be even deeper.

"It's pretty quiet in here," he remarked. "There isn't much conversation going on."

"I think it's peaceful," she said, eyes glowing. "It's such a refreshing change from the constant noise we used to get in the Ea-Zone."

Several people sitting near them stopped talking and stared at them.

"Let's talk about something different," Kalen said, feeling uncomfortable.

"I've been given a laboratory at headquarters and I'm going to be briefed on my new assignment tomorrow."

"Have you been given a Duplicate yet?"

"The supervisor mentioned it, but he said there would be a delay," she replied, moving a thin hand in a jerky, birdlike gesture. "I'm sure I'll get one soon."

"I haven't been assigned a Duplicate either, which is a bit unusual."

"I expect you'll get one when you get back from Three-Craters."

"Are you hungry? Do you want to get some food?" he asked.

She nodded in agreement. "I'm famished! I haven't had anything to eat all day, I've been so busy."

They got up and walked between the tables, towards the serving station. The other diners stared at them and Kalen kept his gaze level as they made their way towards the food. He had been naïve to think that he could transfer to the U-Zone and be accepted immediately. They were strangers here and he would have to earn their trust in time.

At the serving station, he stared at the food. One dish contained a lumpy yellow casserole whilst another dish had a red mashed vegetable in it. Beside those, another plate had circular black slices on it. An unappealing bitter smell emanated from the food.

"Do you know what any of this is?" he whispered to Sera. "I've got no idea what's in them."

"Neither have I," Sera replied. "Just choose something. We're holding up the line."

He didn't think any of it looked tempting but in the end, he picked the yellow casserole and hoped that it tasted better than it looked. It was going to take him a while to get used to things. After following Sera back to their seats, he picked up his fork to eat.

Sera gave him a sharp look. "Aren't you forgetting something?"

"What?"

"We must pray first. Weren't you listening this afternoon?"

"I'm sorry." Kalen put his fork down.

He remembered her tearful confession about the tenets. She wasn't just going through the motions to conform. She really was religious. That was the second thing he wouldn't have guessed about her, recalling the night on the shuttle. She was a contradiction in lots of ways.

Other people were openly staring at them now with expressions of disapproval. Sera closed her eyes and began to say a prayer, her long lashes nearly touching her cheekbones. She briefly touched the Divine pinned to her top with her fingertips while she moved her lips. He lowered his eyelids and looked down at the table respectfully. *I'm not going to be able to put up with this for long,* he thought. *Was it like this throughout the U-Zone or just on Taidor?* He would have to find out. It might be possible to get a transfer to another planet.

When Sera had finished the prayer, she opened her eyes and took up her fork. He copied her and tucked into the yellow casserole. It had a strange flavour of herbs and something that he couldn't identify, but bland, he decided, despite the bitter smell. People nearby were still staring at them while they ate and he tried to ignore them. He cleared his plate and watched Sera while she finished her food. She looked up and smiled.

"I wanted to thank you for bringing me here. It was your idea to see Javed Durton and if you hadn't persuaded me to come with you, I wouldn't be here now. I'd probably be on a prison planet somewhere."

"I think it was the right decision. Both of us were in danger." Religion aside, Unity was the best place for them, he thought.

Her hand rested on the table and he reached for it, but she snatched it away before he could touch her. A man near them put his knife and fork down and glowered, shaking his head.

"I think it's time for us to go, other people need the seats." Kalen began to push his chair back.

"You're right, it's selfish of us to keep these seats when we've already finished."

Sera got up and he followed her out of the canteen, careful to avoid catching the eye of anyone staring at them. He thought they were an unfriendly lot and considered saying as much to Sera once they were outside, but she seemed oblivious to the hostility. The passageway was busy and they negotiated their way through a number of people to get to the bank of elevators at the end.

"I'll see you to your door. At least they've put us in the same block, even if you're on a different level," he said, pressing the switch to call the lift.

"They know how close we are," she replied and glanced at him sideways.

He noticed her look but didn't make any comment. Other people had joined them and stood silently, staring at them. They boarded the lift in a crowd and then exited several levels higher up, stepping out into one of the main corridors where the lights had been dimmed for the evening. He accompanied her down the corridor and then she turned into another passageway and walked to a door at the end. There was no one else in the passageway. In the dim light, her eyes glowed and the frown line between them had disappeared. He took a step towards her and tried to embrace her.

"You can't," she said, squirming out of his arms. "You mustn't hold me like that. Not in public."

"But no one can see us."

"It doesn't matter. If we're caught, we would be shamed."

"Then open the door and we'll go inside." He remembered the way she had kissed him passionately in the shuttle.

"You can't come in."

"Why not? There's no rule against touching in private."

She put her index finger to her lips. "Shush… someone will hear you. We can't be alone together at the moment because we could be accused of having an improper liaison."

"Then when will we be able to be alone?" Kalen asked, frustrated.

"If you want to make a commitment to me, then we can be alone after the commitment ceremony." She gazed at him candidly. "It's immoral before a commitment and I don't want to sin anymore, Kalen. I've sinned enough in the past and look how God has punished me. From now on I want to live in purity so that I can be filled with the God-force."

She was talking about a commitment ceremony but they'd never discussed it. Did she really believe what she was saying? Perhaps the ordeal she'd been through had affected her, but how well did he really know her? This was a different woman to the girl that he'd held in his arms in the shuttlecraft. Had she really changed or was she just trying to adjust to life in Unity? It was too early to tell. She was searching his eyes now, waiting for him to say something.

"Of course, it was silly of me. I wasn't thinking. Please forgive me."

"What about a commitment? I love you," she persisted.

"You're very special to me but we haven't discussed this before." He had to think of something to put her off. "Let's talk about it after I've been to Three-Craters. It might be a good idea to wait for a short time until we're both settled in here and used to the place. I'll be away for a few days, but I'll see you when I get back."

"I wish you didn't have to go."

"I have to, you know that. At least let me make sure you're safely inside."

She opened the door but remained standing at the entrance, her eyes luminous.

"I'll be back soon. Goodnight Sera."

He turned on his heel and quickly walked away.

Chapter Thirty-Four

Kalen travelled to Three-Craters with Javed, and when they arrived, they went straight to the laboratory where Paul Neill was already working. Paul paced the room with excitement.

"I've been trying to find a way to activate the trident," Paul said. "I thought I'd try it at different places, on different levels of the site. When I got down to the levels below forty, I started to get results. I also decided to try the trident near the areas where that new mineral, Uveid, has been found."

"Paul thinks he's found something significant," Javed interjected.

Paul continued, "I've been experimenting at the lower levels in places near the Uveid deposits and I've managed to activate the trident! If we could only find out what it's for and how to use it, we might have a valuable tool."

"So there's a connection to the Uveid?" Kalen was puzzled.

"Yes, I tried activating the trident near one of the heavy deposits and it worked!"

Javed turned to Kalen. "You wanted answers didn't you? Well it's time that I gave you some more. We've found that the Uveid gives off a form of energy when it's in situ. The rocks emit an energy field."

"What sort of energy field? Could it affect machinery and cause power failures?" Kalen asked.

"Possibly, although the individual stones are small, some of the seams running through the levels are extensive," Javed replied.

So that would explain most *of the problems at Three-Craters,* Kalen thought. *Weak Uveid seams were causing the rock-falls and giving off an energy field that affected the power supply. But it still didn't answer everything. Why had the Division wanted him dead?*

"We're still investigating the Uveid's effect, but it may affect machinery," Paul agreed. "The effect of the energy field is very small in the laboratory and gradually fades within a day or so of the samples being taken. The samples that were taken back to Central don't produce an energy field at all, but the large natural deposits at Three-Craters are producing a strong field, so it's possible that could affect the power supply and machinery. We're investigating the energy at the sub-atomic level and if we can establish its properties we might be able to find a way to harness the energy."

"Harness the energy?" Kalen asked.

"Yes, that's the value of the rock," Javed explained. "The Uveid has internal energy and if we can find a way to harness it we could use it as a source of fuel. It would be an incredible breakthrough, but the Ea-Zone won't co-operate with us. They want to keep the benefit of it for themselves. The form of energy is new and we haven't been able to analyse it yet or discover how the Uveid contains and releases it. If we can understand it, we can find ways to use and control it."

"How long have you known about the energy? I was told to treat the Uveid in the same way as any other weak mineral." *Had the Division known about the alien energy when he was at Three-Craters? Why hadn't they told him?*

Javed gave a short laugh. "That's just the Ea-Zone's official line. The Ea-Zone has been carrying out research on the Uveid for months to try and find a way to use the energy but without much success. Originally, Early discovered the Uveid at Area Nine but they suppressed the information, didn't advise the U-Zone, and the rocks were never officially categorised.

"The Ea-Zone didn't expect Sera Ethern to find Uveid at Three-Craters and didn't make the connection between the power failures and the Uveid, until she reported the find. At that point, the Ea-Zone realised that the Uveid might be causing the problems but they didn't want Unity to know about the Uveid's internal energy, so they tried to cover it up by reporting it was simply another weak sort of rock. When you refused to go along with the cover up and carried on investigating they decided to get rid of you."

Kalen steeled himself to ask the question, "Did Halle Rison know? Was she part of it?"

Javed replied, "It's doubtful because the Division knew about her relationship with you. She probably wasn't told anything about the Uveid but she's bright so she may have found out about the rocks by herself, but the Division wouldn't have made her a party to any plan to kill you."

"She tried to persuade me to leave." He visualised her face as clearly as if he had just spoken to her. Blue eyes, blonde hair, and a worried expression as she explained to him that he had to give up on Three-Craters, that he had to leave and she would make sure he was re-assigned.

"She would be following orders but I expect she also found out that something was going on and wanted to get you out," Javed said. "Our intelligence reports that she's been disciplined by the Division for mishandling the situation. But that's not relevant now. We need to concentrate on the trident."

"So what is the connection between the Uveid and the trident?" Kalen asked, turning to Paul.

"The trident has to have a power source to work but I couldn't see one. I speculated that it could have been designed to draw power from the Uveid stones, so I brought it here to try out near the heavy Uveid seams," Paul said.

"Where have you tried it?" Kalen asked.

"I've tried it in several places but I got a good result on level fifty-two. It starts off with the clicking and then vibrates and then something strange happens. I still think it's some kind of communications device."

"Does it give out a message?" Javed asked.

"I don't know if I would call it that," Paul said. "Nothing I can interpret. Rather than describe it, I would prefer to show you. That's why I wanted you to come here. The building on level fifty-two is nearly finished but there's a spot where there's still a strong energy field. We can go down there and I'll show you what I've found."

***

They took the express elevator to level fifty-two and stepped out into a blaze of lights and activity. Several workers were moving furniture and electrical equipment into offices while others were finishing off the décor of the corridors. *This looks nothing like the last time I was here*, Kalen thought as he followed Paul and Javed. Paul carried the trident in a small box and walked ahead until he came to a corridor that led to one of the control rooms and stopped beside a wall.

Javed looked at Paul questioningly. "Why are we stopping?"

"This is the place I tried it. I know it doesn't look much but the geologist told me that there is an Uveid seam running several metres behind this wall. Apparently, the plans for this floor had to be altered to avoid it. I want one of you to try activating the trident to see if you get the same effect that I did."

Paul got the trident out of the box and held it towards Javed.

"What? Here?" Javed asked with a look of consternation on his face.

A worker pushing a trolley of electrical equipment brushed past them and disappeared into the control room.

"Just a minute, I'll get Security down here and we'll seal off this part of the corridor." Javed walked to an intercom on the wall and spoke into it. "Security is coming now."

Two security guards arrived, Divines shining on the breasts of their grey jackets, and both gave a palm forward salute to Javed. "Sir?"

"Clear the control room and seal off this end of the corridor. We don't want to be disturbed. We'll be here for a few minutes."

The guards went into the control room, escorted a worker out, and positioned themselves at each end of the corridor.

"Okay, we can start now. Is the artefact safe to use?" Javed asked.

"Yes, do you want to try it? The proximity of the Uveid should set it off. It's safe so far as I know, but the effect is strange."

Javed reached to take the trident and then hesitated and drew his hands back.

"I'll try first if you want," Kalen volunteered, wondering what the trident would do. It was only two bits of metal slotted together and he'd held the central piece countless times before.

Javed nodded and Paul handed Kalen the trident.

"Hold the trident in front of you with both hands," Paul instructed.

"Which marks do I press?"

"Try a simple sequence first. After pressing the central prong, run your fingers along the outside marks like this." Paul showed Kalen. "You press the top of the centre prong firmly once and hold to stop it."

Kalen found the marks on the sides of the tubes and pressed the indentations in the sequence that Paul had shown him. He repeated the simple pattern continuously until the trident emitted clicking sounds, and then pressed only the last two marks alternatively. The device continued to click in a repetitive staccato rhythm that increased in speed, and then began to vibrate. The vibrations were mild at first and then became stronger until the device hummed between

Kalen's hands, becoming warm, gently caressing his palms and fingertips. The trident became hotter and Kalen relaxed, letting the vibrations travel up his wrists and into his arms, enjoying the soothing sensation. He closed his eyes and focused on the clicking and the feel of the piece. The subtle oscillations seemed to invade him until he was filled with nothing but the quivering of the object and the repeating clicking sequence.

His thoughts faded away until his mind was empty except for the clicking that played again and again in an alien language until the sounds became familiar. He became only aware of the sound and feel of the trident that consumed all of his consciousness. Shapes began to emerge, colourful spheres floating in a void, moving and transforming into ovals and irregular flowing forms that touched and merged with each other. He had a sensation that they had surrounded him and were lifting him up, that he was floating amongst them, and he recognised them. Then they merged with him and he was part of a rainbow of swirling globes.

In his mind's eye, he looked down and saw himself standing in the corridor with Paul and Javed, who were blind to the colourful masses around them. Then he was back with Jorge and Lars stumbling through the darkness of the caves, clumsily blundering through clouds of multi-coloured forms, ignorantly disturbing their sublime existence. Then the images faded, and the vibrations and clicking slowed. He was unaware that he'd pressed the centre prong but the trident stopped, and he opened his eyes to see Javed and Paul watching him.

"Did you see the shapes?" Paul asked, excited.

"Yes, but what are they? They're the same shapes I saw when I got the miners' sickness."

"I think they're in the energy field, but let's go into that later, after Javed's had a go," Paul said. "Then we need to discuss the next step because I think that the trident does more, but I haven't been able to get anything else out of it yet."

Kalen watched while Javed took the trident and played the sequence. Javed's face lost expression as the clicking increased but when the device began to vibrate, he closed his eyes and his mouth curled into a smile. After a few moments, Javed pressed the centre prong and opened his eyes.

Javed smiled. "That's fascinating. I saw the shapes." He turned the trident over in his hands, studying it. "It's difficult to believe it could do that. It just looks like a bit of old metal." He glanced towards the security guard standing several metres away. "Let's go back to the laboratory and discuss this in private."

Javed handed the trident back to Paul and turned to leave.

"Dismissed!" Javed barked as they passed one of the guards. The man saluted and began to walk towards his companion at the other end of the corridor.

Kalen followed the others to the elevators, wondering about the trident. He had seen the forms from the caves. Same shapes, same sensations, but this time engineered.

When they reached the laboratory, Paul put the box holding the trident on the desk and Javed sat behind it.

"Sit down," Javed said, motioning to seats in front. "Now we've all had a go with the trident, we know what we're talking about. What did we see, Paul? What are those shapes?"

"I'm not sure. I've been experimenting with different sequences and I've managed to call up the shapes each time, but their movements differ depending upon which sequence is employed. I've worked out fifteen different sequences so far. Some of the sequences produce nothing except the vibrations, but others bring up images of floating spheres that keep changing shape. I've also seen round objects that move like balls being thrown, as well as oval shapes that dart about. Sometimes the shapes form other patterns."

"Any theories?" Javed pressed.

"So far as I can tell, this device enables us to 'see' what's in the energy field, or rather it's our brain's interpretation of the field when it's exposed to it. What we see are patterns carried by the energy," Paul continued.

"So is the energy field responsible for the miners' sickness?" Kalen asked.

"I think so. They get the hallucinations when they're exposed to the Uveid energy."

"Then why are they hallucinating about all sorts of things?" Kalen said. "When I got sick I saw the shapes but the miners don't see them when they get ill."

"The hallucinations are just a product of the field's affect upon the brain," Paul replied. "But the trident actually enables us to see inside the energy. It channels it, so to speak, to allow the brain to interpret the information correctly. In your case, your brain was able to interpret the field without the trident. One explanation could be that you've been directly exposed to the Uveid before, even if you were not aware of it at the time, whereas the miners who had unrelated hallucinations haven't had direct contact with the rocks."

"So are you saying that the device lets us see something that's real?" Javed asked, frowning.

"I think we're seeing something that exists in the energy. So yes, in a sense it's real. It's in the energy field, rather than something produced by the brain."

"So are we seeing alien shapes?" Javed asked again.

"Only so far as that's the way our brain sees them. There's something there that our brains see as spheres, but that could simply be the closest that the brain can get to recognising them."

"If the spheres are real, what are they? You said originally that you thought the artefact could be some kind of communication device," Javed said.

"It could be. The device is interpreting the energy field so that we can see what's in it, so the shapes could be a form of communication and contain a message. We just can't read the message yet."

Javed sighed. "You know there are strict protocols. Officially, we can't continue development if there is alien life here. If we get any evidence that there's intelligent life here, Unity will have to suspend development at Three-Craters and there will be an enquiry."

Paul countered quickly, "I think it's premature to think along those lines. Although the energy field could be connected to an alien civilisation, the device may have been made millennia ago, and if so, the message may be historical. The intelligence that made it would have died a long time ago. There's no reason to think that the message is current and that we're dealing with an alien presence that's still alive."

"Can we use it to stop the energy field affecting our machinery?" Kalen asked. He had no interest in historical conjecture. It seemed to him that the only purpose of experimenting with the device was to see if they could make it work in some useful way.

"My team's working on it," Paul confirmed. "I'm hoping that once we understand how the trident works we'll have the means to prevent the energy field from interfering with our equipment."

"We need to do something about the hallucinations as well," Kalen said. "The sickness is also causing a lot of delays and it's been demoralising the men."

"What sort of message do you think it's trying to give us? If it's alien then it could be something to do with Taidor. Is there any way you can work out what the message is or when it was made so that we know what we're dealing with?" Javed asked.

"I'm confident that we'll find a way to decode the message and control the energy field, but it will take time.

Once we know how to control the energy field we'll find a way to stop the hallucinations," Paul said.

Javed shifted in his chair. "Still, the divisional director is adamant that Unity will abide by the protocols on alien life forms. I have to prepare a full report, and I suspect that I know what the result is going to be."

"You think that he'll order the site to be shut down? I thought this site was important to the Division?" Kalen questioned.

"I think he'll order a suspension of the work until it's fully investigated, unless Paul can come up with the answers quickly. We need to be sure that there's no sentient life on Taidor, however unlikely that seems. If there is sentient life here, we can't ignore it. It would be immoral as well as illegal."

"I'm convinced that the trident does more than just show the forms in the energy field, but I just haven't found the key yet," Paul said.

"It may be worth trying it in the direct proximity of the Uveid at one of the deeper levels," Kalen suggested. "At a place where there is direct access to a seam. Those seams are huge and if the trident does more, it will react."

"I haven't tried that yet. All my experiments have been on the levels where the work is at a fairly advanced stage and the Uveid is shielded by the walls and several metres away."

"We'd have to go down to one of the undeveloped levels which have just been excavated," Kalen said.

"You know this site well, where you do suggest?" Javed asked.

"I need to see the recent incident reports and the charts showing the areas where the Uveid seams have been found. The accident sites should give us a good idea where the energy fields are strongest."

"Our geologist has collated the location of the Uveid deposits. You can talk to him now. I can also give you the incident reports and details of reported hallucinations, if that helps," Javed said.

Kalen considered this. "That should be enough to work out where the effect is strongest. We can try several locations."

"In that case, let's meet again at the main elevator shaft in an hour," Javed said.

Chapter Thirty-Five

Kalen decided to begin at the fifty-ninth level, resisting the strong temptation to return to the site of the drill crash and cave-in on the fifty-fifth. A dark curiosity tugged at him to go back. The clear up operation would have begun and he tried to imagine what the level looked like now. But it made no difference. He didn't need to see it. He no longer faced charges over the drill.

When he got to the bank of elevators, he found Paul and Javed waiting for him. Both had breathing tubes and wore hard hats and Paul carried the box containing the trident. Paul fiddled nervously with straps attached to the box and Javed looked ill at ease.

"According to the geologist they found another Uveid seam on the fifty-ninth yesterday. It's a large seam and already some of the equipment nearby is playing up, so it's a good place to start. When we get below, just do as I say. You'll be fine—it's not too bad down there," Kalen said.

He set the controls of the elevator to take them to the fifty-eighth level.

"We need to collect full breathing kits before we go down—the tubes won't be enough," he explained. "Level fifty-nine has just been opened up and the air is too thin to breathe and very dusty. The first elevator has been installed so you're lucky we don't have to use the auto-lifts."

After collecting the breathing sets on the fifty-eighth level, they took the elevator to the fifty-ninth level and when the doors opened the roar of machinery and pounding drills engulfed them. Muggy air and dim lighting gave the gallery an almost surreal quality through which drills, trucks, and men moved erratically. Kalen turned on his radio headset and indicated to the others to do the same. Paul fought with the switch on his helmet and then fixed the box to his belt so he could use both hands. Kalen led them over the main construction area, taking a route that avoided the line of rubble trucks that skimmed across the floor, whistling and stirring the air as they went past.

"Don't sidestep the trucks," Kalen said. "They're designed to avoid you. If you try to dodge them at the last moment, you'll cause an accident. Just walk where I walk."

He sensed Javed moving closer to his back, shadowing him, and a strange thought came to him. This should be Halle, not Javed. Halle should be with him now. Halle should be following him across the gallery. For a brief moment, he missed her and this surprised him, but before he could examine the feeling, he came to the primary drill that he was looking for and was forced to turn his attention back to the matter in hand.

He waved towards the drill. "The drill uncovered a cave. It's a few metres away, along this wall."

Kalen passed the drill and began searching along the wall until he came to the black fissure marking the cave's entrance. The cave was not lit. He switched on the light fixed to his hat before stepping inside. He also took a torch from his belt and turned that on, swinging the beam in an arc around the cave.

"According to the preliminary surveys, this is the beginning of a massive cave system that stretches for hundreds of metres, but the geologist says the Uveid seam is near the entrance," Kalen said.

Kalen had a sudden dark sense of foreboding but he could not see anything dangerous in the cave. Just natural anxiety, he told himself. He hadn't been down to the lower levels since the drill crashed.

"Switch your lights on. We're not going in very far, but it's dark in here. Careful, watch your feet—the ground is uneven," Kalen said, moving further into the cave.

Kalen walked a few paces forward, flashing the beam of his torch around him. Strange cone-shaped rock formations up to half a metre thick and several metres high grew out of the floor and the walls were etched with unusual swirling patterns. There was a deep crevice in the north wall and he made his way through the cones towards it. Something glittered in the beam of his torch. When he shone it inside the crevice, myriad blue stones blazed in the light, shaped like tiny pyramids. The dense centre of the deposit was two or more metres in diameter and at its outer edges the stones were more sparsely distributed with little grooves running between them.

"There's the Uveid seam," Kalen said, illuminating the stones for the others to see.

Javed stared at the stones. "I didn't realise the deposits were so compressed. I thought we were talking about sparse distribution."

"You need to speak to your geologist about that. Some of the seams may have a lower density. I don't know if it makes any difference to the stability of an area."

"I'll check that out. But presumably the more Uveid there are, the more powerful the energy field is?"

"That sounds logical," Paul interrupted. "I've never seen the Uveid in situ before. There are so many of them, it's unbelievable. We should be able to get some kind of result here."

Paul took the trident out of the box and faced the interior of the crevice so that he was almost touching the tiny blue rocks.

"I hope we can get something out of this," he said. "If it works, then I'll try and replicate the conditions in the laboratory. Here goes."

Holding the trident in front of him, Paul pressed its centre prong and the sides of the outer prongs in sequence. The tubing immediately started clicking, softly and slowly at first, and then increased in volume and speed, until it began to vibrate in Paul's hands. Paul closed his eyes and his face adopted a blank expression. Kalen and Javed stood on each side of him watching. The clicking sounds settled into a regular pattern that echoed aggressively around the cavern but when Paul stopped moving his fingers along the markings, the trident continued to throb regardless. Paul gripped the device tightly, his knuckles white.

Suddenly, a groaning noise filled the chamber and Kalen swung his flashlight around to try to identify it. The groaning became a thunderous roll and he spun around and shone the beam of his torch at the Uveid. The stones swam before his eyes as if they were moving and merging and the grooves that ran between them were expanding. A low rumble came from beneath his boots and the ground trembled. He whirled around to see Paul's arms elevated with the trident held high at face level.

"Stop now!" Kalen shouted. "Turn it off. The wall's going to come down."

Paul did not react and stood with his eyes shut and face blank. He continued to stand motionless, except for his hands and arms that trembled from the vibrations of the trident, seemingly oblivious to Kalen's cries, and then the crevice lit up with a burst of blinding white light. After the flare died, the Uveid turned yellow and the stones glowed in the inky blackness like feline eyes and then deepened to orange, pulsating like fire, even as Kalen watched. The rivulets that ran between the Uveid filled with a deep fiery orange light as they widened and cracked the rock-face.

"My God, what's happening?" Javed shrieked.

"We have to stop the trident and get him away from the wall," Kalen yelled.

Kalen took hold of the trident and tried to wrench it from Paul's hands. He found that he could not dislodge it so he pushed Paul away from the crevice instead. Paul remained in the trance and stumbled backwards before regaining his footing, but the trident still vibrated hotly in his hands. Kalen guessed that even if he pushed him over, it would not stop the device.

"Javed, we have to get the trident away from him," Kalen shouted, launching himself at Paul again and taking hold of the trident with both hands and giving a violent tug.

"Don't break it! We need that thing!" Javed cried in alarm.

"If we don't get it away from him and turn it off, we won't need anything! That wall is about to come down!"

Javed paled and took hold of one of Paul's hands and began to prise his fingers off the trident's prongs and together they forced one hand away. The vibrations began to slow and Kalen yanked the device out of Paul's hands. The trident throbbed violently for a few moments and then became silent. Kalen shoved the trident in his pocket and turned to help Javed drag Paul away from the wall. Behind them, the Uveid had turned red and the crevice began to fill with a brilliant scarlet light that seared Kalen's eyes.

"We have to get out of here!" Kalen shouted, taking hold of one of Paul's arms.

Paul's eyes opened but he appeared stunned and did not resist. They pulled Paul to the entrance as crimson light illuminated the cavern and the patterns on the walls swirled around them, moving now as the rock shifted. The rumbling base became a roar and they reached the entrance just as the wall exploded in a red flare. Huge chunks of rock smashed to the ground throwing up clouds of dust that looked like smoke in the fiery light.

Outside, Kalen turned back and shone his flashlight into the mouth of the cave. Only mounds of boulders and rubble were left. The strange cone growths were gone and the wall where the seam had been and most of the ceiling nearby had collapsed. His hands were shaking and the beam of his flashlight wavered. He let go of Paul, who leaned against the wall, looking confused.

"What happened? Why did it explode like that?" Javed asked, sweat trickling down his forehead and pooling at the top of his oxygen mask.

"It must be the energy from the Uveid. I don't know what the trident is, but I don't think it's for communication," Kalen replied.

Paul held his face in his hands and shook his head, as if trying to clear his mind, and then got his flashlight out of his belt and shone the beam inside the cave.

"Where's the trident? We haven't lost the trident have we?" Paul demanded. "If it's in there, we'll never find it."

"Don't worry, it's in my pocket. How do you feel?" Kalen re-assured him.

Paul looked relieved. "Thank God for that."

"How do you feel?" Javed repeated. "I mean what happened in there? Did you see anything? Why did the wall come down?"

"It was amazing. They were all around me. The feeling of power was incredible," Paul said.

"Feeling of power?" Javed echoed.

"It was just a feeling that I can't really explain. I saw the shapes again, but this time it was almost as if I was directing an incredible force. Tremendous power, far greater than anything we've ever developed before."

"I think we should leave now. This whole area might be unsafe," Kalen said.

The feeling of foreboding hadn't left him and it had grown into something else, something more than anxiety. If he could label the feeling, he would call it fear. It was a dark primeval fear that he couldn't rationalise. He felt as if he was being sucked into a black pit that smelled of death. Area Nine. For a moment he heard the screaming, but it hadn't been his fault! He didn't have to think about it. Why didn't it let him go? What was it that he'd forgotten?

Chapter Thirty-Six

After Kalen returned to Central he saw Taily in the city again. She was walking a few metres ahead of him along one of Central's main streets. Her long black hair swung in a ponytail from side to side as she walked. When she turned to take a side street, he caught sight of her striking profile. He remembered the tiny skirt she wore at Three-Craters and her long legs, but here she had on trousers under a long tunic. How had she got into the U-Zone? He had to find out and tried to increase his pace. A man in front of him glanced over his shoulder and frowned.

He reached the entrance to the side street and rushed down it. He narrowly avoided brushing against a woman with a small child. Several people stared at him as he weaved between them. Now only a handful of people were in his way and he sidestepped around the nearest and squeezed along the wall. He found that people moved to one side when they sensed he was coming through as if they were frightened he would touch them.

"Taily?" he called out. She stopped suddenly and for a moment, there was confusion in the throng and then people adjusted their course to walk around her, leaving a small island of space into which Kalen stepped. She turned around and her eyes widened.

"I thought it was you. What are you doing here?" Even in daylight, she was still as beautiful as he remembered. He stared into her green eyes and for a brief moment, she held his gaze and then her eyes went blank as if a light had been flicked off.

"I don't know you." She turned her back on him and began to walk away.

"It's me, Kalen. We met at Three-Craters." He put a restraining hand on her arm and she flinched away from him.

She glared at him. "Leave me alone. I don't know you."

He followed her. "It's okay, I'm here legally. I asked Unity for asylum and I live here now."

"My life in Early is over and I don't want to be reminded of it," she said coldly.

"We don't have to talk about Early. We're both here now. We can see each other."

"My name isn't Taily. I've got a new name and a new life. I can't have anything to do with you."

"Why not? Do you have a partner here?"

"I have a new life and I have to try and make it work. I can't associate with anyone from Early."

"I want to see you, even if it's just as friends."

"You don't understand. It's dangerous for both of us. Forget me and get on with your own life. If you don't leave me alone, I'll call that guard."

She nodded towards a security guard who was standing at the street corner and increased her pace. Kalen let her go and fell back. He watched her long ponytail swaying ahead of him in the crowd until other people obscured his view. There would be other days and other opportunities.

***

That evening Kalen sat with Sera at their usual table in the block canteen. She wore a blue top without any adornment except for her Divine, and black trousers, and was trying to engage him in a discussion about religion. He sat listening to her while he tried to eat the purple stew in front of him. It reminded him of the purple vegetables he had seen in the plantation, but had an oily smell. Red lumps floated in it that he thought tasted like carrots but he wasn't sure.

"You've been missing the daily instruction, Kalen. You'll never reach a state of joy if you don't attend."

"I can't always get to the sessions. My work has to take priority."

"But if you miss them, you'll fall behind. The instruction is important so that you can understand the power of the God-force and how it affects your life. You must pray daily to become filled with the God-force and advance from the first grade. At least promise me, that if you don't get to one of the instruction meetings, that you'll make the time to pray instead?"

"Of course I will," he replied in a soothing tone. "I'm just not used to praying in public, that's all. I do my praying privately."

She looked relieved and then frowned. "I'm glad that you pray, but you have to pray in public here. You have to pray with other people so that they can see you praying and know that you're filled with the God-force. You must come to the session tomorrow."

"I'll try," he said, looking down at the food on his plate.

"The priest has been instructing us on the nature of evil and how we can sin without knowing it. I didn't realise how far I'd fallen when I was in Early and I feel ashamed, but with prayer and guidance, I can cleanse myself. If you don't cleanse yourself of sin, the God-force can't fill you. There's always a residue of evil left and that can taint your purity."

She took a mouthful of food and then went on, "Looking back, I can't believe how we could have lived in the Ea-Zone, amongst those people. There was so much sinning that nearly everyone was tainted by it. I can feel the goodness of the people here. They live good lives. It's something that I never felt in the Ea-Zone. You can feel it, can't you?"

He looked at her thin, pale face, her eyes beseeching him. "I can feel it Sera. The people here are good and there are no men here like Lars Mason. It's easier to walk in the streets, people are much more considerate of their neighbours and everything is quieter. The doctors have treated my leg and for the first time since Area Nine I can walk without pain."

But boring and restrictive, he thought. She hadn't let him touch her since they'd arrived. Taily's face came to mind and he remembered running his hands up her long slim legs at Three Craters. That was something he would enjoy doing again.

"What are you thinking?" Sera asked.

"Nothing, just how close we've become," he replied guiltily. She said she loved him, but she couldn't. They didn't know each other well enough. And she'd changed. What had happened to her? All she talked about was religion and the tenets of Cinall.

"So you'll come with me to the meeting room tomorrow? We can walk there together."

"I have to find out what the work plans are for tomorrow before I know whether I can come. I promise I'll try and get there." He smiled at her and then became aware that a large man had stopped beside their table. He looked up at the man expectantly.

"Unity," the man said, putting up his hand in a formal greeting, with palm forward.

The salute seemed out of place in a canteen and Kalen stared at the man.

"I hope I'm not intruding," the man said. "I wanted to welcome you to Unity and apologise for our earlier rudeness."

"That's right," another man said, coming to stand next to the first and giving a brief salute. "We didn't know who you were before, but now we've heard about the way you rejected the unbelievers and decided to serve Unity instead. God has brought you to us."

Around them, people had stopped talking and were looking in their direction, nodding their heads.

Sera beamed. "Thank you for welcoming us."

"I'm Cirroc," the first man said. "And this is Tyn." The man indicated his companion.

"We want to formally welcome you to the block," Tyn said. "We are the lead men here and we should have introduced ourselves earlier. We have regular block meetings and now that you're part of our community we would like you to be involved."

"It must have been very difficult for you to live in Early amongst all the unbelievers. We've heard about the promiscuity and corruption there," Cirroc said. "But God spoke to you and now you're here with us."

People at the surrounding tables were listening, waiting for Kalen to reply. He decided against trying to set the record straight—they'd been indoctrinated and wouldn't listen if he tried.

"Sera and I survived, that's the main thing, and we're grateful to Unity for giving us asylum. Thank you for making us welcome."

Cirroc said, "We must let you get back to your supper now. But if you need anything please let us know." He saluted again and left to sit at another table with Tyn. Kalen turned back to Sera who had a wide smile on her face.

"Isn't this a great place?" she said.

***

Javed was working at his console when Kalen entered his office at headquarters. Kalen still thought of Halle every time he came here. He automatically looked towards the stand where she usually hung her jacket before he remembered that she would have left several hours earlier. Of course, she couldn't leave her things. There was nothing here of her except a trace of lingering perfume.

"Sit down," Javed said, smiling. "I've just got back from Morten and I've got some news. Paul's working on ways to use the trident so that we can utilise the power of the

Uveid rocks. I've reported to the Division and they're very pleased. You are to be commended for bringing the artefact to Unity. Without the piece you brought to us, we wouldn't have the device."

"So you think you can use it?"

"Yes, Paul thinks he's found a way to adapt the trident so we can control the energy, but in the meantime, the Division has referred my report to Unity's Colonial Council. I've now been notified of their decision about Three-Craters."

Javed sat back and tapped the fingertips of both hands together almost in an attitude of prayer as if considering what to say.

"What are they going to do?"

Javed cleared his throat. "The U-Zone considers that while there is some doubt that there is a sentient alien presence at Three-Craters, it would be unconscionable to continue the building work there, until the question is resolved one way or the other."

"What does that mean in practice?"

"Unity has resolved to suspend all building work and evacuate the site, pending a resolution. We can't continue with the work if it invades an alien habitat. It's unfortunate but necessary," Javed said gravely.

"You're pulling everyone out? I thought that Unity wanted to finish the work on site quickly?" Javed wasn't making sense. Neither zone would abandon Three-Craters for a bit of tubing, alien or not.

"Unity does want to complete construction at Three-Craters!" Javed shot back. "But we can't compromise alien life. It goes against the tenets and would be sinful. Everyone will leave except a small research team."

"What about the Ea-Zone? Have they agreed to stop work as well?"

"The Ea-Zone has been informed that we've found an alien artefact at Three-Craters and there may be sentient alien life there. We've formally asked them to evacuate the site in accordance with the protocols. We haven't told them anything else about the trident and we're not giving them access to it. Unity will conduct its own research on the trident."

"And the Ea-Zone has agreed to stop work at Three-Craters?"

"We're still waiting for their official response. They're unbelievers and have no regard for alien life. We think they'll refuse and try to ignore the protocols."

"You can't force them to comply," Kalen said reasonably, but his mind was spinning. Even Javed had called the Ea-Zone unbelievers.

"Yes we can, if we have to. God brought Unity the trident for a purpose and that is to manage the situation on this planet."

"Manage the situation?"

"Yes, the trident should give us the means to control the Ea-Zone. Until you brought us the missing part of the trident, Unity and Early's forces were equally balanced, but now we have the trident, we will have the advantage. We can use the trident to put pressure on Early to leave Three-Craters. The protocols were set up to protect the sanctity of alien life and the Ea-Zone must obey them. If they don't comply, Unity can force them to leave."

"You would force them to leave?" Kalen tried to keep his expression neutral.

"Yes, if we have to. We have the means to enforce the protocols now. Paul thinks that he's found a way to channel the alien energy with the trident. You carried out God's purpose when you brought us the alien piece, although you may not have known it at the time."

Javed's words screamed in Kalen's mind. God's purpose? Force them to leave? "When will you know the Ea-Zone's response?" Kalen heard himself ask. The Ea-Zone would never agree to leave Three-Craters and Javed knew that.

"I'll hear very soon and I'm hoping the closure of Three-Craters is only temporary. The threat of force will probably be enough to make Early see sense and we won't actually have to use it." Javed settled back in his chair. "Anyway, I called you in today to find out how you're getting on in Unity? You must find it a refreshing change after the Ea-Zone."

"Very well, thank you. I wear my Divine all of the time." Kalen touched the brooch on his jacket.

"And you're attending religious instruction regularly? That's very important, you know. You can't get on here unless you climb the ranks. The higher you climb, the more you will understand God's purpose. And to do that you must also obey the rules."

"I have been, or at least I try to obey them."

"Really? You've been bothering one of our citizens on the street. Put a hand on her in public," Javed said meaningfully.

"I'm not sure what you're talking about?"

"Oh come on, you know perfectly well," Javed snapped. "The woman you followed. You must leave her alone. Do you understand?"

"I thought I recognised her but I made a mistake. I didn't mean to frighten her. It won't happen again."

"I don't think you understand. Unity is a good place to live, but our laws are for the benefit of all. These are God's laws given to us for a purpose. If you break the law, you will be punished. Without complete compliance from everyone, the selfishness of a few destroys the peace and harmony of the many. Leave her alone."

Chapter Thirty-Seven

Several days later Kalen found himself waiting in a line of people to get through the Gate to his accommodation block. The first siren of day end sounded and the people in front of him shuffled impatiently. Ahead of him, a ponytail of black hair caught his eye. He couldn't seem to get Taily out of his mind. He'd found himself looking into the faces of women he passed on the streets to see if they were Taily. Now he was doing it again, but he had to look. Right height, slim build, and ponytail. Could it be her?

With mounting excitement, he moved forward, watching the ponytail. She was with another woman and they were talking. He stepped closer to the scanner. She was in the Gate now and then gone. A family in front of him went through together and then it was his turn. He nodded curtly at the guard and walked briskly through. Looking around he caught sight of the ponytail at the end of the corridor and then she disappeared around a corner. Hurrying to the end, he caught a glimpse of the ponytail before she turned another corner. He sprinted after her and turned the corner. She was getting into an elevator. The doors closed behind her and she was gone.

"Hell!" he muttered. A man nearby glanced towards him.

He strode to the bank of elevators. The lights indicated that the elevator was ascending to floor twenty-five so he called another elevator and punched the button for floor twenty-five. There might still be enough time to catch her, he thought. The elevator whistled upwards and let him out into a long corridor. Further down, he saw her going into an apartment. He walked to the door and pressed the entry plate, heart thumping.

After a few moments, the door slid open.

"What are you doing here?" Taily's emerald eyes flashed in her pale face.

"I wanted to see you," he stammered. Doubts suddenly crowded his mind. Perhaps he shouldn't have come here. Perhaps she lived with someone.

"You shouldn't be here. You have to leave," she hissed.

"I'm not leaving until you tell me why," he replied resolutely. Now he had found her he had to know why she was here. Why had she come to Unity? Why didn't she want to see him?

"Please Kalen, leave me alone." She glanced up the corridor. "You must go before anyone sees you."

"I've thought about you a lot since Three-Craters and I want to talk to you. What are you doing in Unity?" he persisted.

Two women appeared at the end of the passageway. They chatted in subdued tones as they came in Kalen's direction.

Taily looked towards them and whispered, "Come inside before they see us."

She stood aside as Kalen came in and closed the door behind him. The room was similar to Kalen's accommodation with basic furnishings. Taily had taken her jacket off and it lay strewn over a chair. She wore a greyish blue top and trousers and no makeup. She didn't offer him a seat but remained standing in the middle of the room.

"I want to see you," he said, trying to draw her to him, but she pulled back.

She shook her head. "I enjoyed your company for one night but it was only a bit of fun. I can't associate with you here. I have commitments. I shouldn't even be talking to you."

"Why can't you talk to me? No one knows I'm here."

"I can't be seen with you," Taily said.

"I don't understand. Why can't I talk to you even in public?" Kalen insisted.

"I've told you before. You're from the Ea-Zone so I can't be seen with you. I'll be punished if they find out I've been talking to you."

"But Unity has granted me asylum and I'm no longer a citizen of Early."

"It doesn't make any difference. You'll always be regarded as someone who came from the Ea-Zone even if you're living here now."

"But you're from the Ea-Zone as well? You must have asked for asylum like me."

Taily stared at him for a moment then said, "You're wrong. I'm not from the Ea-Zone and I didn't ask for asylum. I've always been a citizen of Unity."

"But you were with the tour group?" Now he was puzzled. How had she got on an Ea-Zone tour from the U-Zone? She couldn't have got on that tour from the U-Zone. What was she telling him? A nasty suspicion began to bubble in his mind.

"You mustn't tell anyone I was in the Ea-Zone. That's why I can't see you." She wrung her hands and pleaded with her eyes.

"If you want me to leave you alone you need to tell me what's going on. I've never discovered why Palum Kingston fell into the drill, and you were there."

Taily's face got whiter and she slumped into a chair, shoulders hunched.

"If I tell you, will you promise to leave me alone?"

He pulled a chair alongside her and took hold of one of her hands. "If you tell me the truth I'll leave you alone, if that's what you want. But I need to know what's going on."

"I need you to understand how dangerous it is for us to be seen together. If you keep on trying to see me, you're putting my life in danger. If you care anything about me at all, you must leave me alone. If I tell you, will you promise never to tell anyone what I've said and leave me alone?"

"If that's what you want," Kalen agreed. "But I have to know what you were doing at Three-Craters and why I can't see you now."

"Okay, I'll tell you. Palum Kingston wasn't a tourist; he was one of the Ea-Zone's scientists. Unity learned that Early was secretly sending a scientist to Three-Craters to collect samples at the site. They knew he would be posing as a tourist and I was sent by Unity to watch him."

"You're a spy? How did you get into the Ea-Zone and into the tour group?"

"I was given the identity of someone from the Ea-Zone who had died in the colonies. I was sent to Lavoar as if I had just arrived on Taidor. I had to get a job and pretend that I'd always lived in the Ea-Zone, and then I waited until I was needed for an assignment. But I miss it Kalen! I miss it! I didn't want to come back here!"

"But how did you get back into the U-Zone after you left Three Craters? Security is rigorous on Taidor. I've experienced the Gate myself."

"Unity has other agents in the Ea-Zone, people who live and work in Early for years, waiting to be useful to Unity. There is a certain Gate in Lavoar where one of Early's guards is actually a U-Zone agent. He got me through."

"I should have known that you wouldn't be the only spy Unity had in Early," Kalen said. "What about Palum Kingston? Was it an accident?"

"I saw him pick up a piece of bent tubing from the rubble when we were near the drill. He seemed to be fascinated by it and was playing with it, instead of looking where he was going. He was so distracted that he got too close to the drill and walked into it."

Taily met his eyes and he thought he saw genuine fear there. As if she was desperate for him to believe her.

"What happened to the tubing?"

"He dropped it and I picked it up," she replied.

"But you didn't say anything about it? Why did you tell me that story about someone waving Palum Kingston over?"

"I was ordered to keep anything that I found and bring it back to Unity. I didn't want anyone to know about the tubing in case it was important. I made the story about the worker up."

"What was the piece of tube like?"

"It was bent into a 'U' shape and had lines along the outside of the tubing. It was only a few centimetres long and made of some kind of metal. I gave it to the Division."

So Taily had brought the tubing back, not Luther. Had she really picked the tubing up or had she snatched it from Kingston? He studied her now. An open face and slender frame, but probably not strong enough to push Kingston into the drill. Perhaps she was telling the truth.

"It was part of an alien device," he said.

"I'm not a scientist, but I guessed it was an artefact." She gazed at him with large green eyes. "I'll always remember the night we spent together. I loved being in the Ea-Zone. I didn't know that people could live so freely. I didn't want to come back to Unity, but I had no choice. Now I'm stuck here."

He took hold of both of her hands and stroked them with his thumbs. "Surely things aren't that bad? The Ea-Zone has problems too."

A piece of jewellery on a side table caught his eye. It was the pendant that she had worn at Three-Craters, but there was no light inside it now. He got up and took a step towards it.

"Don't touch that!" she snapped.

"Why?" he asked, picking it up and swinging it on its chain.

"Please! Give it to me."

She reached to take it from him but he had already turned it over to look at its underside. There was a small switch and when he pressed it the back opened to reveal a tiny electrical circuit. It was a miniature laser. He knew in an instant that she had used it to dazzle Kingston. A flick of the switch and he would have been blind. He looked at her questioningly.

She stared at him defiantly, as if challenging him to say more. He said nothing and handed her the pendant.

"I hate it here," she said vehemently. "In Early I could be myself. I could just let go, but here I have to live by the rules."

"So is your name Taily?" he asked curiously.

"It's Mejel."

"There are restrictions and there's the religious instruction, but it's easier to walk along the streets here and quieter. There's a lot to be said for that on a world that's so over-crowded," he said reasonably.

"How much instruction have you had? You're still at the first stage aren't you? They believe that the more you pray, the more you contribute, so the more you're entitled to share the benefits."

"Of what?" For the first time he noticed the number seven on her Divine.

"Of the God-force. The philosophy is that all power and goodness comes from God, but you only receive the God-force in proportion to what you contribute. So if you've contributed a lot by praying a lot, and built up the God-force in yourself, then you are entitled to more benefits. This is recognised by the stage you've reached."

"Most places have some kind of pecking order."

"It's worse than that. The fifteen stages represent states of purity. Someone at a higher stage has more of the God-force in them, and can contribute more of the God-force to the whole, than someone at a lower stage."

"Isn't that the same in most religions?" he asked.

"You're not getting the point. The higher you are on the path, the worthier you are." She waved her hands in a frustrated way.

"I'm still not sure what you're driving at? What does it matter whether you're a number one or a number fifteen? You mean you need to get a higher number for promotion?"

She took a deep sigh as if explaining something to a child. "Once you are at a higher stage, you are literally worth more, to society, to the U-Zone. Those at the lower stages are worth less. Children are expected to reach certain stages depending on their age."

"Surely not everyone follows the religion. There must be dissenters?"

"There aren't any dissenters. No one dissents here." She gave a brittle laugh.

"There aren't many religious people in the Ea-Zone. The majority of people believe in science," Kalen pointed out.

"Unity regards the people in the Ea-Zone as corrupt and worthless. They think that they're all unbelievers and contribute nothing to the God-force. They hate them. Unity doesn't believe that it should share the planet with them."

"They hate them? People they don't know?" People like Halle. People like his family.

"The people here despise Early. They've been told that the population of Early is immoral and immodest, that there are sexual liaisons without commitment, that there is lying and dishonesty, and gambling. They've been indoctrinated to believe that everyone in the Ea-Zone is a sinner, that they have rejected God and neglected their souls. They believe that they have turned their backs on God and the God-force and are filled with evil."

"Where does that leave me?"

"You've been given some leeway because you're new. They value your input but you must try and get through the stages as quickly as you can. If they see us together they'll suspect you've been talking to me about Three-Craters and they'll arrest both of us."

"I've been told they're suspending work at Three-Craters to investigate the alien artefact."

"They won't withdraw entirely because the site is too important to them," Mejel said.

"They're going to withdraw all personnel apart from a small research team and insist that Early does the same," Kalen explained.

"They won't do it, just wait and see. Unity will insist that the Ea-Zone removes its personnel, and then they'll take over the site. They've got strong moral grounds for arguing that work is suspended, but the artefact is just an excuse. Unity wants Three-Craters for itself." Mejel paused and then added, "You have to leave now, before anyone sees you."

"Can I see you again?"

Mejel's expression softened. "Not in the foreseeable future. Perhaps in a few months or maybe years, when you've earned the trust of the U-Zone, but for now, you must stay away from me, for both of our sakes."

***

Kalen was already in the administration building when he received Javed's summons.

"Come to my office, there's someone I want you to meet," Javed said. The screen went blank before Kalen had a chance to reply. Who would it be this time? Perhaps it was another scientist. He switched off his desk screen and picked up his hat.

Javed was sitting with a tall thin man who had his back to the door when Kalen entered his office. The visitor stood up when Kalen came in. Dressed in a chief engineer's uniform, his sparse brown hair had been cut neatly over a broad intelligent forehead. His bright eyes and long narrow nose reminded Kalen of a teacher rather than an engineer. The Divine on his jacket had a figure nine on it.

"I believe you know each other? Let me introduce you formally to Luther Stonway." Javed beamed with satisfaction.

"Unity!" Luther saluted. "It's good to meet you at long last."

"Unity," Kalen responded. "It's good to meet you too." He took a step forward before he remembered that no one shook hands in Unity.

"Luther has just been giving me his report, but I thought you two would like to meet before he left."

Luther remained standing. "Javed has been telling me about your defection from the Ea-Zone. I hear that you brought an important alien artefact to Unity. I'm glad that God has shown you the right path. We used to work so well together that I always suspected on some level that you had the God-force and were one of us."

"That's right," Javed interrupted. "Luther was telling me that you are such a good engineer, he always had difficulty thinking of you as an Earlian."

"An Earlian? I haven't heard that term before."

"You haven't been here long enough," Javed said, with a faint smile, the light catching the figure twelve on his Divine. "A citizen of Early: someone with no God-force."

"They're not the same as us, they've denied their souls," Luther said. "But I didn't feel it when I worked with you. I'm glad you've joined us."

"They're sinners and full of evil," Javed said, pursing his lips as if he had something nasty in his mouth. "They contaminate our cities, our streets, our meeting halls, our restaurants. I feel physically sick when I come into my office in the mornings and know that this chair, this desk, has just been used by someone without any God-force. Sometimes I can even smell her perfume! We shouldn't have to live like this. We shouldn't have to share the planet. We're crowded on a world with sinners, being tainted by them every day." He noticed Kalen's expression and stopped abruptly.

"I don't think Halle saw herself like that," Kalen ventured. He was on dangerous ground. "But you're right. The Ea-Zone treated me badly and acted sinfully." He emphasised the last word. "When I realised how corrupt they were I came to Unity for help. I owe my life to Unity."

"Of course, I forget for a moment that you knew the woman!" Javed exclaimed. "That's part of the sinfulness of it. They have no insight into what they truly are. They're like hollow mannequins that have denied the true God-force and filled themselves up with evil instead. We need to shield ourselves from their corruption, but how can we do that when we have to share space with them?"

"I agree. The situation is untenable," Luther said. "I have to leave now, but I'm pleased that you're with us, Kalen, and I hope that we can meet up again in the future." He gave Kalen a brief salute and strode out of the office.

"Have a seat," Javed said. "There have been developments at Three-Craters. The Ea-Zone refuses to leave. Unity's Colonial Council is considering the use of force to remove Early from the site. Paul has developed a weapon based on the trident, and we're confident that it will give us the upper hand in any military engagement."

"You're planning to attack Early?" Kalen's thoughts reeled.

He had never intended to give Unity a weapon. He pictured Halle in this office, sitting where Javed now sat, and working at her desk, unaware of the storm that was brewing. He had betrayed his own people. He should have destroyed the small cylinder when he found it. He should have thrown it into the depths of the reservoir at the fourth crater. He should have done anything other than give it to Javed.

"The Council are discussing the alternatives. Unity may decide to remove Early from all of the major building sites. We can't continue to live like this. It isn't right. The Ea-Zone has demonstrated yet again their lack of morality and how evil they are. They can't be allowed to pollute places like Three-Craters. Early is jeopardising the well-being of everyone in Unity and also putting an alien culture at risk. We simply can't allow this to continue." Javed thumped his fist on the desk. "We have God on our side. We've been given the God-force and the power to remove them. We can't ignore God's command any longer."

"When will the Council decide?" Did he have time to warn Halle? Find a way to stop the attack? Without the tubing, Unity wouldn't have had a weapon. He cursed himself again for giving it to them. Somehow, he had to put this right.

"In a few days," Javed said vaguely, and turned to stare out of the window at the city below. "We've waited a long time for this."

Without more to discuss, Kalen left Javed and walked back along the familiar corridors of the administration building. The passageways were quiet except for the sound of the staff's light quick footsteps. In his imagination, he could almost hear the echoes of laughter and idle chatter of the people who had walked the same corridors a few hours earlier. Halle leaving her office to go to lunch, chatting to her friends, tying the latest belt she'd bought around her waist. Somehow he had to warn her about what Unity planned to do.

Chapter Thirty-Eight

That evening, Kalen walked Sera back to her room after supper.

"I'm sure I'm being followed during the day," he said carefully, watching for her reaction. "I think the Division is monitoring where I go. Do you get that feeling?"

"I haven't really thought about it. We're new here so I expect we're bring watched. They have to be sure we're not spies and that they can trust us. I thought someone was following me the other day, but it doesn't bother me."

So they were following her as well. He had to think of another way.

"Unity wants to suspend work at Three-Craters to investigate the alien artefact. There are protocols if there is the possibility of alien life."

"I know about the protocols. I always have to be on the look-out for anything that could be alien when I'm taking samples."

"Early have refused to leave Three-Craters and Unity might use force to remove them."

"That's terrible," she said, turning to him with her large brown eyes and an expression of deep concern. "They should leave."

"Unity might attack the Ea-Zone if they don't agree to leave."

Sera frowned. "The Ea-Zone must comply with the protocols, they can't ignore them. Alien life must be protected."

He tried again. "It seems they refuse to. If Unity attacks Early people may be killed."

"The Ea-Zone is wrong," Sera said crossly. "They can't ignore the protocols and set themselves up above Unity and what is right. It makes me sick to think that we used to live there."

"If the Ea-Zone is attacked, there could be a war and people will be killed and injured." Didn't she care about the people that she'd left behind? Then he recalled that her family were safely on Borle.

"But we would win, wouldn't we? God is on our side. If the Ea-Zone continues building at Three-Craters, they could harm any alien life that might be there, or at least they might destroy relics by mistake. The Ea-Zone mustn't be allowed to continue building if there's any possibility of alien life. The U-Zone can't just stand by and let them break the law. Something has to be done."

"Even if it means that people will be killed?" he asked softly.

"We have nothing to fear, we have the God-force."

"But what about the innocent people in Early that are going to get caught up in this?"

"They're not innocent and they have no God-force. If they can't change their ways, they deserve what they get!" she snapped. "You do believe that, don't you?"

She was staring at him now with bright eyes. He would get no help from her. He realised that he had never really known her.

"I was just testing you," he said and smiled, as if he had been teasing her. "Unity must act to enforce the protocols."

"Thank God you feel that way," she said with relief. "For a moment I was worried that you were an unbeliever. I would hate to lose you."

***

Kalen left Sera at the door to her room and walked away, thinking hard. Warning the Ea-Zone required a personal visit, but he wouldn't make the same mistake as last time.

He had to think of another way. Somehow, he had to get into the Ea-Zone and warn them.

He returned to his quarters and changed into civilian clothes. He turned off the light and waited for an hour before emerging and making his way towards the Gates. He couldn't see anyone following him. It appeared his ruse of retiring for the night had worked. It was after day end and his route took him along internal passageways. He walked through the sprawling accommodation blocks that lined the west side of the crater for several kilometres, until he was in the corridor leading to the Gate that was farthest away from his personal accommodation.

At the end of the corridor, a strong metal door closed off the Gate and security cameras lined the walls. He discretely studied the locking mechanism and thought about the possibility of disabling it. It would be difficult to do without being seen. The cameras and traffic in the corridor were obstacles he couldn't overcome. Backtracking, he found an alcove, stepped into it, and stood for several minutes. No footsteps. He hadn't been detected.

Leaving the alcove, Kalen explored the immediate area. On this floor, there was a zone canteen, a small meeting room, two offices, and a security station. The door to the meeting room was open and the sound of praying came from inside. He stopped at the door and peeked in. The room was half full of people praying, including two security guards who sat at the back. Next, he walked past the security station and glanced in the open door. Two guards sat at a desk and on the far wall, there was an equipment locker. One of the guards looked up and saw him.

"Do you need something?" the guard asked, remaining seated.

"I'm looking for the prayer hall. I arranged to meet someone there."

"It's down the corridor on your right," the guard replied.

"Thank you." Kalen turned back towards the meeting room.

Kalen assessed the situation. Were there more guards out on patrol or was the total contingent only four at this Gate during the night? If so, they might take turns praying. A timetable on the wall told him that the next sermon was due to start in a few minutes at twenty-two hundred hours. He went into the meeting room and found a seat where he could watch the entrance and pretend to pray.

Just before twenty-two hundred hours the two guards from the office came in and switched places with their colleagues. People flooded into the room until there were no seats left. On the hour, the priest arrived dressed in a blue tunic and trousers and everyone stood up.

The priest stood on the dais at the front and gave the formal salute. "Unity!"

"Unity!" the crowd responded and remained standing.

More people tried to get into the room and the area near the door became choked. The priest began chanting and each time he shouted the crowd repeated his words. After a sharp glance from a man near him, Kalen joined in.

"Unity is freedom!"

"Unity is freedom!"

"God is all powerful!"

"God is all powerful!"

"God is purity!"

"God is purity!"

The priest paused and motioned with his hands for the gathering to sit. When everyone had sat down, the priest drew himself up and began to give the sermon in a booming voice.

"We shall be purified by letting in the force of God and his command shall prevail throughout our daily lives.

"Those that do not follow the true path and follow lives of depravity and sin shall not know God.

"Those that neglect their souls shall not be worthy to receive the God-force.

"If your neighbour should turn from the path of righteousness you shall seek him out and disclose the error of his ways so that he might be saved.

"And those that persist in living lives of wickedness shall be removed from the company of the true believers so that they will not taint them.

"We shall live without the unworthy contaminating our cities and our lives!"

The crowd erupted in cheering and everyone stood up.

"We shall cleanse this planet!" the priest ranted, his eyes blazing.

"Cleanse, cleanse!" the crowd began to chant.

"We shall be free of evil!" the priest screamed.

"Free! Free!" the crowd shouted back.

After several minutes, the priest motioned the crowd to silence.

"Now we must pray to understand God's command and to gain the power to take our freedom. One day we shall live on Taidor free of the evil burden that we have to endure every day. We shall be free of the unbelievers and free to live in our cities in purity. We shall be free to live without sharing our cities with evil. We shall be free to control our lives without pandering to the wishes of the unbelievers!"

The priest's voice rose in a crescendo and the crowd cheered again and bowed their heads in prayer.

Kalen bowed his head as well and muttered the prayers that he had been taught. He shouldn't have come to Unity. At the time, he'd believed that he didn't have a choice, but he could have chosen to stay in the Ea-Zone. He could have stayed and fought to make the problems at Three-Craters public. Instead, he'd run like a coward. He'd run, leaving no one there to stand up to the Division and tell the truth about the site. *The easy option isn't always the right one*, he thought ruefully. He would go back to warn them. He would go back, whatever the consequences.

***

Kalen waited until after supper on the following evening before returning to the Gate that he had reconnoitred the night before. It was still open and there were several guards manning it, but there were only two guards in the office and two more in the meeting room. He checked the sermon timetable and then lingered by the canteen entrance. Just before nineteen hundred hours, the two guards left their station without closing the door. Kalen estimated that they would be gone for three minutes at the most.

Darting into the office, he reached the locker on the far side, opened it, and grabbed a uniform and hat. Stuffing it under his jacket, he vaulted the desk and walked quickly down the corridor until he found a bathroom to change in. The jacket and trousers fit him and he put the hat on, arranging it low over his forehead. Rolling his clothes up to put down the rubbish chute, he remembered his Divine and pulled it off. Pinning the Divine to the guard's jacket, he checked his reflection in the mirror and then left the bathroom to stroll nonchalantly towards the Gate.

"Unity!" he saluted the guards on duty.

The guards saluted in response and stood aside. Kalen took out his own identity card and held it to the scanner, then waited for the green light to come on before walking swiftly through the Gate. On the other side, he discovered that the crowds parted to let him through and people avoided catching his eye. He reached the city centre quickly and then took a moving walkway eastwards towards the Ea-Zone blocks and the Gate nearest to Halle's accommodation.

The first siren of day end sounded and he continued eastwards, passing fewer people as he went on. Eventually, he got within sight of one of the closed Ea-Zone Gates. A group of ten guards stood in front of it. Taking a deep breath, he walked nonchalantly towards them. He had nearly reached them when the final siren of day end went off and the group split up and disappeared into the buildings.

A few moments later, four more guards emerged from a side alleyway and he watched them walk a few metres down the street and go into a complex of meeting rooms. Kalen strode towards the entrance to the complex, and then slipped around the corner and into the alleyway. There was a rubbish receptacle to his left and to his right there was a doorway. If he could get inside, he could hide until the Ea-Zone came on shift, he thought. He tried the keypad at the doorway.

A voice behind him asked, "Where are you going?"

His heart missed a beat and he turned around. A guard was standing behind him, staring at him suspiciously.

"I thought I saw someone in the alley."

"There's no one else out here. I've never seen you before. Which squad are you in?"

"I've just got this job. I'm in the twenty-first."

"The twenty-first? Are you sure? This area is patrolled by the fifteenth."

Three more guards appeared.

The first guard stared at the Divine on Kalen's jacket. "This man says he's with the twenty-first but I've never heard of them. Show me your identification."

The guard continued to stare at Kalen's Divine and Kalen found his own gaze resting on the Divine pinned to the guard's jacket. It said six. He glanced around at the other guards. They were all sixes. If he could outrun them, he might have a chance, he thought wildly. He slowly took his identity card out of his pocket. He turned it around in his fingers as if checking it was the right card and then proffered it to the guard. When the guard reached to take it, Kalen wheeled around and ran.

There were shouts behind him. "Get him! Don't let him get away!"

He ran down the alleyway and rounded the corner into the main street, then veered around another corner and bounded up an escalator before taking another turn at the top. The guards' boots thundered behind him and their warnings rang in his ears.

"Stop! We order you to stop! Stop, or we'll fire!"

A bright flash missed his head and he sprinted around another bend but the guards were gaining on him. He hurled himself down an escalator and threw himself off it just before he reached the bottom, under the overhang of a building. He hit the ground hard but he picked himself up and carried on running almost without breaking his stride. Another burst of fire just missed his shoulder and he ran back out into the main street.

The guards were gaining on him and he was nearly out of breath. He ran down the side of the street, as near as possible to the buildings, and then swerved into another narrow passageway just before one of the large intersections. Seeing a recessed doorway, he flung himself behind the edge of the wall out of sight from the main street. Pressing his back against the wall he listened to the thud of the guards' boots as they ran past the side turning towards the junction.

He stayed in the recess for a few minutes to get his breath back and take his bearings. He was nowhere near the east Gates now.

He heard voices, "Clear! Clear!"

Peeking out, he saw guards wearing Divines on their jackets coming up the street. He was in the path of the search and soon they would all be looking for him. His only chance was to blend in and try to get back to Unity. With luck, he wouldn't be recognised or associated with the incident. The only thing he could do now was return and think of another way to try again.

Chapter Thirty-Nine

The next day, Kalen attended a series of instruction sessions held near his block and then began to walk into the city centre for an appointment with Javed at the end of the afternoon. Stepping onto a moving walkway, he thought about Javed's request to see him. It was late to be going into headquarters, but Javed couldn't know about the previous evening. He had got back without difficulty and he didn't think that he'd been reported.

Joining the steady flow of people, he passed the open door of a meeting room, and for a moment, in his mind's eye, he saw a band and people dancing in colourful clothes, and then the picture faded and he found himself staring at people standing praying. He walked in the middle of a throng. At a junction, he was forced to stop and wait with the people around him, while a dozen guards marched past. Further on, another file of guards walked through the crowds and people stood aside to let them pass.

Suddenly, the people in front of Kalen stopped walking. He bumped into the back of the man ahead of him and was struck from behind. All around him, people stood stock still. He couldn't see anyone moving on the street. It was as if everyone had abruptly frozen where they were. People began to come out of the buildings and when they saw the motionless crowds, they stopped also. Questioning voices began to babble around him. Peering over the sea of heads, Kalen saw that a corps of soldiers had blocked the end of the street. An army officer strode out in front of the soldiers and a hush fell over the crowd.

"We're evacuating the city. There's a meteor storm on the way and you must return to the accommodation blocks," the officer shouted.

Above Kalen, sunlight shone through the roof of the dome. He could not see any sign of a storm, but the soldiers had already fanned out. Within moments, they began to drive the crowds back along the street westwards, towards the U-Zone Gates. The majority of people turned around and began to walk back in an orderly way, but others panicked and started pushing and shoving those in front of them. Kalen found himself propelled forwards by the crowd's momentum and began to sense the tension of the people around him in the press of bodies.

Someone near him shouted, "Let me out! Let me out!"

The shouting was quickly amplified by other voices, and a palpable charge of fear rippled through the crowd. Kalen found himself pushed from behind and the pressure on his back mounted until he had no option but to allow himself to be pushed into those in front. Near him, a woman screamed and began to fall but a man grabbed her arm and hauled her back up. A small child let out a piercing cry and was scooped up into a woman's arms, but then someone fell and several people went down. People scrambled over them to get out of the melee, ignoring their screams. At the edges of the throng, people began running, knocking down people in their path.

"There's no need to run! There's plenty of time!" the officer shouted.

The mob around Kalen forced their way forwards, pushing down those in front and trampling them. The screaming became continuous and drowned out the soldiers' shouts for order. A woman next to Kalen tripped and went down, but when he bent to pull her up, he was pushed over by the press behind him. He tried to use his hands to break his fall, but another man fell on top of him and they both went down in a sprawling heap. Feet clattered over him but the other man's body shielded him from the worst of it.

After no more than two or three minutes, the other man rolled off him and Kalen tried to scramble up. The thick of the throng had gone, but people were still running by. One of them kicked him and another stamped on his hand when he tried to get up. Farther down the street, there were still knots of people and Kalen could still hear screaming. The woman who had tripped lay unconscious nearby and Kalen called over one of the soldiers to help her.

"Okay, I'll deal with her, sir," the soldier said. "Best get out of here. When the storm comes it's going to be a big one."

Leaving the soldier to tend the woman, Kalen looked around for a route to headquarters. The dome's safety roof had not moved and there was nothing but brilliant sunshine coming through it. He realised that he had never seen it closed before. How far away was the storm? Surely he would have seen some sign of it by now? The soldiers had dispersed the crowds and only a few remained to herd the stragglers. Spotting a side street, he turned down it and began to run towards headquarters.

Shouting and screaming echoed in the distance and three or four times, when he ran past a junction, he glimpsed soldiers, all marching eastwards. The safety roof remained drawn back and sunlight still bathed the city. The roar of engines overhead drew Kalen's eyes upwards. A shuttle was leaving and when it disappeared from view, he watched as three more shuttles left the city in quick succession.

Nearing the Division's headquarters, the screaming faded away but the shouts of soldiers sounded louder. Kalen rounded a corner and stopped. A thick metal barrier, about ten metres high, had been built across the street in front of the headquarters building. He looked for a way in and found that the barrier extended around the building leaving access only from the west side. Heavily armed guards had been stationed on top of the barricade and at the gap in the barrier.

They trained their guns on Kalen when he walked towards the entrance.

"Where are you going?" an officer barked at him, eyes flitting over Kalen's uniform and resting on his Divine. The corners of the man's mouth twisted briefly into a sneer and then his eyes returned to Kalen's face.

"I've got an appointment with Javed Durton." Kalen showed him his identity badge.

At Javed's name, the soldier's expression changed. "Okay, come with me."

The officer led Kalen through the barrier and into the building. There were no civilian staff in the lobby and it was empty except for soldiers and security guards. They were barricading the doors and windows with metal panelling and a feeling of dread pervaded Kalen as he walked across the empty hall. He followed the officer into an elevator and wondered if Halle had used this lift when she left for the evening twelve hours before. He imagined her cheerfully leaving, unaware that she wouldn't be coming back.

They exited the elevator and the soldier accompanied him to the door of Javed's office and left him there when the door slid open. Javed was standing at the window when Kalen entered, and he turned to greet him.

"There you are. Did you have any trouble getting here?" Javed asked excitedly, eyes bright.

"Unity!" Kalen gave a perfunctory salute. "I had an escort into the building."

Javed turned back to the window. "Come over here and see what's going on."

Kalen joined him. Looking out, Kalen could see the city spread out to the east, and below, the barrier and soldiers. The streets were nearly deserted, apart from groups of soldiers and guards moving about. Even at this distance, he could see the soldiers' Divines glinting in the sunshine on their jackets. The shuttle port had closed and the transparent roof of the dome covered the city as usual.

"Look, you can see the Ea-Zone blocks from here, right at the crater's edge," Javed said, his voice cracking with tension.

"I can just make them out," Kalen said. "What's going on? The soldiers have moved everyone off the streets because of a meteor storm but I can't see any sign of one?"

Javed began to pace up and down the room, stroking his Divine on his chest, and then stopped suddenly and faced Kalen.

"This is the best way," Javed said meaningfully. His eyes had glazed over as if he was deep in thought, and he nervously fidgeted with the Divine pinned to his jacket, one moment stroking it, and the next, fiddling with its clasp.

"What do you mean?" The heavy feeling of dread began to seep into Kalen's innards. Something was wrong. Very wrong, and it hadn't got anything to do with a meteor storm.

Javed smiled slowly. "Early has refused to leave Three-Craters. The Council has voted and there can be no diplomatic solution. The Ea-Zone insists that there's no alien presence and want to use the energy field as a source of fuel. Can you believe that? They want to destroy alien life and use it for fuel!"

"What has that got to do with a meteor storm?" Kalen asked.

"There's no meteor storm, it's just a pretext. The Council has voted to use force against the Ea-Zone to enforce the protocols to protect alien life. It would be unconscionable to allow Early to continue developing Three-Craters when there's a risk that they could be destroying an alien habitat," Javed said in a monotone, as if he had been rehearsing his words for days.

"So the Council has voted to use force? I thought that any action was going to be limited to Three-Craters and the building sites?"

"That wouldn't be enough. We're going to take over Central. It isn't right that we have to share the city with them. They are sinful and corrupt. Their plan to use the energy field as fuel shows a total disregard for other life forms and is immoral. We're not going to open the Gates at day end," Javed spat out.

"I don't understand?" He couldn't be hearing this. It was impossible. They couldn't trap the Ea-Zone in the accommodation blocks.

"We're not going to let Early back into Central!" Javed's eyes burned with fierce intensity and his voice rose in fury. "We're going to stop them. We're not going to share Central with them any longer!"

Kalen stared at Javed. "But you can't do that! They can't stay in the blocks for long. There isn't enough space!" The dread had become horror and now shock filled him. He had to do something. Kill Javed? Plead with Javed?

"It isn't right that we have to share the planet with them!" Javed ranted. "They contaminate everything! They're unbelievers and they have no God-force! They have no right to live with us!"

"You mustn't do this! The Ea-Zone will fight; they'll never let you take over Central. It will mean war! No one will win! You must stop this!" Kalen pleaded.

"We will win because we have God on our side. We're going to destroy their accommodation blocks. God has told us to do this! God has shown us their sin!" Javed raved.

"Destroy their blocks?" Kalen cried. The words hit him. For an instant, he pictured people running and screaming through the corridors of the Ea-Zone blocks. Halle, Ije, Reinhard, his daughter and her children, all trying to shelter from the onslaught. "You can't do this. You can't!"

Javed's eyes blazed as he screamed, "They're immoral, depraved, and worthless! Unity is taking action to bring this abomination to an end. We're going to destroy their blocks before they realise what's happening. This is the only way to cleanse the city."

"Cleanse the city? You'll kill all of them! They've got nowhere to go!"

"We must cleanse Taidor of the Earlians! They have no God-force and pollute the planet. We're closing the safety roof in case of air strikes." Javed's face was a mask of hatred.

"Air strikes?" How extensive was the attack?

"Oh yes, we're co-ordinating the action throughout the planet. We're hitting the other cities at the same time," Javed said in a calmer voice and stared out of the window again. "I asked you to come here so that you could watch. You brought us the missing piece of the trident. It was the evidence that we needed to challenge Early. It was also a weapon that, even now, we're deploying at the construction sites. Without you, none of this would have been possible. God sent you to Unity."

A loud groaning noise echoed over the city, a growling that sounded like slow thunder, and Kalen saw the edges of the safety roof start to move over the dome. The black wings emerged slowly from two sides of the rim, sliding across the dome to meet at the centre, plunging the streets into darkness, one by one, as they blotted out the sun.

He had seen the wings before. They were the black wings of the crow that fixed itself to his back while he lay crushed beneath the rubble at Area Nine. Suddenly he remembered it all.

He remembered the instant that he was hit by the rock-fall at Area Nine and crushed beneath its weight. His consciousness had floated upward, leaving his battered body, and then begun to dissipate and fragment. As he lost the thread of his individuality, he had known that he was dying. With his sense of self fading into the eternal energy, the oval and round shapes had come and surrounded him— colourful spheres that transformed as they encircled him.

They had pushed him back down into his broken body and he had lived. How could he have forgotten?

The shapes had been with him since then, just outside the reach of his consciousness. And his mind, irritated by their presence, had tried to grasp the hidden memory by taking him back to the cave, again and again, to the point of his death. But the Uveid's power had been too strong and he hadn't recognised the infection. The Uveid had saved him for a purpose. Javed was wrong. It wasn't God that had sent him to Unity; it was the Uveid. He was the unwitting catalyst of all this, a pawn in an alien game of destruction.

As if in a dream, he watched flickering lights move along the dark streets of Central. Suddenly a bright flare lit up the eastern side of the city and the thunderous growling merged with the sound of an explosion. He heard screaming and the shrill crying echoed across the dome, the sounds bouncing off the metal safety roof.

"It's started," Javed said, his voice quivering with excitement. "We're destroying their accommodation blocks. God has told us to do this."

"You must stop this madness! It isn't God that told you to do this. It's the Uveid. Please stop now!" Kalen shouted, but Javed ignored him.

"This must give you great satisfaction after the way they treated you." Javed raised his voice. "You've chosen the right side. God is with us."

"Don't you understand? You've been infected by the Uveid. It's controlling you!"

Javed appeared not to hear him and remained focused on the scene outside. Numbing shock threatened to paralyse Kalen. What was Halle going through now? What were his people suffering now? He had betrayed them. It would have been better if death had taken him at Area Nine rather than be used as a catalyst for war. But it was too late for regrets.

He couldn't change what had already happened, but he could change the future.

The last sliver of sunlight pierced the city in a line that cut across it dead centre and then it was extinguished as the safety roof closed completely, leaving only the explosions to illuminate the buildings. The day end sirens sounded automatically, but Kalen could hardly hear them above the noise of the attack. He saw that most of the eastern side of the city was on fire, but the Ea-Zone had started to defend itself. Tracers from laser fire flashed backwards and forwards and then there was a blinding light and an explosion near the barricade. Smoke rose from the streets, and when pockets of it cleared, Kalen saw that buildings had been damaged and part of the barrier had been blown away.

"Ah, they're retaliating," Javed said. "We expected that. They're destroying the centre of the city but the dome will hold."

A loud explosion nearby shook the headquarters building and the city lit up in one final brilliant tableau before the streets plunged into darkness again. Another explosion hit the building and now Kalen smelled burning and heard heavy running footsteps and shouting in the corridor. The door burst open and a grime smeared face glanced in.

"We've been hit. We're evacuating the building," the soldier shouted, panting for breath. "We're pulling back to the west Gates and blocks."

The soldier disappeared and Kalen heard his boots hammering down the corridor towards the stairwell.

"We have to leave! What's the point of it all? Tell me? What's the point?" Kalen cried and started for the door. "If you go to the blocks, what have you achieved? Central will be destroyed and no one will have the city!"

He reached the door just as the room began to fill up with smoke. Outside, one end of the corridor was ablaze, tongues of flame licking the walls and ceiling, spewing out suffocating black smoke that burnt the inside of Kalen's lungs. The stairwell at the other end was still clear, but the fire was gaining and soon they would be trapped. He paused at the door and glanced back at Javed who still stood by the window.

"We'll rid Taidor of evil. We'll win. We have God on our side! Our cause is right! This is only the beginning!" Javed screamed.

Kalen turned away and ran for the stairs, Javed's words still ringing in his ears. There was nothing more that he could do here. He scrambled down the stairs, the smoke thick in places, passing where the fire burned fiercely. Reaching the ground floor, he ran for the doors and the exit through the barrier. Outside, the soldiers ignored him and explosions and laser tracers erratically illuminated the black city. He sprinted through the barrier, then took a side street, and began to run east.

END

About Lucy Andrews

Lucy Andrews grew up in the north of England and studied law and psychology at University. After working in London for most of her professional life, Lucy now lives by the sea in Sussex.

Social Media Links

Facebook:
https://www.facebook.com/LucyAndrewsAuthor

Twitter:
https://www.twitter.com/LAndrewsWrites